SECRETS OF DEATH

SECRETS OF DEATH

STEPHEN BOOTH

sphere

First published in Great Britain in 2016 by Sphere

1 3 5 7 9 10 8 6 4 2

A CIP catalogue record for this book is
available from the British Library.

Hardback ISBN 978-0-7515-5998-9
Trade paperback ISBN 978-0-7515-6000-8

Typeset in Meridien by Palimpsest Book Production Limited,
Falkirk, Stirlingshire
Printed and bound in Great Britain by Clays Ltd, St Ives plc

Papers used by Sphere are from well-managed
forests and other responsible sources.

MIX
Paper from
responsible sources
FSC
www.fsc.org FSC® C104740

Sphere
An imprint of
Little, Brown Book Group
Carmelite House
50 Victoria Embankment
London EC4Y 0DZ

An Hachette UK Company
www.hachette.co.uk

www.littlebrown.co.uk

On the day of my birth, my death began its walk.
It is walking toward me now, without hurrying.
– Jean Cocteau

1

Day 1

And this is the first secret of death. There's always a right time and place to die.

It was important to remember. So important that Roger Farrell was repeating it to himself over and over in his head by the time he drew into the car park. When he pulled up and switched off the engine, he found he was moving his lips to the words and even saying it out loud – though only someone in the car with him would have heard it.

And he was alone, of course. Just him, and the package on the back seat.

There's always a right time and place to die.

As instructed, Farrell had come properly equipped. He'd practised at home to make sure he got everything just right. It was vital to do this thing precisely. A mistake meant disaster. So getting it wrong was inconceivable. Who knew what would come afterwards? It didn't bear thinking about.

Last night, he'd experienced a horrible dream, a nightmare about weeds growing from his own body. He'd been pulling clumps of ragwort and thistles out of his chest, ripping roots from his crumbling skin as if he'd turned to earth in the night. He could still feel the tendrils scraping against his ribs as they dragged through his flesh.

He knew what it meant. He was already in the ground. *Ashes to ashes, dust to dust.* Wasn't that what they said at your graveside as they shovelled soil on to your coffin? The dream meant his body was recycling back into the earth. In his soul, he'd already died.

Farrell looked around the car park. There were plenty of vehicles here. Although it was the middle of the week, a burst of sunny weather had brought people out into the Peak District in their droves. They'd come to enjoy the special peace and beauty of Heeley Bank, just as he had.

Of course, in many other ways, they weren't like him at all.

He let out a sigh of contentment. That was the feeling this scenery gave him. The green of the foliage down by the river was startling in its brightness. The farmland he could see stretching up the sides of the hills was a glowing patchwork between a tracery of dry-stone walls. Cattle munched on the new grass in the fields. Further up, a scattering of white blobs covered the rougher grazing where the moors began.

The sight of those sheep made Farrell smile. He'd always associated them with the Peaks. This landscape wouldn't be the same without sheep. They'd been here for centuries, helping to shape the countryside. And they'd still be here long after he'd gone.

It really was so green out there. So very green.

But there's always a right time and place.

A silver SUV had pulled into a parking space nearby. Farrell watched a young couple get out and unload two bikes from a rack attached to their vehicle. One of the bikes had a carrier on the back for the small girl sitting in a child seat in the car. She was pre-school, about two years old, wearing a bright yellow dress and an orange sun hat. Her father lifted her out, her toes wiggling with pleasure as she felt the warm air on her skin. The family all laughed together, for no apparent reason.

Farrell had observed people doing that before, laughing at nothing in particular. He'd never understood it. He often didn't get jokes that others found hilarious. And laughing when there wasn't even a joke, when no one had actually said anything? That seemed very strange. It was as if they were laughing simply because they were, well . . . happy.

For Roger Farrell, *happy* was just a word, the appearance of happiness an illusion. He was convinced people put on a façade and acted that way because it was expected of them. It was all just an artificial front. Deep down, no one could be happy in this world. It just wasn't possible. Happiness was a sham – and a cruel one at that, since no one could attain it. All these people would realise it in the end.

With a surge of pity, Farrell looked away. He'd watched the family too long. Across the car park, an elderly man hobbled on two sticks, accompanied by a woman with a small pug dog on a lead. She had to walk deliberately slowly, so that she didn't leave the man behind. The pug tugged half-heartedly at its lead, but the woman yanked it back.

These two had probably been married for years and were no doubt suffering from various illnesses that came with age. Did they look happy? Farrell looked more closely at their faces. Definitely not. Not even the dog.

He nodded to himself and closed his eyes as he leaned back in his seat. His breathing settled down to a steady rhythm as he listened to the birds singing in the woods, the tinkle of a stream nearby, the quiet whispering of a gentle breeze through the trees.

As the afternoon drew to a close, he watched the vehicles leave one by one. People were taking off their boots, climbing into cars and heading for home. All of them were complete strangers, absorbed in their own lives. They could see him, of course. An overweight middle-aged man with a receding hairline and a distant stare. But they would never remember him.

A few minutes later, a young man jogged past on to the woodland path, checking his watch as he ran, as if he knew the time was approaching. A black Land Rover eased into a spot opposite Farrell's BMW, but no one emerged.

And finally, the lights went off in the information centre. A woman came out and locked the front doors. She took a glance round the car park, seemed to see nothing of any interest to her, and climbed into a Ford Focus parked in a bay reserved for staff. Farrell watched as she drove away.

4

When it was quiet and there were only a few cars left, he leaned over into the back seat and unzipped the holdall. Carefully, Farrell lifted out the gas canisters, uncoiling the plastic tubing as it writhed on to the seat. He placed the canisters in the footwell. They looked incongruous sitting there, painted in fluorescent orange with their pictures of party balloons on the side.

It had taken him a while to find the right brand of gas. Some manufacturers had started putting a percentage of air into the canisters, which made them quite useless for his purpose. That was when things went wrong, if you didn't check and double-check, and make sure you got exactly the right equipment.

Still, you could find anything on the internet, as he well knew. Information, advice, someone to talk to who actually understood how you were feeling. And the inspiration. He would be nothing without that. He wouldn't be here at Heeley Bank right now.

And this is the first secret of death. There's always a right time and place to die.

Farrell said it again. You could never say it too often. It was so important. The most important thing in the world. Or in *his* world, at least.

He reached back into the holdall and lifted out the bag itself. He held it almost reverently, like a delicate surgical instrument. And it was, in a way. It could achieve every bit as much as any complicated heart operation or brain surgery. It could change someone's life for the better. And instead of hours and hours of complicated medical procedures on the operating table, it took just a few minutes. It was so simple.

With black tape from a roll, he attached the tubing to the place he'd marked on the edge of the bag, tugging at it to make sure it was perfectly secure. Everything fine so far.

Farrell had spent days choosing a piece of music to play. The CD was waiting now in its case and he slid it out, catching a glimpse of his own reflection in the gleaming surface. He wondered what expression would be in his eyes in the last seconds.

Despite his reluctance to see himself now, he couldn't resist a glance in his rearview mirror. Only his eyes were visible, pale grey irises and a spider's web of red lines. His pupils appeared tiny, as if he were on drugs or staring into a bright light. And maybe he *was* looking at the light. Perhaps it had already started.

The CD player whirred quietly and the music began to play. He'd selected a piece of Bach. It wasn't his normal choice of music, but nothing was normal now. It hadn't been for quite a while. The sounds of the Bach just seemed to suit the mood he was trying to achieve. Peace, certainly. And a sort of quiet, steady progression towards the inevitable conclusion.

As the sun set in the west over Bradwell Moor, a shaft of orange light burst over the landscape, transforming the colours into a kaleidoscope of unfamiliar shades, as if the Peak District had just become a tropical island.

Farrell held his breath, awed by the magic of the light. It was one of the amazing things he loved about this area, the way it changed from one minute to the next, from one month to another. Those hillsides he was looking at now would be ablaze with purple heather later in the summer. It was always a glorious sight.

For a moment, Farrell hesitated, wondering whether he should have left it until August or the beginning of September.

And then it hit him. That momentary twinge of doubt exploded inside him, filling his lungs and stopping the breath in his throat until he gathered all his strength to battle against it. His hands trembled with the effort as he forced the doubt back down into the darkness. As the tension collapsed, his shoulders sagged and his forehead prickled with a sheen of sweat.

Farrell felt as though he'd just experienced the pain and shock of a heart attack without the fatal consequences. His lips twitched in an ironic smile. That meant he was still in control. He remained capable of making his own mind up, deciding where and when to end his life. He was able to choose his own moment, his own perfect location.

There's always a right time and place to die.

Roger Farrell took one last glance out of the window as the light began to fade over the Peak District hills.

The place was here.

And the time was *now*.

2

Detective Sergeant Diane Fry was standing on the corner of a street in the Forest Fields area of Nottingham, examining a display of toilet rolls and multi-pack crisps in the window of Pound Stop Plus.

Around her were rows and rows of red-brick terraces, cars parked on and off the kerb, the soft, hopeful murmuring of pigeons gathering for an evening feed. The scent of warm spices mingled with the faint aroma of fish and chips. A sign on a nearby wall encouraged her to book early for next year's Hajj. But she had no plans for a trip to Mecca right now. The suburbs of Nottingham were the ultimate destination of her journey.

Fry pulled her phone out of her pocket as it buzzed on vibrate, and glanced at the screen. There had been two calls from her sister, Angie. She could guess what they were about. Angie only had one subject of conversation recently. It could get tedious after a while.

'I *will* call back later,' she said as she put the phone away. 'I promise, Sis.'

For a moment, she wondered why she had to say

that out loud to herself, when Angie couldn't hear her. She seemed to be doing it more and more often recently. Probably because there was no one else she could talk to about the things that were going through her head.

A woman in multi-coloured leggings and ankle boots tottered past, her lank blonde hair as long as the tassels of her shawl. An old man in a flat cap came out of a convenience store with his lottery tickets and crossed the road towards the Polish delicatessen. He gave Fry an inquisitive look from under the peak of his cap.

Behind the old man, a group of Asian men had stopped on the pavement and were discussing something with shakes of their heads and emphatic hand gestures. Next year's trip to Mecca, perhaps? It was a sign of status if you could afford to make the pilgrimage. Fry could hear their voices from here, speaking in a mixture of Urdu and English. They were probably Kashmiris and Mirpuris. The Punjabis tended to live in other parts of the city.

Fry turned her head as she heard a different noise. Fifty yards up the road, a halal butcher's stood between an off-licence and an Indian jeweller's. Beyond them, a NET tram was rattling past the junction, heading north up Noel Street towards the Asian Women's Project. Its sides advertised a local law firm and home deliveries from Asda.

She shaded her eyes with a hand against the dazzle of sunlight. The shadows of the parked cars were lengthening towards her. The sun was gradually getting lower in the west over Aspley, where the geometric shapes of the vast housing estates had looked like crop circles on the satellite photos they'd studied when this operation was being planned.

Fry watched the driver of a white Transit van park by the butcher's and leave his doors open as he walked up the pavement. He stopped and leaned against the wall, half hidden from her view by one of the big black commercial wheelie bins. He seemed to be making a phone call.

Her personal radio crackled into her earpiece.

'Is that him, Diane?'

'No, I don't think so,' she said. 'We're looking for a Caucasian male, aren't we? This one's Asian.'

'Right.'

Her boss from the Major Crime Unit was parked across the other side of Noel Street. Detective Chief Inspector Alistair Mackenzie didn't want to put himself out on the street. He'd argued that he would look more conspicuous, that he was a more obvious copper than DS Fry. And he was probably right. But sitting in his Mercedes, a middle-aged white man on his own, doing nothing but watching – well, that might make him look like someone equally unwelcome in Forest Fields. That was a thought Fry had only expressed to herself.

'DC Callaghan is going to call at the target's house again,' said Mackenzie. 'We must have missed him. He's got by us somehow.'

'Understood.'

Fry shrugged. She thought he was wrong this time, but Mackenzie was in charge of the operation. She'd learned that there was no point in contradicting him unless she had an undeniable argument.

She turned back to the toilet roll display, saw a member of the shop staff staring back at her through the glass, and switched her attention to the window of the sari shop a few paces away. She chastised herself silently. She was starting to lose concentration. It had been a long day and it was warm in these narrow streets – not like sitting in an air-conditioned car. The glare of the sun was making her eyes feel tired. Still, she didn't think she'd missed anyone.

The East Midlands Special Operations Unit was proving to be a challenging assignment. That was what she'd wanted of course, after her spell in Derbyshire E Division CID, out there in the rural wastelands of the Peak District. The remit for Northern Command covered the whole of Nottinghamshire and Derbyshire, which suited her fine. She felt less chained to one area, the way she had been on divisional CID in Edendale.

Of course, her work at EMSOU had turned out to be demanding in unexpected ways. Life at St Ann's police station, where the unit's Northern Command was based, had complications she hadn't anticipated. One of those complications was Detective Constable Jamie Callaghan.

Fry glanced at her phone again. No more messages from Angie. But there would be more later on. Her sister had probably realised she was working late on a job and would try another time. Fry had been surprised by how happy Angie seemed in her new relationship. It had lasted a couple of years now, which was something of a record. So it was possible.

'There's nothing doing,' said Mackenzie. 'Callaghan has called at the house again and there's no one home – no lights on, nothing. So I'm calling it off for today. Do you want to join us up the road at the Lion?'

'Why not,' said Fry.

She turned and saw a Muslim woman in a niqab slipping into a house behind her, a quick flash of suspicious eyes directed her way before the woman disappeared. Fry hadn't even noticed her as she passed. She wondered if her own eyes looked equally suspicious.

The Lion Inn was just up the tram tracks off Shipstone Street and almost overshadowed by the bulk of the old Shipstone's brewery. They could have gone to the Clock on Craven Road, which was nearer. There, though, the attractions were soul and curry nights or evenings of spiritual mediumship, rather than lunchtime jazz sessions. Worse, they would probably have been questioned by the regulars about who they were.

When Fry entered the Lion, she found that Mackenzie had already laid claim to a corner of the pub. It had bare brick walls, but comfortable stripy chairs arranged round a low table near an upright piano.

Jamie Callaghan was at the bar buying the drinks. Oddly, Callaghan reminded her of a Bulgarian police officer she'd known briefly when he visited Derbyshire to liaise on an inquiry a few years ago. Not that Callaghan was Eastern European. There was nothing

Slavic about him. It was more the way he moved, the confident swagger, a swing of the shoulders.

He was definitely the kind of man she shouldn't be attracted to, especially as he was recently divorced, escaped from a marriage that had only lasted a year or two according to the gossip at St Ann's. They said his wife had been caught having an affair with a Nottinghamshire dog-handler. That detail might have been invented for the sake of the cruel jokes it provided the opportunity for. Who knew whether it was true or not?

But then, who knew why any marriage ended? There were always two sides to any story. She had a strong suspicion that Jamie Callaghan would be telling her his side before too long.

'Have we lost him, sir?' asked Callaghan, setting a round of drinks down on the table. He hadn't asked Fry what she wanted, but he didn't have to. Vodka when she needed it. A J_2O apple and mango flavour when she was driving.

'What do you mean?' said Mackenzie, accepting a bottle of Spitfire.

'Has Farrell skipped? Left the area?'

Mackenzie clutched his beer bottle tightly as his face twisted into a grimace of frustration. 'Someone must have tipped him off, if he has.'

'I suppose it might just be a coincidence. He could have headed out for an evening with friends just when we decided to come for him.'

'We didn't identify any friends,' pointed out Fry as she took a chair at the table.

'That's true. But it doesn't mean he hasn't got any.'

'A man like Farrell doesn't have friends,' she said.

Callaghan grinned, looked as if he was about to say something, then stopped. Fry wondered if he'd been going to make some joke about her not having any friends either. It was the kind of sly dig she'd heard often from colleagues during her career. Everyone thought twice now. It was hard to tell when banter crossed the line.

Instead, Callaghan chose something worse.

'He might have picked someone up in the past few days,' he said.

Fry shuddered. 'No, don't say that.'

'Well, it's a possibility.'

He was right. But it was a possibility that didn't bear thinking about as far as Diane Fry was concerned. That was what they'd worked so hard to prevent, after all.

Mackenzie shrugged and took a drink of his beer.

'Well, we'll just have to find a way of tracking down Mr Farrell,' he said. 'He can't hide from us for very long.'

Fry's phone buzzed again. And of course it was Angie. She had waited for her sister to get home, but she was still sitting in the pub. Fry saw that she'd been sent a photo. As soon as she clicked to open it, she knew perfectly well what it would be. The squashed-up Winston Churchill features of a hairless, goggle-eyed baby stared out at her from the screen. Fry flinched. She was finding it really difficult getting used to being an auntie.

'What is it, Diane?'

She put the phone away hastily before Callaghan saw the picture. 'Nothing important. Just my sister.'

'Oh, okay. I thought it looked like bad news.'

Fry squinted at him nervously. He wasn't supposed to be so observant. That would never do.

'Do *you* think Roger Farrell has done a bunk, Diane?' asked Callaghan as they left the pub.

'No, I don't,' said Fry. 'He just isn't the kind. He's the sort of man who'll try to brazen things out to the end. He'll turn up somewhere. I'm certain of it.'

3

Day 2

Well, that was really odd. Not the ideal start to the day. Marnie Letts sighed irritably as she pulled on the handbrake. And it wasn't even Monday. Those were the worst days of the week. She always felt ill when she woke up on a Monday. Nothing was actually wrong with her. It was just knowing that the rest of the week stretched ahead.

Marnie had been the first to arrive at work that morning, which was unusual in itself. On every other day Shirley was already at the visitor centre before her, with the lights on and the kettle boiling in the kitchen.

Six months ago, Shirley had been appointed manager at Heeley Bank Information Centre, and opening up was part of her job. She unlocked the doors in the morning and locked up again at night. If the burglar alarm went off in the early hours of the morning, Shirley got the call-out. That was why she was paid more. Marnie didn't even have a set of keys. And that was the way she liked it. She wouldn't have wanted the responsibility – not for just a few pounds extra every month. She certainly wouldn't want to get called out in the middle of the night. She had better things to do with her time. If that was what promotion meant, the likes of Shirley Gooding were welcome to it.

So Marnie sat in her little Nissan in the staff parking area and listened to the news as it came on the radio. She was tuned into Peak FM and they didn't waste much time on the headlines. Their listeners were more concerned about traffic alerts – the latest closure on the motorway, the length of delays on the A61, a reminder of the temporary lights in Baslow, where visitors were already queuing to get into Chatsworth.

Marnie tapped her fingers on the steering wheel as she listened. None of it was relevant to her on her drive out of Edendale to the visitor centre. She lived on the Woodlands Estate, close to the northern outskirts of the town, and she always took the back roads to reach Heeley Bank. They were narrow and winding, but always quiet. Just a few farmers on tractors, a herd of cows on the way back to the fields from milking. Who wouldn't prefer a commute like that?

She frowned when she noticed the car. She recognised it as a BMW. One of her neighbours on Sycamore Crescent had one. It was always left out on the street in everyone else's way, and she'd often had bad things to say about BMW drivers. One night, someone on the street had keyed the paintwork, so she obviously wasn't alone.

This one was neatly parked and undamaged, though – unlike the condition of a stolen car that Marnie had seen abandoned here a few months ago. The BMW

17

sat in the car park under the shade of the trees on the banking above the river. There had been a bit of mist overnight and the car was covered in condensation. In a few minutes' time, the sun would reach it and the moisture would begin to clear.

Marnie hesitated, looking round at the entrance but seeing no sign of Shirley. That was typical of her. When there might be a problem, she wasn't there. It could wait until she arrived, couldn't it? Shirley was the manager, after all.

But something made Marnie open her car door and walk across the gravel towards the BMW. The car was sitting there silently, mysteriously. It seemed to be drawing her towards it. She believed very strongly in fate, always read her horoscope in the newspaper every morning. She was a water sign, Scorpio, and was led by her instincts.

Her footsteps sounded unnaturally loud in the early morning air. She moved confidently at first but found her feet gradually slowing of their own accord as she approached the car. She could see nothing through the windscreen because of the condensation. Had someone slept in their car overnight? Perhaps two people? She had heard of all kinds of things going on.

If you were doing that, you'd leave the windows slightly open to let in some air, wouldn't you? These were all rolled firmly shut. So the BMW was just abandoned, then? That must be it.

Marnie rapped on the driver's side window. There was no response, no sudden movement rocking the car, no startled noises. Relieved now, she ran her sleeve across the glass and stuck her face close to it, shading her eyes against the glare of the sun as it broke over the trees.

At first, she couldn't understand what she was seeing. It didn't seem human, or animal either. Her brain whirled, trying to make sense of it. A shop window dummy, a practical joke of some kind?

She tried the handle and found the door unlocked. As she pulled it open, the realisation hit her. She knew it was no practical joke. A man sat in the driving seat. A real man, flesh and blood. But there was something wrong with his head. Something very wrong.

By the time Shirley Gooding arrived, running late from dealing with a child too sick to go to school, she was amazed to find Marnie Letts standing in the middle of the car park screaming.

Every morning, Detective Inspector Ben Cooper set off to work with his car full of sound. He needed it to insulate him from the world outside. The traffic passing in the street, the people on the pavements, the market stalls setting up in the square – all the bustle and activity of Edendale on a fine summer's day. Sometimes, it could be too much.

For the past few weeks, he'd been listening to Bruce Springsteen. 'Dancing in the Dark'. It was always the first track that started up when he switched on the ignition. Always the same CD in the player, always the same opening chords. He hadn't bothered changing it. One day, he supposed he'd get tired of it. For now, it suited him fine. It was like a switch that turned him on for the day, clicked him into professional mode and prepared him for the hours ahead, when anything could happen.

He halted in traffic at the Hollowgate lights, reflecting on how his feelings were mirrored by the outside world. During those few minutes of his drive to West Street, Cooper always passed from dark into light. Everywhere he looked, he caught his town in the process of changing its character. He could see it taking off one face and putting on another. During the past few hours, Edendale had hidden away its night-time turnover of drunks and clubbers staggering between takeaway and taxi rank in noisy clumps, shadowed by weary police officers with their high-vis jackets and riot vans. They had to be ushered indoors with the coming of daylight, like vampires retreating from the sun.

The morning brought an influx of visitors to the town. The roads got busier, the car parks filled up, the coaches crawled through the narrow streets, and the pavements became hazardous with boots and hiking poles. All the gift shops and visitor centres propped open their doors; the newsagents put out their ice cream signs.

Edendale looked so different in the sun. And it felt different too. The atmosphere was much more relaxed, the flow of movement slower. Walking groups met at their rendezvous points, chatting and adjusting their equipment for so long that you'd think they weren't planning to do any walking at all. The pavements were full of strolling retired couples who'd decided to have a day out in the Peak District, with a nice lunch in a pub garden and a doze on a bench by the river. Japanese tourists stood gazing into the windows of the Bakewell pudding shops or took selfies on the old bridge over the Eden, forcing passers-by into the road.

Unlike the visitors, Cooper could see through the façade. That darkness was never dispelled completely. He could sense it lurking in the background. He'd seen enough of it to know it was always there.

Cooper waited for the barrier to open and drove into the staff car park off West Street. Very little money had been spent on Derbyshire Constabulary's E Division headquarters recently. As a result, the 1950s stone building was looking a bit the worse for wear. The guttering had come loose on the custody suite, creating an outdoor shower in the winter months. The tarmac of the car park was cracked in the north corner, where the riot vans were parked. Everybody expected one of them to disappear into a sink hole some day, probably in the not too distant future. On the first floor of the headquarters building, some of the offices were permanently empty and locked up. No one could remember who'd worked there now.

Across the road, Edendale Football Club had been doing well lately. Their ground was on West Street, and the windows on this side of the building looked out over Gate C and the back of the East Stand. These days, when the club had an important home match, the streets were filled with cars, which hadn't been a problem when Edendale FC were struggling in the lower leagues. If they became any more successful, access might become a problem on match days: a

21

response officer trying to get to an emergency call would get blocked in and there would be trouble.

Cooper hadn't quite reached his own office next to the CID room when he heard his phone ringing. He broke into a jog, though he knew it was against health and safety regulations to run in the corridors.

But the phone stopped before he could reach it and his mobile began ringing. It was Carol Villiers, this morning's duty DC, somewhere outside Edendale at the scene of a sudden death.

'What kind of sudden death?' he said.

Villiers was always cautious, reluctant to commit herself. He didn't remember her being like this when they were youngsters growing up together. She must have learned it in the services. Make a risk assessment, analyse the intelligence, don't go into anything until you're absolutely certain of the situation. It helped a lot in this job. More police officers got themselves into trouble by reacting too quickly than by standing back and doing nothing.

'Heeley Bank,' said Villiers. 'Do you know where it is?'

'Of course.'

'There's a body,' she said. And then she added the crucial words: 'A body in a car.'

'I'm on my way,' said Cooper.

Diane Fry had a couple of rest days after last night's abortive operation. Today, DCI Mackenzie would be exploring the possibility of getting a search warrant on Roger Farrell's address. It wouldn't have been needed if they'd made an arrest. The search would be going on right now, while Farrell was being questioned in custody. But things hadn't gone the way they had planned.

Fry was renting a double-bedroomed top-floor apartment with its own parking space in a modern executive development in the suburb of Wilford. One of the roads on the development was called Halfpenny Walk – but her rent had cost her an awful lot more than that.

The properties were surrounded by neat grass verges and little access roads. There was barely a sign of human occupation but for lights behind curtained windows and a car parked in front of a garage door. She always had to remember to clear the burglar alarm when she let herself in. She didn't have anything worth stealing – she'd never felt the urge to surround herself with material possessions – but it seemed like an obligation here, like being careful where you put your wheelie bin so that you didn't make the development look untidy.

She hadn't met any of her neighbours in the apartment block to speak to, and she probably never would. She'd nodded to one or two people as she passed them in the hallway or while getting into her car. She didn't know who they were and had never stopped to chat, though sometimes they showed indications of wanting to introduce themselves before she could escape.

One couple downstairs had put a card through her door inviting her to a drinks party when they moved into their apartment. She hadn't gone, of course. For a few hours she'd listened to the faint sound of cheesy nineties pop music and hollow laughter drifting up the stairs, and told herself how glad she was she hadn't accepted the invitation.

The rooms of the apartment had sounded very empty and strange when she first moved in. She hadn't realised how accustomed she'd become to living in a shared house with students and migrant workers coming and going at all hours. The place in Grosvenor Road had never been quiet.

Here in the suburbs, she was only twenty minutes from the city centre with its pubs and shops and theatres. There was even a tram line now, cutting the journey time yet more. And the location suited her just fine. She liked the comforting roar of traffic on the Clifton Bridge, which carried the A52 over the River Trent.

That morning, Fry looked out of the window of her apartment as a car turned in from the direction of Clifton Lane and drew up in front of her building. It was a silver-grey Renault hatchback. Nothing unusual about that at all. But something about the occupants caught her eye, and she watched curiously as the engine was turned off and the door swung open.

Her heart sank when she saw a figure get out and open the tailgate.

'You've got to be kidding me,' she said.

A pushchair came out first, then a bag full of goodness knew what – bottles, teats, steriliser, wet wipes, extra clothes. And packs of nappies. Nappies. God help her.

She looked around the apartment, anxiously scanning for anything left out that she didn't want seen. She wasn't big on tidying up and dusting, because she never expected visitors. It was too late to do anything about it. That empty vodka bottle should go in the bin, and the box from last night's pizza delivery. Oh, and the one from the night before.

Cursing, she burst into activity to make the sitting room at least look presentable. She was sweating from stress and effort by the time the door buzzed and she had to let her visitors in.

'Sis! What a surprise.'

Angie stood there on the threshold of her apartment. Her sister. Barely recognisable now because of the weight she'd put on, which concealed her usually thin, angular frame. And because of the object clutched to her chest in a sling, something wearing a white floppy sun hat with pictures of animals on it.

'Hello, Di,' said Angie. 'We thought we'd call in and see you.'

Diane heard a car engine and quickly stepped to a window in the entrance hall to gaze down at the departing Renault.

'Who was that?' she said.

'A friend.'

'A male friend?'

'Yes.'

'*The* male friend?'

'Sis – is this an interrogation or can we come in?'

As she led the way into the apartment, Diane flinched at her sister's use of 'we'. People did it all the time when they'd just got married or formed a long-term relationship. But Angie didn't mean that. She meant herself and the baby. They were a duo now, a permanent pair. Angie and the child . . .

'So how is . . . Zack?'

Diane was impressed by her own ability in remembering the new baby's name. She'd tried quite hard to forget it. Zack Fry sounded too much like today's special from a Chinese takeaway.

'Oh, he's grand,' said Angie.

'Grand,' repeated Diane, her brain empty of all the other words she ought to use about a baby. *Beautiful, bonny, gorgeous, cute*? They all stuck in her throat the second they came into her head. Silently, she reminded herself of an important rule. Must say *him*, not *it*.

Angie walked into the centre of the sitting room, the weight of the sling making her look slow and ungainly. She looked around critically. Diane was glad she'd managed to clear away some of the debris at least.

'What a beautiful apartment,' said Angie. 'You're so lucky. We'd love to have somewhere like this to live. Wouldn't we, Zack?'

Zack didn't answer, which was a relief. In fact, he hadn't moved since she opened the door. He was asleep presumably. His head was leaning against his mother's body, the brim of the sun hat twitching occasionally, a foot in a tiny woollen sock protruding from the sling.

Looking at her sister, Diane was momentarily overwhelmed with horror at how unalike they'd become, how little they had in common now. They used to be so close. As a teenager, she'd hero-worshipped her older sister, had been devastated when they were separated. Finding her again had been an obsession that had ruled her life for a while. She used to see an older version of herself when she looked at Angie. Now she saw a slow-moving middle-aged woman – which she herself would never be. She saw a woman who had only one topic of conversation and who talked to an unconscious creature attached to her chest. Diane felt as though she were in a remake of *Invasion of the Body Snatchers*. An alien had taken possession of her sister's body.

'So – are you visiting Nottingham for some reason? A day out shopping?' she said.

Privately, she suspected the reason for the trip up from Birmingham was probably to do with some business of the driver of the silver-grey Renault, the mysterious man friend whom she hadn't been introduced to yet. And there was probably a good reason for that. Angie's boyfriends had always had reasons to avoid meeting police detectives. What was this one's name again? Craig something?

'Actually, we were thinking of having a break for a few days.' Angie smiled. 'Don't worry – we've brought everything we need.'

Diane was baffled for a moment.

'I'm sorry?'

Angie smiled again. 'Well, you *do* have two bedrooms in this beautiful new apartment, don't you, Sis?'

Horrified, Diane opened her mouth, but found nothing came out. Like *beautiful, bonny, gorgeous* and *cute*, the words stuck in her throat.

Then the bundle strapped to her sister's chest stirred and the head inside the hat lifted. A wrinkled face turned to look at her. After a second, the baby's eyes seemed to focus. His face burst into a smile and a tiny hand reached out towards her.

For a long, long time, Diane Fry was still without words.

4

Irritably, Ben Cooper swatted at something that landed on his face. Flies were swarming round the car. When he gazed across the car park, it looked as though every fly in North Derbyshire was zooming in on Heeley Bank. Their instincts were amazing. Did the first to arrive put up a sign: 'Fresh meat here'?

And the flies had judged it right. The body in the blue BMW was already starting to look swollen. The smell inside the car was definitely over-ripe.

That was the trouble with summer. A corpse would normally be cold by now. But this one had been sitting in a car in full sun since daylight. As the interior heated up, so had the body. On a warm day in an open space, the interior temperature of a car could rise by five degrees Celsius in five minutes, ten degrees in ten minutes. The heat could reach a lethal level within half an hour, a much shorter time than many people thought.

At Heeley Bank, the ambient temperature outside was about twenty-two degrees by now. Inside the BMW, it had reached an uncomfortable thirty-eight. That sort of temperature in an enclosed space was enough to kill a child or a dog. And it was enough to make a dead body begin to bloat.

Winter was so much better for this kind of thing. Normally, the body began to cool down immediately after the heart stopped beating. It was the stage they called *algor mortis*, the death chill. Body heat fell about one degree Celsius each hour until it reached the temperature of the surrounding environment. On a cold day, you stood a chance of gleaning information about the time of death from the difference between the two, when you took the various factors into account. Body fat and layers of clothing were good insulators – they retained heat that would otherwise be lost as the blood stopped flowing and the muscles relaxed. Children and the elderly lost body heat faster than adults. A victim who had been in ill health would also lose heat more rapidly.

Yet here it was all irrelevant. The nature of the victim's death had destroyed his first line of forensic examination.

'Mr Roger Farrell, aged forty-five, with an address in Nottingham,' said Carol Villiers. 'The BMW is registered to him and his driving licence is in his wallet, along with credit cards, a Tesco Clubcard and a National Trust membership card. Not much cash, but I don't suppose he needed it today.'

Cooper pointed at the windscreen, where a parking ticket was stuck to the glass.

'Just enough for the parking charge.'

Carol Villiers had always been an outdoor girl and

the first bit of sun brought out the colour in her face. Sometimes Cooper was struck by how pale her eyes were. Sandy, as if bleached in a desert climate. They'd gone to school together, studied for their A-levels at High Peak College at the same time, got a bit drunk with a group of mates in a local pub when they received their results. She had been a good friend whom he'd been sorry to say goodbye to when she'd left to sign up with the RAF Police. She'd be the first to say that she'd changed now. She was much tougher, more confident. Experience had shaped her in those years she'd been away.

Though he'd known her for such a long time, there were subjects Carol Villiers never talked to him about. One was her husband, Glen, who had been killed in Helmand Province on a tour of duty in Afghanistan.

The medical examiner was straightening up from a crouching position, half in and half out of the car. His scene suit rustled and Cooper could see he was sweating underneath it. Trickles of perspiration ran from his temples into the neck of the suit. He'd been in the job for a long time and was probably unfit. He would never make it as a police officer, though he was a person they often had to reply on.

'There isn't a hope of getting a time of death,' he said, confirming Cooper's suspicion. 'Not from the body temperature, anyway. *Rigor* might tell us something. In my opinion, you'd be better looking for witnesses or other circumstantial evidence to establish how long he's been dead.'

Cooper nodded. Oh, great. Another one who was

reluctant to commit himself. But it was understandable in this case.

He looked around the car park and scanned the roof line of the information centre, searching for cameras.

'CCTV?' he said.

Villiers shook her head. 'Nothing. It's been discussed because the woods here are supposed to be a well-known dogging site. But there's no money in the budget.'

'No big surprise there.'

It was one of the things you got used to in a rural area, outside the centre of town. No coverage from CCTV cameras.

'So who found the body?' he asked.

'One of the staff at the information centre,' said Villiers. 'Her name is Marnie Letts. She's still a bit upset, I'm afraid. The experience has knocked her sideways.'

'We'll treat her gently.'

It was standard practice for staff at sites like Heeley Bank to alert the police in these circumstances, though usually it was just a stolen vehicle, abandoned by joyriders in a quiet spot. With luck, the car would be relatively undamaged and could be returned to its owner. Occasionally, a vehicle was found burned out and stood ruining the view until the insurance company arranged its removal.

Not this one, though. The BMW was different.

Villiers read from her notes. 'When Miss Letts turned up for work this morning, the blue BMW was still in the car park from yesterday. She wiped the moisture off the window and said she could see the shape of a man slumped in the driver's seat. His face was turned away from her and his head had slipped sideways at an unnatural angle. When she made the emergency call, she kept saying, *"There's something wrong with his head. Something very wrong."'*

'Let's talk to her, then.'

The information centre had been closed for the time being. A stream of visitors' cars were being turned away. Through the trees, Cooper could see vehicles creeping along the road, their occupants craning their necks to see what was going on in the car park. Rumours would be going around soon enough.

Heeley Bank was a popular visitor location, just a few miles outside Edendale. It had a large car park, a toilet block and picnic area. Below the centre, marked trails wound their way through the woods down to a loop of the River Eden, where it ran fast and noisily through a steep limestone gorge, bubbling over rocks and weirs.

Above the road, the hillside rose and rose through banks of heather and gorse to a gritstone moor topped by the outlines of weather-worn tors. Cooper had seen those tors up close. There were rock formations called the Old Man, the Witches, the Howling Dog. They created a dark and ominous landscape.

'Yes, the car was there last night when I left,' said Marnie Letts. 'The blue BMW. I do remember it. Most makes of car I don't recognise, but I know a BMW when I see one.'

She was a slight woman in her late twenties, with dark hair cut into a short bob. She was wearing a baggy mauve T-shirt with a logo on the chest. Cooper supposed it was a kind of staff uniform. It didn't do her any favours. But then it probably wouldn't have suited anyone.

'Did you take any notice of the driver?' he asked.

'None at all. I don't think I really saw him.'

Cooper nodded. It was probable that the driver hadn't wanted anyone to notice him. If someone had, if just one person had seen him properly and realised something was wrong, the outcome for him might have been different.

'What other vehicles were parked near the BMW last night, Miss Letts?' he asked. 'Can you remember that?'

'I couldn't really say. Well, there was a family in a big people-carrier sort of thing. A couple with bikes on the back of their car.'

'Where were they in relation to the BMW?'

Marnie waved vaguely around the car park. She wasn't as distressed as he'd expected. Perhaps she'd got all the screaming and panicking out of her system. Some people were like that. They went off like fireworks, then calmed down very quickly. She was still slightly distracted, as if she couldn't quite focus on what had happened. He could understand that. It was a bit unreal for anyone.

'The people-carrier was near the centre,' she said. 'The cyclists were parked over by the toilets. They had a red car, a four-wheel drive, I think. They weren't close enough to see the driver of the BMW.'

'Can you be sure of that?'

She shrugged. 'No, I suppose not. You'd have to ask them.'

'Did you recognise any of these people? Were they familiar faces?'

'Are you kidding? They were just visitors. We get thousands of them in the summer. I only took account of them at all because they were the last here when we closed. When the place is full, I don't notice anybody in particular.'

'Yes, I understand,' said Cooper.

A memory passed across her face suddenly. 'Oh, and there was a black Land Rover,' she said.

'Last night. Where was that parked?'

'Under the big tree in the shade,' said Marnie. 'People who come here regularly in the summer always try to claim that spot if it's sunny, so their car isn't too warm inside when they get back from a walk. It's in sun in the morning, but shade in the afternoon.'

'Did you see who was in the Land Rover?'

She shook her head. 'No. I only noticed it because it looked more like a farmer's vehicle. It's unusual to get them in here among the visitors' cars.'

'She held up pretty well,' said Cooper when they allowed Marnie to leave. 'She would make a good witness.'

'If she'd actually seen anything,' said Villiers.

'She may have seen more than she remembers, I think.'

'There's no way we're going to be able to trace any

of the people in those cars. Unless we put appeals out – local newspapers, social media? The trouble is, they could have been from absolutely anywhere.'

Wayne Abbott, E Division's crime scene manager, had taken the place of the forensic medical examiner and was writing notes on a clipboard. Abbott was a big man with a shaved head, which was revealed when he tossed back the hood of his scene suit. He looked up as Cooper and Villiers approached.

'Gas,' he said. He sounded oddly smug, as if he'd predicted it all along and was gratified to be proved right.

'Gas?' repeated Cooper.

'It's a popular choice.'

Villiers covered her face with a gloved hand as she leaned in to look at the body. She must have thought Abbott was referring to the decomposition of the body.

'What is that thing over his head?' she said.

'It's for the gas. They call it an exit bag. It's used for painless suffocation.'

'An exit bag? Who uses a nickname for a suffocation device?'

'You'd be surprised.'

Then Villiers sniffed. 'But you said gas?'

'Helium. It doesn't have any smell. Or taste for that matter.'

'I was thinking carbon monoxide.'

'Exhaust fumes? Yes, it used to be the traditional method, especially among depressed middle-aged men. A pipe from the exhaust into your car and the engine left running. Carbon monoxide is extremely toxic in high enough concentrations.'

Cooper remembered deaths from the inhalation of exhaust fumes. He'd come across one as a young PC and been struck by how peaceful the dead person looked. And he'd learned a strange and disturbing fact about the human body. Given a choice between carbon monoxide and oxygen, the haemoglobin in your blood would always choose carbon monoxide first and ignore the life-giving oxygen. It seemed a suicidal impulse had been built into the bloodstream of every human being.

'The design of modern cars has spoiled all that business,' Abbott was saying cheerfully. 'Tighter emission controls, you see. That means modern engines produce too little carbon monoxide for the purpose. It's good for the environment – but bad news for the would-be suicide. Of course, most of them don't research their methods well enough in advance to realise they need to use an old car.'

'So how does this work?'

'An exit bag? It's pretty simple,' said Abbott. 'You just have a plastic bag with a drawstring or some other type of closure. All you have to do is fill it with an inert gas like nitrogen or helium. You see, the gas itself doesn't kill you. Its purpose is to cause painless unconsciousness before suffocation occurs. The victim actually dies as a result of the high levels of carbon dioxide breathed into the bag. It can be a bit dodgy, if you don't do it right. If you change your mind at the last minute, for example, there's a good chance you'll end up alive but with serious brain damage.'

Two orange gas canisters stood in the footwell of the car, with tubing snaking up and across the body of the driver. Cooper could see that several inches of plastic tube protruded all the way into the bag, sticking up alongside the dead man's head like a snorkel tube.

Helium. The gas of fun and laughter. Party balloons and people speaking in funny, high-pitched voices. The depths of irony around suicide were limitless.

'So why choose this method?' asked Villiers.

'It's supposed to be the quickest way of killing yourself and the least painful, if it's done right,' said Abbott. 'The right-to-die groups recommend it, I understand.'

'I can see it would be better than drowning or hanging, or throwing yourself in front of a train.'

'Some of those cases can get very messy,' agreed Abbott. 'With this method, the helium prevents panic and the sense of suffocation, the alarm response usually caused by oxygen deprivation. Again, good planning is crucial.'

'Why so? It sounds straightforward enough.'

'There was a report some time ago about a world shortage of helium. As a result, some suppliers have been mixing air into their party balloon tanks. Even a level of twenty per cent air makes a tank unsuitable for use with a suicide bag. With that amount of oxygen, you'd know exactly what was happening to you. The alarm response would kick in and you'd start to panic.'

There was no doubt that Mr Farrell had got it exactly right. His chosen method had worked perfectly. He was as dead as a doornail and had been for some hours.

'It's an interesting method actually,' said Abbott. 'It can make the cause of death difficult to establish if the bag and the gas canisters are taken away before anyone reports the death.' He looked at Cooper. 'People do that to hide the fact it's a suicide, you know. I mean, members of the family. It's the insurance pay-outs, I suppose.'

'Or the shame,' said Cooper.

'Shame? About what?'

'It could be all kinds of things.'

Abbott looked at him with a confused frown. Cooper smiled. There probably weren't many things Wayne Abbott would be ashamed of. Not enough to kill himself over anyway. But every individual was different. Roger Farrell might have had some unbearable shame in his life that had driven him to this final act.

'So I suppose theoretically someone could be murdered this way,' said Villiers. 'And then the killer could remove the bag and canister.'

Abbott shook his head. 'No, there would be clear signs of a struggle. You wouldn't let someone put a bag over your head without fighting them. There's nothing like that in this case. Besides,' he said, 'the bag and the canisters are still here. No one took them away.'

Villiers looked at Cooper as he turned away from the car.

'Another one, then,' she said.

'Looks like it.'

It was hardly the first time. Every week now, someone drove out into the Peak District to spend their final moments in a favourite picturesque location. Heeley Bank was just the latest.

Cooper was struggling to understand the motivation. Did that last glimpse of the hills really make the moment of dying easier? Could the sound of the wind, a running stream or the bleat of a sheep help to ease the pain of that inevitable slide into death?

People must believe it did, he supposed. Unfortunately, no one was still around to testify whether it was true or not.

Cooper reached into the car and picked a handful of items off the top of the dashboard. A parking ticket timed the previous afternoon, which had been stuck to the windscreen. A photograph in a card frame. Two couples, probably in their thirties. One might be Roger Farrell, but there was no point comparing it to the face of the dead man, which had become unrecognisable.

'Is there a photo driving licence?'

'Yes.'

Abbott passed him a plastic evidence bag. Yes, it looked like the same person, though with a bit more hair in the photograph and a bit less weight. In fact, there was a distinct resemblance between the two men in the picture, the second perhaps a few years younger and a few pounds heavier. Two brothers with their wives? They looked close, though appearances could be deceptive.

'There's something else in there,' said Villiers. 'I can't quite see what it is. It's slipped down at the bottom of the windscreen.'

Cooper fished into the gap with a gloved finger and retrieved a card. He thought it was a business card. A bit pretentious, but that was the style in some businesses. Fancy design in your cards. It was all about presentation.

But it wasn't a business card. Not the usual kind anyway. There was no name on it, neither a company nor an individual. There was no office location, no phone number, not even an email address. It simply carried a string of numbers and letters like an online password. And above it were three words:

Secrets of Death.

5

'Suicide tourists,' said Detective Constable Luke Irvine with an exasperated roll of his eyes. 'They'll be organising coach parties next. A cheap day out in the Peak District. No return ticket required.'

Cooper frowned. Suicide tourists? It was the sort of lurid phrase that would find its way into a newspaper headline if it was repeated to the wrong person. And then everyone would be insisting that something should be done about it. Was it the job of the police to stop suicides? Probably – everything else seemed to be these days. Police officers covered for the jobs of social workers, ambulance drivers, paramedics and midwives. Why not counsellors and mental health professionals too?

The real question wasn't why people killed themselves. It was why they were doing it *here*.

Cooper was very aware that it was threatening to have a bad effect on the tourist trade as the height of the summer season approached. Families were getting nervous of bringing their children into the Peak District, for fear of what they might find: a reality of death that would scar their offspring for life.

Given the number of tourists the national park attracted, it was unlikely the average visitor would stumble across a body. In fact, the odds were very much against it. But statistics and probability factors never counted for anything in the face of popular perception. People feared violence, though they had never witnessed it. They were terrified of flying, though they were more likely to get run over crossing the road.

And everyone was afraid of a reminder of death. That wasn't what they signed up for when they were tempted by the national park's tourism leaflets. It wasn't part of the unwritten contract, that promise they were given of peace and tranquillity. Even the sight of a dead sheep or the squashed debris of roadkill tended to attract complaints. A human corpse bloating in a car was no one's idea of a nice day out.

'This Roger Farrell. Who was he exactly?' asked Cooper.

While he and Carol Villiers had been at Heeley Bank, DC Becky Hurst had been busy on the phones making enquiries into Mr Farrell's background. They'd located a sister living in Nottingham and they'd spoken to some of his colleagues at his place of work.

Hurst snapped open her notebook. She had a brisk attitude and a businesslike air that Cooper liked. She was someone who would watch for reactions and absorb impressions, chipping in an unexpected question. She seemed to approach every job the same, big or small, clutching her notebook and phone in her hand, her expression alert and eager. She had been the perfect choice to work with his recently retired old-school DC Gavin Murfin. She'd been the only person who could keep Murfin under control and pointing in the right direction. In the past, when the two of them were working together, Hurst had looked like a young Border Collie shepherding an ageing ram.

'This is what we know so far,' she said. 'It isn't much.'

'Go on, Becky.'

Hurst reported that Mr Farrell seemed to have barely known anyone. His colleagues communicated with him mostly by email from the other end of an open-plan office. Some of them had struggled to remember what he even looked like. For them, Roger Farrell seemed to have been a distant blur in a suit.

So what about his private life? Not much there either. Farrell wasn't a member of any local clubs or organisations, so far as they could tell from the information his sister had provided. He wasn't the kind of man who took part in the pub quiz night or attended any of the nearby churches. He never showed any interest in politics, sport or charity fund-raising.

So Farrell obviously wasn't one of life's joiners. Yet his final decision had been to join the suicide movement. But was that joining? Or was it the ultimate opt-out?

'Heeley Bank seems to have been a very deliberate choice,' said Villiers. 'He'd driven all the way from Nottingham to be there. It's not as if he passed it every day. He made a special trip to end his life.'

'And there was no CCTV at the information centre,'

44

said Hurst. 'That might have been a factor in his thinking. Too many cameras in the city. He didn't want to be on video.'

'I suspect there was more to the location than that,' said Cooper. 'It meant more to Mr Farrell than just a quiet corner without cameras. Remind me – where was that last suicide we had? Monsal Head?'

'That's right. A great choice,' said Irvine.

'Sorry?'

'I mean – if you wanted a good view.'

When Irvine had first made it into CID, Cooper had been reminded of himself as a young DC, not quite knowing what was going on most of the time but reluctant to ask too many questions in case he seemed dim or was laughed at. Irvine had soon got over that phase – faster than Cooper had himself all those years ago. Every generation seemed to mature more quickly than the last. Luke had begun to gain that air of cynicism more associated with world-weary middle-aged detectives like Gavin Murfin.

Cooper sometimes thought the structure of his team was a bit fragile. He'd noticed that Irvine often teased Becky Hurst for her opinions, and occasionally he'd been forced to step in and ask him to tone it down. Politically, it was obvious the two of them were on opposite sides. Not that politics was openly discussed in the office – it was part of their duty to remain impartial. Yet, in conversation, their views often clashed. Hurst particularly hated it when he called her Maggie Thatcher.

'And there was one before that in Upperdale, on the

45

River Wye,' added Hurst. 'Those locations are pretty close together, if it means anything.'

'At least they're going for remote locations outside of town,' said Irvine. 'I mean, we haven't found one sitting on a bench by Lovers' Bridge or dying over a plate of Bakewell pudding in Granny Eyre's tea shop, have we? They're looking for a quiet spot to do it in.'

Hurst shook her head. 'The Heeley Bank Information Centre isn't quiet any day in the summer. Nor is the car park at Monsal Head.'

'Well, not during the day. But at night . . .?'

'I wonder if they might have been in contact with each other.'

'How?'

'The way most of us make contact with people who have similar interests – on the internet.'

'A suicides' discussion group, you mean?'

'I bet there are lots of them out there, if you look.'

'I'll do an online search, shall I?' said Irvine.

Cooper was looking at the card he'd recovered from Roger Farrell's BMW. The lettering was on a black background. Funereal black. The delicate gold edging did little to make it look more cheerful. *Secrets of Death?* What secrets? Did it refer to the methods to use when committing suicide? Surely there was no secret about that. An overdose, a hanging, a leap from a high place, a convenient railway line and a high-speed train. There were limited permutations. People took the opportunities that were available, whatever means came to hand. They weren't always the best methods. And they didn't always work either.

46

Yet the cases they had recorded so far had all been entirely successful.

Secrets of Death. Written with capital letters too, as if it was a name or the title of a book.

'Do that, Luke,' he said. 'And when you're doing a search, look for this phrase in particular.'

'Secrets of Death? Sounds a bit Goth. But okay.'

'It will come down to a question of why, won't it?' said Villiers. 'That's the real secret. The motivation.'

'Depression, bullying, guilt, divorce, a terminal illness,' said Hurst. She rattled off the list like a railway station announcer repeating the litany of station stops for the thousandth time. 'People can just start to feel there's no point in going on.'

'Well, those are some of the reasons,' said Cooper. 'Let's keep an open mind. There could be lots more.'

'But why kill yourself?'

'Endorphins,' said Irvine.

'Endorphins?' repeated Cooper, surprised. 'What do you mean, Luke?'

'Well, you've heard about near-death experiences.'

Villiers and Hurst looked at Irvine, the former stony-faced and the latter with a sigh of exasperation, as if to say 'Here it comes'. Luke had these moments, when he liked to throw in ideas from left field. Cooper suspected he was a regular reader of *Fortean Times*. He always seemed to know about the newest conspiracy theories, the latest UFO sighting, the accounts of mystery big cats in the English countryside.

'Is this relevant, Luke?' said Villiers.

'I think it might be,' said Irvine defensively.

Cooper saw his expression turn mulish. If Luke was discouraged, he would feel excluded from the discussion.

'Let DC Irvine get it off his chest,' said Cooper.

Hurst sighed again and lowered her head as if she was going to bang it on the table. Cooper looked at Irvine expectantly. 'Luke?'

'Well, depending on your beliefs,' said Irvine carefully, 'NDEs can be regarded as hallucinations, spiritual experiences or proof of life after death. But doctors say near-death experiences are due to endorphins released by the body at the moment of death. They create chemical changes in the brain, you see.'

'Yes?'

'Well, everyone who has ever had a near-death experience reports an overwhelming sense of peace and well-being, and a feeling of being separated from the body. The final stage is a perception of walking through darkness towards light. Whatever an NDE might be, it isn't painful. Far from it. It's always described as a wonderfully positive experience.'

'So your point is?'

'Endorphins,' said Irvine. 'That's what it's all about. It's not just about death. These people were all seeking the release of endorphins at the moment of dying. It's a possibility, isn't it? Like a drug that people crave. A special high. And in this case, there's only one way to get it.'

'Actually, I've heard you can release endorphins by eating plenty of dark chocolate,' said Villiers.

'Or just by having a laugh or a good gossip,' said

Hurst. 'Maybe that's why men commit suicide more often than women. Not enough chocolate and not enough gossiping.'

Cooper couldn't argue with that. There might well be some truth in it.

Ben Cooper always felt frustrated when he had to watch his DCs leaving the CID room and heading out to do all the legwork on the ground.

It was one of the downsides to promotion – the responsibility and the need for delegation that came with it. Young detectives like Luke Irvine and Becky Hurst had to be allowed to use their initiative and take some of the responsibility. Which sometimes meant he had to stay in the office, tied to his desk.

And then there was all the paperwork. Of course, he had known it would happen when he'd accepted the step up to DI. If he hadn't known already, there were plenty of people waiting to tell him – some of them with unrestrained glee, knowing they would never get promoted themselves and wouldn't have to deal with it.

The big issue of the moment was overtime. The finance department was being very persistent about it. Police officer overtime was the main controllable cost in an organisation like Derbyshire Constabulary, and the bean counters spent a lot of their time desperately trying to analyse and rationalise the figures from inevitably poor information they were given by front-line staff.

From Cooper's point of view, it was the most difficult

thing in the world to judge how long an officer should spend investigating a crime. At one time, he would have expected a member of his team to explore every available avenue before closing an inquiry on the grounds of insufficient evidence. It was probably what the law-abiding public still expected too.

But that was when resources weren't so tight. Now crime investigation was reduced to a budget calculation. When enough time and money had been spent, the plug had to be pulled. It could surprise and anger a victim of crime when they found out. In the case of house burglaries, if immediate forensic evidence wasn't present at the scene in the form of fingerprints or DNA, there was often little the police could do except issue an incident number for the insurance claim.

Some of it was above Cooper's pay grade. A proportion of the force's budget was spent on partnerships. The suspicion was that the money might be covering the shortfall for local authorities. Only the Police and Crime Commissioner and members of the senior management team would know that for sure.

One thing he definitely had to worry about was the cost of any forensic services he asked for. At the serious end of crime, in a large murder inquiry, money was rarely a major issue. But, in lower-priority cases, forensic resources were too expensive to be justified. Even with the new forensic centre opened at Hucknall in Nottinghamshire to pool resources between neighbouring forces, Cooper had to think twice about whether he could justify the cost.

*   *   *

A few minutes later, Detective Superintendent Hazel Branagh was frowning at Ben Cooper over a new pair of glasses. They made her face look as though all her features had been compressed to a small space behind the lenses. As a result, she looked even more intimidating than usual.

'Too many bodies in too many cars,' she said. 'It's becoming an epidemic.'

'Yes, ma'am,' said Cooper. 'Or a small outbreak, at least.'

He waited, wondering why everyone had started sounding like headline writers. He could guess which phrase was coming next.

'Suicide tourism,' said Branagh. 'That's what they're calling it, am I right?'

'Some of them are, ma'am.'

'It shouldn't be encouraged. It gives a bad impression of our area.'

Cooper nodded. That was all very well, but how did you discourage your boss from using the phrase?

The Detective Superintendent's office had been moved in the latest reorganisation of E Division headquarters. Its new location was as far as it could possibly be from the CID room and the detectives actually working on inquiries.

When he was sent for, Cooper had to climb a flight of stairs and walk down a long corridor that turned a corner twice in its length for no apparent reason. The lights were on time switches and operated by sensors. They came on as he approached, then went out again when he'd passed.

It was a cost-saving measure, of course. The finance department probably had a spreadsheet showing how much the force's spending was reduced by not leaving the lights on. Was it more than the sensors and installation of time switches had cost? That wasn't a certainty. The amounts probably came from different parts of the budget, so weren't actually added up in any way that made sense. Cooper didn't know. It wasn't his area of expertise.

One thing he was sure about, though. On a June day in bright sunshine, those corridor lights didn't need to be on at all.

'Do you think there's something behind it, Ben?' asked Branagh, her use of his first name indicating a more relaxed mood.

'Yes, that's my instinct.'

Some senior officers would have laughed and raised an eyebrow when he referred to his instinct. But Hazel Branagh knew him by now. And, for his part, he trusted his superintendent well enough to know she wouldn't dismiss what he said.

It had taken him a while to warm to Detective Superintendent Branagh. He'd once thought of her as a negative influence in E Division. He'd even pictured her sitting in her office casting a dark spell, like Lord Voldemort. That seemed very unfair now. He'd been judging her purely from outward appearances. It was because she always looked so serious, never smiling at a joke or even at good news. And there was something about the way her face was constructed that made the corners of her mouth turn down and her jaw fall into a disapproving grimace. With her broad shoulders and severe hairstyle, she did look intimidating. Many junior officers were frightened of her.

Cooper had worked closely with her for long enough now to know that it was only superficial, a façade she used when it was useful. Underneath, she cared deeply about the job and about the officers working for her. It was rare enough these days. She was a genuine copper.

Hazel Branagh had gone through the ranks, spent her time on the streets as a PC and working on the front line as a response officer before moving into CID. She'd followed the traditional route, moving with each promotion to a different role, from one division to another, from speciality to desk job, before ending up as crime manager in charge of E Division CID.

Like most officers, Cooper respected someone who'd got the experience under their belt. These days, with fast-track procedures, it was possible to progress from constable to superintendent in seven years. And now the first direct entrants were coming in, recruited from other professions to take on superintendent roles without any experience in the police service at all. They came from finance, law and the civil service. They were expected to bring different perspectives and be from diverse backgrounds. In other words, they were anything but police officers.

'So do these individuals have anything in common?' asked Branagh. 'Apart from suicidal tendencies and a fondness for a nice view.'

'Nothing that we know of yet. But that's the direction our enquiries will be taking.'

Branagh glanced at his summary of the incidents so far. She noticed the widespread and unrelated addresses.

'And really,' she said, 'why are they coming here? Did it have to be our division? It doesn't make any sense.'

'It's because of who we are,' said Cooper.

'You think so?'

'Yes, it's to do with the nature of the area.'

And he felt sure that was true. The Peak District wasn't just the UK's first national park, it was one of the most visited national parks in the world. That was because the Peak District wasn't remote. It was surrounded by a ring of cities and large towns – Sheffield on one side, Greater Manchester on the other. Not to mention Derby and Nottingham, and Stoke-on-Trent and Chesterfield. There was a huge urban population within an hour's drive of the park and they treated the place as their own backyard.

For some people, it was also a place to go to die.

'My feeling is that there's some element of organisation behind this wave of suicides,' he said. 'It's more than a series of coincidences.'

'Organisation?' said Branagh. 'I don't like the sound of that. An orchestrated trend? Are you sure, Ben?'

'Well, no,' said Cooper. 'I'm not. But it's a possibility.'

'I sincerely hope you're wrong,' said Branagh. 'That sounds very disturbing.'

'I agree.'

'We need to get to the bottom of it, anyway. Whether

organised or not.' She looked at Cooper for a moment. 'Are you happy to stay with this, Ben? I can let you have time, and of course your existing team. We'll find a way to ease the current workload so you can concentrate on this issue.'

'It's considered that important?' said Cooper.

'Well, it can't be allowed to go on. It's starting to attract the attention of the media. The press office have been getting enquiries from national newspapers. We can all imagine the headlines, can't we?'

'Absolutely.'

'I appreciate it wouldn't normally be something that lands on your desk, but these are unusual circumstances.'

'We're on top of it already,' said Cooper.

'Good.'

'There's just one condition,' he said. 'If I may?'

Now Branagh did raise an eyebrow. 'And what's that, DI Cooper?'

'I'd like to see Carol Villiers moved up to Acting DS.'

'Really?'

'Her promotion is long overdue, ma'am.'

'She came to us with a lot of experience, didn't she?'

'Yes, from her service with the RAF Police. Besides, we've lost DS Sharma to liaison with Immigration Enforcement.'

'You're probably right.'

Cooper was pleased to hear her say that. He'd been recommending a promotion for Carol Villiers for the past year or so, without any success.

He knew he could always rely on Villiers to support

55

him, and without the sarcastic and dismissive comments he would have got from Diane Fry when she was in E Division. So there was nothing he wanted more than a promotion to detective sergeant for her. The irony was that she might then get transferred away from E Division, since there was no vacancy at Edendale at the moment.

Branagh made a note. It always looked official when she made a note. If she didn't, it suggested she was going to forget what he'd said as soon as he left the room.

Then she looked again at his summary of the suicide cases.

'At least these locations are relatively remote,' she said.

'So far, ma'am.'

'Yes, so far.'

It was a nagging worry in the back of Cooper's mind that an incident would happen one sunny weekend in a packed tourist hotspot like Castleton or Dovedale. That would cause chaos.

The entire population within the national park was no more than the size of a couple of small towns. The people who lived and worked in the area were over-whelmed by the sheer volume of visitors, who numbered in their millions. The Peak District's prox-imity to major conurbations meant that about twenty million people lived within an hour's drive.

Yet the distribution of visitors was very uneven. There were vast areas of the Peaks you could go to where you might see no one all day. You just needed a bit of energy and determination to get there.

On the other hand, Dovedale alone received an estimated two million visitors each year. The famous and much photographed stepping stones across the River Dove were like a tourist highway in the summer, with their own traffic jams and their own incidents of road rage. Or stepping stone rage. So far, there had been no injuries apart from a few wet feet when someone went into the water.

Then there were Bakewell, Castleton, Chatsworth, Hartington – their role as honey pots attracting crowds of visitors created ever more pressure. The last thing they needed was suicide tourism.

'As for the staff situation . . .' began Branagh.

'Yes, ma'am?'

'Of course, the senior management team is very much aware of the pressure on front-line resources,' she said, as if reading from a press release. 'We're currently looking at ways of supplementing staff levels.'

'Really?' said Cooper.

The superintendent gave him a surprised look, as if he'd just flatly contradicted her. But he wouldn't have been able to do that, since he wasn't clear what she was saying.

'That's good news, ma'am,' he said.

'Absolutely. I knew you'd be pleased.'

Cooper left Superintendent Branagh's office and walked back down the corridor, watching the lights come on and off as he passed through the sensors. He was wondering whether he really was going to be pleased, or not.

6

Back in his own office, Ben Cooper sat down with Carol Villiers to go through the reports again. Individually, the cases were sad. Taken as a whole, they were part of a growing tragedy. But was there a pattern?

There were always a small number of suicides to deal with. But the figures plotted on to a chart showed a steep upward trajectory in recent weeks, a worrying trend that couldn't be ignored. Four in April, only two the month before. Then six in May. Now June was looking even worse. It was still early in the month, yet the suicides were mounting up.

So the reports made a large, daunting stack on his desk.

'There are too many,' said Villiers. 'We can't review all these, Ben. And there's no obvious pattern. These earlier ones are such a diverse bunch. A student, a single mother, a disgraced curate, an ex-soldier, a convicted paedophile. And they're from all over the region too.'

'No pattern at all,' agreed Cooper. 'Not on the surface, anyway.'

'So what should we do?'

'Divide them up. You and I will take a look at the most recent. As many as we can examine in detail. We'll let the rest of the team handle the older cases. They can trawl through them and see if they can come up with any connections.'

Villiers took a file from the stack and slid it on the desk.

'Okay, how about starting with this one?' she said.

On the twenty-first of May a young man had been found sitting on the bank of the River Wye at Upperdale. His motorbike was standing in the adjacent lay-by. It had recently been polished and still smelled of oil. His helmet was placed neatly on the seat. Underneath it was an envelope addressed to his mother.

Three weeks earlier, he'd been made redundant from his job at a theme park, where he'd been helping to maintain the rides. Then his long-term girlfriend had left him when she'd discovered she was pregnant. Not because the child wasn't his, but because she knew perfectly well he was the father. He'd been present at the conception, but she didn't want him there for the birth. Or for the rest of the child's life either.

He'd lived in the Allestree area of Derby, renting a small one-bedroom flat close to the Park Farm shopping centre. He paid a month's rent in advance – probably about all he had to his name after he'd bought food and a tank of petrol for his bike. How had he imagined he was going to support a family? Well, perhaps that was a question he'd asked himself and been unable to answer.

The young man's name was Alex Denning. He was twenty-two years old.

'I can't imagine how anyone would get so desperate at that age,' said Villiers, touching the file softly with the palm of her hand, as if she couldn't be quite sure it was real. Or as if she was trying to read more from it than the printed words actually said.

Cooper shook his head over the report. 'I don't know for sure, Carol. I think you can reach that position at any age, where you can see no point in going on. There *has* to be a point, doesn't there? At least, we have to believe there's one.'

'But he had his whole life ahead of him. Okay, a couple of things hadn't worked out for him, but that's the way life is for everyone. He would have found another job. Someone else would have come along. Someone better. And it won't happen for him now. It's such a waste.'

'Mr Denning couldn't see that, I suppose. He wasn't looking that far ahead, just to the next day, the final tank of petrol, the last ride out into the Peak District.'

'He must have had family or friends he could talk to. He rode a motorbike – bikers tend to hang around together, don't they?'

'Yes. But I think they only talk about bikes.'

She put the file aside reluctantly and picked up another.

'Who's next?' asked Cooper.

'David Kuzneski, aged forty. He was a credit controller for one of those outsourcing operations that have contracts with local authorities and large companies.

He'd been there for five years, was well qualified for the job and well regarded by managers. Kuzneski worked in an office in the centre of Sheffield, but he'd been off work due to illness for several months. He lived on the outskirts of the city, at Totley. And he's the only one on our list who was married.'

'And he was found at Monsal Head,' said Cooper, picturing the location.

'That's right.'

'Cause of death?'

'An overdose of lithium carbonate. The pathologist's report says that the minimum fatal dose for lithium carbonate is fifteen 300mg tablets. When we examined his computer, we found that David Kuzneski bought sixty tablets for less than thirty pounds on a US internet site, without the need for a prescription.'

'He can't have taken all sixty.'

'No, surely not. Even fifteen tablets are a lot to take at once. A larger number becomes physically difficult to swallow.'

'So have we found the ones that were left?'

'Not yet. We're still looking.'

'They could be important,' said Cooper, though he didn't know why and was glad that Villiers didn't ask.

'Kuzneski?' she said instead. 'What do you think . . .?'

'It's a Polish name.'

'Yes, but he isn't a recent immigrant. He was born in Sheffield and his family are from Sheffield too.'

'He probably had a grandfather who settled in the area after the Second World War. There were quite a few Poles here already before the EU. They just didn't have the delicatessens.'

'There's no indication here that he left a note,' said Villiers.

'No, and that's odd, isn't it?'

'Why?'

'If he was married. There would usually be a letter or a message of some kind for the wife, even it's to say, *"It's all your fault".*'

'Perhaps we should ask Mrs Kuzneski again. She might have been treated with kid gloves at the time of the death.'

'Whereas we can be tougher on her now?' said Cooper. 'So which of us is going to play bad cop?'

Villiers grinned. 'I know you can't do it, Ben. But I can.'

'That's why I like you.'

'Thank you,' she said. 'By the way, there's a note in the file here that Kuzneski's funeral is this week.'

'Interesting. That's worth bearing in mind.'

Villiers looked up and met his eyes. 'Lithium carbonate,' she said. 'It's prescribed for the treatment of bipolar disorders. What they used to call manic depression.'

'I know,' said Cooper.

'David Kuzneski had been suffering from a bipolar condition for nearly eighteen months before his death. It was why he'd been on sick leave from his job for a while. The condition was getting worse, despite the medication.'

'Then he bought himself an extra supply of lithium

carbonate tablets online, presumably without his doctor's knowledge.'

'And he took enough of them to end his own life.'

'Mmm,' said Cooper thoughtfully. 'I doubt his GP told him what a lethal dose would be, though. That would be totally unethical.'

'Of course. What are you thinking?'

'That he must have got the information somewhere else, of course. And what about our latest case, Roger Farrell. He's from Nottingham?'

'Right. Forest Fields,' said Villiers. 'We've managed a good geographical spread, haven't we? Just in these last few cases, we've got Nottingham, Derby and Sheffield. It's almost as if they've been chosen to have as little connection as possible.'

'And their jobs too. Farrell worked as a sales representative.'

'Yes, for a company producing memory foam beds, orthopaedic mattresses and back-care products.'

Cooper shook his head. 'I don't see any connection from these reports. Quite the opposite.'

'Nor me.'

'We need to look at each individual and check their online activity. Look for any connections between them, any links or references to suicide websites.'

Villiers made a note. 'Okay. And there's this one too,' she said. 'I don't know if it fits, though.'

'Why?'

'It's a man called Anson Tate, who attempted suicide from a bridge here in Edendale.'

'I remember that,' said Cooper. 'The bridge incident.'

And it wasn't just any bridge either – it had been the seventeenth-century Bargate Bridge, much photographed by tourists, where water foamed over a stone weir and the riverbed was littered with dangerous rocks.

Mr Tate's leap into the River Eden had been prevented by passers-by at the last moment. He'd left a note in a bag on the pavement, which had been picked up by a community support officer. In the note, he blamed loneliness and isolation, a feeling of worthlessness, the fact that no one cared about him, that there was no future for him to look forward to. It was the standard sort of suicide note, blaming no one in particular but society and life in general. It was a letter written by someone who saw himself as a victim.

Anson Tate had certainly been a loner, according to his details. He was aged fifty, a former journalist with a major newspaper group who'd gone freelance when his job had been rationalised out of existence, but had struggled to make a living. He had no family locally, having moved to Nottinghamshire from the Northeast of England many years ago. He had never married.

'Mr Tate was the first one,' said Villiers. 'Well, the first of this recent surge.'

'A survivor,' said Cooper. 'He's the one we should talk to. He might have some useful information.'

'A failed suicide, though. He won't be feeling any better about himself, knowing he can't even do that right.'

'It says here he was referred to the mental health team. He should have been getting counselling since the incident.'

'Working on his feelings of failure?' said Villiers doubtfully. 'Well, I suppose it works for some people.'

'We need to track him down and talk to him.'

'There's an address for him in Mansfield. I'll get someone to check it out and see if he's still there.'

'To see if he's still alive even.'

Villiers collected the files together. 'So what do you want to do, Ben? How are we going to handle it?'

'We should visit Roger Farrell's home first,' said Cooper. 'That's probably all we've got time for today.'

'Nottingham? I'm ready.'

'And tomorrow I'd very much like to visit some of these locations.'

'To do what?'

'To look at the view,' he said. 'And to think about death, of course.'

'You know, my mother always used to say it was caused by the weather,' said Cooper as he and Villiers sat in his Toyota in the West Street car park.

'What was?'

'Suicide. It was an old belief, I think – that the cold and rain, and the long nights of winter, were what led people to get depressed and want to kill themselves. *The weather of our souls reflects the weather of the skies.*'

'Is that what she said?'

'It was something like that.'

'She was quite a wise woman, your mother,' said Villiers. 'I think I remember her. Or I remember people talking about her anyway.'

'Wise woman? You make her sound like the local witch.'

'No, not that. But she was full of local lore, wasn't she? Everyone used to quote her, just as you did now.'

Cooper nodded. 'You're right, Carol. I don't know where she got it all from. My granny probably. She was just the same.'

'I can imagine.'

They were silent for a moment, watching police officers and civilian staff passing in the car park.

'It's not true, though,' said Cooper. 'It's nothing to do with the weather or even the long dark nights. Statistics show that the suicide rate falls in the winter and starts to increase again in the spring. I looked it up.'

'Really? So the actual peak time . . .?'

'Is about now, yes.'

'I don't understand why that would be. Look at it – the grass is growing, the flowers are out, the lambs are in the fields. And the air . . . well, you can feel it in the air, can't you?'

'Of course,' said Cooper. 'But that's exactly the problem, don't you think?'

'What do you mean?'

He paused, trying to find the right words to explain himself properly. He hadn't analysed it fully in his own head, but as he was speaking to Villiers he found his thoughts clarifying.

'It's seeing and feeling everything around you bursting into new life, while your own existence is still frozen in some desolate, permanent winter. It emphasises the chasm between you and everyone else. It makes you realise you don't belong in the world. That your time is over, along with the winter.'

Cooper knew he had finished the thought sounding too convincing for comfort. As he spoke the last sentence, he heard Villiers catch her breath. She seemed to be avoiding looking at him. An uncomfortable silence developed in the car, the kind of atmosphere he'd been used to with Diane Fry, but not with Carol. Slowly, Cooper began to realise that he might have gone too far, expressed too much.

'Shall we move on?' she said finally. And at least her voice sounded normal.

'Yes, let's do that,' said Cooper, and started the car.

7

It took them almost an hour and a quarter to reach the Forest Fields area of Nottingham via Chesterfield and a trip down the M1. Traffic was already beginning to stream out of the city towards the suburbs, so at least they were heading in the right direction: going in.

Roger Farrell's address was in Berridge Road, a semi-detached property with a bay window and a small glazed porch, and a dormer window in the roof where an attic room had been converted. These properties weren't big, and some of the houses a few doors down were in poor condition, with tiles missing and weeds sprouting from the guttering. Cars were parked tightly on both sides of the road. The space caused by the absence of Farrell's blue BMW had already been claimed by the driver of a white Transit van.

But the area was close to the city, seconds from the tram line and with schools within walking distance. Farrell's street ran straight as an arrow downhill to the Forest recreation ground and the trees beyond the park-and-ride, so from here he seemed to be looking out into the countryside rather than towards Nottingham city centre.

They were met in the house by Roger Farrell's older sister. Fay Laws was a woman in her mid-fifties who looked as though she'd dressed in a hurry. Her hair was blonde with grey streaks, and strands of it had escaped in a random fashion.

Mrs Laws had been visited by local uniformed officers earlier in the day and had travelled to the mortuary in Edendale to officially identify the body of her brother. As she unlocked the door of the house, Carol Villiers asked her how she was. She said she was fine, which was what people always said, even when they weren't.

She went on to tell Villiers that she lived on the other side of Nottingham, in West Bridgford, with her husband and two grown-up children, one of whom was still living at home, though he was in his twenties.

Cooper didn't know West Bridgford, but he thought it must be a different type of area from Forest Fields. Mrs Laws looked over her shoulder twice as she was unlocking the door. Even while she was talking to Villiers. She ushered them into the hallway, then checked outside again before locking up.

'I'm sorry if the identification was distressing,' said Villiers.

'I don't suppose it could be any other way.' Mrs Laws stood hesitantly in the passage, gazing at three identical doors that led off it and looking up a flight of stairs.

'How long had your brother lived here?' asked Cooper.

'About ten years. He moved here when Natalie died.'

'Natalie?'

'His wife. She was killed in a car accident. A multiple pile-up on the M1 in fog. Roger gave up the house in Arnold, said he couldn't bear to live there any more. He changed his job too. He left the car dealership where he was making good money as a salesman and he came here to be nearer his new job. He said it would be convenient.'

She said the word *convenient* in a tone of disbelief, as if it couldn't be an important quality in a property you were considering.

Cooper watched her as she continued to hesitate. He had the impression that she didn't know which door to open.

'Did you visit your brother here much?' he said.

'Not often, no.'

Well, there was no hesitation about that. Maybe she had never been here at all – though she was in possession of a set of keys, so perhaps her brother had lived in hope.

'Roger has a daughter, you know,' said Mrs Laws. 'Ella. She lives in Spain.'

There was a definite emphasis there. *She* lives in Spain. The daughter had much more sense than to be here in Forest Fields.

'I'm sure she's been informed,' said Villiers.

'Yes, she knows what's happened. She's flying over tomorrow.'

Cooper was surprised to see that Fay Laws was crying. Quietly, unobtrusively, but the tears were definitely

70

creeping down her cheeks. She wiped them away with a damp-looking tissue.

'It feels like a punishment,' she said suddenly.

'What does?'

'Roger's death. The way he died. As if he's punishing those of us left behind. Punishing *me*, anyway.'

Cooper and Villiers exchanged glances. They could both see what was happening. Mrs Laws hadn't cared enough about her brother for the past ten years and now she was feeling the full, devastating impact of guilt.

'Did your brother ever mention having suicidal thoughts?' asked Villiers.

'Once or twice he said that he wished it was all over, that he didn't have to go on. It was only when he'd been having a particularly bad week. So I didn't think he meant it. People say things they don't mean all the time, don't they?'

'Yes, that's true.'

'Well, I suppose I should have taken more notice. I ought to have told him to get help, to speak to someone about the way he felt. But I never did. I was so sure he wasn't serious. That means it's partly my fault, doesn't it? I let him down.'

'There's always a feeling of guilt in these cases,' said Cooper. 'People who commit suicide get rid of the pain by leaving it behind for everyone else.'

She looked at him then, calmer on the surface but with something flickering uncertainly behind her eyes.

'Well, he's done that,' she said. 'He's certainly done that with me.'

Slowly, they went through the rooms. The place was untidy but in a lived-in sort of way. Newspapers had been left in a pile on the floor by an armchair. In the kitchen, dishes had been washed but left to dry. Only one bedroom had been in use, the duvet thrown back on the bed for the last time, a washing basket full of clothes that would never be washed.

Cooper picked up a photograph. 'Is this your brother's wife?'

'*Was* his wife,' said Mrs Laws. 'Yes, that's Natalie.'

'She's been dead for ten years, you said?'

'That's right. I didn't like her much, but she was good for him. She kept him on the straight and narrow.'

'Really? You're suggesting he went off the straight and narrow when she died?'

Mrs Laws shook her head vigorously. 'Roger changed, that's all I mean. He lost touch with his family and friends.'

Cooper wondered if that had been Farrell's own choice. Or was it the other way round – his family and friends had gradually dropped all contact with him? It was probably academic, unless something in Farrell's own behaviour had been the reason for the split.

He put the photo back. He'd recognised Natalie Farrell from the picture her husband had with him in his car when he died. Two couples, one of them a younger Roger Farrell and this woman, no doubt taken in happier times. He might have lost contact with the rest of his family but he'd still remembered his dead wife. As he used his exit bag, had he been thinking about her death in that crash in fog on the motorway? There was no way of telling. No way of knowing what went through someone's mind as they died.

In the sitting room, Cooper automatically checked the mantelpiece over a blocked-up fireplace. It was the traditional place to leave a note. But there was nothing except a thin layer of dust.

A thick folder and a laptop were on a table in the dining area. Cooper opened the laptop and switched it on. He saw it was password-protected. He would have to pass it on to the high-tech crime unit for examination if he wanted information on Farrell's recent emails or online activity. The same with the small pile of USB memory sticks in the drawer of the table. He unfastened the folder and flicked through the papers. They seemed to be mostly household utility bills – council tax, bank statements, MoT certificates. So he bagged up the laptop and memory sticks, then turned to the next room.

He was looking for a sign of some kind. Anything that might explain why Mr Farrell had killed himself, or what he'd been thinking. Even a hint of his intention. Whatever Cooper could find might be useful, could cast the faintest of lights on what was happening.

In one of the neighbouring divisions, a teenage girl who committed suicide had been found with a semi-colon drawn on her wrist in ballpoint pen, like a temporary tattoo. It had become a well-known symbol, indicating that the individual was suffering depression, anxiety or suicidal thoughts, or was self-harming. A semi-colon was said to represent a sentence that the author could have ended but chose not to; the author was you, and the sentence your life.

Roger Farrell hadn't left a note, though. He didn't even say goodbye. Well, who did he have in his life to say goodbye to? They all seemed to have left him already.

But wait. Here was what he'd been looking for. An envelope, pinned to a corkboard in the kitchen. One sign, such as it was, that Roger Farrell had planned ahead, had been thinking past the moment of death and that flood of endorphins. Inside the envelope was a reservation for a plot at a woodland burial site in the Golden Valley near Ripley, booked about three weeks ago.

Cooper knew exactly where the site was, too. It lay barely a stone's throw from Derbyshire Constabulary's headquarters and was bounded on one side by a heritage railway line. Mr Farrell had booked himself a single grave there with a tree, costing him a little over £800. There were woodland burial sites around the Peak District too. Buxton, Hope, Thornsett. There, the dead helped to create new woodlands and provide habitats for wildlife.

For a few moments, Cooper looked at the booking form and brochure, wondering what they really told him about Roger Farrell's intentions. The location of the burial site stood out. The Golden Valley. It sounded exactly the sort of place you might expect to end up when you reached that distant white light.

When they left, a man was leaning over the fence from the next house, watching them. He was black-haired and unshaven, and his arms were covered in tattoos.

The man laughed as Mrs Laws ducked her head, turned away from him and scurried back to her car. He narrowed his eyes as he faced Cooper and Villiers.

'You look like police,' he said bluntly.

'Yes, sir,' said Villiers, showing her ID. In Edendale, it was usually considered a good thing to have neighbours keeping an eye on each other's property.

'What are you doing here, then?' he said.

'Making enquiries about your next-door neighbour, Mr Farrell.'

'Oh, him. What's happened to him?'

Cooper waited while Villiers weighed up how much information to give out. It was hardly a secret, though. The fate of Roger Farrell would soon be in the local news.

'We've found his body,' she said.

The man grinned as if she'd just told him he'd won the lottery.

'Topped himself, did he? Not before time.'

Villiers looked taken aback.

'Do you have no concern at all that your next-door neighbour is dead?' she said. 'No curiosity about what might have made him do that?'

'Oh, should I pretend to care?'

'You could try, sir. But it would be a bit late now.'

The man nodded smugly, as if he'd just won an argument. 'There you go, then.'

'Do you know your neighbour well, Mr . . .?'

He didn't fall for that one. He was somebody accustomed to police officers trying to get his details.

'My name doesn't matter,' he said. 'I dare say you can find it out if you want to. And I didn't know *him* at all.'

'You must have had some contact,' put in Cooper. 'Mr Farrell had lived here for ten years.'

'Oh, I saw him. But that's all. He meant nothing to me. Nothing.'

A few minutes later, Cooper turned the Toyota on to Noel Street and followed the tram lines south to work his way through the Hyson Green shopping area towards Bobbers Mill and the M1.

'I saw him, but he meant nothing to me?' said Villiers as they stopped at lights on Radford Road opposite a store with a vast display of vegetables all along its frontage. 'That's really sad, isn't it?'

'I don't think we can blame the neighbour,' said Cooper.

He was thinking of the initial reports about Roger Farrell brought in by Luke Irvine and Becky Hurst. The description of a man whom his work colleagues hardly knew, who had no interest in joining local organisations, or in going to the pub. The ghost in a suit and tie. His own sister had never visited him. So it was hardly surprising that even his next-door neighbour denied knowing anything about him.

Yet Farrell couldn't have been completely anonymous, could he? So what had he done with his time in that house in Forest Fields?

'After all, who *did* Mr Farrell mean anything to?' said Cooper as the lights turned green and he drew away.

It was a question that troubled him all the way back from Nottingham to Edendale.

Diane Fry had told lies to get out of her own apartment. She didn't feel proud of it. But there was only so much she could take at short notice. She'd been entirely unprepared for the arrival of her sister and the child. It had come as a shock to her system.

And it was one of her rest days, for heaven's sake. She deserved a break. A break from, well . . . most things. There *were* a few exceptions.

So she'd told Angie she had work to do. Angie had protested and scoffed at her dedication to the job. But she knew from experience that there was really no point in arguing. She'd got used to Diane being a police officer a long time ago.

'Well, don't worry. We'll manage on our own for a while, won't we?'

Half the time, it wasn't clear who Angie was talking to – her sister or the baby. When she was holding the child, she hardly ever looked up from him. So Diane had to work it out from what Angie was saying and the tone she said it in. The babyish voice was a clue. Though sometimes she forgot and spoke to Diane the same way, as if her sister were an overgrown toddler with minimal language skills.

'You know where everything is,' said Diane, hastily pulling on her jacket.

'Have you got any beer?' asked Angie.

'There's some white wine in the fridge. And half a bottle of vodka.'

'That will do. Won't it, little one?'

Diane resigned herself to finding all her booze gone when she returned home. She should probably call at the Co-op on Wilford Green to stock up. They had an offer on Chardonnay, and she might be in for a siege.

Jamie Callaghan was on a rest day too, after the job the previous evening. He was surprised to get a call from Fry. He was just finishing a session on the benches and cross trainers at a fitness centre in Chilwell.

'Give me half an hour,' he'd said.

So Fry found herself in a beer garden overlooking the water at the Castle Marina, drinking cappuccino. The marina itself was packed with narrowboats and small pleasure craft. Every few minutes, one of them chugged slowly by near her table to pass under a foot-bridge into the Nottingham Canal.

The last of the office workers from the Castle Meadow Business Park were just leaving to go back to their desks at Her Majesty's Revenue and Customs after their lunch break, so there were plenty of tables empty. No one would overhear their conversation.

'I thought you'd be doing some shopping on your day off,' said Callaghan, shading his eyes against the glare of sun off the water.

'Shopping?' said Fry.

Callaghan laughed at her tone. 'We're next to a retail park, if you hadn't noticed. Furniture Village, Home Sense, Mothercare . . .'

'Oh, thanks. I'll bear it in mind.'

He sat across the table from her, his back to the

marina. His shoulders seemed to block out the sunlight.

'You're restless, I expect,' he said. 'You don't like being away from the job, do you, Diane?'

'Not at a critical point in an inquiry, no.'

'So you'd rather be in the office than taking your rest day.'

Fry sipped her cappuccino. 'I suppose so.'

Callaghan had ordered a southern fried chicken baguette, and his cappuccino was topped with cinnamon. The aromas mingled with the scent of his deodorant. His hair was still slightly damp from the shower after his workout.

'Are you sure you don't want anything?' he said, waving a piece of baguette.

'No, I'm fine.'

Fry watched another narrowboat go by, a small dog perched on the bow as its owner cautiously negotiated the turn. Across the water, at the entrance to the marina, was a sign for the chandlery. She had never known what kind of items they sold in a chandlery. She wondered if it was worth paying a visit just to find out, since she had nothing else to do. But it might feel a bit too much like shopping.

Callaghan was watching her curiously, as if trying to read her thoughts.

'How do you think the boss is getting on?' he said. 'Will it be good news for us when we go back in?'

'I doubt it,' said Fry.

'So what are you thinking about? I'm sure it's something do with the Roger Farrell case.'

He was right, of course. She had been turning over

the details in her mind ever since she'd escaped from the apartment in Wilford.

'Yes, it is.'

'You're worried that Farrell might have picked someone else up in the last day or two. I only mentioned it as a possibility. It's not very likely, you know.'

'It isn't that,' said Fry.

'So what?'

'Well, it's those witness reports we've had,' she said. 'Someone asking questions around the Forest Road area.'

'Questions about Farrell.'

'Exactly. I'm thinking we ought to be looking into that a lot more seriously than we are. I'm going to press Mr Mackenzie on it tomorrow.'

'I'll back you up, Diane. You know that.'

'Thanks, Jamie.'

He finished his baguette and wiped his fingers on a napkin. 'It's a pleasure. Is that all it was?'

'No.'

Fry hadn't really acknowledged it to herself, but there was more to her worries than that. She was becoming increasingly anxious about the possibility that Roger Farrell had somehow slipped through their fingers at the last moment.

'I'm wondering if whoever was asking those questions might have something to do with Farrell avoiding our attempts to arrest him.'

'They might have helped him to skip town, you mean?'

'No, not that,' she said. 'It occurs to me that they might not be helping him at all.'

Callaghan squinted at her, as if the sun was now directly in his eyes.

'What do you mean?'

'I'm wondering,' said Fry, 'if they might have arranged for him to disappear completely. And for ever.'

8

Ben Cooper had made a major decision in his life. It was probably one of the biggest steps he would ever take. It tied him down for many years to come, putting him under an obligation to people he would rather not have been forced to deal with. But sometimes you had to take this sort of step. It was all part of moving on, facing facts.

He'd bought himself a house.

The village of Foolow was barely a stone's throw from where he'd grown up at Bridge End Farm. He wasn't sure if that was a good thing or not. Of course he liked to go back and visit often, to see his brother and sister-in-law, and his nieces, who were getting taller by the day. On the other hand, he had a sneaking anxiety that it might be a sign of weakness, that he'd allowed himself to be drawn back towards the security of home when he'd been so close to breaking free completely.

His little flat in Edendale had been the first stage. His planned marriage to Liz and the future they'd mapped out for themselves would have been the second.

There would have been no need to look back at the past if it had all worked out. No necessity for him to be buying a house on his own if Liz hadn't died.

And this wasn't the property Liz would have chosen to live in. He was very aware of that. She had wanted something modern, a three-bedroom semi on an executive housing estate to the south of Edendale, a blank canvas she could make her mark on. But this cottage was old and small. Its stone walls oozed with history and the steps to its front door were worn smooth by generations of previous occupants.

It was squeezed into its village setting as if it had always been there, as if it had grown organically over the centuries, jostling with its neighbours for the available space and light, as much a natural part of its environment as the trees and the grass and the heather on the hills.

So here he was, the owner of a house, a limestone cottage half covered in ivy. He'd looked at many other properties before this. In the end, it was the way the front garden was advertised that swung his decision. The estate agent's details described it as having a pleasant outlook over the surrounding village and rolling hills, with ample room to sit out, read a book and enjoy a glass of wine. If it made even an estate agent feel that way, he knew he would probably like it.

Its name was Tollhouse Cottage. Like all the others in the row, it was nearly three hundred years old, built for farm labourers or estate workers at a time when houses were intended to last several lifetimes. The walls were solid, not those timber and plasterboard things you could put your fist through. Without the door or a window open, he could hear nothing from outside.

It also had a cellar. Just a small one – what they would have called a keeping cellar in the old days, for the storage of items that needed keeping cool in the days before fridges. It *was* cool down there too. He shivered as he stood at the bottom of the short flight of stone steps. The walls were bare, with a slab raised a few inches off the floor. It wasn't just the cold that made him shiver, though. There was damp in the walls. He could see it in patches and feel it seeping into his bones. He was a few feet below ground here, so it was inevitable that it would feel this way, like standing in his own grave.

He went back up the steps, closed the hatch and dragged a rug back over it. He couldn't think what use he would have for a cellar. It wasn't as if he'd brought so many belongings with him from the flat in Welbeck Street. His stuff would fit into this house with room to spare.

'So what do you think, Hopes?' he said. 'I suppose a cat flap is the first priority.'

The cat didn't answer. She was too busy exploring all the corners of the house, making sure she'd claimed every room as her territory. She'd be back to the kitchen soon when she got hungry.

One of the other attractions of the cottage for Cooper was the wood-burning stove. It was a smaller version of the one at Bridge End Farm and he'd already ordered in a stack of logs. He was determined it would be cosy in here during the winter.

He would miss his local in Edendale, of course. The Hanging Gate had been his refuge for the past few years with its scenic Peak District views on the walls, the same old sixties and seventies pop classics playing, the Banks's Bitter and Mansfield Cask Ale. It had been a familiar and unthreatening place to retreat to of an evening, where he could enjoy an hour or two of anonymity.

Foolow had its own pub, the Bull's Head. But this was a small village. They would soon get to know who he was here.

He turned as his brother Matt came through the front door carrying a huge cardboard box.

'It's almost as bad as those caravan people,' said Matt. 'You should see the amount of stuff some of them arrive with. You'd think they were heading out on a polar expedition.'

'They must have heard you have a reputation for being primitive.'

'Don't let Kate hear you saying that. She's in charge of facilities for the site, not me.'

Against his better instincts, Matt Cooper had put one field of Bridge End Farm aside for use as a caravan site. Most farms in the national park were small, less than a hundred acres. That size of farm could only be run as a part-time enterprise, with the farmer and his family taking second jobs or diversifying into the area's biggest industry – tourism.

Tourists were the only reliable source of income for a Derbyshire hill farmer. As well as a small number of static caravans, Bridge End had a few pitches for touring caravans and camper vans. From Easter onwards, there had been a steady flow in and out of the site. Matt had watched each one arrive with a scowl of contempt, until Kate made him stay in the cowshed out of the way.

'You've to get used to having the caravanners, Matt,' said Ben. 'Think of the money they're bringing in.'

Matt grunted as he put the box down on the sitting room floor. 'I'm not sure if it's worth the hassle,' he said. 'They're all townies.'

Ben smiled. Of course, most of the visitors were fine – quiet, friendly, undemanding and no trouble to their hosts at all – but occasionally a family lived down to all of Matt's expectations. He muttered the word *townies* so often now that it had started to lose any meaning. After a while, he had begun to do it unconsciously, as if he had a mild form of Tourette's syndrome.

Matt saw his smile and scowled. 'Well, you know what it's like. They come down the lane towing one of those massive things behind an underpowered car and they block the whole place up for miles around. Some of us are trying to make a living at farming, you know.'

'And not doing very well at it. That's why you need another source of income, isn't it?'

His brother didn't answer. He squatted on the floor to unpack the box, distributing the contents at random around the room without even looking to see what they were. Ben wished his sister-in-law Kate could have been here. She was the organised one. Kate would have this place in perfect order in no time. With Matt's

86

involvement, it would take months to get things right. There would probably be essential items he would never find again.

'The girls seem to like the caravanners, though,' said Ben, remembering seeing his two nieces chatting happily to the visitors on his last call at Bridge End.

Matt shook his head. 'I don't know why. It's not as if they're going to meet any young people of their own age. What self-respecting teenager would want to go on a caravan holiday with their parents?'

He held up an electric toaster as if he'd never seen one before and had no idea what its function was. He put it down on an armchair. Then he straightened up and looked round the room, seeming satisfied with his efforts.

Ben thought he and Matt had little in common physically, except perhaps a look of their father around the eyes and nose. Their mother had been blue-eyed, but the eyes of both her sons were brown, their hair dark where she was fair. Matt had also inherited their father's size, the wide shoulders, the enormous hands – and the uncertain temper.

As he aged, Matt was beginning to look more and more like their father. In years to come, he would look exactly the way their father would have, if he'd lived.

His character was different, though. A rebellious side of his personality was gradually being revealed, which could only have come from their mother. Recently, Matt had joined protests against milk prices, angry at the way he and other milk producers were being prevented from earning a proper living by the pressure to drive down costs for consumers. Farmers had been emptying supermarket shelves of milk, blocking roads outside dairies with their tractors and even taking cows into stores. And Matt had been present at several demonstrations in and around Derbyshire.

Ben had watched with surprise and a certain amount of admiration. Once a dyed-in-the-wool conservative, his brother was in danger of turning into a hot-headed radical. Something had finally pushed him over the edge.

'You've got plenty of space here, anyway,' said Matt, pacing the room to gaze out of the window.

'You mean it looks a bit empty, don't you?'

Matt shrugged. 'There's nothing wrong with a bit of space.'

'I'll get some more stuff when I've finished decorating.'

Matt looked at the pile of paint tins and rolls of wallpaper that had been accumulating in the hallway.

'Are you planning to redecorate the place completely, Ben?'

'Why not?'

'It will take a while if you're doing it on your own.'

'I'll be fine,' said Ben. 'It will give me something to do in the evenings.'

'Rather you than me.'

Matt paused. Ben could hear him breathing heavily and fidgeting with some coins in the pocket of his jeans. It was a habit he recognised, one he'd noticed in his brother before. Not that often. Just when he was building up to saying something important.

'Have you thought,' said Matt finally, 'that you might be doing all this as a sort of displacement activity?'

Ben laughed, then looked at his brother with a burst of affection and understanding. *Displacement activity?* That wasn't a phrase Matt would have thought of himself. He probably had no idea what it meant. His reading matter was confined to *Farmers Weekly* and *Classic Tractor*. There were no psychology textbooks on the shelf in his office, just box files full of movement records and cattle passports. Ben knew it must have come from Kate. Matt had come primed with the right questions to ask.

'Displacement activity?' said Ben. 'What exactly do you mean by that?'

Matt sucked in his breath as if someone had just stuck a needle into his finger. He'd been afraid his brother would ask him to explain.

'All this,' he said, with a vague wave of his arm around the room. 'Taking on this house. Deciding to redecorate the whole thing yourself when it doesn't really need it. You're keeping yourself busy all the time. To avoid having to think about anything else.'

'Is that so wrong?' said Ben gently, feeling sorry for his brother.

Matt looked at him, a puzzled and slightly pleading look in his eye. 'No,' he said. 'I think it's what I would do too.'

'Then there's no problem, is there?'

With a deep sigh, Matt went back to moving the paint tins. 'None at all.'

Ben watched him for a while. 'I'm fine, Matt,' he said. 'Really I am.'

After his brother had gone, Ben took the opportunity to enjoy a few moments of peace. He opened a bottle of beer and sat out on the patio to take in the view and the evening air.

After a wet spring in Derbyshire, summer had burst into life with a vengeance. The brightest greens were blinding in their brightness; the darker shades looked damp and cool.

People in other countries, or even in the cities, didn't realise how green England was until they flew over it. He felt so lucky to be living in one of the most beautiful parts of it. And the Peak District was certainly beautiful. Though it could also be dangerous.

Small puffs of cloud drifted across the blue sky. When he looked out from here over the patchwork of fields, the sun broke through the clouds sporadically, highlighting one field and then another, changing the colours in the landscape as it went, catching a white-painted farmhouse here, casting shadows from a copse of trees over there.

The tracery of white limestone walls was like a map laid over the landscape, so painstakingly constructed that it seemed to hold the countryside together. He sometimes thought that if you followed the right lines on that map you could discover any story, find the clues to any mystery. All the answers might lie caught in this gleaming web.

Ben found himself thinking about his father, Sergeant

Joe Cooper, and wondering what he would have thought of the new house. He would probably have scowled and kicked the plaster and muttered something about rising damp and the electricity bill.

He and Matt had never talked about their father properly. Not ever, in the whole of their lives. And when Joe Cooper died, it was too late to start. The subject had become far too big even to grasp at. So Ben had never told his brother how much he'd come to resent the memories he had, the fact that so few of them were positive. He suspected that their father was still an idol for Matt, in a way. The older brother always had a different experience. And Matt still blamed the police for their father's death. That was an unspoken, but unavoidable fact.

Ben shook himself and took a drink of beer. He had to relax. But having Matt in the new house didn't have that effect on him.

He gazed out at the countryside, wondering who his second visitor to Tollhouse Cottage might be and hoping it wouldn't be too much of a shock.

9

Day 3

For Gordon Burgess, Surprise View was no longer a surprise. He still remembered the first time he'd seen it, though.

He'd been driving over from Sheffield past the Fox House towards Hathersage. As he crossed over Burbage Bridge, he'd been distracted by the dramatic sight of Carl Wark, the Iron Age hill fort brooding on the northern skyline like a shattered stone reminder of the past. It had been set against a foreground of purple heather, acres and acres of it sweeping up the hillside.

A few hundred yards later, he'd passed a roadside car park hacked out of the heather and bracken, and he'd wondered why it had been placed just there. Then came white chevrons indicating a sharp right-hand bend as the A6187 blasted through the gritstone. A battered lump of rock was in front him as he swung the wheel to the right.

And bang – there it was. A huge, astonishing vista had opened up. He found himself looking down across Hathersage to the whole of the Hope Valley as it snaked its way up through Hope and Bamford to Castleton.

The distinctive bare face of Mam Tor, the Shivering Mountain, stood at the head of the valley, with a glimpse of the dark plateau of Kinder Scout on the horizon. The rolling White Peak hills swept in from the south, lapping gently against the hard gritstone tors of the Dark Peak. Dense woodland formed clumps and swirls across the landscape. The view was lit by a hazy summer sun that made the scene look magical, something idealised and unreal from a dreamscape.

It was impossible to stop at that point on the road as it began its descent towards Hathersage. In the year since, doing that same journey, Burgess had seen many brake lights come on as he followed visitors' cars into the Hope Valley, with drivers hitting the pedal in that instinctive reaction to an astonishing panorama suddenly opening up in front of them. He could see them looking for a pull-in where they could reach for the camera to capture the vista. But there was nowhere safe to stop. Surprise View was so beautiful that it was dangerous.

So that was the reason for the car park. It was located a hundred yards or so before the bend, tucked into the hillside below the twisted rock tors of Mother Cap and Over Owler, where the broken slopes marked the site of an abandoned millstone quarry. Its location meant you had to know what you were approaching, otherwise you were past the bend on the descent into Hathersage and you had to circle all the way back.

That suited Gordon Burgess. It meant fewer random visitors getting lost and asking questions. Those people ended up down in the valley bottom.

A jet airliner roared overhead, the voice of a climber drifted clear in the air, a partridge rattled in the heather. In the distance, a rocky edge curved and twisted like a giant snake, two figures visible on top of the rocks, near the trig point.

Looking up the Hope Valley, he couldn't quite make out the cement works at Hope, which visitors sometimes complained about as a blot on the landscape, ruining an otherwise perfect view. Yet the cement works were a major employer for people who lived in the area, as were the limestone quarries, the massive excavations of which scarred the hillsides. Without people living and working in the national park all the year round, this landscape wouldn't exist.

Three vehicles were already in the car park, clustered close to the entrance: a Fiat Panda, a Peugeot Escapade, a Citroën Cactus. Burgess wondered about the names and whose job it was to come up with new models. There were so many that they no longer seemed to bear any relevance to what they were – just machines on wheels, after all.

Perhaps the naming of cars symbolised the whole of life. All surface gloss and pretence, with no meaning behind it. No meaning at all. It had always baffled him that so many people went through their lives not recognising that fact but accepting the meaningless gloss. They thought it was important what kind of car they drove, what letters were on the number-plate, what postcode they lived in, what brand of clothes they wore.

Of course, a few like him saw through it all, recognising the utter meaninglessness of life. Certainly of their own lives. He thanked his lucky stars that he'd found that out in the end, learned that he wasn't alone in the world.

Lucky stars? Well, maybe he could thank God soon and do it in person. If that was what lay beyond death.

There was just one last goodbye to say. *The second secret of death.* He hoped that everyone understood it, particularly his mother. He'd been saying goodbye to her for years, in a way. She just hadn't noticed yet.

He watched a couple leave the Peugeot with a spaniel on a lead. They walked towards a belt of trees and on up the hill towards the moor. None of the visitors had paid the parking charge yet. Surprise View had a card-only payment machine, and the screen was unreadable early in the morning until the sun reached it and cleared the condensation from inside the glass.

But Burgess was going to pay, when he could. It was £4.50 for the day on his credit card. He wouldn't leave with a debt to his name. Especially not when he knew the money would go towards preserving the landscape of the national park.

He'd arrived early to make sure of his place. He didn't want to be stuck in some far corner staring at a patch of bracken and an overflowing litter bin. It was bad enough being on your own without that. He was here because it was his favourite place. The only place in the world he wanted to be right now.

A muffled thump in the back of the car reminded him that he wasn't entirely alone. There was one last job to do.

*　　*　　*

95

Parts of Edendale were crumbling rapidly. And it wasn't just old age, though the town had existed for several centuries. From what Cooper had heard, it was mostly due to the number of cars on the roads. The sulphur dioxide and carbon monoxide in exhaust fumes combined with rain to form an acid cocktail, a toxic mixture that ate away at sedimentary rocks like sandstone.

Cooper could see the results in some of the buildings around the market square as he drove through Edendale from Foolow that morning. The walls of the town hall and the tourist information centre had been partially dissolved up to about knee height. The process had left dangerous-looking holes with a few trickles of sand spilling out of them, as if some monstrous creature had chewed on the tastier bits of the buildings, licking the hollows smooth and spitting out the grit.

According to an article in the *Eden Valley Times*, the district council had considered using a preservative spray, in the hope of saving the most vulnerable areas of the town from collapse. They'd been deterred by one factor – the spray made buildings look pink.

They were probably right. The people of Edendale weren't ready to live in a pink town. But in the end, it might prove better than no town at all.

For Cooper, the best thing about Edendale was that it still retained its own character, a proper sense of place. It had its distinctive smells and sounds and sights, an accumulation of sensations that gave it a unique identity, so that you always knew where you were. The same couldn't be said of many towns and cities, where the high streets had begun to look indistinguishable.

The businesses in the market square were mostly banks and building societies, estate agents and pubs, with a town hall clock that always sounded too loud in an empty square, when its clangs reverberated off the taller buildings.

There was a baker's shop in Clappergate, with wicker baskets, a painted milk churn and a delivery boy's bicycle strung with onions standing outside on the pavement to attract customers. There used to be a New Age shop there too. You could always tell you were near it from the smell of aromatherapy oils and scented candles. But the scent had gone now, along with the Tarot cards and crystals. Other towns were considered more New Age than Edendale.

Cooper particularly liked the narrow lanes and arcades in the oldest part of Edendale, between Eyre Street and the market square. He could wander for hours among the shops selling pine furniture, chocolates and malt whisky, antiques, coffee and books.

Edendale's character made it attractive to outsiders, and not just tourists. Recently a television crew had been filming around the town. Their vehicles and equipment blocked the streets around the market square, attracting crowds of spectators but annoying shopkeepers, who complained they were losing business, and residents, who had to step over lengths of cable snaking across the pavements.

At West Street, Cooper checked his internal emails

and phone messages, read some memos and signed a few reports. There was one memo that he didn't fully understand, but which seemed to refer to what Detective Superintendent Branagh had been telling him yesterday: 'Supplementing staff resources'. It sounded good, but the devil was always in the detail with these things. He would withhold judgement until he saw for himself what it really meant. If he walked into the CID room one day and he had extra staff, he might believe it.

Currently on his desk was an abstraction request, already approved. Three days ago, immigration officers acting on intelligence had raided two local restaurants and arrested four men. The raids took place in Underbank and Lowbridge at about 6 p.m. Staff were questioned to check if they had the right to live and work in the UK. Taken into custody were a Nepalese man and a Pakistani man at one restaurant, and two Pakistanis from the other. All had overstayed their student visas.

One man was detained while steps were taken to remove him from the UK. The others were ordered to report regularly to the Home Office while their cases were progressed. Businesses were liable to a financial penalty of up to £20,000 per illegal worker, unless they could show that the correct pre-employment checks had been carried out.

According to the intel, these arrests could be just the tip of the iceberg. Reports suggested that an organised scheme was being run from a location somewhere in Derbyshire, supplying illegal workers for restaurants, bars and takeaways. It was one of the difficulties for intelligence teams and divisional officers alike that many migrant workers were perfectly legal if they came from a European Union country or had the correct documentation.

So his detective sergeant, Dev Sharma, had been requested and assigned to liaise with the immigration officers. They wanted his experience in the city of Derby, where he'd been based before his transfer to E Division.

Extractions were a headache when you were trying to manage a small team. They were unpredictable and hard to refuse.

Cooper made sure his DCs were occupied, which was hardly necessary, and he collected Carol Villiers.

'Where first?' she said.

'Monsal Head, I thought. Before it gets busy.'

'Kuzneski,' said Villiers.

'That's the one.'

Cooper drove as they headed south out of town on the Buxton Road. It climbed and climbed until it reached a plateau where the limestone quarries competed with the moors as background scenery. The stone slates of the roofs were gradually left behind, petering out along the course of the River Eden.

Edendale sat astride a wide valley in the gap between the two halves of the Peak District. Nowhere was the contrast between the White Peak and the Dark Peak more striking than on the climb southwards out of Edendale, past the last of the houses, past the sports field and the religious retreat run by the Sisters of Our Lady.

It promised to be another warm day and their visors were down against the sun already glaring through the windscreen. Cooper could barely keep his eyes off the landscape as he drove. It was a constant pleasure to escape from Edendale into the surrounding hills, where the changing moods of the scenery always fascinated him.

Of course, appearances could be deceptive. Even the White Peak bore its scars – the great crude gashes where the limestone quarries and opencast workings had been blasted and ripped from its hills.

'David Kuzneski vanished from his home in Totley without telling anyone where he was going,' said Villiers, reminding Cooper of the case. 'He took the family car and disappeared without a word.'

'And, unlike so many cases where someone goes missing, his wife was worried straight away,' remembered Cooper.

'That's right. She phoned the police and tried to convince the call handler that her husband was a vulnerable person. But David Kuzneski was forty years old and therefore low priority. He wouldn't be classed as a missing person for a while.'

Cooper reached the A623 and headed west to Wardlow Mires, turning the Toyota on to a road that skirted the hills above Cressbrook Dale towards Ashford-in-the-Water.

It was almost impossible for him to drive around this area now without passing locations he'd been brought to while pursuing a murder inquiry, often in the company of Diane Fry. Here was the village of Wardlow, with its old red phone box still standing near the church. And not far beyond lay the little overgrown graveyard called the Infidels' Cemetery.

'And that was too long in this case,' he said.

'He was found close to death at Monsal Head before a search had even begun.'

Cooper nodded. From the moment he left home, David Kuzneski had been given time to do whatever he wanted. And what he wanted was to end his own life.

When he saw the first visitors' cars parked in a lay-by, with their owners pointing cameras over the wall, Cooper knew he was at Monsal Head. A few yards further down the hill, he turned into the view-point car park by the Monsal Head Hotel.

Unlike many locations in the national park, you could park all night at Monsal Head for no more than a pound. One of the parking areas overlooked Monsal Dale itself and the spectacular viaduct, with a narrow road plunging down to the River Wye and twisting its way north along the valley bottom towards Cressbrook.

Cooper and Villiers got out of the car. Behind them, the hotel, Hobb's Café and the Stables Bar were all doing good business. A queue had already formed at the ice cream van in the corner of the car park.

Hobb's Café. Cooper smiled to himself. Only in Derbyshire would a café be named after an evil spirit. The rock formation known as Hobb's House was on the hillside a few hundred yards north of the viaduct.

He could see its outline from here, though he suspected most of the visitors who came to Monsal Head weren't aware of it, or what it was said to be. In this case, Hobb was a giant who emerged at night and threshed the farmers' corn – but only as long as you rewarded him with a bowl of cream.

It was a glorious vista from here, though, with the river forming a dramatic horseshoe below the Iron Age hillfort of Fin Cop. Upstream, the peaceful river turned to a raging torrent under the rock spires of Chee Tor. Here, the River Wye wound through a peaceful dense green landscape.

And above it was the dramatic Headstone Viaduct, three hundred feet long, with five fifty-foot-span arches. It soared forty feet above the dale to connect with the opposite hillside. It had once served the Midland Railway, though it was now part of a walking and cycling trail.

The building of this railway line had been a spectacular example of bold Victorian engineering. They had cut a route directly through the limestone landscape of the Wye Valley between Hassop and Buxton, creating no fewer than eight tunnels, two major viaducts and several smaller ones within a distance of just eleven miles. Yet the line had lasted hardly more than a century. In the 1960s it had become a victim of the Dr Beeching cuts.

When it was built, this viaduct had been a particularly controversial project. The writer John Ruskin complained bitterly that the view had been destroyed purely so that 'every fool in Buxton could be at

Bakewell in half an hour, and every fool in Bakewell at Buxton'. It was a passage often quoted, even today.

Nature had performed its magic since Ruskin's time. The raw slashes of the original cuttings had been covered over by vegetation and merged back into the landscape. Now the viaduct was a tourist attraction in its own right, forming the focal point of the spectacular view. People came from both Buxton and Bakewell to admire the vista from Monsal Head, as well as from much further afield.

David Kuzneski had chosen well, thought Cooper. When the tourists and ice cream customers had gone home, there was no better place to spend a few quiet minutes. Even if those minutes were going to be your last. Or perhaps especially if they were your last.

'Where exactly was he found, Carol?' he asked.

'On one of the benches. Just stretched out as if he was asleep, according to the member of the public who came across him.'

'And the cause of death was lithium carbonate poisoning.'

'That's right.'

It wasn't a very common form of suicide. Lithium was sold under several brand names and was used for the treatment of recurrent bipolar depression and affective disorders. It evened out the highs and lows, the mania and depression. In some cases, it was added to the medication for patients who didn't respond to antidepressants alone.

David Kuzneski had been prescribed lithium carbonate for a bipolar condition. Yet he'd also bought an extra sixty 300mg lithium carbonate tablets for less than thirty pounds on a US internet site, without the need for a prescription.

Kuzneski had taken the tablets as he sat on this bench at Monsal Head. He had still been alive when found, but only just. Despite medical intervention, he was pronounced dead on arrival at hospital.

In the viewpoint car park, a series of wooden benches overlooked the dale and the viaduct. Each bench had a plaque attached to it, dedicated by families in memory of some deceased relative.

'This one,' said Villiers.

The bench David Kuzneski had chosen bore a plaque. Cooper stood looking at it, reading the words.

Rest here a while, it said. *When you go, leave all your troubles behind.*

Upperdale was close to Monsal Head. It lay just down in the valley, a slightly hair-rising drive along a narrow, winding road, where he had to dodge tourists' cars coming the other way, as well as walkers and cyclists.

At the site of Alex Denning's suicide, they found a dozen cars tucked into a pull-in deep in the dale, their bonnets pointing towards the river. Beyond Upperdale, the Monsal Trail ran on through two more tunnels at Cressbrook and Litton.

'Sleeping pills. Benzodiazepines. They're not as dangerous as barbiturates used to be. Well, not unless you take them in combination with alcohol or an opioid such as methadone or tramadol,' said Villiers.

'Which did Alex Denning combine them with?'

'Both. Meth and a bottle of vodka.'

'He would have experienced all the symptoms of impairment of the central nervous system. Intoxication, drowsiness, lack of balance, slurred speech.'

'Someone who saw him earlier on at Upperdale said he was drunk. They thought he'd stretched out on the grass to sleep it off.'

'I suppose that's exactly what he did,' said Cooper. 'In a way.'

Who had called sleep 'the brother of death'? It was terrifyingly true. In a way, we died every night, he thought. He wondered how many people went to sleep at night not feeling entirely sure that they'd wake up in the morning. Or whether they wanted to.

But people craved certainty, didn't they? A definite end. The finality of death. That might be preferable to the ceaseless uncertainty of life.

Alex Denning's home was in a seven-storey block, six storeys of flats above a row of garages and service areas at ground level. It was almost opposite the Park Farm Shopping Centre, an outdoor precinct where Cooper could see a Boots, a Wilko and a Co-op.

From a communal entrance, he walked into a tiny hallway. A sitting room, a bedroom and a kitchen with modern units. The neutral decor in all the rooms looked quite recent. The bedroom even had a small balcony overlooking the shopping centre car park. The place looked as though it must have come unfurnished. The contents were sparse and randomly matched. The sofa might have come from one of those charity shops selling second-hand furniture. Yet the TV screen was new and attached to a Sky box.

Denning was a former pupil of Woodlands School, just a few streets away from his flat. He wasn't a low-achiever. He'd done reasonably well in his A-levels, but had never been able to find a well-paying job. He'd been unemployed and on Job Seeker's Allowance for eighteen months before the theme park opening came up. And that hadn't lasted long.

Cooper found a framed photograph on the window ledge. It showed Denning standing on a bridge with his arm round a young woman, presumably the now-pregnant girlfriend. They both looked happy and untroubled. The bridge spanned a river – Cooper could see a weir to one side and dense trees on the other bank.

Then he looked more closely. He realised it was the Lovers' Bridge in Edendale, but before it became completely covered in padlocks. Just a few were visible, near the standing couple. In fact, the locks seemed as much the focus of the picture as the young people themselves.

In the car on the way back to Edendale, they were both quiet with their own thoughts. They were within a mile of West Street when Carol Villiers broke the silence. It hadn't been an uncomfortable one, like the many long, awkward pauses he had experienced with Diane Fry. But he was glad when she spoke. It was better than the thoughts that were going through his head.

'So how is the new house, Ben?' asked Villiers.

Cooper smiled. A safe topic.

'Fantastic,' he said.

'Foolow?' she said.

'That's right. It's perfect. Come and see it for yourself. Call round for a drink tonight, if you like. I've got some beer in the fridge. One of the first priorities, after feeding the cat.'

'No, I can't. I'm going out tonight.'

'Oh?'

Cooper knew Villiers had an active social life. She had plenty of friends in the area, old mates she'd picked up with again when she returned to Derbyshire from her career in the RAF Police. She was a member of a couple of sports clubs in the Eden Valley and probably knew lots of people he didn't. So usually he didn't wonder where she was going and who she was going with. Yet he found himself wondering now and hardly daring to ask.

'Anywhere interesting?' he said, as casually as he could.

'Derby,' said Villiers. 'For the book festival.'

'There's a book festival in Derby?'

'Of course. Didn't you know?' She laughed. 'Oh, I forgot – it's the city. Outside your experience.'

'You almost sound like Diane Fry,' said Cooper. 'But I know you're not really a city girl yourself.'

He saw her face crease uncomfortably at the comparison, but didn't know how to backtrack. Even to him, it sound like an insult now he'd said it.

Villiers let it pass. 'They've got a couple of good authors on. Military history, you know.'

'Oh, I see.'

'Not your sort of thing.'

'I suppose it might be interesting.'

Villiers smiled. 'I hope so. I'm going with a friend.'

'Right.'

Cooper felt irrationally disappointed. Not that she was going to the book festival with someone else – he was only a workmate, after all. And not even that really, since he was her boss while they were at work. It was the fact that she didn't tell him *who* she was going with specifically. It looked like a deliberate withholding of information, as if she didn't want him to know who her friend was. He wasn't sure he liked that. Not from Carol Villiers.

10

Becky Hurst looked up brightly when they returned to the CID room at West Street.

'We've tracked down that failed suicide, Anson Tate,' she said. 'Believe it or not, he's moved from Mansfield and is right here in Edendale. Do you want the address?'

'Of course.'

Cooper took the note with Anson Tate's address. It was out on Buxton Road, where many of the properties were large Victorian houses divided into flats.

He hesitated. Something was nagging at him, something that had been left undone.

'Carol,' he said, 'did you check for recent calls on Roger Farrell's mobile phone?'

'Yes. He hadn't made any calls for several hours before his death. In fact, his phone was switched off when we found it in the car.'

'Of course it was,' said Cooper. 'I suppose he didn't want any interruptions to his final preparations. Some randomly generated sales pitch from a call centre would ruin the moment.'

'It ruins any moment,' said Villiers.

'Nothing else?'

'Well, there was one call from a pay-as-you-go mobile, which must have come in while he was parked at Heeley Bank. But there was no voicemail message left. So that gives us nothing either.'

Cooper hated getting nothing. And it didn't feel right in this case.

'Carol, can you stay here and chase up some of those earlier suicides?' he said. 'We really need to pin down more connections. At the moment, we're just not putting the facts together.'

'I'm on it.'

Recently, a number of asylum-seekers had been dispersed to Derbyshire, and some were housed in Edendale's vacant properties, including a series of sprawling houses in the Buxton Road area. The first appearance of Syrians and Somalis had been met with a degree of hostility in the Eden Valley. Racist slogans had been scrawled on walls and the British National Party were said to be holding recruitment meetings in a local pub. Cooper felt sure it would be short-lived.

This was one of the few areas in the older part of Edendale where the streets weren't lined on either side with parked cars. At least, there were no cars evident in front of the house where Anson Tate lived. But a gravel drive ran alongside the house and disappeared around the back. Perhaps there were garages, an old coach house, or just some space cleared from the garden for residents' parking.

The house hadn't been painted in recent years and

some of the window frames on the upper storeys were beginning to rot from the damp. A set of buttons by the front door had flat numbers on them rather than the names of residents. Probably the occupants changed so often that it wasn't worth listing their names. That, or they preferred to remain anonymous.

Cooper pressed the button for flat 5 and waited. Nothing happened, so he tried again. He couldn't hear anything from inside the house and he wasn't sure the bell was working. Then there was a thump of footsteps descending stairs and a vague shape moved behind the leaded glass of the door.

When he finally answered the bell, Anson Tate turned out to be a rather insignificant-looking man. He was a few inches shorter than Cooper, running slightly to flab, with a narrow mouth and anxious eyes. Well, he was insignificant except for his hair. It was receding, but he'd gelled it forwards into a stiff wedge that came to a point on his forehead. It looked oddly aggressive.

Cooper introduced himself and showed his ID. Tate was initially reluctant to let him into the house. That was perfectly normal. Even innocent people resisted his presence, unless they'd actually sent for the police.

'It's nothing to worry about, sir,' said Cooper. 'I just want a chat.'

'A chat?' said Tate sceptically.

'Yes, that's all.'

Tate led him slowly upstairs. The staircases and corridors were wide, and the ceilings were high, with Victorian architraves and elegant mouldings from which the plaster was peeling. The property would have housed an affluent family at one time, with servants living on the top floor. It was exactly the sort of place that was now in multiple occupancy, divided up into cheap flats and bedsits for people who had no intention of staying long.

'So what can I do for you, officer?' asked Tate.

'I'm hoping you might be able to help me with some enquiries we're making.'

'Helping with enquiries, is it? I didn't realise that old cliché was still in use.'

'I'm sure it will disappear when we find a better one.'

Tate smiled, though it was a smile without humour. 'Sit down, please. Make yourself at home. Such as it is.'

'You haven't lived here long,' said Cooper.

Tate recognised that it was a question. 'No, just a few weeks. Temporary accommodation really.'

'I see.'

'Well, you must know about me,' said Tate. 'The only thing that's of any interest about me, anyway. The fact that I'm still here, when I shouldn't be.'

'I wondered if you would mind talking to me about what led to your attempt to take your own life,' said Cooper, feeling that he was speaking more carefully than was really necessary with this man.

'Oh, all that,' said Tate. 'All that stuff I was planning to leave behind me.'

'I'm sorry if it's distressing for you, sir.'

Tate stared at him, seeing something far distant

112

from the walls of the little flat. Then he took a deep breath.

'I haven't got any coffee,' he said. 'But I can offer you a herbal tea.'

'That will be fine.'

'Peppermint, or lemon and ginger?'

'Er, lemon and ginger. Thank you.'

'I won't be a tick.'

Cooper looked around while he waited. The flat was depressing. The furniture looked cheap and ancient, scuffed by the feet and elbows of countless previous tenants careless of someone else's property. The carpet had a threadbare patch in the doorway, the torn pile held down by a strip of tape. Because they were on the top floor, the windows were small and set high in the walls. The old servants' quarters. Servants famously had no need of air and light, or even heating. There was probably a view of Edendale from here if you took the trouble to stand on a chair and peer through the grimy panes.

Although the lights were on, the rooms seemed dark and dismal. Anson Tate had looked quite at home in the gloom, but Cooper felt uncomfortable. It was as if the June weather and the sun-bathed Peak District had disappeared for the length of his visit. He hoped they would still be there when he left.

'He was Canadian, you know,' called Tate from the kitchen area, above the sound of a boiling kettle. 'From Vancouver.'

'Who was, sir?'

'The man who interrupted me that day. On the bridge,

I mean. He stopped me going over. He was a lot bigger than me and very strong. He had a grip like a vice. Perhaps he was a lumberjack. I never bothered to ask him.'

Tate put his head round the door. 'Would you like to see my bruises? They're still there. I probably ought to sue him. Don't you think?'

He put a cup in front of Cooper on the table. Aromatic steam rose from it, filling the room with the smell of hot ginger.

Before coming, Cooper had thought about how to approach Anson Tate. He wasn't a suspect. He had no criminal record of any kind. All he'd done to be of interest was try to kill himself. That made him a victim, of a kind. Vulnerable. If he'd been in a cell at the West Street custody suite, he would be on regular suicide watch.

Tate sat down opposite Cooper, nursing his cup. He'd made peppermint tea for himself. The two aromas mingled in an exotic mist between them. Ginger and peppermint, and a chat about suicide. Sometimes, this job seemed very strange.

'I suppose you want to know why I wanted to do it?' asked Tate.

'Well, if you'd like . . .'

'I had a job once,' said Tate, without needing any more encouragement. 'It was a rubbish job. Boring and pointless. It was badly paid too. I spent all day doing things I had no interest in with people I cared about even less. It was *my* job, though. It made me feel as though I had something, that I belonged somewhere. When I put that ID card lanyard round my neck, it was like putting on a disguise. All the people who passed me in the corridor, or saw me in the canteen – they accepted my right to be there. Some of them even knew who I was. One or two actually said hello now and then.'

There was a book on the table, a bookmark protruding from a page about halfway through. Tate absent-mindedly picked up the book, opened it at the book-mark and closed it again. Cooper couldn't see the cover, but it looked like a novel. Dark colours, a splash of red. A thriller, perhaps.

'I suppose it doesn't sound much, does it?' said Tate. 'But it was *something*. It gave me a purpose. I don't have any of that now. And I've got to ask myself – if I can't do anything with my life, what's the point of being alive at all?'

'Surely . . .'

'Well?'

Tate leaned closer, as if hoping for a meaningful answer. Yet Cooper didn't have an answer at all. He'd asked himself the same question many times.

'I see.' Tate sighed. 'When you're living alone, you become invisible. We're surrounded by invisible people. It's no surprise that they long to do something, anything, to make themselves visible to the world, if only for a while. It doesn't mean they're cowards.'

Cooper blinked. Was it cowardly to plan your own death, to face up to that final unknown prospect and meet it without flinching? On balance, he thought not.

Yet Tate seemed oddly angry. Cooper wasn't sure

what target his anger was directed at – life, fate, society, himself? That was probably a question for his psychiatrist or his counsellor to be asking.

'Doesn't it seem wrong to you that sick animals are put out of their misery by vets, but we aren't allowed to end our own wretched existences?' said Tate. 'What is it about a human life that makes it so different, so sacrosanct? We're just animals too, aren't we? Why should we be forced to suffer?'

He stopped talking. Cooper stared at him through a swirl of herbal steam.

'Do you understand?' said Tate. 'I hope you do.'

He looked at Cooper, his eyes darting anxiously back and forth across the detective's face, as if seeking something.

Then Tate smiled a small, sad smile.

'No, you're too young,' he said. 'You still have delusions of hope.'

'Hope is important.'

'Really? Do you know the three most common regrets that people express on their deathbeds? They say "I wish I hadn't worked so hard" or "I wish I'd stayed in touch with my friends". And they regret not letting themselves be happier. I wish I'd known that. I've never had friends, I've never known happiness. All I had was my work. And when my eyes were opened and I saw the futility of that . . . well, what did I have left? I'm sure there are lots of people like me. You must see them yourself.'

'We see all kinds of things in this job.'

Tate nodded. 'Well, perhaps you've heard people say

this before. That every day you've got this awful thing nagging at you, as if there's something terribly wrong. And then suddenly you see the truth. You know what wasn't right. And you know what to do about it too. It's a kind of release.'

'It's the people left behind,' said Cooper. 'The family and friends. A spouse, the parents. The children.'

'I know,' said Tate. 'Everyone talks as if suicides are selfish, that they don't care what they're doing to other people. But when you've reached that stage in your life, you genuinely think you're doing everyone a favour. You believe that your family and friends will be better off without you, that their lives will be easier when you're gone. And do you know what? For many men, that's actually true.'

Cooper took a drink of his lemon and ginger, gathering his thoughts. He'd lost control of the interview, of course. It was understandable. Tate had been using him as he would a counsellor, pouring out his feelings, his justifications. Somewhere in there might be a useful detail.

'Though you're right about the people left behind,' said Tate. 'No matter who you are, your death isn't just your own experience. It affects other people. The final event of your life will live on in the memories of your loved ones. Wouldn't you prefer their memory of you to be one of freedom from indignity and pain? My mother . . . my mother never had that choice.'

'Your mother?' said Cooper.

That hadn't been in the notes on Anson Tate's suicide

attempt. There was nothing about his mother. No mention of her in his suicide note either.

'What happened to your mother, Mr Tate?'

Tate fiddled with the bookmark, sliding it in and out of the page in his book.

'She died of pancreatic cancer. Do you know the survival rate for that type of cancer? Two per cent. It took her a long time to die and she was in constant pain and distress.'

'I'm sorry. I didn't know that.'

'Why should you? But I had to watch it happening. She had chronic pain from the tumour pressing against her internal organs. She also had all the effects of the medication, the use of opioids – the thirst, the nausea, the itching, the constipation, the despair . . .'

Tate took another deep breath before he continued.

'As a result of that illness,' he said, 'she left me with memories of seeing her in constant agony and of her loss of dignity. In the end, I was unable to see her as the person I wanted to remember. The fact is, if I'd been allowed to end her life before she got to that stage, I would have done it gladly. I'd have done it in the knowledge that she would thank me for it, if she could. But mercy has become a crime.'

'I don't think that's true, sir,' said Cooper.

'For me, it was.'

Cooper looked round the tiny flat. He was trying to ease the atmosphere, to give Anson Tate a moment to collect himself and become calmer. Seeing the sparseness of the surroundings reminded him of an important question he'd come here to ask.

'Do you have a computer, Mr Tate?'

'No, I don't need one. Why?'

'When you started to think about going down that route,' said Cooper, 'I mean, about taking your own life – did you go to anyone to get advice, support or information?'

'No, it was my own decision,' said Tate. 'Entirely my own.'

Cooper nodded. That wasn't quite what he'd asked. Tate had used a common evasion technique, answering a different but similar question.

'Did you look on the internet for guidance, for example?' said Cooper.

'On the internet? Why would you ask that?'

And there was another technique. A question answered with another question.

'It's what people often do these days,' said Cooper. 'Everyone checks out their own symptoms online before they go to the doctor. It's second nature to Google for information.'

'It didn't occur to me.'

'One final thing, then, sir.'

'Yes?'

'When you made your suicide attempt, you were living at an address in Mansfield, Nottinghamshire.'

'That's correct,' said Tate.

'But since then, you've moved to Edendale.'

'Yes.'

'Can I ask why?'

Tate smiled. 'Because I like it here.'

Cooper felt the hairs on the back of his neck stirring

uncomfortably. This was a man who had travelled nearly thirty miles into the Eden Valley to kill himself. He was one of their suicide tourists, though an unsuccessful one. When he came the first time, he'd wanted to die in Edendale. And now he'd decided to live here. Because he 'liked it'.

From anyone else thinking of moving into the area, that would have sounded fine and Cooper wouldn't have questioned it. He understood why anyone would want to live in his town. Well, almost anyone.

From Anson Tate, the motive had to be questionable. Was he here in Edendale just because it was a nice place to live? Or was it because he found it more convenient? Next time he decided to kill himself, it would save the hour-long commute.

'Thank you, sir,' Cooper said. 'I think that will be all for now.'

Tate showed him to the door.

'Detective Inspector,' he said, as Cooper turned to leave.

'Yes, sir?'

'Don't judge anyone's choice. Not until you know what options they had to choose from.'

Emerging into the sunlight on Buxton Road was like coming out of a cinema after watching the matinee of a two-hour horror film. Stepping back into daylight, Cooper found the real world difficult to adjust to.

He was disturbed by his conversation with Anson Tate. When did the right to die become a duty?

Yet he still had nothing. And there ought to be something. In particular, there should have been some sign left by Roger Farrell before he took his own life at Heeley Bank. But there had been no note or letter with the body, no goodbye to a loved one.

And then it occurred to him. He rang Carol Villiers back at the station in West Street.

'Carol, have you listened to the outgoing message on his voicemail?' asked Cooper.

'No. Why?' said Villiers.

'Try it, will you?'

'I've got the number here. I'll ring it.'

'Put it on speaker.'

Villiers dialled Roger Farrell's mobile. They heard the phone ringing. Twice, three times, four times. Then the recorded message cut in. It seemed strange hearing Farrell's voice. He sounded entirely calm and unperturbed, almost content. Cooper was reminded of the bereaved relatives who constantly called the number of someone they'd lost just to hear their voice and remember them the way they'd been in normal life. It became a unique form of reassurance, a suggestion that their loved one might still be there at the other end of the phone, just too busy to take their call right now.

But this wasn't Mr Farrell the way he'd been in normal life. He'd recorded his message when he was preparing for death. From the background noises, he may already have been sitting in the car park at the Heeley Bank visitor centre. Was that his first task when he arrived? He'd composed a farewell message, then turned off his phone so that no one could contact him in those last few hours. His words were quite simple, but chilling:

'So this is the first secret of death. There's always a right time and place to die.'

11

The mortuary behind Eden Valley General Hospital was an inconspicuous building with hardly any windows. It was no more welcoming inside. Cooper was glad he didn't work here all the time. Daylight and fresh air were among his essential requirements.

The people working in a gloomy mortuary like this should really be pale, hairless trolls with lopsided grins who wheeled dead bodies down endless corridors. In fact, they were quite the opposite.

Dr Juliana van Doon had been working here for a long time and was one of the most experienced forensic pathologists in the region. Today, she had a younger woman with her, whom she introduced as her colleague Dr Chloe Young.

Dr Young was no more than five feet six, possibly less. Her hair was dark, almost black, with a sheen that caught the light reflected from the stainless steel dissecting table and autopsy instruments. She wore it knotted at the back in a kind of French twist, leaving the smooth lines of her face clear.

When he came in, she removed a pair of protective

glasses and studied him through cool green eyes. Or were they brown? Perhaps hazel. He couldn't decide and he realised he was staring too hard trying to work it out.

Cooper had become so used to seeing Dr van Doon in the Edendale mortuary that he'd developed a fixed idea of what pathologists looked like – that lean, hunched posture, with an exasperated expression, a sharp eye and a mouth turned down in disapproval. Dr Young looked nothing like that at all.

He was conscious that Juliana van Doon was getting close to retirement. She had even hinted at it once or twice with the suggestion that the only reason she hadn't left already was because there was no adequate replacement. Was the replacement going to be Dr Young? From Cooper's point of view, it didn't look like a bad swap.

'So, Detective Inspector Cooper,' said Dr van Doon. 'Your suicide case. You seem to be making a habit of suicide recently. Is there something you'd like to tell us?'

'I wish there were. I was hoping there'd be something you could tell me.'

'Well, no surprises here,' she said. 'I'm sure that's the way you like it.'

'Suffocation?' he said.

'Certainly. Death would have been quick and painless, given the method used. Very efficient.'

She sounded admiring. Perhaps it was the response of one professional for another at a job done well.

'Anything else?' asked Cooper.

'There's nothing obvious on toxicology. No alcohol or drugs in his blood. No sign of physical trauma or disease. The heart wasn't in great condition, but that's no surprise either. A well-nourished Caucasian male aged around fifty. It's pretty much what we'd expect.' The pathologist gave him a sardonic look. 'This gentleman ought to be alive really. Not lying on my examination table.'

'I can't argue with that.'

'As if you would,' said Dr van Doon with a thin smile.

Cooper had spent years being slightly in awe of the pathologist, ever since he had first encountered her as a young detective and realised that even the older, more senior officers were a bit frightened of her.

'By the way, my colleague here has obtained permission to take some samples of brain tissue,' she said. 'Dr Young has been taking part in a neurobiological study of suicidal behaviour.'

'Oh, really?'

Cooper had a sinking feeling that he was about to be baffled with science. He had almost no idea what 'neurobiological' meant. Unlike many of the younger officers recruited to Derbyshire Constabulary over recent years, he'd left the education system at eighteen with a couple of A-levels and had never tried to get into university. He'd never even considered it. High Peak College had been the limits of his ambitions, because a degree hadn't been necessary back then. And even if he had taken a degree, it wouldn't have been in neurobiology.

His lack of academic qualifications sometimes made him feel uncomfortable, with that sneaking suspicion he'd walked into an environment where he didn't belong. Right now, he felt sure Chloe Young was going to say something before long that he wouldn't understand.

'It's a global problem, of course,' said Dr Young. 'Nearly one million people take their own lives every year, according to the World Health Organisation.'

'I didn't really think it was limited to the Eden Valley,' said Cooper. 'But we do seem to have had a bit of a surge recently . . .'

'Quite an epidemic,' said Dr van Doon cheerfully.

Cooper looked at her in surprise – partly because he knew 'epidemic' was an unscientific term, but also because it echoed the expression used by Detective Superintendent Branagh. He wasn't used to her sounding quite so cheerful either. Perhaps she preferred cutting up suicides to performing post-mortems on murder victims. Or maybe she just liked having the companionship of Dr Young in the examination room. He couldn't blame her for that.

'I believe all your suicides have been male,' said Dr Young.

'Yes, that's right. I'm aware the rate of suicide is higher among men.'

'There are well established socio-economic reasons for that. It's the underlying pathology that isn't very well understood.'

Cooper made a non-committal sound, as he didn't know how else to reply.

'Suicides and suicide attempts are usually associated with mental disorders, or with alcohol and substance abuse,' she said. 'The socio-economic factors have been well identified. But the neurobiology is less clear.'

'Dr Young, I'm not sure . . .'

'I'm talking about studies that are looking into biological abnormalities associated with suicidal behaviour. In particular, there's work on the hypothalamic-pituitary-adrenocortical axis.'

Cooper nodded helplessly. Then she seemed to recognise that she was talking a language he didn't understand.

'Well, anyway,' she said, 'that work requires materials such as blood cells, cerebrospinal fluid and plasma. So post-mortem brain samples from suicide victims are essential for research.'

'As you probably know, Detective Inspector,' said Dr van Doon, 'brain tissue degrades very easily. So particular care is required in collecting samples. That's Dr Young's speciality.'

'Forty-eight hours,' said Dr Young. 'Samples for post-mortem study should ideally be taken no longer than that after death, otherwise they degrade too much to be useful for study.'

'It sounds fascinating,' said Cooper. 'It's a pity I don't have more time. I'd like to hear more about the suicide study.'

Dr Young smiled. 'Another day, perhaps?'

'That would be great.'

'So where are you headed now, Inspector?' asked Dr Young.

'I've got a funeral to go to this afternoon.'
'What a fun life you must lead.'

David Kuzneski's funeral was held on the outskirts of Sheffield. Cooper found the large cemetery among a network of tree-lined streets.

The suburbs themselves were flanked north and south by two supermarkets, Sainsbury's and Morrison's. Their orange and yellow signs seemed to beckon like the colours of rival football clubs. Well, perhaps the decision about where to shop was a bit like choosing to support Wednesday or United. Shoppers cherished their loyalty cards rather than season tickets, flaunted their branded carrier bags instead of a scarf and replica shirt.

The crematorium had been built in the middle of the open space, with memorial gardens around it. The supermarkets met all the needs of daily life. The cemetery provided what the supermarkets couldn't.

'Just here to watch?'

Cooper turned at the sound of the voice close behind him. He hadn't heard anyone approaching, which worried him. His instincts must be letting him down.

The woman looked about thirty, dressed all in black. Tight black jeans, black boots with rows of beads up the seams, and a wide-brimmed floppy hat of the kind his mother might have worn to a wedding – if it had been white, rather than black. Her long, straight hair seemed to confirm his initial impression. Forty years too late to be a hippy and couldn't quite go all the way with the Goth thing.

'Something like that,' he said.

'There are people who find funerals fascinating,' she said. 'Or just graveyards. I can relate to that.'

'Are you a relative of Mr Kuzneski's?' asked Cooper.

She laughed. 'Ah, so you do at least know whose funeral it is. I'm a cousin. My name is Haynes. Lily Haynes.'

'I'm Detective Inspector Cooper.'

'A police officer. I thought you must be,' she said.

'Did you know your cousin well?'

'We weren't all that close, I'm afraid. Not recently. Our parents used to visit each other a lot when we were children, and my brother used to play with David and his sister Dawn. But once you grow up . . . well, your lives diverge, don't they? I saw less and less of him in the last few years.'

'So you wouldn't have any idea about what was going on in his mind, what his mental state was?'

'Whether he'd been thinking about suicide for a long time, do you mean?'

'Yes, I suppose that's what I meant.'

'I couldn't say. David was a strange man in many ways. Obsessive. He thought about death a lot, you know.'

'Why?'

'Well, I don't really know.'

'Was he terminally ill? If so, that wasn't mentioned at the inquest.'

'No, not that I'm aware of. I don't think he had any more reason to worry about dying than anyone else. It's just that the rest of us tend to go about our lives not thinking about it. We have far too many other things to concern ourselves with, don't we? Trivial, unimportant things – that's what David would have said. He thought everything was meaningless, except for the fact that we die one day.'

'I suppose he had a point,' said Cooper.

She looked at him thoughtfully. 'That's a very depressing outlook, though. There's far more to living, isn't there? We can't go through our lives thinking about the day we'll die. Well, I know I don't.'

Cooper smiled. 'And I'm sure you're right. You seem very sensible and well balanced. Unfortunately, not everyone is.'

'And those are the ones you have to deal with, I imagine,' she said. 'It must distort your perception of people.'

He watched the funeral party making its way slowly to the graveside, led by the coffin bearers and the vicar. It wasn't a huge crowd – the immediate family in black and a straggle of friends and acquaintances awkwardly trailing in the rear, some glancing at their watches and mobile phones, as if they'd done their duty and should now be somewhere else.

'Do you know everyone here?' asked Cooper.

'All the relatives, of course. Most of the others are David's former colleagues – I spoke to a few of them before the service. I think the rest are neighbours and some of Stephanie's friends here for support.'

'Anyone who *shouldn't* be here?'

She threw him a curious look. 'Why are you asking me that?'

'Because I think you're a good observer. There might

be someone here who stands out to you. A stranger who doesn't know anyone else, but stands to one side and watches everything.'

'Yes, there is one like that,' she said.

'Oh, who?'

'You.'

Cooper laughed. 'Good point.'

'You do look a bit suspicious. Everyone is wondering who you are. If you want to stay incognito, I'll have to tell them you're my boyfriend or something.'

'It doesn't matter really,' said Cooper. 'If you're sure there's no one else.'

She looked more serious. 'It's important, isn't it?'

'It could be. I can't say more than that.'

'Fair enough. But the answer is no – there's no one who stands out. No complete stranger, no one who looks suspicious or shifty. Apart from yourself, there's only one person here who has clearly never met any of the mourners before and knows nothing about the deceased.'

'And who is that?'

'The vicar,' she said. 'He's useless. He just read from a script he'd been given.'

Cooper watched the party around the grave as the coffin was lowered in and the first spadefuls of soil were scattered. A mound of dirt lay ready to finish the job. If Dev Sharma were here, he would no doubt have been telling everyone that Hindus were cremated. They believed that burning the physical shell released the soul from the body.

Cremation was becoming more and more common

among other groups too, especially since space in village churchyards began to run out. Yet on the far side of the cemetery was the Muslim burial ground. No cremation was permitted in Islam.

Cooper wondered why the beliefs around death differed so much. He'd heard there was a current fashion to bury favourite possessions with the deceased, as if they were Egyptian pharaohs or Celtic princes. Surely no one in the twenty-first century believed that physical treasures could be carried over into the afterlife. He'd even seen bereaved relatives addressing their lost loved ones on social media, as if the dead spent their time in heaven checking out Facebook.

He turned to Lily Haynes.

'Is that Mr Kuzneski's widow by the grave?' he said.

'The pale, thin one who isn't speaking to anyone? Yes, that's Stephanie. Do you want me to introduce you to her?'

'If it's convenient. It might look less intrusive.'

Lily Haynes's hat flapped in a sudden breeze across the cemetery and she clutched at it with a hand, the fingers of which were covered in rings.

'Much good it will do you,' she said. 'Stephanie isn't in much of a state to talk.'

When the mourners began to disperse, Cooper and Lily Haynes walked over and he was introduced to Stephanie Kuzneski.

He offered his condolences first. He was aware that commiserations probably sounded hollow and Mrs Kuzneski seemed to feel the same. She nodded vaguely at his words. Then he asked if he might call on her at home next day to ask a few questions. She gave no answer, but instead just nodded again, a glassy look on her face.

Cooper realised Mrs Kuzneski had been listening politely without taking in a single word. And she had not looked him in the eye when he was speaking. Instead, she watched his mouth, as if his lips were saying something quite different from the words he used. It was very disconcerting. What did she read there that she couldn't see in his eyes?

Of course, he'd seen this before. Mrs Kuzneski was a woman who wished she were anywhere else but here, who wanted to be hearing anything except all these well-meaning platitudes she was bombarded with. Her mind had probably disconnected her from the reality of the cemetery and taken her somewhere else.

All he could do was repeat his request.

'I'm sorry to bother you with this, Mrs Kuzneski,' he said. But he might as well have been talking to the wall of the chapel.

A male family member standing nearby stepped in, told Cooper with a scowl that it would be all right, then took Mrs Kuzneski by the arm and led her away.

Cooper said goodbye to Lily Haynes and walked back through the cemetery to the car park, passing among rows and rows of gravestones, memorials to generations of the dead of Sheffield. How many of these had died natural deaths or had decided to take their own lives? It was a fact never recorded on a gravestone. It was an act no one wanted to acknowledge.

*   *   *

Bethan Jones sat looking out over a hillside at the upper end of the Eden Valley, then stared at her wrists. The skin seemed very pale over her veins. Pale, thin and translucent. Where they snaked over the tendons, her blood vessels were like a tracery of branches from some strange blue plant. The more she stared at them, the stranger her wrists looked. They were like the limbs of an alien creature or a lifelike plastic model.

Bethan had plenty of time. But she knew it was already working. This was how you did it. You trained yourself to see your body as nothing but an object. It wasn't the real you, it didn't contain your soul, it was just a shell. Shells were made to be cast off, like a used skin. Sometimes your body became useless. Less than useless – a burden, a pain, a torment.

All of the dialogue had already taken place inside her head, with her own voice dominant and insistent as she ran through her arguments. Irrefutable arguments. She didn't need to be convinced any more.

She had the door and windows open to let in the summer air. From the big window running the width of the lounge area, she was looking straight across the valley. There wasn't another human being in sight. On the far side of a dry-stone wall, she could see a herd of black-and-white cows grazing. Half an hour ago, she'd watched them ambling back to their field from milking. The air of serenity hanging over them made her smile.

Beyond the cows, the valley itself looked deep and green, a place to dive into like a cooling lake. Sheep dotted the opposite hillside and the moors blended into the sky as they ran away into the far distance. A helicopter passed overhead. Somewhere nearby, a child laughed.

Bethan took another drink of water. She thought about her sister and then about all the plans she'd made. She'd done what she could. There was no more. Nothing left for her to do with her life.

She pushed back the door of the shower unit. The water would be nice and hot now. Then she unwrapped the small packet on the worktop and carefully slid out the first razor blade. She tested the edge with her finger. A tiny drop of blood oozed from her skin and fell on to the worktop. She was more than ready.

12

That evening, Ben Cooper was sitting in the backyard of his new house enjoying the early evening sun, when he heard voices. He frowned. One of the voices seemed familiar, but he couldn't place it and he couldn't hear what was being said.

After a few minutes of conversation, two or three people laughed together. Now he recognised one of the voices. It was *very* familiar. Yet it was so out of context that he'd failed to put a name and face to it. Even now, he couldn't quite accept this was true.

He got up and peered cautiously over the low wall. His neighbours from up the row were just about to go back into their house – the one with the wrought-iron gate. And ambling towards him along the path was a third figure.

Cooper pulled open the gate. 'Gavin – what are you doing here?'

'Well, that's nice,' said Murfin. 'Can't I visit an old mate in his new home? Are you too posh to have common folks like me calling by now you're a middle-class property owner?'

'Come in,' said Cooper, taking Murfin's arm to steer him towards the back door.

'Ah, I see you've got the booze out to welcome callers,' said Murfin.

'You'll be driving, if I'm not mistaken. I don't suppose you were out for a country ramble and happened to be passing through Foolow.'

'No, I was drawn by the unmistakable odour of money and success,' said Murfin, gazing around the room. 'Very nice too. Needs a bit more furniture, I reckon.'

'I'm working on it.'

Murfin sat down on the settee without being asked. The cat strolled in nonchalantly and gave him a once-over.

'Gavin, what were you doing talking to my new neighbours?' said Cooper.

'Have you forgotten what my job is? I'm a property enquiry agent. Would you like a card?'

'No, thanks.'

'Well, I appreciate it's a bit late for you, like. Since you seem to have gone ahead and purchased the property without calling on my services – a bit of a risk that, you know. Impetuous. Not like you, Ben. What was it that tempted you? I bet it wasn't the council tax band or its energy efficiency rating?'

'I just liked it,' said Cooper defensively.

'Ah. You've no idea how often we hear that when it's too late.'

'So you're telling me you've been checking out my neighbours?' said Cooper.

'That's what I do. And in your case the service comes free. Call it a housewarming present, if you like. You'll be pleased to know that the old biddy next door will be no trouble to you, as long as you make a fuss of her cat. The couple two doors down are a different matter. She's a teacher and you know what they're like.'

'Gavin, I don't want to know any of this.'

Murfin shrugged. 'Suit yourself. You'll thank me for it one day.'

'I don't think so. Just imagine if they thought I'd been snooping on them. That would be a great start.'

Murfin looked round the room again. 'So no beer, then?'

'How about a coffee?'

'That will do.'

Murfin and the cat stared at each other while Cooper went into the kitchen to put the coffee on. When he came back, Hopes had turned away, as if deciding that it was nothing she hadn't seen before. Gavin looked smug, as if he'd just won a staring match.

'So how is the job going?' asked Cooper. 'Is it still the best decision you ever made?'

Murfin's expression changed. 'It's pants really. Dealing with members of the public all the time. It's like . . . well, you know what it's like.'

Cooper laughed. 'Yes, I do. But didn't you expect that when you went into the business, Gavin?'

'I thought I'd be dealing with a better class of person.'

'And aren't you?'

'No such luck. I don't spend my time in nice villages

like this. People keep sending me to housing estates in Edendale. I know the streets up there like the back of my hand. Can you believe it, some kids on the Woodlands Estate keyed my car the other day.'

'They probably thought you were still a copper.'

Murfin sniffed dismissively. 'Do I look like a copper these days?'

'Not really,' Cooper admitted. 'You're much too unfit now. They'd never have you.'

'Exactly.'

'But then, you've looked like that for years. I was surprised you lasted that long.'

'Me too, to be honest,' said Murfin.

'So it's not working out? It's not what you imagined yourself doing when you left the job?'

'You wouldn't credit it,' said Murfin. 'People see houses advertised on the Woodlands Estate and they're fooled by the road names. They actually think Elm Street will be lined with elms and Sycamore Crescent is a shady little wooded dell. I've never seen anything less like woodland than the Woodlands. The only similarity is the amount of grass the Woodies smoke.'

Cooper found himself smiling broadly as he listened. Hearing Gavin Murfin complaining about the residents of the Woodlands Estate was so comfortably familiar that he could easily have been sitting in the CID room at West Street a time long ago, when they were both detective constables and Gavin was the one he looked up to because of his age and experience. Times changed. But some things stayed the same, and Gavin was one of them.

'Have you actually found any Woodies who'd make suitable neighbours for your agency's clients?' he asked.

'Are you kidding? Not unless they're obsessive social workers in their spare time and like the challenge of having a dysfunctional family of scumbags next door. You don't come across many of those.'

'So what do you tell them? Without putting them off completely, I mean.'

Murfin hid his face behind his mug. 'There are ways,' he said. 'A certain form of words you can use.'

'You lie, then.'

'It's a business,' said Murfin, suddenly gloomy. 'A way of earning a living.'

'You put in your thirty years, Gavin. You've got your pension to fall back on.'

'It doesn't go as far as you might think. Not these days. Not in the circumstances.'

'Circumstances?'

Murfin didn't seem to want to elaborate on the circumstances that were leaving him short of money. And that was something you didn't pry into, if it was personal. Not unless the other person volunteered to share his problems.

'I'm sorry to hear it anyway. I thought you'd got yourself set up nicely.'

'The best-laid plans and all that, like. But you're doing all right for yourself. Bounced back, Ben?'

Cooper stared at the floor. 'In a way.'

'Yep.'

And that was all they needed to say. Cooper and Murfin sat in silence drinking their coffee for a while.

No traffic passed outside. Somewhere a dog barked, the noise reaching far across the hillside from a distant farm.

'And other irritations out of your hair,' said Murfin finally, without feeling the need to explain what he was referring to.

'Yes,' said Cooper. 'That too.'

After their evening meal, Diane Fry spent ten minutes going through some gentle exercises, winding down from the day. She always did it after a day at the office, but today had been just as stressful for a different reason. The presence of her sister and the baby in her apartment had disrupted her life in a way that she could never have imagined.

She stood up and looked through the door into the sitting room. Angie was on the sofa, watching TV. The child was sleeping in a carry cot. Thank goodness he was asleep at last. For a while, the noise had been unbearable. She had expected her neighbours down-stairs to be banging on the door at any moment to complain.

'Everything okay?' she said.

Angie didn't even look up. Her eyes were glued to the screen. Some reality show was on that Diane had never heard of.

'Fine. We're fine.'

'Great.'

What she really wanted to ask was when her sister was planning to leave. Angie was here for now, she'd been forced to accept that. When the bed in the spare room was made up for her, Angie had scoured the room like a Secret Service agent to make sure it was safe for a small child. No exposed wires or bare flames, no dangerous wild animals or monsters lurking behind the curtains.

Diane wondered what was wrong with her. She'd observed other people's reactions to babies, but couldn't understand them. Women were supposed to feel a particular emotion – an instinctive warmth, a maternal affection. But she didn't have those feelings at all. So that meant there was something wrong with her, didn't it?

Yet she would never have imagined Angie as a mother either. Perhaps there was some disastrous change that happened to you when you reached a certain age. A catastrophe in your hormones or a loss of rational thinking in your dying brain cells. That was something to dread in the future, then. How nice.

'What are you watching?' she said.

Angie didn't look up from the screen. '*Strictly.*'

'Strictly what?'

That made her sister stare. Diane didn't watch much TV. Well, that wasn't true, she did watch quite a lot, but it didn't really register with her what was on. She switched it on when she came home for the sake of a bit of noise in the apartment. But the sense of it sort of bypassed her brain, like background music in a lift. She could tell from the music whether it was drama or comedy, or news. Otherwise the screen just showed faces, talking.

'*Come Dancing,*' said Angie with a mocking lift of the eyebrow.

'Sorry?'

'*Strictly Come Dancing*. Don't tell me you haven't heard of it.'

'I suppose I have.'

'They're doing a summer special.'

'Great.'

'Normally, it would be *Bake Off*.'

'Right.'

Diane's colleagues at St Ann's never mentioned these programmes. They talked about football, of course, or some other sporting event. Apart from that, the titles they referred to were *Game of Thrones* or *The Walking Dead*. No crime dramas. They hadn't seen one they liked yet.

But *Strictly Come Dancing*? Never. It sounded very middle class to Diane's ears – the kind of programme the *Daily Telegraph* would write headlines about after *Downton Abbey* had finished, when the red-top tabloids were still writing about *EastEnders* and *Coronation Street*.

She didn't feel like talking about it. But Angie looked settled for a while.

'I'll be going to bed soon,' said Diane.

'Seriously?' Angie made a pantomime of looking at her watch. 'What are you, twelve years old?'

'I've got work in the morning. I like to be in the office early.'

Angie laughed. 'Oh, of course you do. I'd forgotten.'

'And the traffic can be a nightmare getting across Nottingham from here.'

Her sister had lost interest already. The audience was

hooting and cheering on the TV, and her attention was drawn back to the screen.

'Will I see you tomorrow?' asked Diane, forced to raise her voice as Angie increased the volume with the remote. The one thing she didn't want to do was seem to be shouting, but it was happening despite her intentions.

'Yes, we'll be here,' said Angie.

'Is your friend . . .?'

She didn't finish the sentence and Angie wasn't listening anyway. She wanted to ask if her sister's boyfriend with the Renault would be coming back to pick her up when he'd finished his business in Nottingham. She had a suspicion he would be here during the day as soon as she'd left for work.

But she'd just realised that she didn't want to see him. She didn't want to know anything about him. Diane nodded to herself. Yes, that was definitely for the best. Some things were better not faced up to.

She produced a package she'd been saving for the right moment. This wasn't the right moment, but if she waited any longer it would never arrive.

'Here,' she said, handing it to Angie.

'What's this?'

'It's something I bought for you. Well, for . . . Zack, really.'

Angie ripped open the packing and pulled out the contents. It was a romper suit with a cartoon of a car on the front and the slogan 'I'm a Little Classic'.

'It's lovely,' said Angie. 'Where did you get it?'

'I went into Mothercare.'

144

Angie's mouth fell open in surprise. 'Sis. You never.'

'Well, I happened to be passing.'

'Really?'

'So make the most of it,' said Diane. 'Because I'm never going in a place like that again for the rest of my life.'

13

Day 4

Ben Cooper called at Bridge End Farm on his way
from Foolow into Edendale next morning. He'd remembered that he still had some items in storage at the
farm, left there when he'd moved into the flat in
Welbeck Street and hadn't had room for them.

He knew there were some books and a box of CDs,
perhaps even some small pieces of furniture that would
make the new house look more like home. They were
stored up in the loft of the farmhouse, but he could
probably manage to get them down on his own if Matt
was too busy on the farm.

The track down to the farm had been resurfaced
when the caravan site was developed. Visitors would
never have made it through the immense potholes
and Matt Cooper's makeshift repairs with rubble and
broken bricks.

Ben missed the old track, though. It had been part
of the character of the farm, so familiar from growing
up there that he knew he was coming home every
time his suspension hit the biggest hole on the bend
before the yard gate. Driving down to Bridge End on

a level tarmac surface felt wrong, as if part of his childhood had been smoothed out and erased.

He parked the Toyota in the yard in front of the farmhouse door. He could hear Matt's dog Tess barking, but the noise was coming from the shed behind the house, where she was kept when she wasn't out with Matt.

The field used by the caravanners was just to the south of the barn. When he looked over the gate, Ben saw his brother and he knew straight away something was wrong. He could see Matt running up the field, his hands held away from his body, palms raised as if he was praying. He could see his brother's face contorted in distress.

And then he saw the blood.

Diane Fry pulled into the forecourt of the BP filling station on Clifton Lane, where she withdrew some cash from the ATM, filled up the tank of her Audi and bought a couple of bottles of water in the shop.

A set of InPost lockers stood in a corner of the forecourt next to the air pump. She had a medium-sized locker of her own for items she'd bought on Amazon or eBay and was never at home to receive. She scanned the QR code from her phone to open the locker and smiled at the CCTV cameras overhead. She slid out a bright yellow box and clicked the locker shut again.

She cast a glance at the small Christadelphian chapel next to the petrol station. Fry had no idea what a Christadelphian was or why they'd chosen this spot for their place of worship. It looked faintly suspicious.

Then she got back into the car and swung through the roundabout to join the roar of traffic towards the Clifton Bridge. She would be in St Ann's in twenty minutes' time, though it ought to be less, considering the distance was no more than four miles. The most direct route was eastwards, but that took her past Trent Bridge and both the Forest and County football grounds, then right through the city centre past the Motorpoint Arena. In the morning, the volume of traffic could add another quarter of an hour to her journey.

Instead, she crossed the Trent on the Clifton Bridge and cut north of The Park estate to St Ann's Well Road. She felt so much more at ease having a multitude of routes and side roads she could choose from if her way ahead was obstructed.

When she had first transferred to Edendale from the West Midlands, she'd been amazed to find that the Snake Pass had no way to turn off it once you were on it, no side roads or alternative routes, for fourteen miles, all the way from Ladybower to Glossop. Fourteen miles! And that was the A57 for heaven's sake, one of the major routes between Sheffield and Manchester. She couldn't understand how people coped with it, especially when the Snake was frequently closed by snow in the winter. The road ought to be littered with abandoned vehicles, left there by frustrated drivers who'd given up and decided to walk.

Soon Fry had dodged the trams to get across the city and reached St Ann's. When she got out of the

Audi, she took a deep breath of air. There had been a distinct smell from it, which grew stronger during her journey, perhaps as the car got warmer in the sun. It was something rancid and unpleasant that she couldn't identify. She looked around the outside, but could see nothing. She wondered whether she ought to take it into the garage to be checked out or just to the car wash for a good hosing down. That would have to do later on.

She keyed in the code number and entered the building. St Ann's was a modern police station, unlike the building she'd worked in at Edendale with its leaking roof and draughty corners. The small windows, screened by blue louvre blinds, looked out on a road and a sprawling housing estate, with perhaps a glimpse of the office blocks in the city centre or the old cinema that was now a cash and carry warehouse.

Jamie Callaghan and DCI Mackenzie were already waiting for her when she arrived upstairs, as if she was late for work, which she never was.

And the looks they gave her as she came in seemed significant, expectant. Was she in trouble? She'd done nothing wrong. She knew she hadn't, not since she'd been with EMSOU, probably not ever in all her time as a serving police officer. In her personal life, yes. There had been a lot of mistakes, things she'd done that she'd known were stupid. But professionally, no. In her job, she was confident in her own ability to do the right thing.

'Good morning,' she said cautiously. 'Is something up?'

Mackenzie nodded. He was perched on the edge of a desk, trying to convey a casual air. It wasn't working.

'Roger Farrell,' he said. 'He's been located.'

'Well, that's great. How far did he get?'

'Not far. But far enough.'

Fry frowned. Mackenzie was being uncharacteristically cryptic. Her DCI didn't do enigmatic. He said what he thought, which was one of the reasons she liked working for him.

'It's bad news, Diane. In a way.'

'What is?'

'Farrell is dead,' said Mackenzie.

'Topped himself,' added Callaghan.

She looked from one to the other, wondering when they had turned into a double act. Ant and Dec had no reason to worry.

'It closes our inquiry, then?' she said.

'We always prefer to get a suspect into court, Diane.'

'Of course. Although . . .'

'It *is* convenient,' said Callaghan. 'I know what you mean.'

'That wasn't really what I meant.'

Callaghan smiled at her. She detected sympathy in his eyes. She didn't like that very much either.

DCI Mackenzie cleared his throat. 'Well anyway, a report has come in from our colleagues in Derbyshire that Roger Farrell was found dead the day before yesterday in a car park.'

'Derbyshire?' said Fry.

'Near Edendale. A place called Heeley Bank.'

Fry bit her lip, anticipating the worst. 'What on earth was he doing there?'

'Topping himself,' said Callaghan. 'Obviously.'

At Bridge End Farm, the furthest caravan was still cordoned off by police tape, with a uniformed officer trying to look casual as he guarded the scene under the inquisitive gaze of the remaining visitors.

'One family left at lunchtime,' said Matt. 'They said it was spoiling their holiday.'

Ben nodded. 'Yes, a sudden death does that.'

'I wouldn't know. I'm only used to the odd dead sheep.'

'So what happened exactly, Matt?'

'It's one of our caravan people. A woman staying in the six-berth at the far end of the field. She particularly asked for that one when she booked.'

'I know the one you mean. It has a view over the valley, doesn't it?'

'That's right. It's popular with couples because it's quiet, a bit out of the way of the other caravans. You can be pretty much on your own down there.'

'And this woman was alone?'

'Completely.'

'Do you know if she'd stayed here before? Perhaps with a husband or a friend?'

'I've no idea. I'll get Kate to check. She keeps records of all the visitors. To be honest, I don't really notice them unless they cause trouble.' Matt's expression became sheepish. 'Not that I'm complaining she's caused us trouble by dying. That makes me sound a bit callous, I suppose.'

'God forbid.'

Matt shook his head. 'I don't understand why she'd do it here, though. You'd think she'd go somewhere more . . . private, like.'

'That doesn't seem to come into their planning,' said Ben.

'Who's "they"?'

'I honestly don't know.'

'You don't really know much, do you?'

'Not as much as I'd like to.'

Matt stared across the field at his caravans. 'It's all a bit of a secret, then,' he said. 'And I suppose that's the way she wanted it.'

Ben was silent. It was an unusually perceptive remark from his brother. And he didn't want to ruin the moment.

Cooper found DC Becky Hurst leaning against a Scientific Support van. She looked pale and she was clutching her arms around her body as if she was cold. Yet it was warm out here, even in a field at Bridge End.

'Are you all right, Becky?' he asked.

She straightened up when she saw him. 'Yes, I'm fine.'

Cooper wasn't convinced. Her reassurance just made him more concerned.

'Are you sure?'

Hurst shook herself and blew out a long breath. 'It's being so near,' she said. 'So close to someone in death that you can smell their blood.'

Cooper knew exactly what she meant. A body

glimpsed from a distance was one thing. A still shape shrouded under a blanket or zipped up in a body bag, that was an occupational hazard. But when you got up close it was a different matter.

And yes, it was the smell of blood. He could smell it himself – that unmistakable metallic tang of substantial bleeding. It was that, and knowing the dead person must have been able to smell their own blood too, in those final moments.

He wondered if he'd become too used to it, that he should need a DC like Becky Hurst to point it out, to remind him how upsetting a violent death could be. He ought to feel the effect of it more, shouldn't he? At one time, he would have cared deeply about what drove these people to their deaths. Yet when he set off from Foolow this morning he'd been thinking of them as a major nuisance at best.

Maybe there was something wrong with his routine. Perhaps he should put a new CD on for his morning drive to West Street.

'She cut her wrists,' said Hurst. 'Sliced right through the arteries with a razor blade.'

Cooper winced at the thought. 'Take a break for a while anyway, Becky,' he said. 'We'll manage fine here.'

Carol Villiers was here too, and once more Cooper was impressed by the cool way she'd taken control of the situation and begun to establish the facts.

Whenever a dead body turned up, whatever the circumstances, the first officers to arrive had to assess the scene and take steps to protect evidence before the chain of command began to shift upwards. For

Ben Cooper, the moment of interpreting the scene was critical. If he set up a murder investigation when it turned out to be suicide or natural causes, he would be criticised for wasting resources. If he got it wrong in the other direction and a post-mortem revealed suspicious circumstances, this initial decision would have hampered the investigation.

Everyone knew the first twenty-four hours after a sudden death were the most important. But the assessment was always made under pressure and it took good judgement and a lot of luck to get it right on limited information. Death could be messy, even when it resulted from natural causes. Blood could confuse the interpretation, especially for officers with little experience in dealing with death.

Cooper had come to rely on instinct, a gut feeling. From experience, he trusted his instincts, the sense that something wasn't right. He would hear a warning bell going off in his head, telling him to step back and review the situation. Death was suspicious until proved otherwise.

'Are we sure it's suicide?' he asked Villiers.

'No suspicious circumstances,' she said. 'No evidence of anyone else being present.'

'Okay. Name?'

'Bethan Jones,' said Villiers. 'She's from Cheshire. We've made contact with a next of kin.'

'And who is that?'

'Her sister, Megan. It seems Miss Jones had been diagnosed with cancer. Until the last few weeks, she wasn't really suffering any symptoms, but she knew she had limited time to live. Her sister says she'd started getting pain recently, but she'd stopped talking about it. "As if there was no point in talking any more." That was the way the sister described it.'

Cooper nodded. 'I bet her affairs were in order, though.'

'Absolutely. Bethan left a list of all her bank account details with her sister, showing that her utility bills were in credit and her funeral was already paid for. And she'd chosen the music.'

'The music?'

'Of course,' said Villiers. 'That's the first thing you'd think of, isn't it? The music makes a difference to what sort of funeral you get. You can make them play something cheerful as a celebration of your life or you can pick something really moving and sad to make everyone cry in church.'

'I hadn't really thought of that.' Cooper glanced at Villiers curiously. 'Have you planned your funeral?'

She shrugged. 'Well, you know – when you're on active service, it's something you think about. Making a will and all that. You never know what's going to happen.'

'No, of course. You're going into a dangerous situation. You can't choose the time and place you die. Most people can't do that. But our suicide tourists have.'

Matt Cooper was still standing around, outside the tape that had hastily been strung around the caravan. He looked like a bull that had just been stunned and was waiting for the slaughterman's knife to finish him off.

'It's a six-berther, if you fold everything out,' said Matt glumly. 'We wouldn't normally rent it to a single person or even to a couple. But Kate says she asked for this one and was very insistent. She booked well in advance and was happy to pay the full price. And it's still fairly early in the season . . .'

'So you don't have many families booked in yet,' said Ben.

'Not until the school holidays in July.' Matt shook his head. 'God knows what we're going to do with this caravan now. It cost a fortune to buy and get on site. Do you think the insurance will cover it?'

'I have no idea, Matt.'

'Bugger.'

Matt shook his head. 'Well, I'll go and ask Kate to check the bookings. She might remember the woman, or she'll be able to look it up.'

He walked off and Ben watched his brother go, noticing his shoulders hunched with tension, and his fists clenching and unclenching. Matt couldn't go on like this, staggering from one crisis to another, the strain and anxiety getting worse all the time. He would drive himself into an early grave. For his own sake, it might come time to give up the farm one day. It would be a very tough decision to make. And what his brother would do instead, Ben couldn't imagine.

It was a big caravan, an Elddis Crusader, twenty-six feet long. The largest static they had on the site. It had a separate washroom at the far end with a shower unit and a cassette toilet. And this was where Bethan Jones had performed her final act.

She'd laid towels on the floor to block the drain, so that water had pooled inside the cubicle. The condensation from the hot water was still running down the walls and the floor was pink with swirling trails of blood-tinged water. Some of it had overflowed into the bedroom and soaked into the carpet.

In the kitchen area, several empty bottles of Buxton Spring water stood on the worktop. A freshly opened packet of razor blades lay by the sink. A used blade had been bagged from the floor of the shower.

'She did a good job of it,' said the medical examiner, removing a pair of bloodstained gloves. 'No hesitation marks.'

Cooper thought about that. Hesitation marks were usually found in suicides who slashed their wrists. It was such a dramatic thing to do that people normally made a number of attempts before getting up the courage for the final slash, or they realised they couldn't do it. He felt sure this woman must have practised. It would fit the pattern of these carefully planned suicides. But what had she practised on? There was probably guidance available on that too.

'She went really deep too. Yes, she definitely did the job properly.'

Cooper had no doubt about that by now. He was sure Bethan Jones would have done it exactly right – not cutting across the wrists, but lengthwise down the forearm. A firm, straight cut. Deep enough to expose the artery. And then a quick switch to the other hand before she lost too much blood.

'What's the significance of the water, doctor?' he said, indicating the empty bottles.

'If you drink plenty of water in the twenty-four hours beforehand, it enlarges the veins and speeds up the flow when the blood vessels are severed.'

'I see.'

'Not that drinking bottled mineral water would make any difference from plain, ordinary tap water in that respect.'

'No.'

'People have their little idiosyncrasies, don't they? Their own preferred brand of water.'

Back outside, Cooper crouched and looked under the caravan. The water from the shower had soaked through the floor and was dripping on to the grass. Drip, drip, drip. It was still falling in a steady, blood-tinged trickle.

A small amount of blood didn't produce any particular smell. There had to be substantial bleeding for the smell to be noticeable. The metallic, coppery scent of fresh blood was very distinctive. And fresh blood was warm. If you saw it close to hand, its surface steamed gently in the air.

But now, hours after the death of Bethan Jones, the decaying blood had begun to produce a sickly-sweet aroma.

Matt came back across the field from the farmhouse clutching a page torn from a notepad, with some dates scrawled on it in his wife's handwriting. Ben glanced over at the house and saw Kate standing in the doorway looking anxiously after her husband. Ben gave her a wave, but she didn't seem to notice, instead ducking back inside.

Of course, he could appreciate how she must be feeling. Kate had been the one who'd talked Matt into setting up the caravan site at Bridge End. It had been an expensive investment for the farm. It was her responsibility, her voice reassuring Matt when he grumbled about townies camping on his land.

And now this, the last thing she could have expected. She must be imagining the worst scenario, what might have happened, with the girls around the farm trying to make friends with the caravanners, asking where they were from, offering to bring them milk and eggs. Kate would be picturing Amy and Josie knocking on the door of the furthest caravan and seeing the body or noticing the blood-tinged water dripping through the floor.

Villiers took the note from Matt, who allowed her to have it like a child reluctantly giving up a toy. Then he nodded at his brother and hurried back to the farmhouse, where Kate would be waiting for him. There would be some difficult conversations at Bridge End.

Cooper turned back to Villiers.

'Whereabouts in Cheshire is Bethan Jones from?' he asked.

'Not this side of the county – somewhere over near Northwich.'

'Northwich? Right in the middle of the Cheshire

Plain. It's barely fifty feet above sea level there, even where the salt mines haven't made the land sink even further. So she came looking for the hills.'

'She could have gone over into North Wales from there.'

'Yes, she could,' said Cooper. 'But Derbyshire has better hills.'

He stood looking at the caravan and at the view across the Eden Valley. This was definitely the best pitch on the site. Nevertheless, it was unnatural to think about death as desirable. He'd grown up with the impression that death was something strange and frightening, an unknown terror that would one day come for him, as it did for everyone sooner or later.

When he was a child, the idea of death had made him think of autumn nights, when darkness came earlier and earlier in the evening until there was hardly any daylight left. On those nights, he would lie in his bed at Bridge End Farm listening to the scream of mating foxes or the blood-curdling screech of badgers as they fought over territory.

Death was like that, wasn't it? A dreadful and unseen presence out there in the darkness, whose closeness only made you cling more tightly to the comfort of life. Or it should do.

14

Ben Cooper was driving on the A50, the noisiest road in Derbyshire. It had a ragged tarmac surface that made his car sound as though it was falling apart and turned every lorry he passed into a rattling cattle truck.

It was a drive of about thirty-five miles from the Eden Valley down through Derbyshire to the Lightwood area of Stoke-on-Trent. On Derbyshire roads, that took well over an hour.

Megan Roberts was married, with a couple of young children, whom Cooper could hear playing somewhere upstairs in her nice detached house. The property had an annexe, which had been converted into a sort of granny flat – except that it had been used to accommodate Megan's terminally ill sister Bethan for the last few months of her life.

'It was the tiredness Bethan complained about most,' said Megan. 'The constant fatigue. In many ways, it was the most upsetting symptom she had. There were so many things she wanted to do before it was too late, but the tiredness meant she often couldn't manage.

Apparently, it's very common with a case of advanced cancer.'

'And then she began to have pain?'

'Yes. It was an annoyance at first, but she knew it would become so bad that it would be debilitating. Sometimes the pain made her irritable and stopped her sleeping properly. She was hardly eating either. She used to enjoy her food, but her appetite had gone.'

'So do you think your sister did the right thing, then?'

Megan Roberts hesitated, as if weighing up what her response should be and how he would react.

'Let me put it this way,' she said, 'I can't argue with what she decided to do. If she felt it was the best thing for her in the circumstances, because of the way she was suffering, how can the rest of us say it was wrong? We can't fully understand what's going on in someone's life.'

Cooper examined the rooms in the annexe. He wasn't expecting to find anything, even though Bethan Jones didn't fit the pattern. Bethan had been too well organised and properly prepared. She wouldn't have left anything behind that she didn't want found. Given that she lived in her sister's house with two young children around, she would have been particularly careful. He felt certain there would be no link to a suicide website left on a Post-it note, no printouts that someone might ask awkward questions about.

On a cushion in the sitting room, he did find something that surprised him: a stack of *Brides* magazines. Cooper had seen these magazines before. He'd been forced to look at them himself, obliged to examine the photographs, asked his opinion on dresses and bouquets and table decorations. He knew it meant only one thing – someone had been planning a wedding.

He glanced at the dates on the covers. They were all published in the last few weeks. Had Bethan Jones been dreaming of her own wedding? And, if so, who had she been planning to marry at such a late stage in her life?

Or was it just one of those dreams that approaching death had brought into sharp, ironic focus? Bethan had been the kind of person who made plans. She'd planned her death and her funeral too. He could picture her sitting down with these magazines, turning the pages and planning a wedding. A wedding that she knew would never happen.

Back at West Street in Edendale, Cooper gathered his team together to review their progress. If another death could be regarded as progress.

'I've found Bethan Jones's profile online,' said Irvine. 'She was very active on social media. She talked mostly about TV shows and animals, shared a few cat videos – that sort of thing. She also did a lot of promotion for charity fundraising projects.'

'Cancer charities?'

'Those, and others. And do you know the funny thing?'

'What?'

'She had more than two thousand friends on Facebook. And none of them seems to know that she's dead.'

'Any luck with a suicide website, Luke? *Secrets of Death*?'

'Not yet. It's very difficult. There are so many of them. You wouldn't believe it. But none I've found so far suggests any connection.'

'Keep trying.'

'Of course.'

'All of these people were disturbed in some way, even if only temporarily,' said Hurst. 'They must have been. You have to be unbalanced to kill yourself.'

Cooper saw that her hand was trembling a bit, though she tried to conceal it. Seeing the body of Bethan Jones had shaken Hurst up more than she would probably care to admit. Yet it seemed to have made her angry rather than sympathetic. It was the reaction he sometimes saw from family members after a death, as if it was something that had been done to them rather than to the victim.

'Unbalanced?' he said. 'Is that the right word?'

'They say one in four people is mentally unbalanced in some way,' said Irvine.

Uncomfortably, they avoided looking at each other. Nobody needed to take a quick head count. There were clearly more than four of them in the room. So which one of them was it?

'It's an average, of course,' said Cooper after a suitable pause. 'There are a higher proportion of mentally unbalanced people in some professions than in others.'

'CPS lawyers?' suggested Irvine. 'Judges?'

'None of these individuals was considered to be so much of a risk to themselves that they had to be sectioned under the Mental Health Act.'

'And there are things you can do before it gets to that stage,' said Villiers. 'There are people you can talk to. Why aren't they getting help?'

'That's the trouble,' said Cooper. 'I think they are.'

'What do you mean?'

'There's a plan,' he said. 'Someone is orchestrating these suicides. Yes, a lot of people reach a point when they badly need help. And sometimes they reach out for help in the wrong direction. They get the worst kind of help.'

'There's absolutely no evidence that these individuals had been in contact with each other in any way. We've been through their phone records, their emails. There's no link through family or work, or even similar interests.'

'There's a connection, though. There must be. Some link that binds them together. Mr Tate is the only one who could tell us, but he's keeping his mouth shut. Whether he's sworn to secrecy or someone has a hold over him, I don't know.'

'Who knows what commitment people sign up to,' said Irvine. 'Perhaps he was thrown out of the club for not dying.'

'Blackmail perhaps?' said Villiers.

'Possibly. A threat that their shameful secrets will be revealed unless they take the honourable way out. So what would a blackmailer get out of that? How would they benefit? There's no financial gain, no suggestion of revenge.'

'No. Unless someone out there just likes to watch people die,' said Villiers.

Cooper looked at her. It was a horrible thought, but it was feasible. Too feasible. Had someone been present at the locations, waiting for victims to reach their final moments? Could there be some psychopath who found satisfaction from controlling other people's lives to the extent that they could dictate how and when they died? And even where?

Well, of course there could. There was no limit to the twisted logic and desires of true psychopaths. And Cooper knew they tended to have another characteristic in common. Psychopaths were manipulative. They were masters at making themselves convincing and credible, at creating a false empathy with their victim. They could be very, very persuasive.

'I need something to put to Anson Tate,' he said. 'To break through his façade. I've got to get him to open him up about what actually happened. Whatever it is, something is keeping him from telling us what we need to know.'

'He's probably ashamed. He feels a failure,' said Irvine.

'Yes. Of course, what interests me,' said Cooper, 'is whether Mr Tate is someone else's failure.'

Cooper went upstairs and along the corridor to report to Detective Superintendent Branagh. During his report, he carefully avoided the use of that word *progress*. It would have felt like a lie. He explained his theory that the suicides had been getting advice and guidance, probably encouragement. That they were someone else's puppets.

'It looks to me as though someone is being very controlling, taking the decisions out of the hands of desperate individuals,' he said. 'They don't have to worry about method and means, about whether it will go wrong or even about where to do it – all those details that potential suicides stumble on, the small stuff that stops people going through with it. It's all done for them.'

'It's presented as an easy option,' said Branagh.

Cooper nodded. 'Or the only option. Once you've signed up, you're made to feel obligated, as if you're engaged in an inevitable process that you can no longer stop, even if you want to.'

Branagh frowned as she listened to him.

'So what direction is your thinking taking you, Ben?' she asked.

'Well, at the moment, I'm asking myself a difficult question. If any of these individuals were persuaded or coerced into doing what they did by someone else, would we have a case against that person?'

'It would depend on the evidence,' said Branagh.

'Doesn't it always?'

'I mean, there would have to be proof of definite intent. Just discussing suicide methods on a website wouldn't count. Putting suicidal individuals in contact with each other certainly doesn't. You might argue that that was a kind of support group. Even talking to someone about suicide doesn't prove anything – you would need a record of that person being actually encouraged to commit the act.'

'It's very frustrating when you suspect someone has

been doing it deliberately. Is there no legislation we can use?'

Cooper had thought about it himself, turning it over in his mind. He came up against the one unanswerable question. You could prosecute for murder without a body. So what could you do with a body, but no suspect or motive?

'I know how you feel, Ben,' said Branagh. 'It's been a frustration to us for a long time. There have been some glaring incidents, even in public. Like that young man in Derby.'

Cooper was familiar with the case she was referring to. A few years previously, police negotiators had spent two hours trying to coax down a suicidal boy from the top floor of a shopping centre car park in the city of Derby. Meanwhile, a group of youths on the street below had shouted taunts at the boy, telling him to 'Jump!' and 'Get on with it'. Some had filmed the incident on their mobile phones and uploaded clips online for everyone to see. Seconds before he jumped, the boy almost touched an officer's hand but was distracted by the taunts. He counted down from ten and hurled himself off the car park roof.

At the subsequent inquest, the coroner had said the taunting youths were partly responsible for the boy's death. Despite the coroner's comments, no one had ever been arrested or charged for their role in the incident. The trouble was, there was no specific offence that people could be charged with if all they were doing was shouting comments.

There had been similar incidents around the country,

168

so it wasn't just a Derbyshire problem. For Cooper, this was more than mindless insensitivity and a lack of concern for another human being. People had become passive consumers of tragedy, incapable of separating reality from entertainment. Now smartphone users were engaging in the tragedy itself, goading a suicide to his death so they could share the footage on Facebook and YouTube.

Like it or not, there were people out there who liked watching someone die.

'So, you're talking about a sociopath or psychopath of some kind,' said Branagh.

'Yes, ma'am.'

He'd realised that on his way up the corridor, as the lights went on and off. In fact, what he had in mind was the very definition of a psychopath. While one in four people might be unbalanced in some way, there was another statistic that was even more disturbing. One in ten went so far as to have socio-pathic tendencies.

And they became the violent psychopaths. Their violence was planned, purposeful and emotionless, reflecting a detached and disassociated mental state. They were motivated by a desire for control and dominance. Their attitude was one of absolute entitlement.

Most of all, psychopaths often possessed an almost demonic ability to manipulate others. They could persuade their victims out of everything they owned, even their lives. He thought of the leaders of religious cults who led their followers to their deaths. They might even believe in their own lies, convince themselves of their own omnipotence.

'Yes, someone out there thinks he's become a god,' said Cooper. 'A god with the power of life and death.'

15

David Kuzneski had lived in the Totley area of Sheffield. His street was right on the southwestern edge of the city, close to the moorland that began almost at the city boundaries. From here, you could see the outline of Blacka Moor, where a footpath through Cowsick Bog had recently been relaid with stone slabs recycled from disused cotton mills in Lancashire and dropped in by helicopter.

Cooper wondered if Kuzneski had spent much time up there, braving the quagmires of Cowsick. A herd of red deer lived on the moor and were said to raid gardens in Totley from time to time. Kuzneski had lived as close as he could to the Peak District while still being in the city.

He'd been on medication for bipolar disorder. But his bipolar extremes had lasted for weeks. His wife said she couldn't remember when he'd been in a condition she would describe as 'normal'. He'd been taking lithium carbonate and valproate, but he was troubled by the side effects of the lithium – diarrhoea and vomiting. When in a manic phase, he simply stopped taking the medication. And the cycle began all over again.

'I did begin to wonder whether David wanted to kill himself,' said Stephanie Kuzneski. 'Whether he was just waiting for the right moment, for everything to come together. He never said anything to me, but it was part of the manic depressive cycle. When he was up, he made plans. When he was down, he knew it was all useless. After a while, I don't think he could convince himself there was a future, no matter how hard he tried. How hard we *all* tried, everyone who cared about him.'

She got up and walked to the window to stare out at the road, with her back to Cooper so he couldn't see her face. He sat quietly and waited, trying to pretend he wasn't there while she collected her thoughts.

'That condition,' she said. 'It possessed him as surely as any demon. And in David's case there was no hope of exorcism. He once told me it was like having your own personal bully. A voice inside your head constantly telling you how rubbish you are, banging on and on about how you've failed in every single thing you've tried to do, destroyed every relationship you've had. It tells you over and over that you've let everyone down. That you might as well . . . Well, you know . . .'

'Yes, I know.'

Mrs Kuzneski took a deep, ragged breath before she continued. 'He told me the voices were saying, "*The pain will never end. It's time for you to die. You know you want to die.*"'

Cooper shook his head in frustration. 'He shouldn't

172

have reached that stage,' he said. 'If things had been done properly for him.'

'I know. But it's a bit late now to look back and say how things might have been done differently. In the end, David was still in control of his own fate.'

'I suppose that's true. Did you ever see a card like this in your husband's possession?' asked Cooper, showing her the *Secrets of Death* business card from Roger Farrell's car.

Mrs Kuzneski went pale. 'Yes,' she said. 'I found one in his jacket pocket.'

'What did you do with it?'

'I burned it,' she said. 'Was that the wrong thing to do?'

'I suppose it can't be helped.'

'And there were some extra tablets too. What was left of the lithium he'd bought online. He must have known exactly how many he needed to take.'

Stephanie Kuzneski gazed into the distance, as if running the whole episode through her mind.

'David hated taking tablets, you know,' she said. 'He insisted it was unnatural. He said the drugs were taking his personality away and changing him into a different person, someone he didn't like.'

'I think that's quite common,' said Cooper. 'It must have been difficult for you to deal with.'

She nodded. 'I often used to nag him to take his tablets. He took no notice of me. And what could I do? He was as difficult to handle in that phase as he was when he was depressed. He was a grown man, for goodness' sake. I couldn't physically force him to take them.'

'Of course not.'

Finally, she turned away from the window and looked at Cooper again.

'I think he was right, too,' she said. 'The medication *had* changed him into someone else. And it was a person I didn't like very much either. Definitely not the man I fell in love with and married. In a way, his death was a release. For both of us.'

As Cooper was leaving Totley, his mobile rang and a number he didn't recognise came up on the screen. He was always cautious about unidentified numbers. They often turned out to be randomly generated sales calls. But something made him answer this one rather than let it go to voicemail.

'Hello?' he said.

'Hi. It's Chloe Young,' replied a woman's voice.

'I'm sorry?'

'Dr Young, from the mortuary. We met over a dead body.'

He heard the laugh in her voice and recognised her then.

'Oh, Dr Young. Of course. What can I do for you?'

'Juliana van Doon found your number for me. I was wondering whether you had more time yet.'

'For . . .?'

'Well, to talk about my suicide study,' she said. 'Informally, you know. Since you said you were interested. I thought it might be good to get another perspective on the subject from an experienced police officer.'

'Oh, I see. When were you thinking of?'

'Tonight?'

Cooper was surprised by his own inner response – that sudden warm rush, the upsurge of hope. It was a feeling he hadn't experienced for a long time, not since Liz's death. But he recognised in himself a growing need for something, for someone new. Perhaps it was time to stop mourning.

'I'll be free in an hour or two,' he said.

'Excellent. Do you know where the Barrel Inn is?'

'The one at Bretton? Certainly. It isn't far from where I live.'

'Seven-thirty or so?'

'Fine. I'll see you there.'

Cooper ended the call. He wasn't quite sure what had just happened. Perhaps he would find out tonight.

In the CID room at West Street, Cooper went first to speak to Luke Irvine, who sometimes needed nudging to get results from the jobs he'd been given. In particular, some hint of a connection to the card in Roger Farrell's car was a priority. *Secrets of Death* was starting to bother him.

'Ben, we've got a result from our appeals in the media,' said Carol Villiers.

Cooper looked round. 'What appeals?'

'For potential witnesses who were parked at Heeley Bank the night Roger Farrell killed himself.'

'Of course.'

Cooper had put the appeals to the back of his mind.

They had just been a gesture really. He hadn't expected anything to come of them. So this was a stroke of luck.

'Anyone credible?' he said.

'A couple from Chesterfield got in touch. We got lucky with them – they weren't too far away and saw the piece in the local news.'

'Are they coming in to see us?'

'They're on their way now. In fact, they'll be here soon.'

'Great.'

Barely half an hour later, Villiers escorted a couple of visitors to the first floor and knocked on Cooper's office door.

'This is Mr and Mrs Cook,' she said.

'Gareth and Barbara,' said the man who stepped forward to shake his hand.

'Thank you very much for coming in.'

'It's no problem,' said Mrs Cook. 'We'll be happy if we can help at all. It was a terrible thing to happen.'

The couple sat down in his little office, which was hardly big enough for three people. They pulled their chairs as close together as possible and Barbara Cook took her husband's hand, as if for reassurance.

Cooper could see from the start that they were the sort of people who had never been in a police station before, not for any reason. Possibly they were among those lucky members of the public who had never even encountered a police officer and didn't know quite what to expect. It might depend what TV crime dramas they were used to watching. Their expectations might have been shaped by anything between *Midsomer Murders* and *The Wire*.

So Cooper smiled and offered them tea, which they declined. He eased them into the session by asking them about themselves and how often they visited the Peak District. He learned that they'd met each other as members of a group of conservation volunteers on a tree-planting project near Grindleford, that they'd only been married two years and had no children yet. He told them he'd volunteered himself once and had been allocated to a footpath construction and repair team on the edge of Bleaklow.

'It was January,' he said. 'We were soaked and freezing cold. I admire the people who keep going back time after time.'

He watched them relax and they began to tell him about their visit to Heeley Bank. They'd been there for a walk in the woods and down to the river. They'd also bought some flapjacks in the information centre and eaten them in their car with a flask of coffee. Cooper gathered that the Cooks were keen people-watchers. They noticed things.

He slid across the photograph of Roger Farrell.

'And you recognised this man?' he said.

Barbara Cook grimaced. 'Yes, we're quite sure it was him we saw. Aren't we, Gareth?'

Her husband nodded. And then he described seeing Farrell leave his BMW and go into the information centre. That was news to Cooper. Marnie Letts hadn't mentioned it.

'What time would that be?'

'Oh, perhaps about four o'clock. Not long before we left.'

'He wasn't in the centre for long,' said Barbara. 'He came out again. And then he spoke to someone.'

'He did? Who?'

'We don't know. Sorry. It was just a man, standing over by the toilet block. They only spoke for a minute or two.'

'We couldn't really see them very well because of the sun,' said Gareth. 'It was shining from that direction and they were in the shadows. You know what I mean?'

'Yes.'

Cooper questioned them gently for a few minutes to see if they could remember any other details, but they seemed to have exhausted their information. They were trying very hard, too, he could see that.

Finally, he ran out of questions and sat back to look at them. The Cooks stirred in the chairs, as if about to leave. Then Gareth Cook reached into his pocket.

'Oh, and there's this,' he said.

'What is it?'

He handed Cooper a small blue case containing a memory card.

'We have a dashcam,' said his wife. 'Gareth bought it after he had a collision in the car last year and the other driver wouldn't accept liability.'

'It was a total nightmare,' said Gareth. 'I was going backwards and forwards with insurance companies for months and the worst thing was they didn't seem to believe me. I lost my excess in the end. Three hundred pounds. So now I've got proof, if it happens again.'

'Unless someone hits you from behind,' said Barbara.

'Well, I'd have to install another camera on the back shelf to cover that, wouldn't I?'

Cooper held up the case. 'You're telling me you had your dashboard camera operating during the time you were parked at Heeley Bank that day?'

'Only while the engine was running, obviously. But there should be some footage to look at. It's a sixteen-gigabyte micro SD card and we get nearly three hours of recording from the camera before it starts to over-write the earliest files.'

'Thank you, Mr Cook,' said Cooper, feeling genuinely grateful for something for the first time all week.

'You're welcome. We hope it helps, we really do.'

'It was a terrible thing,' said Barbara.

When the Cooks had left West Street, Cooper took the memory card to Luke Irvine.

'What's this?' asked Irvine.

'It's footage from a dashboard camera.'

'Do you want to view it?'

'Of course.'

'No problem. This PC has a card reader.'

When the video started, the quality on screen was surprisingly good. Unfortunately, the first half-hour had recorded the Cooks' journey all the way from the drive of their home in Chesterfield. There were glimpses of a Tesco Extra, the Proact Stadium where Chesterfield FC played, then a scenic drive out past the Old Pump in Barlow before they even reached the boundary of the national park near Unthank.

179

Cooper straightened up. 'I'm going back to my desk. Let me know when they reach Heeley Bank,' he said.

It seemed a long time before Irvine came to fetch him again.

'They got to Owler Bar and stopped for lunch,' he said apologetically. 'And they seem to have taken the scenic route to Heeley Bank.'

Irvine restarted the video. Cooper saw the familiar view of the hill on the approach to Heeley Bank and watched as the Cooks' car slowed and turned into the car park. The place was full when they arrived and it was hard to make out any individual vehicles, except a green VW camper van they parked opposite, which was captured in beautiful detail for a few moments before the dashcam stopped when the engine went off.

'I think they left the car here,' said Irvine.

'They went for a walk in the woods.'

'Right. But here they come back again.'

A different vehicle was facing the Cooks' car when the dashcam came back on. A small blue car, a Vauxhall from the look of the badge on the radiator grille. The car park was beginning to empty. Two vehicles passed in front of the camera on their way out. And then Cooper realised there was now a view up the car park towards the information centre. He couldn't see the door of the centre, but he could see the toilet block clearly. A couple of figures stood talking nearby, but he couldn't make out any details. There was no way he would be able to recognise anyone, let alone Roger Farrell, whom he had never seen alive.

'Well, that's a washout,' he said.

'Sorry.'

'Not your fault, Luke.'

Then Cooper looked more closely at the last bit of footage from the dashboard camera. There was a vehicle parked close to the corner of the building. He could catch just a glimpse of a wing, dark and half obscured. But there was something distinctive about the shape of it. Surely there was only one type of vehicle that still had that shape of wing?

It was the familiar boxy outline of a Land Rover.

Marnie Letts had an address on the Woodlands Estate. It was way up in the north of Edendale, an area that was hardly part of the town itself, as far as Cooper was concerned. Their natures were certainly very different.

Victoria Park was the point where the character of Edendale changed. On one side of the park stood the Royal Theatre, just off Hulley Road, with the new courthouse development across Park Street. To the north of Victoria Park, Edendale's largest housing estates began. They'd spread way out of town that way now. Passing the park gates, he could see the Devonshire and Cavendish Estates, but he knew there was much more housing creeping up the hillsides behind them.

Cooper had patrolled the beat on the Devonshire Estate when he was a young bobby, watching out for stolen cars being raced round the streets or gathering information on local drug dealers who operated from the sprawl of prefabricated concrete houses slung up in the 1960s.

The estate occupied low-lying land in the valley floor that had once been water meadows until they were drained for the housing scheme. For decades the damp had been creeping back into the foundations of the houses, staining the walls with mould and rotting the doors and windows. When some of the houses became virtually uninhabitable, with fungus growing through the floorboards and water pouring through the roofs, the council decided to act and had carried out a major remedial scheme on the entire estate, redecorating, replastering and re-roofing. They'd spent millions of pounds on the project and it had taken three years. But it hadn't stopped the damp creeping back in.

The Woodlands Estate was more modern and bigger, stretching all the way across to the Manchester Road. Addresses on the estate were instantly recognisable: Elm Street, Sycamore Crescent, Chestnut Avenue, Lime Tree Close. It seemed as though the house-building had only stopped when the developers ran out of tree names.

He recalled Gavin Murfin talking about working on the Woodlands Estate. He had some sympathy with Murfin. Residents were known universally as Woodies. The name had taken on connotations that summed up all kinds of prejudices and preconceptions.

Cooper drove up into the estate with his windows open. He passed a shopping parade in the middle of it. Most of the shops had steel shutters pulled down over their windows and doors, as if preparing for a riot.

The local supermarket was about to close for the

evening and teenagers had begun to gather in the car park. They clustered round a yellow hatchback with its doors and windows open and loud grime music banging out into the summer air. Cooper didn't need to get any nearer to guess what the kids were smoking. He could smell it from here, its distinctive odour mixing with the tang of lager.

At her address on Sycamore Crescent, Marnie Letts looked as though she had been doing some baking. She was wearing an apron and there was a smudge of white flour on her face. She looked uneasy at getting a visit. Cooper remembered her at Heeley Bank. She'd been calm and composed after the initial shock and once she knew what was happening.

'I'm taking the chance to catch up on some jobs,' she said. 'Pete is working and it's much easier when he's out of the house.'

'Your husband?' said Cooper.

'Yes, he's a tree surgeon.'

'We've had a couple of witnesses who responded to our appeals,' said Cooper when she let him into the house. 'They say they remember the man in the BMW – Mr Farrell. They saw him come into the information centre that afternoon. It would have been about four p.m.'

'I don't recall him,' said Marnie. 'But then – what did he actually look like?'

Cooper realised that Marnie Letts would not have seen Roger Farrell's face, except when it was obscured by the exit bag after his death.

'Haven't you seen the story in the papers?' he asked.

'No. I didn't want to read about it. Not after that morning . . .'

'I see. Well, here. This is Mr Farrell.'

Cooper showed her the photograph of Roger Farrell they'd been using. She ought to have been shown it earlier, if he'd thought about it. Too much else had been happening.

Marnie looked at the photo, squinting her eyes as if seeing Farrell against a burst of sunlight, then shook her head.

'No. I still don't remember him,' she said. 'That's not to say he didn't come in. We were quite busy that day. I don't remember people very well, to be honest. Some of them don't actually buy anything, you know. They just browse the books and postcards, then pick up a few free leaflets before they go out again. I'm sorry.'

'Thank you anyway.' Cooper took the photo back. 'According to our witnesses, when Mr Farrell came out of the information centre he spoke to someone near the toilet block.'

'I definitely can't help you there,' she said. 'I can't see in that direction, not when I'm working behind the counter. If I happen to be standing near the door, I can. But, like I say, we were busy. So I was probably serving a customer at the counter.'

'I understand. It might not be important, but we have to check these details. The evidence from our witnesses does confirm the presence of a dark-coloured Land Rover, by the way.'

'If that's what it was,' said Marnie.

'Yes.'

She could see that Cooper was disappointed.

'I'm really sorry I can't be more help,' she said.

Cooper smiled. 'Everyone says that.'

As he was leaving the Woodlands Estate, Cooper noticed a crowd of Woodies gathered at the corner of Sycamore Crescent. They were probably building up to a fight between the Sycos and the Elmers. It was the normal evening entertainment around here.

16

Luke Irvine had left the office promptly at the end of his shift that day. There was no overtime on this inquiry. In fact, it was as rare as hen's teeth these days, unfortunately.

Irvine had been living in Bamford for a couple of years now. It suited him nicely – a village location that reminded him of his family home back in West Yorkshire, a good community atmosphere and a fantastic pub. What more could he ask? It even had a little railway station on the Hope Valley line, so he could get to Manchester or Sheffield without driving – though the nature of the Peak District landscape meant he couldn't get to Edendale, which lay over the hill in a different valley.

Since he'd arrived in Bamford, Irvine had been sharing a house on Old Post Office Row with two web designers. He had a room overlooking the fields between The Hollow and South View. When he opened his window in the morning he smelled fresh horse manure.

When he got home that evening, he parked his Kia half on the pavement. He wasn't stopping long and parking was a problem, of course. These villages were built before people had cars. The older properties had no off-street parking and the roads were narrow, so there was always a bit of competition for spaces. That was one of the compromises you had to accept.

Irvine let himself into the house, went up to his room and changed into a T-shirt, jogging bottoms and trainers, then went straight out again. On the pavement, he paused and looked around the village.

The house was positioned halfway up the long hill that Bamford had been built on. One Sunday morning at about half-past ten, not long after he'd moved in, Irvine had walked down the hill and into the village church, St John the Baptist, attracted by the smell of fresh coffee. He'd spent the previous evening in the Angler's Rest and wasn't quite awake. He discovered that the service on the first Sunday of the month began with coffee and cake.

Irvine hadn't been to church much since he'd left Denby Dale, where he grew up. His mother had been a church warden and was very serious about the role, which had probably made him react against anything with a whiff of C of E ever since. St John's had a curiously tall, thin tower with bells that he heard being rung for practice every Wednesday evening when he was at home. He'd been told that bodies exhumed from the village of Derwent had been brought here for reburial after it was submerged during the construction of Ladybower Reservoir.

And, while he was drinking coffee and eating cake there, he'd met the female vicar for Bamford, who covered three parishes and lived down the line in Hathersage. And somehow, he'd found himself being roped in to help with the village carnival, climbing ladders to put up bunting and acting as a marshal for the parade. He found it oddly satisfying. He was starting to be absorbed into the community.

But today when Irvine got back in the Kia he headed uphill. Not far above Bamford, he hit the lower end of Ladybower Reservoir, where the dam held back twenty-eight million gallons of water from flooding Bamford and the famous eighty-foot-wide plugholes created swirling vortexes on the surface of the water, as if Ladybower was draining away into another dimension. Most of the water flowed southwards from here along the Derwent Aqueduct to be distributed to the populations of Derby and Leicester.

He crossed the bridge, turned left at the lights and drove on to the narrow road that ran up the northern arm of Ladybower. The reservoir formed an enormous stylised letter 'Y' in the landscape. The Fairholmes Visitor Centre lay right at the tip of Ladybower's northern arm, where it was separated from Derwent Reservoir by another dam with castellated twin towers. Though Fairholmes was run by Severn Trent Water, there was a ranger service station here, as well as a cycle hire centre. A bus service ran all the way between Fairholmes and Fearfall Wood on the side of the A57.

As Irvine was parking, his phone rang. He saw straight away that it was his parents, calling from Denby Dale because they knew he ought to have finished work by now. They worried that he'd get too obsessed with the job and be working all hours of the day and night, with no social life, no proper meals and far too much alcohol. They'd watched so many TV crime dramas that they had a distorted view of police work which he couldn't get out of their minds, no matter how often he tried to explain the reality to them.

'Hello? Mum?' he said.

It was usually his mother who made the call. Sometimes she passed him on to his dad, but she was the one who waited impatiently by the phone until the clock said it was okay to ring.

'I'm just out for a run,' he said. 'Ladybower. No, *Lady*bower. The big reservoir. You know, I showed it to you and Dad when you came down. Yes, like Ingbirchworth but a lot bigger.'

He put his money into the parking machine and stuck the ticket on his car, shooing away a Mallard duck pecking at his trainers. An enormous flock of ducks owned the car park at Fairholmes. When you drove in, you had to wait for dozens of them to waddle slowly across the tarmac to make way for your car. When you walked towards the café, they followed you. When you came out, they clustered round your legs, making hopeful little quacking noises. If you sat at a picnic table, they gradually surrounded you, until you were sitting in a sea of gently undulating feathers.

'No, I haven't started going to church regularly, Mum,' he said. 'Don't start asking me why not. I don't have to say why not. I'll go if I want to.'

Irvine rolled his eyes. Near the far wall of the car park, an elderly woman was ripping up chunks of bread and scattering the pieces on the ground. It prompted a surge of movement around the site and a waddling tide converged on her.

'No, I'm fine,' he said. 'I'm eating properly. Busy at work, but . . .'

He began to do his warm-ups. A group of walkers were picnicking at a table. A man sat smoking a cigarette. A minibus pulled away, carrying a group of people home from a day out. Two exhausted-looking cyclists unfastened their helmets. A motorcyclist checked over his bike.

A dog was barking. And, while two women chatted at a table, their pre-school children ran around the grass throwing sticks at the ducks. The ducks didn't seem unduly worried, though. They outnumbered everything at Fairholmes.

'No news, then?' he said. 'Just calling to check up on me? Yes, I'm eating properly – I just said that. I'm off for my run now, Mum. Okay? See you, then.'

Irvine tucked his phone in a pocket and headed off on the trail away from the visitor centre. He noticed that the water levels were low in Ladybower for the time of year. In a dry summer, the water could get even lower, exposing the sandy shallows at the edges. And sometimes other things appeared if the reservoir was low enough. Though Irvine had never seen it himself, he'd heard people talk about the long hot summer of 1976 when the walls of houses and a church had been visible, the submerged remains of Derwent village, which had been lost when the valley was flooded. An old man he'd met leaning on the bar in

190

the Angler's Rest had claimed to have seen the church spire still rising out of the water before it was blown up in 1947.

The Peak District was known for its rainfall. It was why so many reservoirs had been built over the years to store water supplies for cities like Manchester and Sheffield. It was frightening to think of the amount of water already held in those reservoirs. More than ten million gallons were contained in the Upper Derwent Valley alone.

Irvine had been running for fifteen minutes when he heard shouting. He rounded a corner of the trail and saw a small group of people milling around near the edge of the water. Some of them were pointing at the surface of the reservoir, though there was nothing to be seen out there. For a moment, it crossed Irvine's mind that some townie had imagined they'd sighted the Loch Ness monster or its Derbyshire equivalent. What would the equivalent of Nessie be at Ladybower? Bowie?

So Irvine was smiling at his own joke as he jogged up to the group. He was about to pass, but they all turned and looked at him as if he was exactly what they'd been hoping for. He noticed a small pile of clothes on the bank.

'He's gone in,' someone said. 'Gone in and gone under.'

'Who?'

'We don't know. He was here when we passed earlier on, but now he's gone.'

'How long is it since you saw him alive?'

'It must be nearly two hours.'

'Oh, shit.'

Although it was June, the water in the reservoir would be very cold and there were powerful undercurrents. Even a strong, healthy swimmer could be affected by the temperature and get into difficulties.

Irvine gazed out at the reservoir, shading his eyes against the dazzle of sunlight off the water. A light breeze was blowing down the Upper Derwent Valley, kicking up little waves and ripples here and there on the surface, confusing the eye. It was hard to make out anything too far from the shore. This was a reservoir, after all. Though some of the banks looked sandy in places, there was a steep drop and the water would be colder and colder the further out you got.

'What are we going to do?' asked one of the group. 'We've called 999. What else can we do?'

'I don't know.'

Quietly, Irvine cursed to himself. So a body was in Ladybower somewhere. There were five hundred and twenty acres of it, with thirteen miles of shoreline along its two arms. Twenty-eight million gallons of water could hide a lot of bodies, unless they surfaced. How could anyone ever hope to find it? He'd have to call out the water search team with their boats and divers.

But no. There it was, just fifty yards out. He could see it, bobbing on the surface like a dead fish. A human body. Was the person alive or dead?

He pointed. 'There. Right there.'

Everyone had seen it now. A man stripped off his shirt and plunged in. Another one followed him. Irvine waded into the shallows and helped them drag the limp body ashore. The victim wasn't breathing. For several minutes Irvine and one of the other men took it in turns to do CPR until they were exhausted from the chest compressions.

'Should we put him in the recovery position?' said someone anxiously.

Finally, an ambulance arrived and the paramedic took over. As he stood watching, Irvine came to the unavoidable conclusion that the victim was dead. Yet no one had seen him go into the water. Could he be sure the man had drowned?

Irvine tried to recall the details of his training. How did you determine a drowning? Note the appearance of the victim's eyes. The eyes of a person who'd drowned could appear glistening and lifelike. It helped to determine that the victim had died in the water and not beforehand. And the skin condition. A body immersed between one and two hours had a wrinkled appearance. Longer than two hours and the skin started to separate and slip off the hands, like a pair of crumpled gloves.

Well, this body certainly looked wrinkled, but there was no sign of the skin separating. The eyes glistened, so the victim must have drowned within the last two hours.

Irvine looked into the dead, glittering eyes. They did look as though they were still alive, still staring at something in the distance. He wondered if they'd seen the tunnel, if even now they were approaching the light.

He made the call to the control room. It would be interesting to see if he was right in his assessment.

After he'd finished calling in the details, Irvine found himself standing there on the side of the reservoir with nothing else to do until more help arrived, except to stare at the waterlogged body with its glistening eyes and wrinkled skin. It was only then that he started to feel horribly sick.

17

Cooper parked his Toyota at the edge of the road opposite the Barrel Inn, slotting in alongside half a dozen vehicles already there.

He'd always thought the Barrel had the best views of any Peak District pub and that was saying something. It stood at the side of a road that climbed from Foolow up Eyam Edge, then ran along the top of the edge to Sir William Hill, reaching a height of over fourteen hundred feet at its summit before descending to Grindleford. This had once been a turnpike road from Buxton, but now it wasn't much used except for trips to the Barrel.

He glanced along the line of parked cars to see if anyone was in them. During the last few days, he'd found himself being influenced by the unnerving expectation of death. Every time he saw someone sitting in a parked car, he automatically checked to see if they were still alive.

Sometimes it was difficult to tell. Drivers who were sitting with their heads back against the seat and their eyes glazed over turned out to be listening to Coldplay on an iPod or engaged in a tedious phone conversation with their sales manager. Occasionally, in Edendale, someone was actually asleep at the wheel, dozing while they waited for a partner to come back from the shops or finish a dentist's appointment.

Was he getting paranoid about it? Probably yes.

Cooper nodded to himself. 'Paranoid,' he said. 'That's me. But for good reason.'

And he wasn't alone. Extra police officers were out on the streets in Edendale to keep an eye out – or 'high visibility patrol', as managers preferred to call it.

He was a bit early arriving at the Barrel, so he leaned on his car for a few minutes. Immediately in front of him was a steep drop and an immense view towards the southern horizon. Not only was this the highest pub in Derbyshire, but he was standing right on the divide between the White Peak and Dark Peak. A hundred yards below him was the top of the limestone layer, which rose to form the plateau to the south. Riber Castle was supposed to be visible on the skyline on a good day. That was over the other side of Matlock, nearly twenty miles away.

Cooper looked down again and could see the village of Foolow nestled in a cluster of trees. It looked very peaceful from here. And it was his home now.

Looking at the landscape from this vantage point, it struck him that he was living only a few fields away from Carol Villiers. She was still staying with her parents, Stan and Vera Parry, who ran a bed-and-breakfast on the high street in Tideswell. Would she come to visit his new house, perhaps when she wasn't out with a friend in Derby? Or was she staying away from Foolow for a reason?

He shaded his eyes against the sun as he searched for Tideswell in the landscape and thought he could make out the pinnacles on the tower of St John the Baptist, the church they called the Cathedral of the Peak. When Carol Villiers returned to Edendale, she had been older, leaner and more tanned than when he'd last seen her. And there had been something else different: an air of confidence, a firm angle of the jaw and a self-assurance in the way she held her head. Her pale hair was pulled back from her face in a more masculine style. Despite that, he'd recognised her immediately.

Well, Carol Villiers was no Diane Fry. His mother would have approved of Villiers, for a start. Back in their school days she'd been a lively, sports-obsessed girl who was into swimming and running half-marathons and had talked a lot about some female role models who had been prominent in athletics at the time, but whose names he'd long since forgotten.

Yet there had been an extra dimension to her by the time she returned to Derbyshire and joined the police – a shadow in her eyes, a darkness behind the professional façade. Part of that darkness might be explained by the loss of her husband in Helmand. And perhaps there were other experiences, too, that she was unwilling to talk about.

He remembered Carol showing him a photograph of herself in her uniform, with black-and-red flashes, her corporal's stripes on her sleeve, an MP badge, and a white top to her military cap. The cap was what gave the RAF Police their nickname of Snowdrops.

There had been occasions when he'd wished she was still carrying the Browning nine millimetre she'd been equipped with in the RAFP. In Derbyshire, very few officers were armed. An extendable baton and a pepper spray were all they had as a matter of course, unless a unit with a Taser was available.

Armed or unarmed, he was always glad that Carol Villiers had his back. He wished there were more that he could do for her, to help lighten that shadow in her eyes.

Cooper put Villiers firmly out of his mind. He was here for a different reason and he was unsure how it would go. Perhaps he shouldn't have agreed to the meeting with Chloe Young. It seemed a bit unprofessional. But there was no doubt about it – he needed to be here.

He turned towards the pub. The Barrel Inn dated from the sixteenth century, with ancient stone walls and a slightly wavy-looking roof, and a few tables and chairs set outside on a flagged terrace in a little sun trap. The front of the pub was bursting with colour, flowers blooming in hanging baskets and window boxes, and more in clay pots and stone planters.

Bretton was one of those names on a map that could no longer be called a village, consisting of barely a scatter of houses. Yet it had once had its own peculiar tradition, like so many Peak District villages. Here, they used to cover a ram in soap to make it slippery, then runners had to try to catch it as it raced down the road towards Grindleford. And, like nearby Eyam, Bretton had lost many of its inhabitants to the plague in the seventeenth century. Their graves lay in a field marked with flat little headstones.

A yellow VW Beetle came down the road from the direction of Grindleford, slowed and drew into the parking area a few places up from his Toyota. Dr Chloe Young emerged. He noticed that, like him, she stopped to gaze at the view before she did anything else. He wondered what she saw in the landscape. He had an unaccountable urge to find out.

Dr Young looked very different with her hair down. Cooper found himself wondering how long it took her in the morning to pin it back out of the way in that complicated knot she'd worn when he first saw her in the mortuary. She was dressed casually too, in a light cotton top and blue jeans. She might have been wearing something similar under the mortuary apron and scrubs, but you could never tell.

They ordered drinks and took them out to one of the tables. Cooper was glad that the weather was good enough to sit outside. The subject of their conversation might disturb the customers already eating meals inside the pub. That had happened to him before, when he'd become involved in some discussion of death, murder and violence, only to become aware of the horrified stares and the uncomfortable silence around him.

When Chloe Young put in an order for a baked potato, Cooper realised he hadn't eaten for several hours and decided to join her. The food was good here.

He recalled once eating wild boar when he'd been here with Matt and drinking Marston's Pedigree. But tonight, he had to be totally sober.

'How do you come to know the Barrel?' he asked Dr Young when they sat down.

'My family are from Sheffield,' she said. 'We've always regarded the Peak District as ours. It's our backyard, in a way.'

'People in Manchester say the same thing.'

She laughed. 'They're wrong, though.'

He liked the way she laughed so easily. It was a warm laugh and it made him smile too.

'So you're from Sheffield?' he said. 'You don't sound like a Sheffielder.'

'I'll have to work on that, then. I must have spent too much time down south. After I graduated from Cambridge, I did some postgraduate work and had a spell in a research position in London. Then I came back north and I've been working in Sheffield for the past year. I don't know where I'll end up next.'

'There's going to be a vacancy in Edendale,' said Cooper.

'Oh, you mean when Dr van Doon retires? I think she might be good for a few years yet.'

'Do you?'

'You sound a bit disappointed. Do you find her difficult to work with?'

'I . . .' Cooper didn't want to admit that he did sometimes find Juliana van Doon difficult. It might suggest he was the awkward one. 'No, she's fine. Very professional.'

Dr Young took a drink and gazed across the road at the view. 'I missed the north,' she said. 'I suppose that's why I wanted to come back. I particularly missed all this.'

'Your backyard.'

'It used to feel like my own personal national park. You don't know how lucky you are, living here.'

Cooper nodded. She was right. Sometimes he did forget how lucky he was. When you lived in a place, you tended to take it for granted. It was good to be reminded now and then.

Their baked potatoes arrived and Dr Young began to eat. She seemed quite unselfconscious and at ease with him, as if she'd known him all her life. For a moment, Cooper wondered whether she did know him. Perhaps they'd encountered each other at some time in the past and he'd forgotten – though she was the sort of person he was unlikely to forget.

'Your suicides, then,' she said, with her fork poised in mid-air. 'Your epidemic, as Dr van Doon called it. Though I think I detected that you didn't like the term.'

'No, epidemic isn't a good word. It gives the wrong impression. As if it might infect other people.'

'And that could cause copycat incidents.'

'It could do. In fact, it might have done already. We don't really know.'

'And you said all of your suicides have been males.'

'That was the case when I spoke to you yesterday.'

'You've had another one? A woman?'

'Yes.'

Cooper gave her a brief outline, glancing round to see that no one could overhear the details.

'That's interesting,' said Dr Young. 'It doesn't fit the pattern.'

'That's what I thought.'

'With male suicides, there's a well-established process. The trouble is, men never have anyone to talk to. Not just the loners, but the ones who've been married for a while. They lose all their male friends and their chance of any meaningful conversation vanishes for ever. Unless they have enough sense to get professional help, which too few of them do.'

'Not around here. It would be considered a sign of weakness.'

She nodded. 'And that's often the way it is, until it's too late.'

Cooper remembered attending a seminar once, when the subject of the increasing rate of male suicides was raised. An experienced police officer had voiced the common belief that men achieved a successful suicide, whereas women only attempted it as 'a cry for help'. So when a woman did manage to kill herself with an overdose or a self-inflicted wound, it was an accident, a simple misjudgement. Men planned to die, and most of them did it competently.

'Yet some people live to a grand old age without any friends or family around them,' said Cooper. 'You hear about them all the time. Some ninety-nine-year-old Second World War veteran who's seen off all his contemporaries and spends his last days in a nursing home among total strangers. You see appeals in the papers for people to go to their funerals so the church isn't empty.'

Chloe Young threw out her hands helplessly. 'I can't explain that for you. No doubt there are lots of other factors involved. But the suicide rate among men is substantially under-reported. Coroners bend over backwards not to upset the family with a suicide verdict. And of course there's the question of life insurance. Suicide makes a policy invalid. So the family may try to conceal any direct evidence, such as a farewell note, and hope the death will be recorded as an accident. The trouble is, under-reporting means the seriousness of the problem isn't appreciated and there's no pressure on the authorities to do anything about it.'

'Suicide is still disapproved of, though.'

'In a way.'

Cooper nodded. 'In a way' was right. The righteous denunciation of more religious times had gone. What had once been considered a mortal sin was now something more private and shameful, an act to be swept under the carpet rather than denounced from the pulpit. A form of self-abuse, rather than an insult to God.

Although suicide was still shocking, it seemed to Cooper that it had become respectable in a strange sort of way. An acknowledged problem for society, a suitable subject for study by sociologists and medical professionals. The image was no longer of Romeo and Juliet, romantic and youthful, but more like King Lear, ageing and desperate.

'Statistically, the number of successful suicides

increases with age,' said Dr Young. 'You are more likely to kill yourself between the ages of fifty-five and sixty-five. The young attempt it, but don't succeed as often. They act impetuously, on a wave of emotion, a statement of despair. Older suicides are more careful and more determined.'

'And more usually men.'

She nodded. 'In many cultures, suicide has often been regarded as a logical act by a man. It's the choosing of death before dishonour.'

'I know what you mean.'

Cooper had heard of it even in his own culture. If you believed what you read in classic detective fiction, it had even been offered as an alternative to arrest and trial. There were countless stories by the likes of Agatha Christie and Arthur Conan Doyle in which the perpetrator had been left alone in their study with a loaded revolver and expected to take the 'honourable' way out.

And there seemed to be some truth in it, as far as men were concerned. Many suicides were the result of disastrous decisions in life, men caught out doing something shameful or experiencing the disgrace of bankruptcy or unemployment, or divorce. Not long ago, a serving police officer in a neighbouring county had jumped from a bridge to avoid prosecution for sexual offences committed while he was on duty. He hadn't been able to face that prospect. He'd taken the honourable way out. Or that was what people said.

'It's odd how some suicides are given a sort of legitimacy,' Cooper said. 'They seem to be regarded as an understandable response to circumstances.'

'Yes, there's a whole list of causes that are used to justify the act. But then there are others who are judged to have no legitimate reason for taking their own life, who were regarded as disturbed or irresponsible, or even cowardly. Those are the ones we condemn.'

Cooper looked at Dr Young and realised there was something she wasn't saying or was only suggesting between the lines.

'The ones we condemn,' he said. 'They're usually women, aren't they? They're not considered to have legitimate reasons, no option to take the honourable way out.'

She smiled. He'd said the right thing, had understood what she'd meant without her having to spell it out in words of one syllable.

'Your latest case, the woman from Cheshire,' she said. 'She will be the one the newspapers talk about. Even though she was terminally ill, her suicide will be disapproved of.'

'I think her choice of method will disturb people too,' said Cooper. 'Cutting your wrists is a violent act. Messy. A clean death isn't so bad.'

'I agree. You know, a couple of decades ago, the drug of choice would have been paracetamol. It was readily available and people took them like sweets. There were so many deaths from paracetamol overdoses that the media were asked not to report the amount a victim took in a suicide case. It was believed that printing the details encouraged more suicides.'

'The copycats.'

'Exactly.'

Despite the nature of their conversation, Cooper found he was enjoying the company of Chloe Young too much. Was it possible to enjoy being with someone too much? Well, it was if you were still nervous of forming a new relationship. The memory of Liz was still too fresh in his mind, the experience of her death too painful.

He would never have made the first move with someone he'd just met anywhere, let alone over a dead body in a mortuary under the beady eye of Juliana van Doon. But Chloe Young had taken the trouble to phone him to arrange this meeting, hadn't she? It would have been much too rude to refuse.

It was hard to know how he could move the conversation on. Their relationship so far revolved entirely around the subject of suicide. It wasn't the most promising of starts. Yet it was all he had right now.

'Dr Young . . .?' he said.

'Yes?'

'Most people who commit suicide do it because they lose hope. They suffer some tragic loss, they're grieving or in pain and they end their lives out of despair. Isn't that usually the case?'

'Yes, generally speaking.'

'Why else would you kill yourself?' asked Cooper. 'What other motive might you have, other than to put an end to your own suffering?'

'Oh, I see.' She thought about his question. 'To save someone else? Someone whose life means more to you than your own.'

'I suppose so,' said Cooper. He gazed at his empty glass and the remains of his jacket potato. 'Yes, I'm sure you're right.'

There were so many campaigns to make people aware of the suicide problem. World Suicide Prevention Day took place in September every year, when members of the public were encouraged simply to go up to someone in distress and ask 'Are you okay?' Police officers were issued with guidance on dealing with potential suicides too.

It was a frustrating issue to tackle. The problems suicidal individuals faced were often short-lived. By the time they'd talked their problem through with someone, it was all over and done with. But only if they got the right help, the appropriate response.

During the critical phase, everything could get completely out of proportion or out of perspective, and people became desperate. That was when they were open to the wrong influence, to the dangers of manipulation.

The person who preyed on vulnerable individuals like these had to be a kind of psychopath, an emotionless monster lacking in empathy or compassion. They were as bad as any serial killer, weren't they?

It was still only nine o'clock when they left the Barrel and the sun wouldn't set for another half-hour or so. It was a fine evening, but with a slight chill in the breeze up here, which reminded Cooper that it was still early in the summer. The weather could change dramatically and without warning in the Peak District.

Not many miles to the west was Buxton, where a cricket match had famously been snowed off one June.

Instead of heading to her car, Chloe Young began to walk slowly towards the corner of the pub, where a lane ran up the hill.

'Where are you going?' asked Cooper.

'I remember an interesting spot at the back here. I thought I might go for a walk while it's still light.'

'Yes, Bretton Clough.'

'That's it.' She turned and looked at him. 'Are you coming? You can't have any more dead bodies to look at tonight?'

Cooper hesitated only briefly. 'Okay.'

They walked up the lane through a copse of trees, along verges full of wild flowers and past a sagging dry-stone wall holding back a hillside yellow with gorse. Within a few minutes they reached a footpath that cut across the fields to the clough itself. A few yards ahead was the Duric Well, a spring, the water of which was said to make women fertile. It was hard to find, though, since it was a small stone chamber set into the hillside, barely two feet wide.

Bretton Clough was one of those peculiar landscapes he had only ever stumbled across in the Peak District, the sort of place that made him feel he'd just stepped into a different universe, as though he'd fallen down a rabbit hole or walked through the back of a wardrobe. The bottom of the clough was unnaturally undulating and broke out into a series of odd grassed-over humps, with one of the biggest rising steeply to a peak like a tiny extinct volcano. Cooper had always thought that if he looked hard enough among the bracken there he might find a hidden door.

'It makes me think of hobbit houses in the Shire,' said Dr Young.

'Yes, me too.'

'Lead mining?' she said doubtfully.

'Actually, no.'

In many parts of the Peak District, a landscape like this would have indicated the remains of old mine workings, the spoil heaps and deep hollows left by generations of lead miners. Not here at Bretton Clough, though.

'Back in the nineteenth century, the lord of the manor created a rabbit warren here,' he said. 'They used to produce rabbit fur for London furriers and tie makers. It wasn't a financial success, but the rabbits thrived. They burrowed so far into the sides of the clough that they damaged the land. They made the slopes of shale so unstable that they created landslips. These mounds are the result. So this landscape was created by rabbits.'

'So it's more *Watership Down* than *The Hobbit*, then.'

'Well, the rabbits are gone. But we can still imagine Bag End.'

Cooper watched her walking among the humps. The ruins of five deserted homesteads stood in Bretton Clough, which had once been a thriving community. Nearly three hundred years ago, one of the farms had been the scene of a notorious and bloody murder. A man known locally as Blinker Bland had come here one night intending to rob the farmer of his savings.

He had hit the farmer over the head with a milking stool and fatally wounded him. Milking stools weren't much used as murder weapons these days. So Bretton Clough had earned its place in the criminal history of Derbyshire.

Cooper looked at Chloe Young as she set off to climb back up the track. It was perhaps best not to tell her that story. Murder might always be in his own mind, or not far away, but he was happier to let her go away thinking of rabbits and Bilbo Baggins.

18

A few minutes after he left the Barrel Inn, Ben Cooper turned his Toyota into the car park at Heeley Bank. He turned off the engine and wound down the windows.

The sun was setting in the west over Bamford Moor, turning the sky a spectacular orange as banks of cloud built up overhead. It was twilight now, that eerie stage between day and night when the fading light made everything seem wrong.

The rolling farmland and tree-covered slopes to the south looked welcoming and approachable when lit by the sun. Dry-stone walls broke up the scenery into an intricate patchwork, forming geometric shapes that caught the eye from every angle. But the White Peak was full of hidden depths. Here and there, steep limestone cliffs and the pockmarks of abandoned mine workings were waiting to surprise the visitor. It was a human landscape, shaped by people, but a place where thousands of years of history might lie close to the surface, if you cared to look.

To the north, the moors of the Dark Peak looked

completely different. Forbidding and dangerous. The bare surfaces of its gritstone outcrops absorbed the sun instead of reflecting it as the limestone did. Bad weather seemed to hover around the dark slopes, catching out many ill-prepared hikers, even in the summer.

A large flock of sheep slowly edged their way across the slopes, moving east to west with the sun. In winter those sheep would cluster on the roadside for warmth at night, creating an extra hazard for drivers.

There were still a few cars left in the car park when he arrived. He saw a French car, one with German plates and a dark blue Mazda with a National Trust membership sticker in the windscreen. A party of walkers stood around a pile of hiking poles near the picnic tables. A row of fresh molehills had erupted in the grass behind the toilets and banks of nettles grew along the paths.

He noticed a sign saying: 'CCTV may operate in this car park'.

'Not this one,' he said to himself.

When the last car had gone, he sat with his windows down and listened. A stream gurgled a few steps away, the canopy of leaves stirred gently in the breeze, a rook cawed in the woods. A lone sheep complained, bleating plaintively as dusk fell and the air began to cool.

It felt so peaceful, he could imagine why a place like this drew people who were planning to end their lives. It was a perfect spot to say goodbye to the world, if that was your firm intention.

It made him wonder, though. Did they begin to

think differently as the evening grew late and night gradually fell? When it was dark on the outside, but even darker inside? An uncontrollable drift into the final blackness.

Cooper shuddered. He was finding it too easy to imagine. He would have to stop thinking about it. Focus on something else. But what?

He saw from his phone that Matt had rung earlier on. He ought to call back and see how his brother and his family were getting on after the incident that day.

Ben got out of the car and walked into the dusk. He always felt there was something unnatural in this period between light and dark. Sometimes, its grey malevolence made him shiver.

Matt sounded okay when he answered at Bridge End Farm. Well, as okay as he ever did. He was never absolute sweetness and light when he picked up the phone. If he ever did give up farming, a job as a receptionist or in a call centre would not be top of his list.

'The girls are a bit quiet,' he said. 'Otherwise we're fine. Another family of caravanners left, but we expected that. They were perfectly nice about it, but I suppose we'll be getting negative reviews on TripAdvisor.'

'It was hardly your fault,' said Ben. 'It's not as if it was some failure in the advertised facilities on the caravan site. It could have happened anywhere.'

'Well, it didn't.'

Ben sighed. 'No. And I can't tell you why, Matt. You've given your statement, haven't you? So that's all done with.'

'Yes, I've done that. I suppose I'll start getting all those leaflets now.'

'There's no avoiding it, I'm afraid.'

In Derbyshire, anyone who reported or witnessed a crime became subject to the 'Justice Information Guide Supporting and Advising Witnesses', a clumsy-sounding phrase designed to produce the acronym JIGSAW. It was all about the way the 'jigsaw' of the criminal justice system was pieced together. Sometimes, it wasn't very clear where the victims of crime fitted into it, let alone the witnesses.

Ben knew he must have mentioned it at some time during a spell of grumbling about the bureaucracy and paperwork he was beset by now. Matt always seemed to appreciate those conversations, especially as he'd spent years boring everyone about the bureaucratic nightmare farmers had to cope with. The idea that his younger brother had the same issues seemed to give him a peculiar satisfaction.

'Where are you, by the way?' asked Matt. 'You're not at the new house.'

'How can you tell?'

'I can hear water, a stream. There's a pheasant out there somewhere. And sheep. I know sheep when I hear them.'

'Can you hear all that from Bridge End?'

'Clear enough.'

'I'm out at Heeley Bank, in the car park.'

'At night?' said Matt. 'I didn't know you were into dogging.'

'What?'

Then Ben realised his brother was making a joke. He did it so drily, in such a matter-of-fact tone, that it wasn't always easy to tell. Now Ben felt genuinely reassured that Matt was okay.

Ben turned at the sound of a loud rattling coming towards him in a wave across the adjacent field. He could see nothing at first and it took him a few seconds to work out what was happening. It was only when the first series of impacts hit the edge of the tarmac that he realised what was coming.

He dashed for his car as a scatter of hailstones began to land on his head and shoulders. He slammed the door and sat in the driving seat listening to the drumming on the roof and watching the crystals build up on his windscreen. Within a couple of minutes, the surface of the road had turned white, as if there had been a sudden snowfall.

'What's happening?' Matt was saying. 'Ben, are you there?'

Ben shook hailstones off his jacket and out of his hair.

'It was hailstones, that's all.'

'For a moment, I thought something had happened to you.'

'It was just a shower. It's gone now. I guess it will be heading your way.'

'We're all inside for the night,' said Matt.

'Sounds great.'

Ben ended the call and sat listening for a little while longer after the hailstone shower had stopped. Eventually, as night came on, the noises receded. They left just the lonely call of a bird on the moor and the sound of his own heart beating in his ears.

Cooper was only half paying attention to the road on his way back from Heeley Bank. It was dark now, properly dark in the way it only ever was in the countryside where there were no street lights. The sky had clouded over as night fell and there were no stars or moon visible. There were just his headlights picking out the shapes of the trees and gateways, and the flicker of a sheep's eyes in the darkness.

At first he didn't notice the lights behind him. Though there was little traffic on this road at night, it wasn't so rare as to draw attention. It was only when the headlights steadily came closer and closer that he became conscious of the glare in his rearview mirror.

'What on earth are you trying to do?' he muttered.

Some drivers were far too impatient and took ludicrous risks to overtake in dangerous situations. On this road there was barely room for one car, let alone a safe overtaking manoeuvre. The bends and the stone walls prevented you from seeing what was coming in the other direction, even in daylight. At night, it was only the last-minute glimpse of an approaching headlight that warned you to slow down and swing over on to the verge as you passed. Everyone knew that who was used to driving on these narrow back roads. This must be some tourist, perhaps heading home from an evening at a country pub after too much to drink and deciding to take the scenic route.

Cooper peered ahead, trying to spot a place to pull in so he could let the other driver past. But there were only walls close on either side, a stretch of rocky banking and a gnarled hawthorn tree poking its branches into the road.

The headlights came closer still, until the interior of the Toyota was flooded with light. Cooper found he was clutching the steering wheel tighter.

'Idiot,' he said.

He sounded his horn, a couple of sharp beeps to warn the other driver. The car kept coming, closer and closer. Had the driver taken him for a tourist and decided to have some fun by pressuring him to drive faster and faster on the narrow road? If so, he'd chosen the wrong person.

Cooper switched his hazards on, opened his driver's side window and waved a hand to indicate to the driver to slow down. He couldn't brake, because the other car was too close and the road was slippery after the shower of hailstones: there would certainly be a collision. The Toyota was his own vehicle, not police property, so any damage to his rear end and the subsequent insurance claim would be a nightmare, just like Gareth Cook's experience.

Then Cooper felt a jolt and was thrown forward into his seat belt.

'What the hell—'

He realised the car behind had deliberately hit him. He gazed in surprise into his mirror and was just in time to see the car lurch forward again and collide with his bumper. Cooper put his foot on the accelerator, but had to swing the wheel sharply to the right as he went into a bend.

The other vehicle accelerated too. He could hear the roar of the engine and the squeal of the rubber from the tyres a second before he felt the impact, harder this time, a shunt that spun his Toyota out of control. Though he frantically twisted the wheel, he found himself sliding off the road and bouncing over a grass verge in a hail of scratching branches and stones scraping the underside of the car.

The brakes were useless on this surface as he skidded into a slope. His front wing bounced off something and his view through the windscreen was suddenly obscured by a mass of leaves and twigs from a dense shrub.

By the time Cooper undid his seat belt and pulled himself out of the Toyota, the other car was a hundred yards away, round the bend and out of sight.

Cautiously, Diane Fry unlocked the door of her apartment, pushed it open an inch or two and sniffed.

A pungent odour reached her nostrils. Several pungent odours. They mingled like a fatal disaster in a perfume factory. That meant her sister and the baby were still in residence. Life wasn't yet back to normal.

'It's only me,' she called as she entered the hall.

There was no reply. Perhaps they were asleep. She pictured Angie sprawled out on the bed in the spare room. And the baby? Where would the baby be? You weren't supposed to leave them unsupervised, were you? They could lie in the wrong position and their

218

faces would go flat. She was sure she'd read something like that.

She had to admit that the baby terrified her. It seemed to keep staring at her and demanding things. No, *he*. She was supposed to say *he*, not *it*. His name was Zack. She'd even managed to say it out loud once or twice and she was quite proud of her achievement.

Diane found Angie dozing on the settee in front of the TV, with the baby on her lap and a reality show unwatched on the screen. At least there was no sign of the mysterious boyfriend.

Against her better instincts, Diane felt a rush of affection for her sister. Lying there with eyes closed, mouth open and a pool of baby dribble on her T-shirt, she looked peculiarly vulnerable in a way that Diane hadn't seen her for a long time. It took her all the way back to their teens when they were growing up in foster homes together and were as close as sisters could possibly be. What had happened between them since then to drive them apart?

The baby stirred, kicked its legs, gurgled and woke up. In a moment, it would begin to cry and wouldn't stop for hours.

Well, that was one thing that had come between them. This child had driven a wedge in their relationship. It stirred up so many mixed emotions in her that she could hardly bear to have it in the house a minute longer.

Diane headed to the bathroom for the shower, thinking, Not it, *he*. She supposed she would get used to the idea one day, when baby Zack had grown up, left school and was earning a living for himself. Then she turned the shower up full blast, so that she couldn't hear the baby crying.

19

Day 5

Carol Villiers did a double-take and stared across the staff parking area behind E Division headquarters. She walked over, then stopped and shook her head in disapproval.

'So what happened?' she said.

'Some idiot,' said Cooper, climbing out of the driver's door and gazing at the scratches in the car's paint-work.

'Some idiot what? Some idiot was driving his red Toyota RAV back from the pub and hit a stone wall?'

'Well . . . no, it wasn't like you're thinking.'

'You'll need a new wing anyway,' said Villiers. 'And a respray. Have you made an insurance claim?'

'I might have difficulty with the insurance company.'

'Why? Where had you been?' She looked at the expression on his face. 'Oh, you were at the pub. Seriously, Ben?'

'I was drinking fruit juice,' he said. 'You know me better than that.'

'So what did happen?'

'Someone ran me off the road.'

'Deliberately?'

'I don't know. I can't be sure.'

'You didn't get the registration?'

Cooper sighed. 'Not even the first letter of it.'

He could have kicked himself for that. It was one of the first questions you asked people who were involved in a hit-and-run or a road traffic collision where one of the parties left the scene. Didn't you get the registration number? And so few people did.

'But you're okay, are you?' said Villiers as they entered the building.

At last, she was expressing concern for his welfare rather than only about the damage to his car and his blood alcohol level.

'I'm fine, thanks,' he said. 'Just a bruise or two. I'll let you know if I suddenly develop whiplash. I could be wrong,' he went on. 'It may have been some fool who'd had too many drinks and wasn't used to the road.'

'They didn't stop, though,' said Villiers. 'That's a serious offence right there. They were probably trying to avoid getting breathalysed and banned. You're sure it wasn't deliberate?'

'I don't know,' said Cooper. 'I really don't know.'

He followed Villiers up to the first floor and headed for his office. No, he didn't know for sure what had happened last night. All he could feel certain of was the tangled undergrowth he'd had to clear from the front of his car, the branch he had to wrench out of his wheel arch, the mud covering his headlight.

He also didn't know whether his brief glimpse of

the other car had been accurate. He couldn't be sure that it really had been a Land Rover.

'So what's going on this morning?' he asked when they reached the first floor.

'The body in Ladybower last night,' said Villiers. 'His name was Christopher Yates. You know Luke Irvine was right on the spot?'

'Yes, I heard.'

'Mr Yates was only a young man. Twenty-three. He has an address in Dronfield. We don't have anything else on him yet. Becky Hurst is out taking some statements.'

'Okay.'

Cooper sat at his desk and turned over some paperwork without reading it. He realised Carol Villiers was still standing there watching him. He wondered what she was thinking, what she might see in him that was different this morning. Apart from the dents on his car, that was.

'Carol, what do you think of assisted suicide?' he said.

'Assisted suicide? It's illegal, isn't it?'

'Both active euthanasia and assisted suicide are illegal under English law,' said Cooper. 'Depending on the circumstances, euthanasia is treated either as manslaughter or murder. The maximum penalty is life imprisonment. Assisting suicide is also an offence under the terms of the 1961 Suicide Act. It's punishable by a maximum of fourteen years in prison.'

'You've been looking it up,' said Villiers.

'I don't carry a law book in my head.'

'It's legal in some countries, though.'

'Yes, a handful. Belgium, Holland, Luxembourg. Under their laws, a person's life can be deliberately ended, but only by their doctor or a healthcare professional. Generally they use an overdose of muscle relaxants or sedatives, which causes coma and then death. But it is only legal if the individual makes a voluntary request to end their own life and has the mental capacity to make an informed decision. Oh, and they must be suffering unbearably and have no prospect for an improvement in their condition. The conditions are pretty tight.'

'So what's your point?'

'Well, do you think assisted suicide is wrong?' asked Cooper.

'You just said yourself – in this country, assisted suicide is a crime.'

'Yes. But is it *wrong*?'

Villiers hesitated. It was a question police officers weren't used to being asked. In their world, things were either legal or not. An activity was either an offence or it wasn't. The law was the only rule they could act by, an Act of Parliament their point of reference. If something was defined as a crime on the statute books, how could it *not* be wrong?

'I don't know,' said Villiers. 'I can't judge.'

'No, nor me.'

Well, how could anyone understand or judge those individuals who chose to go down that route, to take a trip abroad to end their lives? Otherwise, their future

224

rested on a decision between enduring the hell of their own suffering or attempting a high-risk suicide. Yet it was said that 80 per cent of those who got the green light for an assisted suicide didn't go through with it in the end.

From the outside, the thought processes were impossible to understand. As Anson Tate had said: '*Don't judge anyone's choice. Not until you know what options they had to choose from.*'

'And attempting to kill yourself isn't a criminal act in itself,' said Villiers. 'It's not like attempted murder.'

'The motive for suicide is the same,' said Cooper.

'What?'

'It's the same reason some people end up committing murder. They reach a point in their lives when they start to get everything out of perspective or out of proportion, and they can't see any other way out.'

'Yes, I think you're right.'

Cooper had always been fascinated by what led people to commit murder, the ordinary individuals who found themselves in circumstances where they could see no other way except the taking of someone else's life. They were rarely evil. Everyone had the potential for good and bad, to be perpetrator or victim. There was often a very complicated prior relationship between the two in a murder inquiry. And, in a way, suicide was the ultimate example. In suicide, the killer and victim were the same person.

He recalled what Chloe Young had said. Men never had anyone to talk to. Not just the loners, but the married ones. Their chance of any meaningful conversation vanished. *And that's the way it is, until it's too late.*

Cooper looked up from his paperwork. What if these men actually had found someone to talk to? Perhaps the only person they could ever talk to about the way they were feeling and explain their suicidal thoughts. And that person hadn't steered them away from taking their own lives. Instead, they'd been guided towards death. But why?

He saw that Luke Irvine had come into the CID room and he went out to speak to him.

'Well done, Luke. That must have been difficult.'

'I couldn't do anything to help him,' said Irvine.

Gently, Cooper put a hand on his shoulder. 'I know. It's bad, isn't it? You want to feel you can do something to help. Sometimes, it just isn't possible. And you have to remember, it's not your fault.'

Irvine nodded. 'I know you're right.'

'Take some time, if you want,' said Cooper.

'No, I'm okay.'

'Good.'

'You know what made it worse?' said Irvine, 'The fact that he was so young. Younger than me.' He shook his head in bafflement. 'Why would you do that?'

Cooper became aware that DC Becky Hurst was standing in the doorway. She was clutching her notebook and he would normally have expected her to bear that eager expression when she had useful information. But not this time. She stood quietly, hesitating as she listened to what Luke Irvine was saying. Hurst

226

almost looked as though she was about to back out again. Cooper waved her forward.

'What have you got, Becky?'

She stepped forward tentatively, glancing from him to Irvine and back again.

'Well, I don't know if this is good news or not,' she said.

'What do you mean?'

She gazed at a page of her notebook, but only to avoid meeting anyone else's eye. She would know what it said by heart.

'The deceased,' she said. 'Mr Christopher Yates. The man who drowned in Ladybower Reservoir.'

'Yes?'

Irvine had turned to look at Hurst, and Cooper could see that he'd tensed up again.

'The fact is,' said Hurst, 'he wasn't a suicide. He decided to go for a dip because it was warm and got sucked to the bottom by the current. He died because his heart failed in the cold temperature.'

'So that was an accident.'

'Or misadventure. On the other hand . . .'

'What?'

'Well, it looks as though we might have missed one.'

'What do you mean?'

'A Nissan X-Trail has been at Surprise View for two days now. We ran the number-plate and it hasn't been reported stolen. The owner is a lecturer at Eden Valley College by the name of Gordon Burgess.'

'Local?' said Cooper.

'Yes, local.'

'Are you sure?'

'He lives in Edendale. Why?'

'He doesn't fit the pattern, that's all. He's not a tourist.'

'Well, pattern or not, he hasn't turned up for work today. And no one knows where he is.'

Cooper looked down at the map. 'It had to happen,' he said.

'What?'

'That one of them wouldn't stay with their car. We'll find him on the Longshaw Estate or up on one of the hills. If we're very unlucky, he'll be somewhere on the moors. There's no chance of finding a body out there at this time of year. Not on the ground anyway. The heather and bracken are too deep; there are too many dips and hollows.'

'I'll request the air support unit, shall I?'

Cooper nodded. 'And mountain rescue. They're the best resource on the ground in these circumstances.'

'They're all volunteers, though, aren't they?'

'They'll come nevertheless,' said Cooper. 'They always do.'

From Surprise View, the panoramic vistas were dramatic, some of the most spectacular scenery in the whole of Derbyshire. To the north, a series of steep edges linked together to form a gritstone barrier dividing the higher moorland from the lower limestone dales.

When Cooper arrived, he could see several liveried police vehicles and a silver-grey four-wheel-drive ambulance from the Buxton Mountain Rescue team halfway up the track towards Carl Wark.

'Yes, we've located the gentleman,' said a uniformed officer in a high-vis jacket. 'Or at least the mountain rescue team did. And do you want the other good news?'

'What's that?'

'He's still alive. But only just. He seems to be in a coma. We've got a problem, though.'

'A problem? Why isn't he in hospital?'

'He hasn't even been examined yet. We can't get near.'

'What do you mean? Are you afraid of getting your feet wet?'

'It's not that. You'd better see for yourself.'

Cooper finished pulling on his boots and followed the officer up the rocky path until they crested a rise and looked out over the moor.

The stone ramparts of Carl Wark rose above him, guarding the boundary of the Dark Peak. Yards of tumbled rocks lay below the summit of the hill fort, boulders of weathered gritstone that might have been tossed there by an angry giant. This site had played a huge part in his imagination when he was growing up. Who knew what had lived out here among the bleak expanses of peat moor and the twisted rocky outcrops?

And Cooper could see the body straight away. It lay in a clear patch of grass between clumps of bracken, the start of a track that led across the moor, snaking between the boggiest parts. Gordon Burgess was wearing a bright blue cagoule and denim jeans. The legs of the jeans were turning black where the dampness from the ground was soaking through.

Yet the man looked perfectly comfortable, lying flat on his back with his arms folded across his chest like the effigy of a dying saint. His face wasn't visible, but the position of his head suggested he had simply lain down to gaze at the sky.

The reason the officers were standing cautiously back from the body was equally obvious. Two long-haired German Shepherds lay on either side of the body, pressed close to their owner as if trying to keep him warm. Their leads lay on the ground where they'd fallen from his hands as he died. When Cooper took a step closer, the two dogs bared their teeth and snarled.

'That's as far as they'll let us get,' said the officer. 'They're protecting him.'

'So I see.'

'We've asked for a marksman. We're going to have to shoot them.'

'What?'

'We can't get near. They're too vicious.'

'I don't think they're vicious,' said Cooper. 'They're just protecting their owner. They're doing their job.'

'Even so—'

'What would you do if that was a human being shouting at everyone and threatening you when you came close?'

'We'd use a Taser,' said the officer.

'So why treat an animal differently?'

The dogs began to bark as an officer came too close

for their liking. The noise gathered resonance from the gritstone slabs around them and echoed across the site of the hill fort.

Diane Fry was sitting in a meeting with Detective Chief Inspector Alistair Mackenzie and other members of the Major Crime Unit at St Ann's.

'What about the other two?' she said. 'Simon Hull and Anwar Sharif.'

Mackenzie ran his fingers over his smooth, bald head to a fringe of hair at the back.

'We can't get to them without Farrell,' he said.

'Is there no way?'

'Have you got any suggestions, Diane?'

Fry looked up at the board on the wall. Three faces stared back at her. One of them was Roger Farrell. The other two were men who had been seen at the same time in the same vicinity as Farrell, either following him or watching him, and just once in an altercation with him on the street in Mapperley. The relationship between them was unclear. Associates, accomplices?

That didn't seem to be the case from the facts they'd gathered during the inquiry. Their presence had been more of a warning or a threat. Farrell had made deliberate efforts to keep away from them when they appeared.

'We do know where to pick them up,' said Fry. 'We have home addresses for both of them. Anwar Sharif works on a business park near the motorway. And Simon Hull has the garage in Radford. We've always considered the possibility that the garage provides a connection with Farrell, haven't we?'

'But we have no evidence against either of them,' said Mackenzie. 'At this stage, they're potential witnesses, not suspects.'

'Unless they were responsible for Farrell's death,' said Fry.

'How could they be? He killed himself, didn't he?'

'Are we sure of that?'

'Divisional CID in Derbyshire seem pretty sure.'

Fry shook her head. 'I don't think that's enough.'

To her surprise, DC Jamie Callaghan backed her up.

'DS Fry is right, boss,' he said. 'We could pick them up and get them in an interview room. One at a time, of course. Then see if we can get anything out of them. It will put them under a bit of pressure and we won't have lost anything.'

Callaghan glanced at Fry and smiled. She wasn't used to that kind of support. It was usually more grudging.

Finally, DCI Mackenzie nodded.

'Let's do it, then,' he said. 'You two can check out the lie of the land today, make sure Hull and Sharif haven't skipped, and we'll put an operation together tomorrow. How does that sound?'

'Great,' said Fry and Callaghan in unison.

Mackenzie smiled. 'Meanwhile, we should make sure divisional CID in Derbyshire aren't queering our pitch with their enquiries into Roger Farrell.'

No major roads ran through Forest Fields, so it was a place most people never visited. To Diane Fry, it seemed to be shut away from the rest of the city. Only since the arrival of the tram route had Forest Fields become visible, as commuters travelled up and down Noel Street between the northern suburbs and the city centre. Yet it still carried an air of neglect.

Forest Fields, Hyson Green and Radford comprised the NG7 area of Nottingham. This district had some of the cheapest housing in the city, so it attracted people on low incomes or benefits. It was mostly street after street of small two-up, two-down terraced houses familiar from *Coronation Street*. Decades ago, the streets would have been cobbled and the toilets would have been outside in the backyard. There were some larger houses near the Forest recreation ground, originally built for the management classes but now divided into flats.

In the 1950s, immigration into Nottingham had been mainly from the Caribbean. But the 1960s had seen a new wave of immigrants, largely from Pakistan. Like other towns and cities, Nottingham had tended to divide itself along ethnic lines. Black Afro-Caribbeans lived in Radford, St Ann's and the Meadows; Pakistani communities settled in Sneinton, Hyson Green and Forest Fields.

Gun crime had been a major problem in this city at one time, earning it the nickname of 'Shottingham'. Fifteen years ago, when Fry was working for West Midlands Police in Birmingham, Nottingham had become the first city in the UK to have armed police officers on regular patrol, carrying Walther P990 pistols on their service belts, with Heckler and Koch semi-automatic carbines in their cars for back-up.

Things were better now. The drug and gun culture that existed on some of the estates had been suppressed, though she was sure it still lingered here and there.

Jamie Callaghan sat alongside her in her black Audi as Fry drove through Forest Fields. As usual, he wanted to chat. Callaghan always seemed to be asking questions about her, as if it was important to find out as much about her as he could.

'Are you hoping to stay with EMSOU long-term, Diane?' he asked. 'Derbyshire Constabulary could still call you back, couldn't they?'

'They could,' said Fry, 'I suppose.'

Yes, it was true, but the thought made her blood run cold. Well, a transfer to D Division in the city of Derby might not be too bad. But a recall to E Division CID? That was her worst-case scenario. If that happened, she would have to resign. No question about it.

'I was already working here in Nottingham,' said Callaghan. 'This is home for me.'

'What – this?'

'Well, not *this*,' he said, gesturing out of the window. 'I mean Beeston. My father was a civilian contractor at the Chetwynd Barracks in Chilwell.'

Simon Hull's car repair business was located in a unit on an industrial estate, reached from the other side of the old Shipstone's brewery. Doors stood open into a couple of bays with ramps waiting for customers' vehicles. The windows on the ground floor were plastered over with signs, the blue triangles for an MoT testing centre surrounded by warnings of CCTV cameras and guard dogs. Hull's black Jeep Grand Cherokee was

234

backed up to a padlocked gate. The yard beyond it was protected by security fencing topped by steel spikes. Blinds were pulled down on the first-floor windows of the building, where there must surely be far too much office space for a business this size.

'There doesn't seem to be much happening,' said Callaghan, showing an ability to state the obvious.

'Isn't that always the case?'

'They don't seem to have any customers. There are no cars on the ramps. Perhaps we've come on a quiet day.'

'Or they've got some other work on.'

A shadow moved on the blinds at one of the upstairs windows. A hand appeared, separating the slats, as if someone was peering out. Fry didn't think they were visible here. There were plenty of vehicles on either side of the street and vans coming and going to the other units.

'We've got a bit of movement,' said Callaghan.

A mechanic in blue overalls emerged from the shadows of the workshop and stood outside in the sunlight to smoke a cigarette, leaning on a trade waste skip and knocking his stub out in a wall-mounted cigarette bin. A moment later, he was joined by a second man, who was talking on a mobile phone.

'That's Hull,' said Fry.

'He's at work anyway. Everything looks normal.'

A recovery truck passed Fry's car carrying a white Citroën with a badly crumpled wing and a missing bumper. It drew on to the forecourt of the garage and the driver unloaded the Citroën from the bed of the truck with a winch. Hull and his mechanic gathered round to examine the damage and began to manoeuvre the car into the workshop.

'Well, that should keep them busy for a while,' said Callaghan.

Fry looked up at the first-floor windows, wondering what the rooms were used for. They might just be storage space, with shelves full of air filters and boxes of spark plugs. On the other hand, you could keep anything, or anyone, hidden up there. She itched to get a search warrant and give the place a going-over. But that wasn't going to happen just yet. Procedures had to be followed.

'Check with the team assigned to Sharif,' said Fry.

Callaghan called using a direct channel on his personal radio and listened for a moment.

'Same at their end,' he said. 'Anwar Sharif is at work as usual.'

'So both Hull and Sharif are keeping themselves busy during the day.'

'It seems they're a couple of law-abiding, hard-working citizens. Nothing to raise a red flag.'

'During the day, yes,' said Fry. 'It's what they might have been getting up to in the evenings that I'm interested in.'

Callaghan shook his head, baffled. 'But what did Roger Farrell mean to them, Diane?'

Fry took one last look at the garage, now busy with work going on around the damaged Citroën.

'That's what we need to find out,' she said.

20

Jessica Burgess had spent the morning picking fleas off her cats and popping them one by one between her fingers. There was something very satisfying about the way the insects burst under her fingernail with a tiny spit of blood.

When the police came to the door, she was baffled and couldn't understand what they were trying to tell her about Gordon.

'No, he's at work,' she kept saying.

She could hear herself saying it and knew from the expressions on the faces of the two police officers that it wasn't true. She said it again anyway, though it didn't satisfy them. It was all she could think of to say.

'No, he's at work. He's teaching today. He's taking extra classes, because they're short-staffed.'

'We're very sorry, Mrs Burgess,' said the female officer, 'but we need someone to identify him. Perhaps there's a relative . . .?'

She bridled at that. Were they suggesting she wasn't capable of recognising her own son without help?

'Where do you want me to go?' she said.

'To the hospital.'

She nodded. Obviously, Gordon was just hurt. They'd got it wrong or she'd misheard.

Without hesitation, she picked up her packet of cigarettes and lighter from the table. 'Are we going in your car?'

'Yes, Mrs Burgess.'

She climbed into the back of the police car and smiled to herself as they drove her to the mortuary.

Ben Cooper got the news soon afterwards. 'Gordon Burgess is dead,' said Carol Villiers. 'He never came out of the coma. He was declared DOA when they got him to the hospital.'

Mr Burgess had died from a gunshot wound. He was found clutching a 1930s Enfield No. 2 revolver, a standard sidearm issued to British Army officers during the Second World War and for many years afterwards in conflicts from Korea to Aden. Burgess's were the only prints on the gun. But where had he obtained it?

'Next of kin?' asked Cooper.

'His mother, Jessica. She's a bit elderly, Ben.'

'I understand.'

The Burgesses lived in the Underbank area of Edendale. Steep streets, old houses. Very different from the sprawling modern estates to the north of the town. It felt more intimate, more friendly. More like a proper community.

The sitting room of the house was crowded. Cooper picked out the elderly Mrs Burgess, but he had no idea who all the other people were. Family members, friends, neighbours? Half the street seemed to be in Mrs Burgess's house.

'Please. Have a seat,' said someone.

'Thank you.'

Cooper hesitated. An armchair had been left conspicuously vacant. The moment he took a step towards it, he knew whose chair it was. He could sense the tension in the room, hear the sharp intake of breath from one of the family. He could feel their eyes watching him – the hopeless, agonised stares of people who could see a bus about to run them over but were too scared to move or protest. They were all too polite to ask him not to sit in the armchair. But he knew it would be a mistake and might stifle the conversation completely. Throughout his visit, they would be looking at him, but seeing someone else in his place. Seeing a ghost.

He turned and looked at Mrs Burgess. He followed her eyes to a dining chair that looked as though it had been brought into the sitting room to cope with an influx of visitors.

Cooper sat down. First, he expressed his condolences, which produced a series of nods and a few tears on faces already stained by too much crying.

He tried to assess the group. There was a large middle-aged woman in a baggy denim trouser suit and a man wearing a black quilted body warmer, with oversized lips and a piercing through his eyebrow. A very frail-looking younger woman sat bundled up in a coat. Where her hands protruded from her sleeves, they seemed unnaturally long and fragile.

A young man of about seventeen kept moving rest-lessly from room to room. His hair was cut very short and his feet were in huge, bright blue trainers. He was talking on his mobile phone, but all Cooper heard him say was, 'Yeah, yeah, yeah. Look.'

Like a lot of teenagers, he seemed to take up more space in the room than was physically necessary. With every movement, he came within inches of bumping into a wall or knocking over an ornament. Cooper was reminded of a large, clumsy dog whose limbs weren't quite as co-ordinated as they ought to be.

This could be family. But his instinct was telling him they were neighbours, crowding in on the pretext of proving support for the old lady while picking up any information they could glean. A prurient interest was natural, he supposed.

He marshalled his first questions in his mind, but found he didn't need to ask anything. Mrs Burgess began to talk, with her visitors chipping in comments occasionally. They barely even gave him chance to figure out who was who in the room.

The information came in no logical order. It was just brought out randomly as it occurred to someone. He gathered that Gordon Burgess was a volunteer with the Derbyshire Wildlife Trust and had recently been working on a badger vaccination programme in the Hope Valley, which was a designated 'edge area' where bovine TB hadn't yet taken hold. His mother seemed particularly pleased with this detail, as she repeated it a few minutes later.

Gordon was a native Derbyshire man, born and raised

in the area. At one time, the idea of such a man committing suicide would have been almost inconceivable. Derbyshire hill people were bred to be stoical. The ability to cope and be imperturbable in the face of a crisis was second nature. And Gordon Burgess had always seemed that way, according to his family. His decision to take his own life was a total shock to them. At some point, Gordon had found it much too difficult to maintain the façade.

'Yes, his father served in the army during the early fifties,' said Mrs Burgess when Cooper got round to asking about the gun. 'When he died, he left a box full of mementos. I never asked what was in it. It was a personal thing between them. I just thought they were medals and such.'

'Do you know where the box is?'

'It's in Gordon's room. At the bottom of the wardrobe.'

Cooper found the box easily. It was a solid metal construction, a bit bigger than a shoe box. A key was in the lock. Inside, there were indeed some service medals, badges, postcards from the Middle East, a shoulder epaulette. And a small, greasy cardboard carton with indecipherable printing, which rattled when he picked it up. Inside were half a dozen bullets.

And there was one other item. A black business card with a string of numbers and letters. *Secrets of Death.*

He closed the box up and locked it before he went back downstairs. Everybody turned and looked at him as he entered the sitting room. They seemed surprised that he was still there or had forgotten who he was.

He had never felt more like an unwelcome intruder, like the title character in *An Inspector Calls*.

'I'm afraid I'll have to take this away with me, Mrs Burgess,' he said.

She nodded. 'Of course.'

'I'll make sure you get everything else back.'

She nodded again. He wasn't sure she understood what he was saying. Perhaps someone would explain it to her later.

'I suppose he wouldn't have felt a thing,' said Mrs Burgess. 'That's what they say, isn't it?'

'So I believe,' said Cooper, realising that she had jumped to the actual moment of Gordon's death, trying to imagine it for herself.

'And the dogs were with him,' she said. 'Abbey and Pepper. They're outside in the garden now. They're devastated. They know that he's gone. Surely Gordon must have realised how much it would affect them.'

Cooper had a flashback to his interview with Anson Tate, the failed suicide. Tate had brought out all the arguments, much as if he'd been quoting them from books he'd read – or, of course, from a website.

Doesn't it seem wrong to you that sick animals are put out of their misery by vets, but we aren't allowed to end our own wretched existences? What is it about a human life that makes it so different, so sacrosanct? We're just animals too, aren't we? Why should we be forced to suffer?

'Abbey and Pepper?' he said. 'I haven't heard those names used for dogs before.'

'They're named after Beatles albums,' said Mrs Burgess. 'Gordon was a huge fan.'

242

'*Abbey Road* and *Sergeant Pepper*,' said Cooper.

Instinctively, he looked around the room for a stereo, or a CD player at least. But he could see nothing. What about a bookshelf? You could tell a lot about a household from the books on the shelf. There were hardly any books either. The shelves held a few ornaments and a couple of crossword puzzle books. And there was a huge plasma TV screen on one wall, which some of the visitors couldn't resist glancing at, though it was switched off. They said you shouldn't trust anyone whose TV screen was bigger than their bookshelf.

'I think you're right,' said Mrs Burgess. 'It was funny, the way he talked to the dogs on the last day. He said he was taking them for a walk, but I knew something was different.'

'Why do you say that?'

'Gordon was saying something to them about learning to let go. He didn't realise I could hear him.'

'He was saying this to the dogs?'

'Yes. He talked to them all the time.'

'Mrs Burgess, can you remember what he said exactly?'

'I don't need to,' she said.

'What do you mean?'

'My memory isn't very good, so Gordon always wrote things down for me. We kept a special notebook that he put things in he wanted me to remember. I don't know why he wanted me to remember this. But I'm sure it was what he was telling the dogs.'

She handed Cooper a notebook. It was filled with dates and notes, most of them written in clear capital letters and some of them underlined to emphasise their importance. On the final page was one last thing Gordon Burgess had wanted his mother to remember:

And this is the second secret of death. You have to let go. You have to learn to say goodbye.

And underneath he'd written, in a more personal handwriting style:

Goodbye, Mum. I love you.

Of course, Carol Villiers was a dog-lover. Her parents had two retired greyhounds adopted from a rescue centre and Cooper remembered how upset she had been by the death of a pet spaniel when she was about fourteen.

'If Mr Burgess really cared about his dogs, he wouldn't have put them through that ordeal,' she said. 'Imagine what it was like for them out there on the moor for two nights with their owner dying.'

'I don't think he intended it to be that long,' said Cooper. 'He must have thought he would be found sooner and the dogs would be looked after. I don't suppose he had any idea that he would lie there so long. If only his mother had appreciated the significance of the note he left, the search would have got under way much sooner.'

'But she doesn't seem to have known that he was depressed. Did he never talk to her?'

'Of course not,' said Cooper. 'He was fifty-five years old and unmarried. Can you imagine him telling his mother he was feeling depressed? He probably thought he was a burden or a disappointment to her. In fact,

I wouldn't be surprised if she'd told him that herself, many times. Mothers can be cruel.'

Cooper recalled his own mother when she was alive, constantly asking him whether he'd been promoted from detective constable yet, pointing out how early in his career his father had made it to the rank of sergeant. Yes, mothers could make you feel a disappointment and a failure. Gordon Burgess might have endured many years of that.

'Fifty-five?' said Villiers. 'Frankly, if you reach your fifties and you haven't come to terms with yourself, you're in serious trouble. You should have got your life sorted out by then.'

'Yes. And if you haven't, and you suddenly realise that you're on a downward slope, I imagine it can knock the ground from under your feet. It wouldn't need any specific event to trigger the deterioration in your state of mind. A slow acknowledgement of the inevitable, undetectable even to his closest relative.'

'It doesn't bear thinking about.'

'No.'

Many individuals *did* think about it, though. When old people died they were sometimes said to have 'had a good innings'. But even living to a hundred didn't guarantee you had the opportunity to do everything you'd hoped to do in your life – or anything you hoped for, in fact. Some individuals went through their entire existence wanting to do something different, to be somewhere else, to spend their time with anyone except those they found around them, strangers and family alike.

It was a tragic but undeniable fact. It made Cooper realise how lucky he was, in spite of everything that had happened to him.

So Gordon Burgess had died from a gunshot wound. He'd aimed at the soft area under his chin, but people tended to flinch at the last second when they did that. As a result, the path of the bullet hadn't been perfect for an instant death. Instead, he'd caused serious brain damage which had put him into a coma and resulted in a much slower death than he would have anticipated. His apparently peaceful pose on the moors did not reflect what had been going on in his head.

Burgess was found clutching a revolver that he'd apparently inherited from his father. That answered the question of means. So how did his death fit in with the others?

There was a twenty-two-year-old jobless biker from Derby who had taken a mixture of sleeping tablets, methadone and vodka. A mattress salesman from Nottingham, forty-five years old and a widower, who had chosen an exit bag filled with helium, causing painless suffocation.

And then there was David Kuzneski, aged forty, a credit controller from Sheffield. The man who hated tablets. So what method of suicide had he chosen? An overdose of lithium carbonate. In a way, it was a logical choice for him, given his history of bipolar disorder. But would it have been his personal preference? It was almost as if a punishment had been devised to fit the crime, a manner of death chosen to fit the victim's life.

'You said Gordon Burgess didn't fit the pattern,'

pointed out Villiers. 'But it's also the woman, isn't it? Bethan Jones. She's an odd one out too.'

'Well, obviously, as the only female.'

'I don't see the logic in her case either.'

Yes, there was Bethan Jones. A twenty-eight-year-old playschool leader who had travelled from Cheshire to slit her wrists. How did that fit in? Cooper had to admit it. Again, there was no pattern.

They had the Ordnance Survey map of the area spread out on a desk. The locations were marked on it. Monsal Head, Upperdale, Heeley Bank, Bridge End Farm and now Surprise View. And in the middle of it all sat Edendale, deep in its green hollow in the hills, as if sucking everything towards it, drawing in individuals who had no resistance left.

Cooper stared at the map. Sometimes people smiled when they saw him spending so much time gazing at maps. It was because he'd been taught to take an overview of a case, a top-level perspective. Looking down on it from above, rather than obsessing all the time about the small details.

'I wonder who is choosing the locations,' he said thoughtfully.

Villiers frowned. 'What do you mean? Surely each one was the individual's own choice.'

'Do you think so?'

'What else could it be?'

Cooper didn't reply. But only because he didn't know the answer.

'It couldn't be anyone else's choice, could it?' said Villiers.

He stood up. 'Well . . . you're probably right.'

Cooper picked up his jacket.

'Where are you going, Ben?'

'There's only one person who can stop this and help us to prevent more people from dying. He needs to be shaken up a bit.'

'I'm coming with you,' said Villiers.

'That's probably a good idea.'

Halfway to the car park, he stopped and turned to Villiers.

'I forgot to ask you,' he said. 'How was the book festival in Derby the other night?'

'Fantastic,' said Villiers. 'We had a great time.'

Cooper nodded to himself as he followed her out. 'Fantastic' had been an echo of what he'd said when Carol asked about his new house. And he still didn't know who she'd gone to the book festival with.

21

Before they reached the house on Buxton Road, Cooper spotted Anson Tate striding up the pavement, his head down, hands in his pockets, as if walking against a strong wind. He was carrying a green shoulder bag.

'Where is he going, I wonder?' said Cooper.

'Could be anywhere. Shopping, to the pub? Or just for a walk? I assume he has a life of some kind.'

'Life? That's not what Mr Tate is interested in.'

Cooper turned the Toyota round and drove slowly back down the road, keeping his distance from the figure a hundred yards ahead. A driver behind him beeped irritably, then pulled out to overtake. A woman waiting to cross the road gave him a suspicious look, as if he was a kerb crawler.

Tate crossed Meadow Road and walked over the railway bridge. He didn't look right or left, but kept straight on. He wasn't just taking a walk, he was fixed on a destination.

'He's turning into the high street,' said Villiers.

'Keep him in sight, Carol.'

Cooper took the corner cautiously, deliberately letting

a van get in ahead of him. His old local, the Hanging Gate, was down a side street to the left. But Tate didn't even glance at it as he strode past.

'There you go, he's probably heading for the shops in Clappergate,' said Villiers. 'He's going to buy his toothpaste in Boots or have his lunch at McDonald's.'

'Or he could be heading for the railway station,' said Cooper. 'Once he gets on a train, he could be in Sheffield or Manchester, or any location of his choice in between.'

'You're paranoid about him.'

'Am I?'

'Look, all he's carrying is that shoulder bag. He hasn't exactly got luggage with him for a trip.'

'I wasn't suggesting he was going on holiday,' said Cooper. 'Or even for an overnight stay. If he's going somewhere, it will only be for one purpose. And he won't be planning to come back.'

'Oh, you mean . . .?'

'Of course. Anson Tate only has one objective in mind and if he achieves it we'll have lost him as a source of information. He doesn't need luggage. Just the specific items for whatever method he's chosen this time.'

Villiers was quiet and Cooper began to think he'd shocked her. But she'd lost sight of Tate in a crowd of shoppers and was concentrating on trying to pick him out.

'Has he turned towards the station?' asked Cooper, as his car came to a halt behind the van.

'No, he's crossing the road at the lights.'

'The shops, then?' said Cooper. 'It looks as though you were right. I was wrong.'

'You were paranoid.'

'Not that paranoid.'

In fact, they were both wrong. As the traffic moved and Cooper coasted the Toyota towards the lights at the bottom of Hollowgate, they could see Anson Tate on the opposite pavement. He'd reached his destination.

'He's going to the library,' said Villiers.

'Well, that's interesting.'

'He's looking for some improving literature? Self-help books?'

'I doubt it.'

Cooper indicated and drew into the kerb, earning himself another angry stare from a passing driver.

Edendale Library was a modern building with a glass frontage on to the high street. Cooper knew there was another entrance at the back, where the public could get access from the bus terminus near the market square. Tate could walk straight through the library and get on to a bus. It would be a classic tactic if he suspected he was being followed. Luckily, the plate glass allowed them to track his movement as he entered. He walked past the counter and the self-service checkout machines to the far end of the library.

'He's sitting down at one of the desks. He's going to use one of the computer workstations,' said Villiers.

Cooper nodded. That made sense too.

'You go inside, Carol,' he said. 'Tate doesn't know you. Try and get a look at what he's doing online. Go and browse the romance section or something. Pretend you're a fan of Danielle Steel.'

Villiers climbed out of the car.

'What makes you think I'm not?' she said as she swung the door shut.

Cooper watched her dodge through the traffic, then slow to a casual stroll as she entered the library. Nobody gave her a second glance.

He pulled back out, managed to force the Toyota into the outside lane and turned right into Hollowgate, where he found a space in the car park behind the town hall. The back of the library was just beyond the bus stops, where a blue Hulleys bus was even now discharging passengers. A couple of them turned and walked up the disabled ramp to the library's rear door.

Inside, Cooper found himself in an entrance lobby, with noticeboards full of information about forthcoming events – a book club, Crafts and Chat, benefits advice and lots of children's story-telling sessions. He was impatiently reading a leaflet about health and safety when Villiers finally appeared.

'As far as I can tell, he's not online. He's writing something,' she said.

'Are you sure? Did you get close enough to see what it was?'

'No. Not without breathing down his neck and looking like a stalker.'

'Okay.'

Cooper opened the doors and walked into the library. He strode down to the line of workstations. Anson Tate was sitting in the middle, with a teenager on one side and a pensioner on the other. The young man looked like a student, with a notepad and a small rucksack. The OAP was looking up flights to Portugal.

'Mr Tate.'

He took hold of the back of Tate's chair and read the screen before he could delete it or close it down. He seemed to be composing a letter to the *Eden Valley Times* complaining about plans for fracking on the edge of the national park.

'What do you think you're doing?' said Tate in an angry whisper. 'I can't talk to you here. It's a library, for heaven's sake.'

'Libraries aren't what they used to be,' said Cooper. 'We won't get shushed by a woman with her hair in a bun.'

Tate began fussing with his bag. 'I'm leaving anyway,' he said.

'We'll come with you. It's a nice day. A little stroll by the river, perhaps?'

'It's harassment,' said Tate. 'I'll make a complaint.'

But from the way he looked round the library, he seemed to be more worried about what other people were thinking of him. Jumping off a bridge in the centre of town was fine, but drawing attention to yourself in the library was unacceptable behaviour in Tate's world.

Cooper and Villiers stuck close to Tate as they left the library and went back out on to the high street. Cooper gently put a hand on his arm and steered him down the steep flight of steps to the river bank. There were benches here facing the water. Tate reluctantly sat down and Villiers sat next to him. Cooper remained standing over him. He was too impatient to sit down, even for a moment.

'I'm trying to live a normal, law-abiding life here,' said Tate. 'I don't deserve this.'

He patted his head, pushing the wedge of hair forward until it pointed between his eyes. Then he shuffled his legs and shifted a few inches along the bench to distance himself from Carol Villiers.

'You do if you're withholding information from us,' said Cooper. 'As far as I'm concerned, you deserve a lot worse.'

'Has something happened since the last time we talked, Detective Inspector?'

'We've had two more deaths,' said Cooper.

'Suicides?'

'Of course.'

Tate nodded. He seemed calmer now, more reassured. 'No one I know, I'm sure.'

'The name of one was Gordon Burgess. He lived here in Edendale. Not a mile away from you.'

'I don't know anyone in this town. I'm a stranger. I speak to no one and they don't bother me.'

'Have you had any visitors since you've been in Edendale?'

'Visitors? I don't get visitors. My flat isn't fit for anyone to see.'

Cooper glared at him. It was almost as though Anson Tate was deliberately presenting a picture of himself as the classic loner, a man who kept himself to himself. He could have taken the image from any newspaper story about a serial killer or from a crime novel he'd picked up in the library. It told Cooper nothing and it felt as though he was being taunted with the fact.

Tate couldn't resist the obvious question.

'How did he do it?' he said.

Cooper knew then that he held something over Anson Tate. He had information that Tate wanted. The man craved details, the facts of some other person's successful suicide. Cooper waited. He could hear the traffic on Fargate behind him and the town hall clock striking the half-hour.

'Are you looking for tips, Mr Tate?' he said finally.

Tate pulled a face and didn't dignify the question with an answer.

'Was he someone like me?' he said instead.

'Not really. He lived a normal life. No one knew he was suffering.'

Tate smiled that sad smile. 'I'm glad you're starting to see it as normal.'

Cooper noticed Tate was looking up at the tower of All Saints Church.

'Were you suffering, Mr Tate?'

'Certainly.'

'So didn't you seek help?' asked Cooper. 'There are plenty of organisations available. Helplines? The Samaritans?'

'There was no help for me.'

He put the emphasis on *for me*, as if there was something unique about his circumstances. That was all part of his façade, the need to feel his decision to end his life was somehow earth-shatteringly important. Yet he was just another suicidal middle-aged man. He was just one small part of an epidemic.

'No help at all?' said Cooper. 'It can make a big difference just to talk it through with someone, to tell them how you're feeling.'

'I know that. But it's not enough.'

'Isn't it? I see.'

Tate looked up at him, shading his eyes. Cooper realised he was standing against the sun. Tate couldn't look him directly in the eye, couldn't tell what he was thinking from his expression.

'What do you see, Inspector?'

'I think you needed someone to do more than that, to be there for you talk to. You wanted someone to give you advice. To tell you exactly what to do.'

Tate pursed his lips, but didn't answer. Cooper pressed on, feeling as though he was on the verge of something but in danger of slipping off track before he got there.

'Because you couldn't make the final decision on your own, could you?' he said. 'Perhaps you didn't know how to do it. Or you weren't brave enough. Was that it? You didn't have the courage. So you needed the right guidance. A voice to say you were doing the right thing. You had to be told by someone else what to do, because you weren't capable of taking your life into your own hands. You were too weak, too cowardly to see it through.'

'You shouldn't be saying these things to me,' said Tate, his cheeks flushing.

'Perhaps not. But it's true, isn't it? You were in touch with someone who encouraged you to take your own life, who told you exactly what to do and where to do it. That made all the difference to you, I imagine. All the weight of responsibility taken off your shoulders. The difficult decisions taken out of your hands. Finally, you'd found someone who understood how you were feeling and knew what to do about it. It must have been like finding God. Who was it, Mr Tate?'

'I have no idea what you're talking about.'

'Whoever it is, they not doing it in your best interests. Don't you realise that? It isn't God, it's just another deceitful and untrustworthy human. You're being manipulated, Mr Tate. Just like all the others.'

'All what others?'

Cooper stepped back in surprise.

'Didn't you realise there were others?' And then he saw Anson Tate more clearly. 'No, of course you didn't. You thought it was all about you, didn't you? You were so self-obsessed and blinded to reality that it didn't even occur to you that you were just one of many, a small, insignificant part of a bigger picture. You're very unimportant. Even to God.'

Tate stood up unsteadily. 'I think it's time you left, Detective Inspector Cooper. I'm afraid I can't help you with your enquiries after all.'

'You went way over the top there,' said Villiers bluntly, when they let Anson Tate leave.

Cooper sighed. 'Yes, I know.'

'It wasn't like you at all, Ben. I've seen you dealing with all kinds of people – individuals who've committed horrible crimes sometimes – and you always manage to have some sympathy or empathy for them. You find the humanity in everyone. You try to understand their reasons for doing what they've done. It's why they talk to you when they wouldn't talk to someone with a less sympathetic attitude. It's one of the abilities I've always most admired in you.'

'Thank you.'

'You weren't able to do that with Mr Tate. I wonder why?'

'I don't know why,' said Cooper.

'Mmm.'

He could tell that Villiers didn't believe him. And of course he did know why. Now that he was out of the man's presence, it was clearer to him what had happened, why he'd treated Tate so badly. It wasn't because he didn't understand Anson Tate. It was because he understood him far too well.

Villiers waited for him to explain. When he didn't, she let it go and moved on.

'Well, anyway,' she said, 'I hope he doesn't make a complaint.'

'He won't do that,' said Cooper confidently.

'No. But you were right, of course,' said Villiers.

'Do you think so?'

'Yes, absolutely.'

'Obviously, he's refusing to give us any useful information,' said Cooper. 'Nothing about who he was in contact with, where he got his advice or assistance from. Not a word. I'm not surprised, though.'

'Why?'

'Well, couldn't you tell? It's written all over him, obvious in every word he says. As soon as he gets a chance, he's going to have another try.'

Cooper had found talking to Anson Tate much too frustrating. Now he took a deep breath, feeling himself beginning to calm down. He looked at Villiers.

'Did you take out a Danielle Steel, by the way?' he said.

Villiers shook her head. 'No. I'd read them all.'

22

And then it was time for another visit to the Edendale mortuary. Eden Valley General Hospital was busy, the visitors' car park full to overflowing, with more vehicles parked on the grass verges and on the side of the road. According to the *Eden Valley Times*, the local NHS Trust had been making millions of pounds a year from parking charges paid by patients and their visitors. It was the same up and down the country. Nothing was really free any more.

A few minutes later, Cooper was inside the mortuary looking at the body of Bethan Jones laid out on the stainless steel examination table.

'You don't need to tell me that she did a good job of it,' he said.

Dr van Doon made a pretence of crossing out a note on her clipboard.

'Well, that's spoiled my act,' she said. 'I hope you're not going to start claiming to know everything, Detective Inspector Cooper. I haven't been accustomed to that since Detective Sergeant Fry deprived us of her company and left for pastures new.'

'I've never claimed to know everything,' said Cooper. 'Only a—'

He stopped. But Dr van Doon gave a dry chuckle.

'Only a fool would do that,' she said. 'I think that's the saying, isn't it?'

'I couldn't confirm or deny.'

The pathologist glanced at her younger colleague, then back at Cooper.

'Have you seen much of DS Fry since she left Edendale, by the way?' she asked.

'Not much. She's busy with the Major Crime Unit. Based in Nottingham, you know.'

'Ah yes, EMSOU.'

Dr Young looked quizzical. 'EMSOU?'

'East Midlands Special Operations Unit,' said Cooper. 'It's part of the collaboration process between the region's police forces.'

'I see.'

'You'll get used to the acronyms in time.'

'I hope so.'

Cooper cleared his throat, wondering whether he'd gone too far. It sounded as though he'd suggested Chloe Young would be here for a while, long enough to learn the police acronyms. Perhaps he had hinted that she might expect to have more contact with police officers, or with one particular officer. He wasn't sure. He would probably have to repeat the conversation to himself later on when he was on his own. And then he probably still wouldn't be sure.

'So,' said Dr van Doon, like a hostess breaking an

awkward silence, 'we have here a Caucasian female, aged in her late twenties. Cause of death was serious lacerations to both forearms. She would have bled out fairly quickly. The cuts are deep and extensive, and they look deliberate. I know you won't allow me to say it, but—'

'She did a good job of it.'

'A most thorough and professional job, I'd say. Of course, I say that was the cause of death. In fact, she wouldn't have lived much longer. Unlike most of my customers who attract your interest, Detective Inspector, this was *not* an individual in good health. She was suffering from advanced cancer of the stomach. Would you like to examine the tumour?'

'No, thank you,' said Cooper.

Dr van Doon's tone softened suddenly.

'I think this poor young woman must have been in considerable pain,' she said.

'She said the tiredness was the worst symptom. The exhaustion.'

'I can sympathise with that.'

'Don't you find it depressing dealing with suicides all the time?' asked Dr Young.

'Yes, a bit. But no more depressing than dealing with murder victims. At least these people made their own decisions to end their lives.'

'True.'

He looked at Dr Young.

'And in any case . . .' he said.

'Yes?'

'Aren't you the woman who spends all her time cutting out bits of people's brain tissue?'

'Ah, but that's science,' she said.

Detective Superintendent Branagh was waiting for Cooper when he got back to the office. She looked concerned about something.

'You've caused a bit of a stir,' she said. 'It seems you've been making enquiries about a person of interest to the Major Crime Unit at EMSOU.'

'Something of significance?'

'It must be important. They've come all the way from Nottingham. I'm surprised they even knew how to find us.'

'They must use a satnav.'

'DS Sharma is free anyway,' said Branagh. 'He'll be coming back to us tomorrow from the immigration case. He'll be free to liaise with EMSOU, if you wish.'

'I'd prefer to deal with them myself,' said Cooper.

Branagh's expression suggested that might be the wrong answer.

'It's up to you, of course,' she said.

A team from the Major Crime Unit had already arrived at West Street. To Cooper's eye, they looked awkward and uncomfortable, like people who'd turned up at a party and found they were the only ones in fancy dress.

They included a DCI he'd seen before, Alistair Mackenzie. It was strange how so many senior detectives seemed to look like accountants. A sober suit with a pale mauve shirt and a striped tie, sensible glasses and a shiny expanse of bald head with a dark fringe of hair at the back. He was clutching a clipboard too, with his mobile phone gripped tightly in his other hand. All he needed was an electronic calculator and he would have been the perfect image of a finance director with a medium-sized company manufacturing cardboard boxes for the pharmaceutical industry.

They seemed to have cloned a number of these DCIs and detective superintendents in recent years. Perhaps there was a special school for them at Bramshill. Cooper thought he'd actually seen this one on TV not long ago reading out a statement on a murder inquiry. He'd sounded like a bad actor who'd just been handed a script – which he probably was.

Well, at least Diane Fry wasn't here, for once.

Cooper turned to the window at the sound of a car approaching and he recognised it straight away. A black Audi. So much for that one consolation.

Cooper had so many memories of Diane Fry. He even recalled their first meeting when he was just back from leave and found everyone at West Street talking about the new arrival in CID from the West Midlands. People were already being less than complimentary about her. 'A bit of a stroppy bitch' had been one of the kindest comments. It had made him feel empathy for her before he'd ever met her.

And then he'd seen her in the CID room, moving

with that calm deliberateness, not meeting his eye, but glancing from side to side as she walked past the desks and filing cabinets, as if searching for evidence of faults among her colleagues. He remembered telling her, 'Nice to have you on board.'

Their relationship had gone through many phases since then – too many for him to keep up with. His last memory was of sitting with Fry in a gastropub in Nottingham, the Wilford Green, looking out at the endless street of suburban housing and roads solid with traffic. It had been another one of those baffling and disturbing moments that had characterised the whole experience.

Throughout that time, Fry had been the one making the running, for good or bad. In a way, it was a relief that she was no longer a permanent presence in his life. And yet he missed her.

Diane Fry's manner was cool. But that suited Cooper. He had nothing really to say to her. Well, he had lots of things to say to her, except none of them would be wise and none of them was suitable for the present circumstances. Best to keep his mouth shut. That was the way he'd been taught.

Fry gazed steadily at him, almost as if she saw him as a stranger. No doubt she felt she'd moved on to better things and had left behind the humdrum routine of life in E Division CID. Since the Major Crime Unit had been established at EMSOU, the work of divisional CID had been focused on volume crime – burglaries, robberies, car thefts, assaults. Major Crime claimed all the glamour and the headlines.

Yet Fry still had *that* look. It was a look that suggested the whole world was a terrible place. Everyone must know how awful it was. If you smiled too much, you must be an idiot, too stupid to see how bad everything was. Stupid enough to be happy.

'So,' she said. 'It seems you've been asking questions about a Mr Roger Farrell. He's a person of interest in one of our inquiries.'

'He's a suicide case,' said Cooper.

'Not just a suicide, though.'

'It seems enough to me.'

'There's the question why . . .'

'He was depressed and desperate. He couldn't see the point of living any longer and he decided to put an end to it. What more is there to say?'

Cooper knew he ought to share his suspicions with her. They were on the same side, after all. Well, weren't they? But his instant reaction to her had been the opposite. He was reluctant to share anything with her. The fact was, he didn't trust her any more.

'He was an associate of a suspect in a murder inquiry.'

'Not any more. Not unless your suspect is on the other side too. Perhaps there's where you should go if you want to interview them.'

Fry's mouth twitched. 'Are you telling me to go to hell? Why don't you just come straight out with it, instead of trying to be clever and saying it in that pathetic roundabout way?'

Cooper dropped his eyes. Fry's plain speaking had disarmed him before. She was right to call him out on his words. He needed some way of defusing the situation if they had to work together.

He wondered if he could ask about the baby. Angie must have had it by now. He'd been out of contact with Diane for months and he didn't know if everything had gone smoothly. It might be intrusive to enquire. You could never tell what Diane's reaction would be.

'And are you an aunty now?' he said finally, trying to make it sound light, but knowing as soon as he got the words out that it was entirely the wrong way of putting it.

'You can keep your cheap jokes to yourself,' snapped Fry, 'if that's what you were thinking of.'

'But Angie—' he began.

'Yes, she's a mother. She had a boy.'

She glared at him, daring him to ask the next question. Cooper was practised enough in these situations to know that you usually asked what name the child had been given. Fry's glower deterred him.

'And Angie's well, is she?' he said instead.

'Yes. She's fine.'

And that was said with unmistakable finality. Diane's sister was out of the conversation.

Cooper wondered what had happened that he'd missed. It could be pretty much anything. He was uncomfortably aware that there was more to Angie Fry's history than her sister suspected. After she'd met him at the Hanging Gate once, he'd followed her through the market square to the corner of the high street. He'd watched her as she approached a car parked on the street and got into the passenger side. He'd managed to take the car's registration number before it drove off, and requested a PNC check. It was a blocked number – the first time he'd come across one in all his years of police service.

Angie had always tried to give the impression she mingled with low-life criminals, that she was herself a drug user. He'd seen plenty of smackheads in Edendale and they were blank-faced and skinny, with discoloured teeth. There were places on the housing estates where kids went to inject themselves every night and the council came round every morning to pick up the needles. Those smackheads had dead eyes, not like Angie's. Diane had been too blinded to see that.

And criminals and drug addicts didn't have blocked numbers on their cars. It was a privilege only for investigators in vulnerable positions or police officers involved in sensitive operations. Cooper didn't think that Diane had ever known that either. He'd felt it in the look that Angie had given him on the few occasions when he'd encountered her since. *She* suspected he knew. But she trusted him not to tell Diane. It had always troubled him and he'd never got to the bottom of it. To be honest, it was one mystery that he hoped never to hear of again.

It was just one of the reasons that talking to Fry

was like treading on eggshells. Cooper was always afraid that he would say the wrong thing.

'So why were EMSOU looking for Farrell?' he said.

'It's quite simple,' said Fry. 'Roger Farrell was a killer.'

23

Diane Fry eyed Cooper critically. He was no longer the slightly dishevelled innocent with the scuffed leather jacket and a crooked tie. He had matured, filled out and smartened himself up. They said what didn't kill you made you stronger. Cooper had come through his recent problems looking as if he could cope with anything.

Promotion to DI suited him too. Some people thrived when they were given responsibility. Everyone who'd said he wasn't ready for it had been proved wrong. And she had been one of those people herself.

She'd also been thinking about DC Becky Hurst, after seeing her at West Street. Fry knew that Cooper really rated her. She was the best of the recent recruits to E Division CID. For a moment, Fry wondered if Hurst would appreciate a move to EMSOU if a vacancy came up. It was something to bear in mind for the future.

'A killer?' Cooper shook his head. 'Roger Farrell had no criminal convictions. Not a thing on his record.'

'That was what we were working on. Our enquiries suggested he was responsible for the deaths of three young women in Nottingham, unsolved murders spread over three years. We had been gathering evidence against him for months. It was a painstaking operation. He was a very careful man. The decision had just been made to go for an arrest, because we'd heard he was getting a bit spooked – perhaps he'd found out we were asking questions and was afraid we might be getting too close. We were going to take him as he arrived home, so that he didn't have chance to dispose of anything in the house.'

'What went wrong?'

'We don't know. He didn't appear that night. He never came home. The next thing we heard was that someone had been into his house, people who looked like police officers. That would be you.'

'But that was after he was dead,' said Cooper.

'You came to Nottingham to investigate a suicide?'

'Not just one suicide.'

Cooper told her about the other cases, but only in vague terms, instinctively holding back on some of the important details.

'I see. A suicide epidemic.'

'Not— Well, we've been trying to establish if there's any connection between the victims.'

'Well, there's no doubt about Farrell.'

'What do you mean?'

'No doubt about why he did it. He must have known he was facing arrest, a court case and concurrent life sentences. He took the easy way out.'

271

'Who is Roger Farrell supposed to have murdered?'

'You want me to share details from our inquiry with you?'

'It seems . . . well, are we going to work together or not?'

Fry thought about it. 'As long as it's mutual. A mutual exchange of information.'

'Of course.'

Still she paused, deliberately making him wait. Cooper was just starting to get irritated when she opened her file and passed him three victim profiles, copies that were already prepared and ready for him to ask for them.

'For a start, there's no "supposed" about it,' said Fry. 'We're confident that we have sufficient compelling evidence to enable us to get a conviction for Farrell. Or it would have done, if he'd waited for us to get our hands on him.'

Cooper spread the profiles apart on the desk and studied the faces of the women whose photos were attached to them.

'Three confirmed victims. It's possible there were others. We very much wanted to question Mr Farrell about them. Now their cases will probably just lie in the archives. Their families may never know the truth about what happened to their daughters.'

Cooper glanced at her. Coming from Diane Fry, the last words sounded like an uncharacteristic burst of empathy. He couldn't see any corresponding emotion in her face, no flicker of sympathy or reflection. It dawned on him that she was saying what she thought

272

he wanted to hear. In fact, she was speaking out loud what she imagined he himself would say in the same circumstances.

So she was manipulating him blatantly. Did she believe he wouldn't notice it? But she knew him better than that. She didn't care whether he saw through it. She knew her strategy would work on him anyway.

And she was right. As Cooper lowered his gaze and read through the profiles, he was already thinking about the other victims, the ones who might never get justice. It was an outcome he had always hated as a police officer. Everyone deserved justice of some kind. He'd said it many times.

Cooper bit his lip as he read. Damn Diane Fry. He was her senior officer, yet she knew how to play him as if he were still a young, inexperienced DC.

'The first one was Sarah Mittal,' said Fry. 'Aged twenty, from Birmingham. Studying graphic design at Nottingham Trent University.'

'A student,' said Cooper.

'They were all students. Nottingham is full of them.'

'And she was found strangled.'

'Yes.'

And there were photographs to prove it – a body lying sprawled in an alleyway and a headshot with the bruises on her neck clearly visible.

He turned the page. A second body.

'Anna Balodis, aged twenty-one, from Jelgava in Latvia. She was in the final year of a degree in health and social care. She was strangled in the same way.'

'He used his bare hands?'

273

'No, he wore gloves,' said Fry. 'No fingerprints. We had some DNA traces, but of course Roger Farrell wasn't in the database to compare them to.'

'Farrell had no criminal record,' said Cooper again.

'Exactly. We needed enough evidence against him to make an arrest so we could get the swabs and do a comparison.'

'I see.'

And then there was another.

'Victoria Jenkins. Also aged twenty, a media student on the Clifton campus.'

'Apart from being students, did they have anything in common?'

'Well, they weren't the most striking of girls,' said Fry coolly. 'Everyone who knew them agrees on that, except their mothers. They also weren't from the most affluent backgrounds. Trent takes a very diverse range of students. These girls were from poor working-class families. There was no money coming in from Mummy and Daddy to help them through their university courses. Nottingham is a big student city, but it can be an expensive place to live.'

'Were they doing part-time jobs to help pay their way?' asked Cooper.

'Yes, they were.'

He looked up at Fry, trying to interpret her expression.

'Are you suggesting they were prostitutes?' he said.

'We call them sex workers in the city,' said Fry. 'I don't know what you call them here.'

'I'm not sure we have any in Edendale.'

'Are you kidding me?'

'Well, they're not mentioned in the visitor guides,' said Cooper.

Fry scowled. 'We're not saying that anyway,' she said. 'Not publicly. And certainly not to the families. It would be difficult and time-consuming to prove. And it wouldn't be considered appropriate to start destroying the reputation of the victims.'

'But . . .?'

'Well, if they were turning a few tricks, it was very much on a part-time basis. I'd call them amateurs, except they were doing it for the money.'

'So there would be no pimp, no madam, no established brothel or massage parlour they were working from?'

Fry shook her head. 'No organisation at all. Strictly casual. Pick-ups in bars or on a street corner.'

'I bet the professional working girls knew all about them, though.'

'Well, they don't like competition. Who does?'

'So perhaps they weren't too upset when these three were killed.'

'They certainly haven't been providing us with information. We might have concluded the inquiry a lot sooner if they had. The feeling was they were glad to see the part-timers go. On an "it could have been me" basis.'

'That's a shame.'

'We pieced the evidence together bit by bit over a prolonged period,' said Fry. 'Hundreds of interviews, thousands of hours of CCTV footage and endless PNC checks on car registrations.'

'You identified Farrell's blue BMW?'

'No, he was too cunning for that. He changed his car between attacks. First he had an old Mercedes B Class, then a Peugeot 508 and a Škoda Octavia, before he switched to the BMW. When we studied the cameras from the streets near the incidents, we never saw the same vehicle twice, no matter how much footage we looked at.'

'Did you do anything else?'

'The murders meant increased patrols from the local cops. High-visibility policing on the streets, but also regular undercover operations by the vice squad. They picked up a lot of men for soliciting, recorded a lot of car number-plates, warned a lot of girls who were out touting for business. You can imagine how popular that was with the sex industry. It was disastrous for their business.'

'Yes, I can.'

'So there are plenty of people in Nottingham who would have been glad to arrange Roger Farrell's death. Some of them wouldn't even need paying. They would have done it for the pleasure.'

'Three girls, a year apart,' said Cooper.

'Yes. So things were just getting back to normal when the next one happened. Assaults aren't unusual. There are plenty of arguments over money. Sometimes a customer gets robbed and goes back for revenge. Occasionally the girls get into fights with each other over territory. These incidents were different. They were cold and calculated.'

'Planned?'

'Undoubtedly. One of our difficulties was that we are fairly certain Roger Farrell had an accomplice or an associate. Some of the women report seeing two men together. And the other man is captured on CCTV, we believe.'

'Have you identified him?'

Fry hesitated. Then he knew she wasn't telling him everything. This had all just been for show. But why?

'No,' she said. 'We haven't identified him. Not definitely. There are some possibilities we have in mind.'

'Can I see the CCTV?'

'I don't think that would be a good idea.'

'So far and no further, then.'

'It's a sensitive operation. We've already had one disaster with the loss of Farrell.'

'And I'm just too much of a risk.'

She didn't answer that. Cooper sat back. He supposed he would just have to be grateful for what he got.

'Trust me,' said Fry.

That was too much for Cooper. One step too far.

'Trust?' he said. 'I'm surprised you don't choke on the word.'

Fry stood up suddenly. 'Come with me. I want to show you something. I want to show you where we've been making our enquiries. It's a long way from your rural backwater in Edendale. Only a forty-mile drive. But a world away.'

Diane Fry slowed down as she turned her car into Forest Road. Evening was coming on, but it would stay light for a while yet. The real business wouldn't get under way until the sun began to set.

A few street girls operated in the area between Mapperley Park and Radford, despite repeated crackdowns by Nottinghamshire's vice squad. It was largely residential and many independent prostitutes worked safely from the flats, all charging their clients a standard rate. On the street, the girls were cheaper and more dangerous. For years, many of them had been teenagers trying to raise cash for drugs, angering the established prostitutes by invading their patch and undercutting prices.

From her own experience, Fry had seen girls going through the care system and straight on to the street. They got hooked on cocaine in their teens and discovered that prostitution was the only way to earn enough money to feed their habit when state benefits weren't available.

You still saw a few of them at night. The older women were identifiable by their mini-skirts, leather trousers, thigh-length boots and wigs. But the younger ones could be any teenager in their jeans and track shoes. The way they were hanging around gave them away. Most of the street girls came out after dark. They would take a position near a convenient side road or alley, or in the recreation ground. Any woman who stood around long enough in the Forest Road area would be asked how much she charged by a man in a passing car.

More recently, some Eastern European girls had been walking the streets off Radford Road. Parts of the district were upmarket middle-class suburbs, streets of solid

Victorian town houses and open parkland. Understandably, residents were exasperated with the area's continuing reputation as the red light district of the city.

Ten years ago, there had been more than three hundred girls known to the Kerb Crawling Taskforce, but the figure had been reduced dramatically. Efforts to eradicate prostitution from the streets of Nottingham had included drop-in centres and outreach programmes, as well as rehabilitation courses for men caught buying sex who weren't charged but given a police caution to cut reoffending.

Of course, everyone knew prostitution hadn't disappeared. It had just moved off the street. Prostitutes worked from a crack house instead of roaming the streets around Forest Road. They had resorted to using mobile phones and computers to get custom.

There were definitely risks for men like Roger Farrell. Street prostitution was illegal and so was kerb crawling. If a police operation didn't catch you, the girls were likely to rob you or leave you with a disease.

'So you think Farrell is right at the centre of your inquiry,' said Cooper, gazing out at the passing streets.

'Yes.'

'And our inquiry too?'

'It would help, wouldn't it? Since Farrell is dead.'

Fry could see Cooper didn't like that answer. He probably thought she was being too flippant. He always worried so much about everyone.

'These suicides of yours,' she said. 'Aren't they just self-created victims?'

'You've never had much sympathy for victims, have you?' said Cooper.

'Not for some of them.'

It was true and she didn't feel guilty about it. Fry thought of all the times she'd observed the behaviour of victims and felt a twinge of contempt at their weakness. Often she'd wanted to tell them that it wasn't so bad as all that, that they should have a bit of backbone and pull themselves together.

She'd seen plenty of genuine victims, individuals whose lives had been destroyed by some horrible crime. But so many people were just self-obsessed narcissists who deliberately over-dramatised their problems because they longed to be the centre of attention. They were the same people who dialled 999 because they'd broken a fingernail or to complain their kebab was cold.

'Where are we going now?' asked Cooper.

'This is one of our few witnesses. At least, one of the few who have been willing to talk to us about what happened. I've been given permission to let you talk to her.'

'Oh, thanks.'

'You might not thank me afterwards.'

The girl was thin and her eyes were sunk in shadows as dark as bruises. Of course, *girl* was the wrong word for her. She was a woman, probably well into her thirties, though she looked and dressed like someone much younger, with the thin limbs of a teenager in tight jeans and a ripped T-shirt that continually slipped off one shoulder.

Cooper guessed that if he met her at night he wouldn't recognise her. He was seeing behind the façade. It was a privilege of a kind, he supposed.

'Of course I'll never forget him,' she said. 'I didn't like the look of him from the word go. But you can't be too fussy when you need the money.'

Cooper opened his mouth to ask what she needed the money for, but Fry gave him a sharp look and he changed his mind.

'Can you describe him for us?' he asked instead. 'What didn't you like about him in particular?'

'He had those spider eyes,' she said.

'He had what?'

'Spider eyes. Do you know what I mean?'

She stared at him, then turned away and looked at Fry, as if suddenly realising that Cooper was a man and wouldn't understand.

'They crawled all over your body,' she said. 'It made my flesh creep where they touched me.'

Fry just nodded. 'And what did he say to you?'

'When I turned him down, he got really angry. He said he'd kill me. He reached out to try and grab me. So I started running and screamed. He panicked then. He got back in his car and drove off. Went hell for leather up towards Alfreton Road.'

From time to time, Cooper thought she looked even younger – almost like a child, as she hugged her knees for comfort at the memories.

'And the other one,' said Fry. 'Tell us about the other man.'

She looked really frightened then.

'You mean the one who came after him,' she said.
'I don't know which was worse.'

'So who was she talking about?' asked Cooper when
they were back in Fry's car. 'The other man?'

'There are two other men who came into our
enquiries,' said Fry as she started the car. 'Simon Hull
and Anwar Sharif. The plan was to arrest Roger Farrell
and question him to establish what his relationship
was with the other two. Now we can't do that.'

'Were they his friends or accomplices?'

'Personally, I don't think so. I believe they knew
what he was doing, though.'

'Might they have being trying to stop him?'

'By what means? Persuasion, intimidation? We don't
know.'

'Blackmail?' said Cooper.

'Ah, now,' said Fry, 'you might be talking some sense.'

'What do you mean?'

'We've been analysing Roger Farrell's bank accounts.
There was some unusual activity during the past year.
A series of large cash withdrawals at monthly intervals.'

'Cash? So you can't trace who it went to.'

'Exactly.'

Fry drove around for a while, then parked in front
of a row of shops. Cooper had no idea where he was
now. Many of the streets looked indistinguishable. He
wasn't sure how he would choose one from the next.
This city seemed to go on for ever and there was no
indication when you'd passed from one area into
another. He supposed people here must know whether

they lived in Forest Fields or Hyson Green, but he couldn't tell.

Fry pointed out a bulky figure in a hooded jacket.

'There. That's Simon Hull,' she said.

'Does he live in this area?'

'Not far away.'

Cooper watched the man but couldn't see his face from here.

'What sort of car does he drive?' he asked.

'A black Jeep.'

'A Grand Cherokee?'

'Yes, I think so. Why do you ask?'

'Oh, it looks a bit like a Land Rover, if you don't know much about cars.'

Fry frowned, but let it pass as an irrelevant comment. She'd got used to having to do that when she worked regularly with Ben Cooper in Edendale.

'And what job does Hull do?' asked Cooper.

'He runs a small garage in Radford. Servicing and MoTs. You know the sort of thing. If I'm right, that may be a direct to link Farrell, given his tendency to change cars so often. Why, what does that make you think of? Land Rovers again?'

'No, I was wondering if he was an internet wizard of some kind. A web designer perhaps.'

'A web designer?' said Fry. 'Oh, that would be Anwar Sharif. He works in managed IT services. His employers are based on a new business park out by the motorway. Companies outsource to them for network infrastructure, technical support, data security, that sort of thing.'

'Interesting.'

Simon Hull disappeared into a house and Fry pulled away from the kerb again, turning the corner into another almost identical road.

'Diane . . .' said Cooper.

'What?'

He gestured out of the car window. 'Is this what you left Edendale for?'

Fry stamped her foot on the brake a bit too hard as a light turned amber, making Cooper jerk against his seat belt.

'Yes, this is part of it,' she said. 'Just a very small part of it. Here in the city is where we see what's actually happening. I don't suppose you can even begin to understand that. You and your rural idyll up there in the wilds of the High Peak. You don't realise how cut off you are from the real world, how divorced you are from what's going on in society.'

'Oh, I'm aware of it,' said Cooper. 'I just don't want to be so much a part of it as you've become.'

'Me? I always was a part of it. You never changed me into a country girl.'

'No, I realise that. It wasn't going to happen.'

'Never.'

Fry took him to the police station at St Ann's, where the Northern Command of EMSOU's Major Crime Unit was based. To Cooper's eye, the St Ann's area was another huge housing estate. And someone had spent money on the building where Fry worked too. There probably weren't any leaky corners here or sink holes in the car park.

The station on St Ann's Well Road was used as a base for officers, but had no front counter and wasn't open for members of the public to visit. It gave the building a different atmosphere from West Street, where the lobby and front reception desk were often busy with visitors.

There was another difference here. Back home, Derbyshire Constabulary was divided into geographical divisions, all of which contained some urban areas. Nottinghamshire Police openly divided themselves into just two – City Division and County Division. It was reminiscent of the days when the city had its own separate police force, before amalgamation in the 1960s. It seemed a tacit admission that policing in the city was different from that in a rural area.

It was late by now, and the station was unnaturally quiet. Upstairs, Fry introduced him to a tall, dark-haired officer who was alone in the MCU office.

'This is my colleague, DC Jamie Callaghan,' she said. 'He's working a late shift.'

'Inspector,' said Callaghan with a brief nod.

Cooper studied the pin board. The photograph of Anwar Sharif meant nothing to him. He was an Asian man aged in his late thirties, with a trimmed beard and gelled hair. But the head shot of Simon Hull made him frown and look more closely.

'What is it?' asked Fry.

'I've seen this man before. Simon Hull.'

'I showed him to you earlier on.'

'Well, not the man himself,' said Cooper. 'I mean a picture of him. A younger him.'

'I don't know what you're talking about.'

'There was a photograph in Roger Farrell's car when we found him. It showed two couples. I'm pretty sure the other man in it was Simon Hull.'

'I'd like to see that.'

'It's at Edendale with the rest of the stuff we recovered from his car.'

'Such as?'

Cooper shook his head. 'Nothing important.'

'If Simon Hull denies knowing Roger Farrell,' said Fry, staring at the photos, 'it would be very useful to have photographic evidence we can present to him to prove otherwise.'

'So what are you going to do about these two men?' asked Cooper.

'We're picking them up in the morning,' said Fry. 'A couple of early calls have been arranged. DC Callaghan and I will be conducting interviews with them here at St Ann's later tomorrow.'

'It sounds like a bit of a fishing expedition,' said Cooper.

'Don't let DCI Mackenzie hear you say that. He might change his mind.'

'Well, I hope that's helped to put you in the picture,' said Fry when they got back in to the Audi. It was dark now and she turned on her headlights as they passed through the barrier on to St Ann's Well Road.

'Absolutely,' said Cooper. 'I appreciate it.'

'So what are your thoughts about Roger Farrell now?'

'It's a different perspective. I'll have to give it some consideration.'

'Is that it?'

'For now.'

Fry gritted her teeth as she drove back towards Edendale. They left the street lights of the city behind and hit the darkened roads of North Derbyshire.

'Isn't it your birthday later this month?' said Fry after a while.

Cooper was surprised. 'Fancy you remembering that.'

'I wasn't planning to send you a card or anything,' said Fry. 'I just remembered that you're Cancer. A crab in its shell.'

'Thanks.'

Half an hour later, Cooper got out of Fry's car at West Street and stood looking at her for a moment before he closed the door.

'By the way, Diane . . .' he said.

'What?'

'Do you know you've got a white stain on your jacket?'

'Really?' Fry looked at the mark and brushed at it ineffectually. 'I don't know what that can be.'

'Strangely enough,' said Cooper, 'it smells like sour baby milk.'

24

Day 6

The clouds had settled over the Eden Valley next day. A thin white layer stretched to the horizon, with a hint of deeper grey that might produce rain. Ben Cooper knew it could happen in the blink of an eye, that change from light to dark, from warmth to chill. Up there on the moors, you had to be vigilant.

Even driving through Edendale, Cooper couldn't get one obsessive thought out of his mind: the expectation of another suicide. That was the way it worked with epidemics, wasn't it? You just got more and more cases until you finally discovered the cause.

At the top of the high street, he turned left at the lights into Clappergate, away from the pedestrianised area. He passed the front of the railway station and the spire of All Saints parish church. He found himself thinking about people who threw themselves off tall buildings. You needed about fifteen storeys to be sure you wouldn't survive the fall and leave yourself with massive injuries instead.

There were no buildings tall enough for that in the town. Well, unless you could get to the top of the spire at All Saints. That would do it, he supposed. He'd never heard of anyone attempting it and he hoped he never would.

There was another thing that had changed in Edendale. And it was one that Ben Cooper regretted. For many years, he and other officers based at E Division headquarters had been calling at May's Café, just down the hill from West Street, for a mug of May's coffee and a meat pie. It had been a tradition, deeply ingrained in the working practices of the police station.

But the café had closed when May Hobson became ill and no one could be found to run it in her place. It was empty now and awaiting a confirmed buyer. Rumours at West Street said it was going to be a hairdresser's or a tattoo parlour. Whenever Cooper walked past it, he still seemed to detect the aroma of coffee and baking – familiar and comforting, like May herself. It was a lesson everyone had to learn. Some traditions passed, because their time was over.

Cooper walked past the door of the CID room towards his office, automatically glancing in to see which of his team were present. At first, he didn't notice anything unusual. He'd reached his desk and was taking off his jacket when he stopped and frowned.

'No, it can't be,' he said.

Slowly Cooper walked back out and gazed into the room. It was as if he'd been hurled back in time, shifted several months into the past when the world was a different place. Yet somehow it also seemed completely right and natural.

The person sitting next to Becky Hurst looked round,

chewing slowly on something. Cooper could have a good guess what it was. A remnant of pork pie or a bite of a cunningly concealed Mars bar.

'Gavin, what on earth are you doing here?'

'Eh-up,' said Murfin with a grin. 'They told me you needed a bit of help. So here I am.'

'That's not possible.'

'Not possible? Think of me as a miracle, then.'

'But why you?'

'I'm available,' said Murfin. 'And I'm cheap.'

'Don't tell me you got sacked from Eden Valley Enquiries.'

'We went our separate ways by mutual consent,' said Murfin. 'We had artistic differences.'

'No, that's what members of boy bands say when they can't stand each other any longer.'

Murfin sighed and picked at something stuck in his teeth. 'I couldn't face one more day on the Woodlands Estate. That's the truth of it, like. It had got so they saw me coming like the bailiffs or the rent collector, and they all closed their curtains and hid. I mean, what sort of private enquiry agent has to stand on someone's doorstep shouting through the letterbox while kids abuse him from the pavement?'

Cooper laughed. 'It didn't work out, then. Not quite up to your expectations.'

'That's the top and bottom of it. So when I heard a rumour that HR were scouring Derbyshire for cheap civilian staff to hire, I decided to bite the bullet and take a pay cut. Just to help out, like. Public duty and all that.'

'You were missing us.'

'After a fashion.'

So this was what Superintendent Branagh had meant when she talked about supplementing staff. In a way it was amazing that Gavin Murfin was the one who'd been brought back. Of course, he was only recently retired, which meant he hadn't lost touch in the way most retirees so quickly did.

On the other hand, he had never made any attempt to toe the line while he was here, never tried to be in anyone's good books. Quite the opposite, in fact. He'd been very free with his comments, his sarcastic asides and sardonic looks. There must be something about becoming a senior manager that destroyed your sense of irony. That was the only reason Murfin had got away with it for all those years.

Cooper looked around the room to see how Murfin was fitting back in. Even Becky Hurst looked pleased to see him.

'So what am I supposed to do with you, Gavin?' asked Cooper.

'I can take statements, make phone calls, prepare files for court, bring fun and laughter to the office.'

'Door-to-door enquiries?'

Murfin sighed. 'If you insist. But . . .'

'But it might be better if we just kept you in the office and away from the general public.'

'That seems to be the general idea. Since I'm not a police officer any more.'

'So whose responsibility are you? Whose authority do you actually answer to?'

291

'The same as everyone else,' said Murfin. 'Human Resources.'

'I wish Hazel Branagh had told me,' said Cooper. 'She ought to have been more specific about what was being planned.'

Murfin tapped the side of his nose. 'I'm a sort of secret weapon, like.'

'No powers of arrest, though.'

'Definitely.'

'Not that I can recall the last time you arrested someone, Gavin.'

'True, it wasn't my speciality in my more mature years. I preferred to use my vast experience to guide my colleagues.'

'Is that a direct quote from your application letter?' asked Cooper.

Murfin smiled. 'You'd have to ask HR.'

'How did it go with Diane Fry?' asked Carol Villiers, changing the subject.

'Oh, it was fine,' Ben said. She knew about his history with Fry, of course. There wasn't much he could conceal from Carol. And she'd worked with Fry too for a while, when Cooper was on extended leave. Villiers had made no secret of the fact that she hadn't enjoyed the experience, in fact had regarded Diane Fry as a kind of interloper.

But was there something more personal between them? Cooper could see Carol's hackles rise as she mentioned Fry's name. Perhaps they were just incompatible personalities. Fry wanted to dominate everyone and Villiers wasn't the kind of woman to let that happen to her.

'Fine?' she said. 'Really?'

'Yes, of course. We're both professionals, aren't we?'

'If you say so, Ben.'

Murfin grinned when he overheard their conversation.

'Detective Sergeant Fry?' he said, drawing out the name with disturbing relish. 'Shallow as a puddle, I reckon.'

'Are you kidding, Gavin?'

Murfin looked surprised to be challenged on his view. 'I can read her like a book, mate. It's all on the surface. She wants you to think there's a lot of depth behind it, but it's all out there really. What you see is what you get. Superficial, like.'

'I think you may have seriously misjudged Diane Fry.'

Murfin winked. 'My instincts are never wrong.'

'I think your instincts have died, Gavin. They're just overdue for a decent burial.'

Cooper filled in his team with an outline of the case against Roger Farrell and the two associates, Simon Hull and Anwar Sharif.

'Farrell's funeral is the one we ought to be present at,' said Villiers. 'It won't happen for a while yet, until the inquest has been opened at least.'

'We can keep an eye out for the date, though.'

'Okay.'

Cooper even had DS Devdan Sharma back from secondment. That meant the team was almost back to full strength, the way it had been when he'd first moved up from uniform to CID.

Sharma came to Cooper's office to give him a briefing on the immigration inquiry, though he didn't need to. It was outside Cooper's remit, not his responsibility at all. But it was courteous of Dev to do that. He was always dutiful in the role of detective sergeant, always had respect for Cooper's position as his boss.

Not everyone showed him that level of respect. In fact, Cooper wasn't sure he liked it. He preferred honesty and he wasn't convinced that Dev Sharma was genuine. There was something else going on in the background, which would take him more time to figure out.

Sharma was a recent addition to E Division CID, filling the role that Cooper himself had left vacant when he was promoted. Cooper had taken him for dinner one night shortly after he arrived in Edendale, in an attempt to get to know him. He always felt it was important with someone he was going to be working with closely. They'd gone to the Mussel and Crab on Hollowgate, and shared a selection of fish and chicken dishes. And yes, Sharma had talked about himself, his background, his family, his police career in D Division in Derby.

But Cooper had come away from the evening feeling he'd failed. He'd been given a list of facts, like a carefully planned character outline, rather than getting right to the heart of the person. He still didn't really *know* Dev Sharma. Perhaps it would just take more time. Some people were like that.

'The group organising and exploiting illegal migrant workers was based in Derby, but there were links to other cities,' said Sharma. 'It was quite a network.'

'Nottingham too?' said Cooper.

'Yes. And Leicester. Even down as far as Birmingham. So the inquiry has moved beyond us now.'

'Was it a useful experience?'

'The illegal workers we picked up were taken to an immigration removal centre near Lincoln,' said Sharma, avoiding the question. 'Right out in the country. It's strange, isn't it?'

Cooper took it that he hadn't enjoyed the assignment but didn't feel able to say so.

'What is?'

'I think most people don't know places like that even exist.'

Cooper had to agree. The location that Sharma was referring to had been a women's prison until a few years ago. Now it was operated on behalf of the UK Border Agency, housing four hundred foreign detainees awaiting deportation. Its new purpose might not be obvious to the casual passer-by. It had maintained a low profile, even after the death of a Bangladeshi migrant worker.

'You wouldn't want to work on Immigration Enforcement, then?' said Cooper.

Sharma shook his head firmly. 'No.'

Cooper was surprised to see his DS looked genuinely shaken by his experience working alongside Immigration Enforcement. It was the first real glimpse of the man behind the facts.

'Well, there's certainly plenty to do here,' said Cooper. 'We'll be able to keep you busy.'

'I'm glad of that.' Sharma hesitated before continuing.

'DI Cooper, I know I haven't fitted in here as easily as you might have hoped. I'm not familiar with this area and I may appear lacking in vital local knowledge at times. But I do appreciate the opportunity of working in E Division as part of your team.'

It was quite a speech and it sounded genuine. Cooper felt himself warming to Sharma.

'Let's get to work, then,' he said. 'Have you heard about our current inquiry, Dev?'

'DC Irvine has told me about what he called "suicide tourists".'

'We're trying to avoid using that term, if possible.'

'I told him it was inappropriate.'

'Good.'

It dawned on Cooper that Luke Irvine might take more notice of Dev Sharma's disapproval than anything his DI said. Now, that could be very useful.

'I'd like you to supervise DCs Irvine and Hurst, who should be sifting through a stack of suicide cases recorded over the last few months. Chase them up. Make sure they let you know any potential links they find.'

'Will do.'

'And Irvine is doing an online search on suicide websites.'

'I could take that over,' said Sharma immediately.

Cooper considered it briefly. 'No, let Luke run with it, but keep a close eye on him.'

Sharma nodded. 'I notice we have DC Murfin back again too,' he said.

'Ex-DC. He's a civilian now. Bear that in mind, but use him wherever possible.'

'And I imagine there are quite a few memos and emails for me to catch up on?' said Sharma.

'Yes.' Cooper smiled. 'Better get on with it, then, Dev.'

Sharma stood up to leave. With his hand on the door handle, he turned back to Cooper.

'You know, DI Cooper – I heard one of our spiritual leaders at the Geeta Bhawan Temple in Peartree talk about the subject of suicide once. He told us it was always wrong because it disrupts karma. He said the important thing to remember is that your suffering is justified.'

'Justified?'

Sharma gazed at him, his brown eyes suddenly intense.

'Yes, justified,' he said. 'People fully deserve what they're experiencing, because it's a consequence of their own actions. Their actions in a former life.'

And of course Diane Fry had arrived at West Street too. She entered the CID room as if she'd never left E Division. With a nod to Cooper, she cast a critical eye around the room.

'Isn't that Gavin Murfin?' hissed Fry when she got Cooper on his own.

'You know perfectly well it is. You worked with him for long enough. You could hardly have forgotten what he looks like.'

'But he retired, didn't he?'

'Yes, a few months ago.'

'And not before time. So what is he doing here?'

'Civilian support,' said Cooper.

297

That was the phrase he'd been given when he asked. That was the job description on Murfin's ID card attached to the lanyard round his neck. Civilian support. It was a nice-sounding phrase. It had echoes of Sir Robert Peel's *Principles of Law Enforcement*: 'The police are the public and the public are the police'.

'Unbelievable,' said Fry.

That sounded unduly harsh to Cooper. It was bizarre and illogical, yes. But very little that senior management did was unbelievable. And Gavin Murfin was very much a believable presence.

He studied Fry more closely. She looked a bit harassed, with dark shadows under her eyes, as if she hadn't been sleeping properly for some reason.

'Are you okay, Diane?' he asked.

'I'm fine. I've just been having a bad week.'

'That's tough,' said Cooper.

If it had been him, if he was going through a really bad week, he would have gone for a drive over the Snake Pass or taken a long walk on the moors, whatever the weather. As far as Cooper was concerned, there was nothing like a good blow to clear the mind and make you feel better. There wasn't any point in suggesting it to Diane Fry, though. Whatever was troubling her, she would deal with it in her own way. If it was a person, she would probably kill them.

'Simon Hull and Anwar Sharif have been picked up this morning,' she said. 'They're being processed now. We're going to let them cool their heels for a bit in the custody suite and consult with their briefs, then we'll be interviewing them fully this afternoon.'

'Can I sit in on the interviews?'

'I'll ask.'

'I suppose they'll go "no comment".'

'It wouldn't be a surprise.'

Cooper nodded. *No comment*. Every police officer had to get used to it. So often in the interview room, he'd grown tired and exasperated by the repeated use of 'no comment', interviewees who gave the same reply to each question, as if they'd forgotten how they answered the last one. Sometimes it was like trying to interview a goldfish, with a memory span of three seconds. What was the point?

'You can examine their phone records, though. Their email, bank accounts. You can give their computers a going-over. Sharif is a web designer. He has the capability.'

'Capability? Oh, you're still thinking there's a website.'

'I *know* there's a website,' said Cooper. 'Or at least there was. *Secrets of Death*.'

'Why are you so sure?'

A bit reluctantly, Cooper showed her one of the business cards in its funereal black with gold edging. He'd kept it back because it felt like the only advantage he had, the one thing that Diane Fry and the Major Crime Unit didn't know about. Now was the time to share it.

'We found this one in Farrell's car, on his dashboard,' he said.

'*Secrets of Death*. What is it?'

'I have no idea. As I said, I'm working on the theory that it's a website of some kind.'

'I see. I assume you've had the card examined for fingerprints?'

'Of course. There were only Roger Farrell's own prints on it.'

'Shame.'

'Two of our other suicides had them too. I recovered a similar card from Gordon Burgess's house, which is under examination now. And another was destroyed by the victim's wife.'

There was a shout from across the room. It sounded like Luke Irvine crying 'Eureka!'.

'What have you got?' asked Cooper.

Irvine was reading out loud from his screen.

'Yes, death. Death must be so beautiful. To lie in the soft brown earth, with the grasses waving above one's head, and listen to silence. To have no yesterday and no tomorrow. To forget time, to forget life, to be at peace. You can help me. You can open for me the portals of death's house.'

'What the heck is that, Luke?'

'It says here it's a quote from Oscar Wilde. *The Canterville Ghost.*'

'Are you reading ghost stories?'

'No, it's this website.'

'You said there are a lot of those websites.'

'Yes, but we matched a phrase on this one.'

'What phrase?'

'There are three secrets of death. It's right there on their home page. It reads: *There are three secrets of death. The first is a secret of the heart, the second a secret of the mind. The third secret of death is one you can only find out when you die.'*

'Let's have a look.'

There was a legal table of suicide methods ranked by lethality, the likelihood of causing death. Disturbingly, it also listed the average length of time each method took and, in a column headed 'Agony', a rating for how painful it was.

By checking through the list, you could choose the quickest or least painful form of death, or you could opt for certainty. Death by firearm was at the top of the list. But by using a shotgun, not a 1930s service revolver. According to the table, a shotgun to the head led the competition with 99 per cent lethality. It was definitely an option chosen in rural areas like the High Peak and Derbyshire Dales, where the possession of shotguns was higher than the average. The method was also quick, taking an average of less than two minutes to produce death, which would pretty much be considered instantaneous in the circumstances. It looked far preferable to being hit by a train, when apparently you could take eighteen minutes to die, or an overdose of illegal drugs, when death could take two hours.

The most painful was death by fire, which didn't surprise him. Cooper had always thought it must be the worst way to go.

He glanced at Sharma. Was it just a coincidence that Luke Irvine had suddenly found what he was supposed to be looking for? Or was it due to the presence of his DS in the CID room? But Sharma's face was impassive. Perhaps that distant manner really worked.

'Can we see the rest of the site?' asked Cooper.

'There must be some private area where you can log in with a password like the one on Roger Farrell's card.'

'Yes, there seems to be a members' area,' said Irvine.

'Can you get into it?'

'Not without registering and requesting a password.'

'Do it, then.'

Irvine hesitated. 'I have to enter my name and address.'

'You can't give the office.'

'Do you want me to use my home address?' said Irvine. 'I don't mind.'

'Are you sure, Luke? It's a big thing to ask.'

Irvine began to type again. 'No, it's all right. I'll survive. By the way, I've also done a WHOis look-up on the domain name, but it's privacy protected. You have to go through the registrar.'

'What's the domain?'

'It's called *secretsofdeath.org*. The website itself is hosted by a company in China. It's going to be tricky getting any information out of them, if not impossible.'

Cooper's eye was caught by a line at the top of the members' log-in page.

And this is the second secret of death. You have to let go. You have to learn to say goodbye.

'The second secret of death,' said Villiers. 'Are there more?'

Irvine turned to look at her. 'At least one more, according to the introduction on the landing page.'

'I wonder what the third secret can be.'

'I have no idea. And I'm not sure I want to find out.'

Irvine checked his phone for an email.

'Yes, here it is. It's an automated message, of course. But there's a password. A string of numbers and letters. Oh, and . . .'

'What?'

'It says I'll get my membership card through the post.'

'Like the cards the others had.'

'Don't say "the others" as if I'm one of them,' protested Irvine.

'Sorry, Luke.'

'So what now?'

'I'm going to talk to Anson Tate again,' said Cooper.

'Who is he?' asked Fry.

'A failed suicide.'

'Am I coming with you?'

Cooper looked at her, noticing the determined set of her mouth in spite of her tiredness. 'Can I stop you, Diane?' he said.

'Probably not.'

25

'Detective Inspector Cooper again,' said Anson Tate when he answered the bell. 'What a surprise.'

'I'd just like to ask you a couple more questions, sir, if that's all right?'

'Well, I didn't say it was a pleasant surprise.'

Tate turned to examine Diane Fry as she appeared at Cooper's shoulder. Because she was behind him, Cooper couldn't see Fry's expression or the look she gave Tate. But the tension between them was immediately palpable. Tate's face tightened and his eyes narrowed suspiciously.

'And who is this person?'

'This is Detective Sergeant Fry. She's my colleague from the Major Crime Unit in Nottingham.'

'Oh,' said Tate. 'That does sound important.'

Cooper restrained a smile as Tate spoke about Diane Fry as if she weren't there, rather than speaking to her, which would have been much more courteous. *Now* he could imagine her expression.

'I can't tell you any more than I already have,' said Tate. 'Personally, I feel we exhausted our useful exchange of information on your last visit. In fact, this is starting to look rather like harassment.'

Fry glanced at Cooper and raised an eyebrow. She could get a lot of meaning into one eyebrow lift. This one expressed surprise and a question she wanted to ask him about what had happened last time. And there was also a hint of approval, a suggestion that, whatever it was, she might have done the same.

'Can we come in?'

'Yes, do that. And you can listen while I phone and make a complaint about harassment.'

'That's your decision, sir.'

When they reached the flat, Tate made no effort to use the phone. Instead, he stood in the middle of the worn carpet and glared at them. There was no offer of herbal tea this time or even for them to sit down in the lumpy armchairs.

'So?' Tate said impatiently.

'I'm hoping you'll change your mind,' said Cooper. 'I'm hoping you'll want to help us to prevent more people from dying.'

'Of course, I would – if I could.'

Cooper showed Tate the printout from the cached web page Irvine had given him.

'Does the name of this website mean anything to you?'

Tate took the printout and stared at it intently. He gazed at it for such a long time that Cooper began to think he'd made a mistake letting him see it. Tate's fingers gripped the paper so tightly at the edges that it crumpled in his fingers.

'*Secrets of Death*,' he said. 'What a strange title. What does it mean, Detective Inspector Cooper?'

'I thought you might know,' said Cooper. 'Have you ever come across it before?'

'I'm afraid not. I would remember, if I had. It's very . . . ominous.'

'Are you quite sure?'

'Does this website encourage acts of violence?' asked Tate.

'In a way.'

Tate looked pained. 'I don't approve of violence,' he said. 'People should be able to die a gentle, painless death.'

Fry had been leaning forward, watching him carefully.

'Jumping off the Bargate Bridge wouldn't have been painless,' she said.

Tate winced again. 'Who can say? No one. Not until you've done it yourself.' He peered more closely at Fry. 'It's my life, you know. No one else's. It's my life, from start to finish. It's the only thing no one can take away from me.'

'Mr Tate, did you ever have contact with any of these people?' asked Cooper, pressing on determinedly. 'Alex Denning or David Kuzneski?'

Tate had already begun shaking his head. 'I've no idea who they are.'

'Bethan Jones or Gordon Burgess?'

'No.'

'And what about Roger Farrell?' added Fry.

'None of them,' said Tate. 'Though wait a minute . . .'

'Yes?'

'Farrell, you said?'

Fry leaned forward a bit more. 'That's right.'

'I read a story about someone . . . yes, here it is.' Tate fiddled in a magazine rack next to his chair and pulled out a copy of that week's *Eden Valley Times*. 'Yes, a man who took his own life at Heeley Bank was identified by police as Mr Roger Farrell, aged fifty, of Nottingham. Would that be the one?'

Fry didn't respond and Tate turned back to Cooper. 'Detective Inspector?'

Cooper didn't like Tate asking the questions. But he wasn't obliged to answer them.

'Have you ever heard of him before?' he said.

'No, of course not.'

Then Tate held the newspaper up as if it smelled of something more than ink and newsprint.

'Do you think he and I have something in common?' he said. 'You imagine we must be old friends, is that it? It's rather insulting.'

'There's always a right time and place to die,' said Cooper, quoting from Roger Farrell's voicemail message.

'Thank you, Detective Inspector Cooper,' said Tate. 'I would actually agree with that.'

'Ugh,' said Fry when they were back outside in the daylight. 'What a creep.'

'You didn't like Mr Tate very much, then?' said Cooper.

'You're always so perceptive.'

'Don't say I should be a detective.'

'Have I said that before?'

307

'More than once, I think. When you thought I was wet behind the ears.'

'Well, that was years ago,' she said.

Fry began to laugh. Cooper glared at her, daring her to say what she was thinking.

'Detective Inspector Cooper,' she said with a sardonic smile. 'I keep forgetting you're a more senior officer.'

'I've noticed that.'

'Oh, have I been disrespectful?'

'That's not the word I would have used.'

Fry laughed again. 'No, don't tell me your word. I'd be shocked.'

'Perhaps you would.'

She glanced sideways at Cooper. 'Tell me something,' she said.

'What?'

'I'm wondering why you haven't transferred to another unit? I know tenure rules aren't enforced any more, but you've been in E Division CID a long time now. Much too long.'

'What unit would I go to?' said Cooper. 'Back into uniform? Traffic? Intelligence Officer? A training role?'

'I was thinking Community Relations might suit you.'

'Thanks for the suggestion.'

'You're welcome, Inspector.'

Cooper shut himself in his office, closing the door firmly against the possibility of Diane Fry wandering in after him. It was one of the few privileges he had, this tiny office of his own. That door was a good psychological barrier.

Within a few minutes, he was getting restless. He paced the narrow strip of carpet for a while, then went back into the CID room. He was no good on his own. He needed somebody to bounce off.

And there was Carol Villiers, the perfect person. Diane Fry was sitting at a spare desk at the back of the room making a phone call.

'What's up, Ben?' asked Villiers when he appeared.

'We mustn't lose Anson Tate,' he said. 'Unfortunately, he's all we have at the moment. Tate possesses vital evidence, I'm sure of it. And I'm terrified of losing his evidence for good. He's never going to make a complaint for harassment, but he's going to make some other kind of move.'

'Do you think so? What, though?'

'I don't know,' said Cooper. 'I would have put some surveillance on him, if only we had the resources. But he knows you and me now, Carol, and he'll be on his guard.'

Cooper turned and looked at Gavin Murfin. He remembered saying how little Gavin looked like a copper. He hadn't done so for a few years. And he wasn't a copper at all now. He was civilian support.

Murfin met his eye and seemed to read what he was thinking.

'Is that within your remit, Gavin?' said Cooper. 'Is it in your job description from HR?'

'No direct contact with a suspect?' said Murfin.

'Nope.'

309

'And I have no power of arrest, remember.'

'You won't need it. He's not a suspect. I don't expect you'll be carrying handcuffs anyway.'

'I haven't been issued with any.'

'There you go, then. So . . .?'

Murfin looked out of the window, probably to check it wasn't raining.

'Do I get a personal radio?'

'Of course.'

'I'll do it.'

'Good man.'

Cooper watched Murfin leave, still not quite able to believe that Gavin was working here again. He turned back to Villiers.

'And what happened to Roger Farrell's daughter, Ella Webster? Wasn't she supposed to be flying in from Spain?'

'Yes, you're right.'

'She hasn't exactly been eager to talk to us, then.'

'I'll chase her up.'

Cooper tapped his foot impatiently while Villiers was on the phone. It was his own fault. This was something he'd overlooked and should have kept track of. There were only so many priorities he could balance at once.

He turned expectantly as Villiers put the phone down.

'I spoke to Mr Farrell's sister, Fay Laws. She says her niece arrived from Spain and has already been talking to the police.'

'What? Which station?'

'Nottingham,' said Villiers. 'St Ann's.'

'That's the Major Crime Unit. Damn.'

Fry had finished her call and had her head down checking text messages. She might not have noticed what was going on or she might be pretending not to hear.

'Diane,' called Cooper across the room. 'Mrs Webster.'

'Who?'

'Ella Webster. Roger Farrell's daughter. The one who's been living in Spain.'

'Oh, she arrived,' said Fry casually.

'I know. And the Major Crime Unit seem to have laid claim to her. You've intercepted her, when we wanted to talk to her.'

'It's all right. You can have her when we've finished with her. She isn't being very helpful anyway.'

'Oh, and I suppose she's going to be thrilled to see us after you and your colleagues have muddied the waters.'

'Don't worry. You'll be a bit of light relief.'

Cooper sighed. 'So you've not been getting anything out of her?'

Fry stood and strolled slowly across the CID room, with Cooper and Villiers watching her. It was a long time since Cooper had seen her so deliberately marking out this room as her own territory. She must do it unconsciously.

He glanced at Villiers out of the corner of his eye and saw a shocking expression on her face, a hostility he had never noticed before. A muscle was working in her jaw and her eyes were fixed on Fry. It was like watching one predator observe the approach of a rival in some blood-and-guts wildlife programme.

'We've been getting nothing useful,' said Fry. 'She denies knowing anything about her father's activities. But then, she hasn't seen him for the past five years, has hardly even spoken to him on the phone. I'd be surprised if they exchanged Christmas cards. Yet she can't explain exactly why they were estranged. Or she won't explain, more likely. They "drifted apart", she says.'

'And you don't believe that?' asked Cooper.

'Frankly, no. Spain seems a long way to drift.'

Cooper thought of Roger Farrell's sister who only lived across the other side of Nottingham in West Bridgford. She possessed a key to her brother's house, yet never seemed to have visited. That wasn't drifting apart. It was staying in the same place, but building an imaginary wall between you.

Perhaps, in a way, it was like those families who went to great lengths to conceal the fact that a husband or father had taken his own life. Suicide was shameful and those left behind felt the guilt of it. There were also families who found themselves forced into a state of denial when they suspected criminal activity by one of their members. Some closed ranks and rallied in support, and might even become implicated. Others distanced themselves as far as possible, either physically or psychologically.

Farrell's family seemed to have fallen into the latter category. It would have made him even more isolated, more focused on his night-time activities, the obsession that must have developed in his long, lonely hours.

Even convicted prisoners serving long jail sentences

were encouraged to have visits from family members. Keeping in touch meant they were more likely to rehabilitate successfully when they were released and fit back into a normal life. No one took that trouble for solitary people living apparently ordinary lives in society. It was a case of the classic loner who kept himself to himself. They lived on the edge of society, thinking their own thoughts and making their own plans.

'Did you ask her about her father's suicide?' said Cooper.

'She says he'd never mentioned feeling suicidal.'

'Do you think she ever actually talked to him about how he was feeling?'

'No.'

Cooper was sure Fry was right. Despite what else he might have done, Roger Farrell had been easy prey for a manipulative sociopath, an ideal victim, mentally well prepared to be led in an inevitable direction. Farrell might have had some deep-seated guilt gnawing at him or a paranoid fear of being caught. Either could have been used against him, or both.

But what if there was someone else he was afraid of too? Had it all been camouflage? Had someone been encouraging people to take their own lives just to disguise a murder among an epidemic of suicides?

'What about Hull and Sharif?' said Cooper. 'Did Farrell's daughter know them?'

'Never heard their names before.'

He could hear the scepticism in Fry's voice. She hadn't believed a word that Ella Webster said. Mrs

Webster had probably seen that plainly enough in her face, since Fry wasn't good at hiding her opinions of people. Would that make Mrs Webster more likely to talk to E Division CID, or less?

'We need to speak to her in any case,' said Cooper.

Fry smiled. 'No worries. I've already been in touch with my office. Jamie Callaghan will bring her back in to St Ann's later.'

Cooper bit his lip. So Fry had been listening to everything. She was ahead of him all the time.

The CID room looked better without the presence of Diane Fry. She'd taken the opportunity to make her exit without waiting to hear what he thought of Ella Webster. Carol Villiers was there, covering for him as always.

'Bad news, Ben.'

'What's going on?'

'We've just heard from Nottingham. Roger Farrell's house has been broken into. It sounds like they've made a mess of the place.'

'Damn. And I bet you and I were the last people to visit the house.'

'Along with Mr Farrell's sister, yes.'

Villiers looked at him and raised an eyebrow.

'I should head straight there,' he said.

26

At Forest Fields, a crime scene examiner handed Cooper a white overall in a plastic bag and a pair of elasticated overshoes. Inside the house, video was being shot, photographs taken, surfaces dusted for fingerprints.

He could see straight away that this was being treated as more than just an ordinary house break-in. Volume crime like burglary must be a regular occurrence in the city. A SOCO might call a day or two after the event for prints and the duty PC would issue a crime number with a shrug of the shoulders about the possibility of recovering stolen items. The resources deployed here looked as though someone had escalated the incident to a serious crime.

In the sitting room, a vase lay shattered on the floor. He could see that a pane in the French windows had been knocked out to reach the handle. Papers were strewn across the floor, a rug was rucked up at one corner. A struggle? Or just a hasty burglar?

'What has been taken?'

'We're not sure, until the key holder arrives.'

'Mrs Fay Laws?'

'That's her.'

'I doubt she'll have any idea,' said Cooper.

He moved into the dining area and looked at the table. It was lucky he'd removed the laptop and memory sticks. He couldn't have known this would happen, but in retrospect his priorities had been right.

Cooper saw that the folder was still on the table, but he had a feeling it had been moved. He could see that the area had already been dusted for prints so he flipped open the folder.

'I did a job the other day,' the crime scene examiner was saying. 'It was a burglary at a big house in The Park. Do you know the area?'

'Yes, vaguely.'

He knew that The Park was a very upmarket private estate near the centre of the city, built on the former deer park of Nottingham Castle. It still had gas lighting and restricted access for cars. Not the kind of place he would be invited to visit.

'The homeowners said the burglars had taken thousands of pounds in cash. It's surprising how much people leave lying around, isn't it? So I asked them, how many thousands of pounds? And they didn't know exactly. So it just goes to show.'

He didn't specify what it showed. But Cooper could guess. It was the sort of comment Luke Irvine would have made. Luke had strong views on the uneven distribution of wealth, the divide between what he called the 'haves' and 'have nots'. And, on his detective constable's pay, he regarded himself as one of the 'have nots'. He was probably right.

Here at Forest Fields, the perpetrator had worn gloves, no doubt about it. There were no prints anywhere, according to the frustrated crime scene examiner.

Through a window, Cooper could see Diane Fry watching officers in scene suits conducting a fingertip search in the alley. One of them reached the edge of the search area at a low wall and stood up, arching his back to relieve the pain from crouching for so long. Cooper saw him stop, lean over the wall and reach into the garden of the neighbouring property. Then he stopped and raised a hand to get the attention of his supervisor.

'What have they found?' asked Cooper when Fry entered the house.

'A pair of latex gloves. It looks as though our man must have used them to avoid leaving prints, then chucked them in the neighbour's wheelie bin.'

'They never think these things through, do they?'

'Not too often, thank God. It makes life a bit easier for us.'

'Do we have any idea when it happened?' said Cooper. 'It must have been within the last four days.'

'There's no way of telling. It was reported by the postman, who noticed the damage this morning. But he hadn't delivered anything to this address for the past week or more, so that doesn't necessarily prove anything.'

'What was he delivering?'

'Oh, just the usual bundle of junk mail. You can't escape that even when you're dead.'

Cooper remembered the neighbour he'd encountered on his last visit to Forest Fields.

317

'Has anyone spoken to the people next door?'

'Of course,' said Fry. 'It's standard procedure, even in Nottingham.'

'And?'

'They heard nothing, saw nothing, don't have anything to say about it.'

Cooper gestured around the sitting room. 'A smashed window, a broken vase, an empty house being ransacked?'

'The gentleman says he has the TV on very loud because he's a bit deaf.'

'Deaf, blind and dumb, then.'

'Pretty much.'

Cooper looked again at the table where Roger Farrell's laptop had been. The folder didn't seem quite as full as when he was here last. He tried to recall what had been in it. Household utility bills, that was all. He hadn't made a closer examination than that. And it still seemed to contain household bills.

So what had been taken and why? Unless a perpetrator was identified from the latex gloves, he might never know.

They found him a spare office to use at St Ann's. Well, it probably wasn't spare like those standing empty at Edendale. It was just vacant for the time being, as if a DI was on leave and would be back any minute.

It felt odd to Cooper sitting in someone else's office, with unfamiliar furniture and a different carpet. And a different view from the window too. The city was out there, a world he didn't belong to.

A short while later, Detective Constable Jamie Callaghan arrived with a woman Cooper didn't recognise. Callaghan spoke to Diane Fry, then came to the office, making a show of knocking on the door before entering.

'This is Mrs Ella Webster,' she said. 'Detective Inspector Cooper. DI Cooper has been investigating the circumstances of your father's suicide.'

'Oh, come in,' said Cooper. 'Thank you for taking the time.'

He'd almost forgotten Ella Webster was coming in, though he'd insisted on seeing her.

'I'll leave you to it,' said Callaghan.

'Er, thank you, DC Callaghan.'

Callaghan smiled as he closed the door. Cooper studied the woman sitting across the desk, looking at him expectantly.

'So, Mrs Webster,' he said, 'there are just a few questions I'd like to run through with you.'

Ella Webster looked nothing like her father or even her aunt, Fay Laws. She had blonde hair and lots of it. Cooper looked closely for dark roots, suspecting it was dyed. She was more tanned than anyone in Derbyshire had a right to be, unless they spent a lot of time on a sunbed. And when she waved her hands around, her fingers glittered with rings. She was wearing a sweater, as if she found it cold.

As he ran through his questions, Cooper could see that Mrs Webster was bored. She'd been through the whole thing once and had lost interest. She gave him the same replies that Fry had reported. She knew nothing and recognised nobody.

He did discover that she had two young children back in Spain, aged five and eight. She mentioned them frequently. They were her justification for needing to return soon, her main concern when it came to arranging a funeral and all the 'fuss' that went with it.

Cooper gathered that the precious children would not be attending the funeral. He was shocked to learn that they had never actually met their maternal grandfather.

Ella Webster shrugged when he asked. 'We weren't close. We hadn't been close for a few years.'

'Three years or so?' he guessed.

She tossed back her hair. 'About that long.'

'Was there any reason for that?'

Her face fell into a stiff mask and her lips pressed tightly together.

'Nothing in particular,' she said. 'We just drifted apart.'

Cooper thought about the prisoners he'd seen when they were released from a long spell inside. Many of them, too, found their families had drifted away from them. They were often cut off from society completely, left at sea with no anchor. It rarely ended well – for them or for society.

Simon Hull was in the first interview room with the duty solicitor. He'd already been interviewed once, but a second session often produced results. Suspects became impatient or frustrated. They got tired of the tedium of walking from a cell to an interview room and back again, listening to the same old questions over and over. Sometimes, they would do and say anything to bring it to an end.

Hull was aged in his mid-forties, with heavy shoulders and large, thickly knuckled hands that he planted firmly on the table when Ben Cooper and Diane Fry entered. Cooper sat to the side and let Fry take the lead. It allowed him to study Hull more carefully. He had sandy, almost ginger hair cut in a ragged fringe. A silver stud glinted in one ear. During his time in a cell, he'd already developed that blank, hooded stare familiar from a thousand custody suite images.

Fry started the digital recording and they introduced themselves. Hull wearily repeated his name, then sat back in his chair as if he'd completed his part of the process. The solicitor glanced at his watch and ostentatiously made a note.

Fry didn't start straight away. She'd brought a dauntingly thick file of papers with her, which she placed on the desk with a thump. Most of the reports couldn't possibly refer to Simon Hull. They were just padding, to give the impression she had far more information than she actually did. She took her time studying it before she looked up, knowing Hull would be watching her with growing unease.

Then she met his eye and smiled. Cooper knew that smile. He hoped it was making Simon Hull even more uneasy.

'You won't have met my colleague before,' said Fry. 'Detective Inspector Cooper is from Edendale CID in Derbyshire.'

Hull looked at him then and narrowed his eyes. 'I don't have anything to tell you,' he said. 'I have no idea what this is about. You're going to have to let me go really soon.'

The solicitor nodded and made another note. Apart from the time the interview had started and finished, he could only have been writing down the names and ranks of the interviewers. But it was all for show, all part of the charade, like Fry's padded file and Hull's protestations of innocence. If the evidence was there, they all knew there would be charges. If not, Hull was right – he would be walking out of St Ann's very soon.

'DI Cooper is here because the death of Mr Roger Farrell occurred in his area,' said Fry. 'But you knew that – didn't you, Mr Hull?'

Hull's eyes flickered. 'No comment.'

'But you did know Roger Farrell? Is that right?'

'No comment.'

Fry drew out a form. 'This is a statement from your previous employers, Arno Vale Motors. They confirm that you and Mr Farrell were both employed at their premises during the same period. I can give you the dates, if you'd like.'

Hull said nothing, but stared back at her.

'You worked together,' said Fry with unusual patience.

'Farrell was a salesman,' said Hull reluctantly. He could see there was no point in denying it when the evidence was right in front of him. 'I worked in the bodyshop. We didn't mix.'

'But you knew each other.'

322

'If you like.'

Cooper expected her to produce the photograph at that point, the one he'd found in Roger Farrell's car. It was indisputable evidence that Hull and Farrell had been friendlier than Hull was suggesting. But she didn't do that. She must be saving it, keeping her cards close to her chest to allow her suspect to show himself a liar.

'So when did you last have contact with Roger Farrell?' asked Fry instead.

'You've asked me this before.'

'I'm asking again.'

'No comment.'

'Have you ever visited his address in Forest Fields?'

'No comment.'

'And where were you last night, Mr Hull?'

'At home.'

'All night?'

Hull couldn't resist a smirk. 'Weren't you lot watching me, then?'

'Why should we?'

He sat back and folded his arms. 'I told you – I have no idea what this is all about.'

'It's about the nature of your relationship with Roger Farrell,' said Fry. 'So what was it?'

'No comment.'

The solicitor cleared his throat and intervened.

'Detective Sergeant Fry, could you clarify what exactly my client is accused of? It might help us to make progress.'

'Accessory to murder,' said Fry.

Hull laid his hands on the table again. 'What?'

'We're investigating a series of murders here in Nottingham. We have evidence that you were associated with Roger Farrell and that you were in the area at the time of at least one of the murders. I would be considering a charge of accessory to murder at least, if not conspiracy to murder.'

Hull's face flushed angrily and he turned to the solicitor. 'Can they do that?'

'Well, it depends on the nature of the evidence.'

'That's bollocks. They haven't got anything.'

Fry didn't react, except with a small, confident smile. That seemed to unnerve Hull more than anything else.

Cooper recalled his impression from the photograph of a physical resemblance between Roger Farrell and Simon Hull. He couldn't see it now. People changed, of course. They moved on in their lives, headed in different directions. Inseparable friends could drift apart.

Fry turned her head slightly towards him and Cooper understood the gesture. It was his invitation to come in. A switch of interviewer kept the suspect off balance.

'So, Mr Hull,' said Cooper, waiting for the man's eyes to swivel his way, 'what I'm wondering is this – which of you went around the Forest Road area asking questions about Roger Farrell? Was it you?'

Hull hesitated for a second. 'No comment.'

That was interesting. Had he been on the verge of denying it for that second? Cooper pressed on quickly.

'Or was it your friend Anwar Sharif? Was that *his* job?'

But Hull shook his head. 'I don't know what you mean.'

'Both of you, then?'

'No comment.'

To distract his attention, Cooper slid across the print-outs Luke Irvine had produced from his online search for *Secrets of Death*.

'Does the name of this website mean anything to you, Mr Hull?' he asked.

The solicitor leaned over to examine the printouts, then glanced at his client.

'Is this—?' began Hull. But the solicitor shook his head and Hull changed his mind. 'No comment.'

'Mr Hull, we believe you knew what Roger Farrell had been doing,' said Fry. 'You were aware that he was responsible for the murders of at least three young women. You found that out in some way, didn't you?'

'No comment.'

'I wonder how you came by the information. It seems to me there aren't many possibilities. Was it some bit of gossip you picked up when you were visiting prostitutes yourself, perhaps?'

'That's ridiculous,' said Hull, going even redder.

But Fry nodded thoughtfully. 'It seems feasible to me. You might have heard something and put two and two together, worked out it was your old colleague they were talking about.'

'No way.'

'In that case,' said Fry, 'I can only conclude that Roger Farrell told you himself.'

That took even Cooper by surprise. He hadn't considered that possibility. Had it come into Fry's mind just now as she was speaking?

Whatever the case, the comment seemed to have struck home. Simon Hull sat dumb, all the colour draining from his face. For a few seconds he was unable to control his reactions. His fists clenched spasmodically and he scowled at Fry, his expression a mixture of anger and fear.

The solicitor looked alarmed too and stepped in to intervene.

'Detective Sergeant Fry, I think I'd like to consult with my client.'

Fry nodded calmly. 'Interview suspended.'

'What do you think?' said Cooper when they left the interview room. 'Was there anything there, behind the "no comment"s?'

'Not much,' said Fry with a shrug.

'But you definitely had a hit with your suggestion about Farrell telling them himself about his murders. That was inspired.'

'Thank you.'

'Hull didn't know how to answer that. You can push him on it later.'

'That's what I intend to do.'

Fry didn't take compliments very well. She had never learned how to do it with any grace.

'And I did wonder about the website stuff,' she said. 'He almost reacted to that.'

'Yes, I thought so too.'

'It's nice that we agree on something.'

Cooper had never heard the word *nice* used in quite that way before. But this was Diane Fry. She could give anything a different meaning.

'And maybe when I put it to him about one of them asking questions around Forest Road,' said Cooper. 'I had the feeling he considered trying to point the finger at Sharif on that one, when I gave him the opportunity. I'm hoping he'll reflect on that.'

'We'll get more out of them,' said Fry confidently.

'Do you think so?'

'We picked them up separately and they've been kept apart since. One of them will let something slip eventually. I think we might be able to tie them in to some of the girls in the Forest Road area. I'm hoping a search of their properties will produce something useful in that respect.'

'Tie them in how?' asked Cooper.

'Hasn't it occurred to you that Hull and Sharif may be running some of those girls themselves? Setting them up in suitable properties, distributing pay-as-you-go phones, arranging the clients? And taking a cut of the proceeds, of course.'

'You didn't mention that theory.'

Fry shrugged. 'It seemed a fairly obvious possibility.'

Cooper forced himself to ignore her tone. Now wasn't the time for being at loggerheads. They had to work together, as best they could.

'Well, it would explain why they might have been trying to intimidate Farrell and scare him off without incriminating themselves,' he said.

'Yes, it would. But it's speculation at the moment. I'll let you know what we turn up.'

'By the way,' said Cooper, 'has Simon Hull's vehicle been examined – the Jeep Grand Cherokee?'

'Yes, why?'

'I'm wondering if there was any recent damage on it.'

'I don't think so. The examiner would have mentioned it, if there was. Did you think there would be?'

'It was just a possibility. I might not recognise a make of vehicle as well as I think I do.'

'I don't know what you're talking about.'

'It doesn't matter.'

Cooper reminded himself that Simon Hull ran a garage and would have had plenty of time to carry out a few repairs and do a respray.

He followed Fry along an unfamiliar corridor to the next interview room.

'Diane,' he said, 'one more thing. The person who was asking questions about Farrell – are you sure it was Hull or Sharif?'

'Our one willing witness isn't good on description, as you might have gathered.'

'What about getting her in to look at some photos, then?'

Fry sighed. 'Yes,' she said. 'If she'll come.'

Before they moved on, Cooper called up Gavin Murfin.

'Surveillance here,' he answered.

'What's Anson Tate doing, Gavin?'

'Nothing. It's all quiet.'

'All quiet' was the surveillance equivalent of 'no

comment'. An accumulation of negatives might eventually lead to something positive. Or so it was hoped.

'He's still at home?'

'He hasn't budged. I've established which is his flat on the top floor and I've found a spot where I can see the window. He's definitely there. He's passed by the window a couple of times. I think he's probably eating his dinner.'

'Okay.'

'So what do you want me to do? I could chat to a couple of the other tenants, see what they know about him.'

'No way,' said Cooper.

'I'm good at it,' said Murfin. 'It's my job, don't forget.'

'It *was* your job. It didn't work out.'

'Oh, yeah.'

'You can knock off,' said Cooper. 'He won't be planning anything now.'

'Fine. I'll get back to my car.'

Murfin seemed to be breathing hard and Cooper pictured him labouring up Buxton Road, which was on a definite hill.

'Then I might pop down to May's Café for a pie and a cuppa before I go home,' said Murfin.

'But, Gavin—'

He was too late. Murfin had gone. He would have to find out the bad news for himself about the loss of May's Café.

Anwar Sharif seemed much more composed than Simon Hull. In Interview Room 2, he sat looking relaxed with a bottle of water in his hand, chatting quietly to his solicitor. And this was his own legal representative, as Fry mentioned before they entered the room. Was Sharif the more organised of the two and perhaps the one with the money?

From his photograph, he'd looked to be in his late thirties. But closer up, in the unflattering light of the interview room, Cooper thought he was probably the wrong side of forty. He was trying hard to look cool, with a neatly trimmed beard and gelled hair.

'Mr Sharif, we'd like you to tell us about your relationship with Roger Farrell,' began Fry without hesitation when the recording had started.

Sharif put down his bottle and stared at her.

'No comment,' he said.

Cooper sighed inwardly. This one would be a hard nut to crack, even for Diane Fry. The only hope was that a search of their homes would produce something.

That evening at home in Foolow, Cooper checked his mobile phone for messages, then the answering machine on his landline. Of course, there was no reason to think that *she* would have his home number. But she'd taken the trouble to get his mobile number, hadn't she? So you never knew.

His frustration was that he hadn't asked for her number when they met at the Barrel Inn the night before last. All he had on his caller list was the number of the mortuary office and that was no use. Of course, he could be misleading himself. It might simply have been an informal meeting to talk about her study into suicides. Was that all they'd talked about? No, it wasn't.

Cooper fed the cat. That was one job he never missed. The cat flap had been installed and he could tell that Hopes had been out exploring the neighbourhood. When he arrived home, she'd been sitting on the adjoining wall between Tollhouse Cottage and the neighbours. And there had been another cat with her, a ginger-and-white tom. His cat was better at making friends than he was himself.

'Well, I'll see you next time,' said Diane Fry. 'Make it very soon, won't you? And Zack – I can't wait to see him walking.'

Angie had everything packed ready to go. A bagful of used nappies had gone in the wheelie bin. The baby was asleep. The sun outside was shining. And Diane smiled.

'Of course, Sis. I hope everything goes well.'

The Renault hatchback turned in from Clifton Lane. The exhaust was a bit too loud, but Diane didn't care. The man at the steering wheel nodded curtly to her, but didn't get out. Angie waved and trotted to the car to begin loading everything. Zack went into the baby seat without stirring. Within a few minutes, they were ready to go.

Diane waved them off until they'd disappeared. Then she heaved a deep sigh, went back into her apartment and poured herself a very large drink.

27

Day 7

First thing that morning, Cooper had to brief his team and give them assignments. In the CID room he was met by a set of expectant faces.

'Anson Tate,' he said. 'He was a journalist, wasn't he?' He looked to Carol Villiers, who always seemed to have that sort of detail at her fingertips.

'Yes, he worked for one of the major regional newspaper publishers, but he was made redundant three or four years ago when they went through a phase of centralisation. Tate went freelance, but couldn't make a living at it.'

'What sort of stories did he cover as a freelance?'

'I have no idea.'

Cooper turned to Irvine. 'Luke, see if you can find out, will you? Research Tate's journalism background. A lot of stuff is online.'

'What am I looking for?'

'Look for any possible links. Did he do a feature at some time about suicide websites? Any stories about actual suicides? There may be some way that he came across the *Secrets of Death* site or the people operating it, and knows more about it than anyone else.'

'It might take a while,' said Irvine.

'Just do what you can, will you?'

'Yes, okay.'

Cooper turned to Murfin.

'Gavin, I want you back on surveillance at Tate's flat. Keep me up to date on what he's doing.'

Murfin didn't look pleased. 'Couldn't you just ask him to come in for a chat?'

'I don't want Tate slipping away from us. It's possible he spotted you outside his flat yesterday.'

'Well, I doubt it. I'm trained to blend in, like.'

'Even so. I don't want him doing anything stupid. He needs watching.'

'But—'

'Just do it, Gavin. You're not here to ask questions.'

'Fair enough.'

Everyone turned then and stared at each other. Cooper knew they hardly ever heard him speak like that to one of his team. He didn't have time to worry about it. Right now there was a horrible thought in his head that he wanted to concentrate on before it escaped him. He took no notice as Murfin slouched out of the room, grumbling quietly.

'Tate could be crucial in making a case against the two suspects the Major Crime Unit have picked up,' said Cooper. 'He's the only credible witness we may have at our disposal. Diane Fry and her colleagues in Nottingham need something concrete to put to Simon Hull and Anwar Sharif.'

'Hull and Sharif?' asked Dev Sharma in a puzzled tone.

Cooper realised that not all his team were aware of the connection with EMSOU's murder inquiry. He brought them up to speed as far as he could.

'It puts a whole different light on Roger Farrell,' said Irvine. 'A pity we didn't know about all this from the start.'

'It couldn't be helped.'

'By the way, we've got some preliminary results from the laptop you recovered from Roger Farrell's address,' said Villiers, picking up a report from her desk.

'Well, that's something.'

Cooper could at least breathe a sigh of relief that he'd made the decision to seize the laptop when he had. Otherwise, he felt sure it would be gone now. And the preliminary results had come through quickly, which was helpful.

'Not really,' said Villiers. 'Unless you think no news is good news. The initial examination reveals no sign of involvement with a website called *secretsofdeath.org*. His browser history and email records contain no references to *Secrets of Death* or anything resembling it. They've drawn out a list of contacts from his address book, so we can have a trawl through those.'

Villiers passed across a list and Cooper ran his eye down it without seeing any name he recognised.

'But otherwise,' said Villiers, 'the forensic examiner says it appears to be a perfectly straightforward device for personal and business use. Farrell did his household accounts on a spreadsheet, wrote letters in MS Word, used online banking and watched films on Netflix. He liked obscure sci-fi movies, apparently.'

Cooper put the list down, disappointed. 'Ask them to keep trying.'

'I will.'

'Okay, there's plenty to get on with. Let me know straight away if you turn up anything significant.'

When the phone rang, Carol Villiers had news that took all Cooper's attention.

'They've found what?' he said.

'A burned-out car. It's been identified as a black Land Rover Discovery.'

'Where?'

'On a track at the top of Sycamore Crescent,' said Villiers. 'That's on the Woodlands Estate. Do you know it?'

'Know it?' said Cooper. 'I've already been there once this week.'

When Cooper arrived on the Woodlands Estate, the burned-out wreck was being winched on to a low-loader. He could see for himself that it had been a Land Rover Discovery. The shape was quite distinctive.

The colour of it was less obvious. The blaze had stripped the paint off the bodywork, leaving bare, scorched metal. It had also melted the tyres, blown out the windows and consumed the interior, leaving just the metal seat frames. The doors, bonnet and boot had all been left open to allow the flames to spread. This was no simple engine fire. Large amounts of accelerant had been used to make sure the job was done properly.

But there would be traces of paint left under the door sills or on other parts of the body that had been shielded from the flames. If a vehicle examiner said it was black, then it was black.

Of course, the number-plates had gone and there would be nothing of any value to recover from the interior. But with any luck a forensic examination would retrieve the chassis number. And then the owner of the Land Rover could be identified.

Cooper turned to Villiers as the wreck was lowered on to the recovery vehicle.

'Did anyone see anything?' he asked.

'What do you think? Joy-riders and burned-out cars are a common occurrence round here. The neighbourhood team says some of the kids keep a stockpile of petrol cans and disposable lighters ready for a bit of fun. The Woodies love a good fire. One thing, though . . .'

'What?'

'A lady at the house over there says she heard someone paid the local kids a few quid to do the job in this case.'

'Oh? And where did she hear that?'

'She's the type who watches what's going on up and down the street. In good weather she leaves her windows open so she can listen to conversations.'

'Is that what she said?'

'No, not in so many words. But that seems to be how she came to overhear some youths talking about it. She couldn't see which youths they were, of course.'

'We could ask around to see which of them has just got in a supply of fags and booze.'

'They probably have other ways of making a bit of money round here,' said Villiers.

'True.'

Cooper looked at the streets around him. There were plenty of other places you could take a vehicle to dispose of it by setting it on fire. So why here in particular?

He could see Marnie Letts' house a few doors down Sycamore Crescent, near the corner with Elm Street. He recalled his conversation with her a few days ago, when she'd claimed not to know much about cars. Marnie had said she wasn't be able to recognise one car from another, except for a BMW, because her neighbour had one. And she drove a Nissan herself. So what about her husband, the tree surgeon?

Cooper shook his head. Why would Marnie Letts mention seeing a Land Rover at Heeley Bank if she knew perfectly well who it belonged to? Perhaps she had taken into account the possibility that visitors like the Cooks might have caught it on a dashboard camera.

A crowd of spectators was gathering at the corner of the street, attracted by the police activity. They were laughing and taking photos with their mobile phones as if they were watching a performance of street theatre staged for their benefit.

When an officer cleared the way to allow the low-loader to exit the street, some of the crowd cheered.

At least they'd provided some entertainment for the Woodies.

Diane Fry took Jamie Callaghan in for another inter-view session with Simon Hull and Anwar Sharif. They were running out of time to keep the two men in custody without making formal charges and this would probably be their last shot.

But Fry had a new piece of evidence at her disposal. DNA traces from the latex gloves found dumped in the neighbour's wheelie bin at Forest Fields had matched the sample taken from Simon Hull when he was arrested. Partial prints had been recovered from inside the gloves too, but they were less clear. It didn't matter. She had the ammunition she needed.

'When we asked you previously if you'd visited Roger Farrell's address in Forest Fields, you declined to answer. Would you care to change your response, Mr Hull?'

'Why should I?'

'Because we have your fingerprints.'

Hull shrugged. 'I suppose I must have been there at some time. Like you said, I did know him.'

'When would that have been?'

'I can't remember. Ages ago. Ages.'

'Were you wearing these gloves at the time?'

'What?'

Fry showed him the latex gloves in their evidence bag. 'That must have been a strange sort of social call.'

'I've never seen those before.'

'It's too late for that, Mr Hull. Your DNA is inside

them. And you left them in the wheelie bin of the next-door neighbour after your break-in. That was foolish.'

Hull looked at his solicitor, who seemed to be getting worried. 'I'm advising my client not to answer any more questions,' he said.

'But that doesn't stop me asking them,' said Fry, sensing that she was close to her objective.

'If you insist, Detective Sergeant.'

Fry turned back to Simon Hull.

'Mr Hull, why did you break into Roger Farrell's house? Was it to remove evidence? I suppose, after he died, you must have panicked and wanted to conceal the fact that you were connected to him.'

'No comment,' said Hull.

'So the question is – were you an accomplice to Farrell's murders? Did you get some kind of pleasure from the murders of those girls? Did you and Anwar Sharif join in or were you just watching? On the other hand, perhaps that wasn't your role. Maybe you helped Farrell afterwards, assisted him to escape the consequences of his crimes? Which was it, Mr Hull?'

Hull's face flushed bright red. Fry was pleased to see it. She knew from the previous interviews that he could be pushed close to the edge by the right questions. Despite his solicitor's efforts to caution him, Hull could no longer hold back.

'No, you've got it all wrong,' he said. 'That's not what we were doing at all.'

'But you were observed by witnesses asking questions about him around the area.'

'No, that wasn't us. We *saw* that bloke, the one asking questions all over the place. He was a journalist. He knew all about Roger Farrell anyway. And he knew about Victoria Jenkins too.'

'A journalist?' said Fry.

Hull scowled. 'Well, that's what he said he was, anyway. An investigative journalist. If you ask me, him and Roger Farrell were a pair made for each other.'

Priorities were always a problem and this inquiry was becoming more complicated. Cooper knew this wasn't an urgent priority, but his instinct was nagging him about something.

He stopped off in the centre of Edendale on his way back from the Woodlands and asked Carol Villiers to wait while he walked down to the river. He'd brought the framed photograph he'd found in Alex Denning's flat in Derby. He held it in front of him as he stepped out on to the river bank. Yes, he'd been right about the place it had been taken.

The modern footbridge over the River Eden had been built with decorative cast iron railings. In the last couple of years, people had begun to attach padlocks to the bridge as a symbol of their eternal love, each couple throwing the key into the water below. The tradition had reached the East Midlands from China, via Paris. In some parts of the world, the fashion had already reached its peak and was dying out. As usual, Edendale was a decade or two behind the times.

At least the trend was a boost for local gift shops. They'd begun selling heart-shaped, personalised padlocks aimed directly at the lovelorn couples market. Eventually, the bridge would be covered in locks like a metallic flower display. It might become another of those quirky Peak District customs with their origins lost in time, like well dressing and money trees.

That was if the bridge didn't fall down first or the river wasn't blocked by a rising dam of submerged keys.

Cooper walked forward until he was at the point where Alex Denning and his girlfriend had been standing. There were dozens of locks here and it took several minutes to go through them, looking at their inscriptions. Finally he found one that said 'Alex and Joolz'. No other indication of who the mysterious Joolz was. He guessed she probably wasn't christened that either. Jules, Julie? It was hard to say.

As he was holding the photograph, Cooper felt something in the back. He prised open the clips and removed the backing. A black business card dropped into his hand. Gold edging, a string of letters and numbers. At least Alex Denning had taken some precautions to keep his *Secrets of Death* password secure.

A group of people went by, their footsteps making the deck of the bridge vibrate uneasily. Cooper recalled that this bridge was supposed to be haunted. A jilted bride who'd thrown herself into the river or something like that.

It was always the most tragic stories that left legends of ghosts behind. Nobody ever claimed to have seen the terrifying spectre of some benign granny who'd died peacefully in her bed from old age. There were no hordes of ghostly flu victims haunting the streets of Edendale, though there ought to have been hundreds of them after the First World War. Legend had just left the murdered and executed, the desperate and helpless. And, of course, the suicides.

You could see the Bargate Bridge from here. It was an ancient stone construction, described in the guide books as seventeenth-century. No lorries or other HGVs were allowed on the bridge now. And the road itself was one-way, because of its narrow width. So cars drove near the middle, which took the strain off the arches and buttresses, and left room for pedestrians along the parapet. That was where tourists stopped to take photographs of the river.

And that was also where Anson Tate had intended to make his jump, until the Canadian tourist had intervened, locking Tate in a powerful grip to prevent him going over. Tate would have jumped without that intervention. He would have ended up in the water below the weir, where wet rocks protruded above the surface.

Cooper wondered about the passing tourist who'd been the first to restrain Anson Tate from throwing himself off. The picture in his mind made a distinct contrast with the incident Superintendent Branagh had referred to in Derby, when youths had taunted a young man on the roof of a shopping centre car park with shouts of 'Jump!'.

But wasn't that exactly what someone had been doing, though more subtly? The owner of the *Secrets of Death* website had appeared to be the friend and adviser of potential suicides. In reality he was just one more person shouting 'Jump!'.

Cooper liked the proportions of Bargate Bridge. They knew how to build bridges in the seventeenth century. Its arches were elegant as well as strong. It looked as though it would stand over the River Eden for ever.

There was one other thing that struck him today, though. The bridge wasn't that high. A fall from that parapet to the water probably wouldn't kill you.

Cooper remained staring at the bridge for a few minutes, until he sensed Carol Villiers standing impatient alongside him.

'Anson Tate,' he said, almost to himself. 'He's much cleverer than he seems. I bet he's a success at everything he sets out to do.'

Villiers looked at Cooper in surprise. 'Mr Tate? Ben, he attempted suicide, but was held back by a passer-by. He's the one who failed.'

'Failed? No, he didn't,' said Cooper. 'He was very successful.'

'What do you mean?'

'Well, think about it for a minute. What is his story? What did he try to do?'

'He tried to throw himself off Bargate Bridge.'

'Did he?' said Cooper. 'There are plenty of high places around here. Good long drops if you were going to jump. Stanage Edge, Kinder Downfall, Peveril Castle. Not that I'm recommending it – it's insane. But if you *were* planning to do that . . .'

'What are you saying, Ben?'

'I'm not saying anything. I'm asking a question. I'm

asking why you would choose Bargate Bridge instead. It's only thirty or forty feet, and you'd land in water. From Peveril Castle, the Peak Cavern gorge is nearly two hundred and fifty feet. So why that bridge?'

Villiers looked thoughtful. 'Because it's more public?'

'You would make more of an impact at Peveril Castle, if you chose a busy time for visitors to the cavern.'

'What other reason is there?'

'Because,' said Cooper, 'there's more likely to be someone passing who will stop you. A Canadian tourist from Vancouver, for example. You could almost count on it.'

Cooper was suddenly overwhelmed with horror at the realisation of what he was saying, at what Anson Tate must have done.

28

Diane Fry arrived in Edendale and drove straight up to West Street. She entered the CID room, stopped and looked around. This was her former territory, yet she didn't belong here any more. One of these desks had been hers, but there was no trace left of her presence, not even her initials carved into the surface.

'Where is Ben Cooper?' she said.

DC Becky Hurst looked up. 'He's out.'

Fry sighed. 'Is this it, then?'

'We do our best,' said Hurst.

Fry hadn't imagined working with DS Sharma and DCs Irvine and Hurst, let alone Gavin Murfin. But there they were at their desks and here she was. It would have to do.

'Stop what you're doing,' she said. 'I've got some important information on your inquiry.'

Hurst and Irvine looked to Sharma for guidance, but he barely responded. Murfin simply shrugged his shoulders and stopped what he was doing without argument.

'I'm not sure how much you know about this

already,' she said. 'But let me explain EMSOU's involvement.'

Fry briefed them on her interviews with Simon Hull and Anwar Sharif, her efforts to confirm their connection to Roger Farrell. She was surprised how little Ben Cooper seemed to have told his team. But perhaps he wanted them to focus on their own particular tasks.

'Now Simon Hull has given us some significant details in an interview this morning,' she said at last. 'He says that he and Sharif were well aware of the person who was asking questions about Farrell. We've been told that he claimed to be an investigative journalist.'

'Oh, that sounds like my territory,' said Irvine.

'And what are you doing, DC Irvine?'

'I've been doing some research into Anson Tate's history as a journalist. Trawling through links to articles he's written in the past.'

'Good. That sounds useful.'

Dev Sharma had been listening intently, leaning forward in his chair, his eyes fixed unnervingly on Fry but not commenting. So when he began to speak, Fry immediately paid attention.

'Some of those prostitutes are trafficked,' said Sharma. 'The Immigration Enforcement team picked a couple of them up during the operation I was liaising on earlier this week.'

'From the Forest Road area?' asked Fry.

'Yes.'

Fry studied him, wondering how much she could rely on him. She liked the look of Sharma and had heard positive things about him. She took a decision.

'DS Sharma, could you speak to Immigration Enforcement and see if one of the prostitutes might be willing to talk?'

'I'm sure they would if they thought they could avoid deportation by co-operating,' said Sharma.

'Get on to it right away, will you?'

She saw Sharma hesitate then. Of course, she had no rank over him. He was Ben Cooper's DS. He ought to take instructions from Cooper, not from this interfering detective sergeant sticking her nose in from the Major Crime Unit.

'I think Ben would appreciate it when he gets back,' she said more gently. 'It will save a lot of time if you do it now.'

Sharma nodded reluctantly. 'All right.' He went back to his desk to make some phone calls.

'We've been going through all the previous suicides in the area,' said Hurst. 'There are quite a lot of them.'

'You've been told to look for connections to the Farrell case?'

'Yes.'

'You're probably wasting your time, I'm afraid.'

A few moments later, the atmosphere in the room changed suddenly and several pairs of eyes swivelled towards the door.

'What's going on?'

Fry turned to find Ben Cooper in the doorway, with Carol Villiers close behind him.

'Sorry. But you weren't here and this couldn't wait.'

'What couldn't?'

'Simon Hull has opened up. We've got what we need from him. And you might not like it.'

Not for the first time, Cooper could see that something had been going on behind his back. Irvine and Hurst looked particularly guilty. He gestured Diane Fry into his office and made her sit down across the desk from him. Now he was in the DI's chair again.

'Let's hear it, then,' he said.

Fry went over the details again, impatient and fidgeting. He nodded as she talked. It seemed indisputable that Anson Tate had been the journalist asking questions about Roger Farrell in Nottingham. The description Simon Hull had given was very accurate and he'd since confirmed the ID from photographs. Anwar Sharif had backed him up on this, if nothing else.

'Farrell is the link,' said Fry. 'Tate is behind your suicides, not Hull and Sharif. They were into the black-mail business.'

'So you've come to the same conclusion as me,' said Cooper calmly when she'd finished.

Fry stared at him. 'You're saying you'd already figured this out?'

'It was starting to seem likely.'

'I see. Well, it couldn't have been one of the successful suicides, obviously. It would have to be someone who is still alive. A survivor, then. Your local man, Anson Tate.'

'He isn't really local,' said Cooper. 'He lives in Edendale now, but he only moved here a few months ago from Mansfield.'

Fry had gone very still. 'Mansfield?' she said. 'Why didn't you tell me that?'

Cooper blinked. 'It didn't seem relevant. Why?'

'One of the murdered students, Victoria Jenkins. She was from Mansfield.'

'It could just be a coincidence.'

'You've never really believed in coincidences, though,' said Fry. 'You're the man who sees connections in everything.'

'I can't see the connection in this case.'

'That's because you're not looking at it from the proper angle.'

Cooper gazed at her. From the start, he'd been trying to look at the situation from above, gain an overview without being blinded by the details. Had he failed to do that? Was there some other angle he could be looking at it from?

He hated to admit that. But Diane Fry was so often right. In the past, she'd nudged him into seeing things differently and it had turned out to be the right way in the end.

'Tate must have spent a lot of time on this,' said Cooper. 'The planning alone had to be immense. So why did he target Farrell so obsessively? Presumably it was something to with the killing of the three girls in Nottingham.'

'That's right.'

'What was so personal about it for him?'

'I don't know. Yet.'

Cooper got up and went back into the CID room, with Fry following him. Luke Irvine had his head down behind his screen, as if trying to avoid any flak that might be flying around.

'Luke, have you been focusing your search on when Tate was working in Mansfield?' asked Cooper.

Irvine had his finger poised to keep scrolling, but he stopped, staring at the screen as if frozen.

'Yes. This one,' he said. 'This is the one.'

'What is it?'

'See for yourself.'

Irvine tapped a couple of keys and several sheets of paper slid off the printer. Fry snatched one up. She hardly needed to read the text. She recognised the person in the photograph.

'Victoria Jenkins,' she said.

'Who is Victoria Jenkins?' asked Villiers.

'Was,' said Fry. 'She was the last of the three murder victims. A media student at Nottingham Trent University. Twenty years old. She was found strangled in an alleyway. And she was from Mansfield.'

'Like Anson Tate?'

'And not only that.' Fry waved the printout. 'He'd written a story about her.'

Cooper took a copy of the cutting. There was a photograph of a young Victoria Jenkins waving a results sheet with a huge grin on her face. The accompanying story was glowing, and felt oddly creepy and syco-phantic when it carried Anson Tate's byline.

'This goes back to two years before her death, before she became a student at NTU,' said Fry.

'Victoria Jenkins was a multiple A-star student in

her A-level results,' added Irvine. 'Tate did an interview with her for the local papers at the time.'

Cooper scanned through the article. Victoria was described as a brilliant student with a promising future ahead of her. In fact, Tate had used the word 'rosy'. There were more clichés and purple prose, but a glimpse of the real girl did emerge.

Victoria Jenkins came from a poor family on a Mansfield housing estate, one of four children brought up by their mother on her own. Victoria told her interviewer about struggling to afford books and having to help look after her younger siblings. But she also talked about her determination to make the most of her opportunities and follow her dreams. She had ambitions to be a TV presenter one day. But there was a problem. She couldn't move too far away to attend university because her mother still had the three younger children at home. So she had been delighted to be accepted on a media course not far away in Nottingham.

Fry put her copy of the article down. 'Is this the reason for Tate's subsequent actions? Did he fall for her? He was a single man, heading towards middle age. It can happen.'

Hurst looked up, aghast. 'My God. She was an awful lot younger than him. Twenty-five years, at least.'

'An unhealthy obsession certainly,' said Cooper. 'I wonder if he visited her in Nottingham.'

'Perhaps he was a customer?' suggested Fry.

Cooper shook his head. 'I can't imagine it, Diane.'

'Well, you never know. He is a man.'

'Tate isn't that type.'

'If you say so. I'm not convinced.'

Cooper sat quietly for a moment, turning over the new information in his mind. There was a lot to take in.

Anson Tate had planned everything so carefully. That *Secrets of Death* website must have been his. For a start, it was no coincidence that he didn't have a computer in the flat but had to use one at the library. He would have disposed of whatever machine he used, right after the death of Roger Farrell. It could be anywhere now and they would never stand a chance of finding it without information from Tate himself.

And it was worse than that. Tate had lured people in and made them practise their means of suicide until they got it exactly right. Surely, if he'd really intended to kill himself that day on Bargate Bridge, he would have done it properly. He wouldn't be alive now and living in his cheap little flat in Edendale. But his hadn't been a genuine attempt. He had never intended to die. He'd chosen too busy a location, had timed his actions so that he would be prevented from jumping by some helpful passer-by.

Yes, Tate had been a very careful planner indeed. He'd even planned his own failure.

When the forensic examiner rang to say he'd recovered the chassis number from the burned-out Land Rover, Cooper hardly needed to ask who it belonged to.

'Anson Tate,' he said. 'That clinches it.'

'Should we go and get him?' said Fry.

'*We?*'

'Well, it's your case, of course . . .' she said.

Cooper smiled. It was the one concession from Fry that he'd been waiting for.

'Come along, then,' he said.

'It would be a pleasure.'

Gavin Murfin was still on surveillance outside Anson Tate's flat. Cooper was about to call him to check that Tate was still at home, when Murfin rang.

'He's on the move,' he said.

'Tate?'

'Yes, a taxi has just pulled up at the house and he's getting in.'

'Are you in your car, Gavin?'

'Yep.'

'Follow him, but at a discreet distance. And keep me informed where he's heading. We're on our way.'

29

In the West Street parking area, Cooper jumped automatically into his Toyota and held open the door. Fry stood on the tarmac staring at the bodywork.

'Get in, then,' said Cooper. 'Or I'm going without you.'

She reluctantly got in and snapped on her seat belt, and Cooper swung out through the barrier into the Edendale traffic. It was almost like old times, having Diane Fry in the car with him on the way to make an arrest. Almost, but not quite. She still had the rank of sergeant. And he was an inspector.

'We could have taken my car,' she said. 'It has less damage on it. So it's probably more legal on the road.'

'There's nothing wrong with the RAV,' said Cooper. 'Just a few scratches. It can survive a lot worse than that.'

As they drove, Cooper was waiting for news of Anson Tate's whereabouts.

'Will he be expecting us to have figured it out, do you think?' said Fry.

'Tate is far from stupid,' said Cooper. 'Evil and manipulative, yes, but not stupid. He knows we'll have been looking at him carefully. And that's my fault, of course. I've scared him by pressing him too hard over the past few days.'

'I hope he hasn't bolted. It would be unfortunate to lose him like we did Roger Farrell.'

Cooper realised he didn't feel guilty at all for putting Tate under pressure. Anson Tate had presented himself as a victim. But he wasn't.

For a moment, Cooper wondered if David Kuzneski's cousin Lily Haynes had been right when she talked to him at Kuzneski's funeral. She'd suggested that his perception of people had been distorted over the years by what he'd had to deal with.

There was no way of avoiding it in this job. You always had to assume someone was lying until you could establish otherwise. The law said people were innocent until proved guilty, but that was only when a case came to trial. During a major inquiry, everyone might be guilty. And that was the way a police officer had to approach an unknown individual. So of course it distorted your perceptions.

Gavin Murfin came on his direct radio channel.

'Tate's taxi is driving out of town. Heading south. Eyam maybe or Foolow. Perhaps he's planning to call on you, Ben.'

Murfin made it sound like a joke, but Cooper went cold at the thought of Tate knowing where he lived.

'What does he mean?' asked Fry. 'You live in Edendale. That little place in Welbeck Street with a cat and the old lady next door.'

'I've moved,' said Cooper.

'I didn't know that.'

'There wasn't any reason why I should tell you.'

'No.'

Cooper had a sudden, sharp memory then of Diane Fry calling unexpectedly at his flat in Welbeck Street on the day he moved in, bringing him a house-warming present. Apart from members of his family, she had been the only person ever to do that. She had claimed just to have been passing. And he recalled her very words as she handed him the gift, because they had made such an impression: *I don't like you all that much, as you know. But I brought you this.* He had pretty much given up trying to understand her since then.

'No, he's past Foolow, so you've had a lucky escape,' came Murfin's voice. 'Looks as though he's turning towards Wardlow.'

Cooper acknowledged the information. He'd driven that route himself with Villiers a few days ago on his way to visit the scene of David Kuzneski's suicide. It was the logical way to Monsal Head.

Cooper put his foot down when they got out of the town. Tate was some distance ahead of them and he didn't know what exactly the man was planning to do. They might not have much time.

'Okay, the taxi is stopping at Monsal Head in front of the hotel,' reported Murfin.

'The viewpoint car park?'

'Yes. Tate is out of the car, paying off the driver. It looks like he's going for a walk.'

'A walk? Are you kidding? Anson Tate? Keep a careful eye on him.'

'Will do.'

Gavin Murfin greeted Cooper and Fry as they parked on the side of the road just downhill from the Monsal Head Hotel. A small group of marked and unmarked police cars began to gather behind them.

'Tate is on the viaduct,' said Murfin. 'Right in the middle. He hasn't spoken to anyone, he's just standing there, leaning on the parapet. He's been there a while now and members of the public are starting to get a bit uneasy about him.'

'What do you think he's planning?' asked Fry.

'A dramatic gesture, I think. A statement. He's winding down his life, but he wants to do it publicly. With us watching.'

'Damn it.'

Carol Villiers had joined them, peering round the corner of the hotel at the scene on the viaduct.

'This explains why he disposed of his Land Rover,' she said. 'He knew he wasn't going to need it any more.'

'We'll have to get him away from there,' said Cooper.

'Tate couldn't have a better vantage point if he tried, though. Our vehicles will be obvious the moment they turn into the car park. And so will we. If he sees us coming . . .'

Cooper tried to imagine a bird's eye view of the area. The viaduct was the focal point of the landscape here, but there was a lot more going on that you couldn't see so obviously.

'Don't worry. I know a way,' he said. 'The Headstone Tunnel.'

'That would work,' said Villiers.

'Can you and Diane work your way round to the other side, in case he legs it?'

Villiers and Fry looked at each other. It was no good: they would have to work together.

'We'll meet you somewhere in the middle,' said Fry. 'I suppose.'

He turned to the uniformed officers. 'Close the trail at both ends of the viaduct. And try to keep the public back.'

Cooper got back in his car, turned by the side of the hotel and drove past the congregational chapel into the village of Great Longstone. He found a side road in the centre of the village and followed it just past a sharp dog leg to where an old railway bridge formed a hump in the road. He tucked the Toyota into the side of the lane with difficulty and climbed out.

Most people got on to the Monsal Trail at Hassop, where they could hire bikes at the café. From there, the trail followed the track of an old railway line, where a deep cutting had been blasted from the rock. At Longstone, this part of the trail was set so deep into the landscape that it was invisible from the surrounding fields.

He ran down the steps and found himself on the Monsal Trail. He'd recalled that this last section before the viaduct passed through Headstone Tunnel. Headstone was the longest tunnel on the line. It had been closed for many years after it fell into disrepair, forcing the Monsal Trail to take a diversion round it. Now it was open for walkers and cyclists. A new surface had been laid and lighting installed.

'It will only take a few minutes for me to walk through the tunnel,' said Cooper on the direct channel to Villiers. 'He won't see me coming from this direction.'

'You could have hired a bike and a cycling helmet. Tate would never have recognised you then.'

'That's actually a good idea. A bit late now, though.'

Near the former Longstone station stood Thornbridge Hall, a wedding venue for which Cooper had once read the prospectus, when marriage had still been a prospect. He'd found the brochure in the flat at Welbeck Street with a pile of others and thrown it out when he packed up to move. Thornbridge had been the home of a railway director, who had direct access to the station via his own set of steps. A later owner had filled it with items from the Duke of Newcastle's home in Nottinghamshire, when his company was contracted to demolish it. In July, a beer festival was held at Thornbridge, when beer enthusiasts camped out in the parkland among the duke's statues and fountains.

Just past the old station, Cooper passed under a bridge that crossed over the trail connecting the fields on either side. He saw the entrance to the tunnel ahead.

The approach was spectacular. The vertical walls of the cutting were buttressed by columns of dark brick, weathered to the same colour as the rock. Trees grew high above the trail on top of the embankments. Dense masses of vegetation swarmed down the rock face, brambles and long, green tendrils of ivy hanging clear as they reached towards the ground. Wild flowers peeped from the crevices, their purples, whites and yellows creating the appearance of an exotic garden. At ground level, bracken and elder saplings threatened to overwhelm the fencing, creeping on to the edges of the trail.

Near the tunnel entrance, the buttresses formed alcoves in the rock, like the walls of an ancient temple. A steel-framed mesh canopy protected walkers from the danger of boulders tumbling down from the broken rock face. A blue sign warned him that the lights were turned off at dusk. But it was almost midsummer, and the longest day of the year was only a week or two away. Dusk was a while off yet.

For the first few yards, the walls were green with moss and lichen. They survived only as far as the light reached. When Cooper was barely fifty yards in, all he could see ahead was darkness but for the long string of overhead strip lights curving away to the right where the tunnel formed a bend on its way towards the viaduct. He could smell the dampness in the walls and hear the strange echo of his own footsteps.

Cooper stopped, turned and looked back for a moment to the entrance. He saw a green arch, an unnatural bright green from sunlight flooding the trail where it ran through the cutting. The light was behind him now and ahead was darkness.

After he'd paused to let his eyes adjust, he realised that the tunnel wasn't really as dark as it had seemed.

The overhead lights created patterns of dark and light, and he could see refuges built into the walls at intervals. He was becoming conscious of the amount of rock and earth beyond those walls and above his head, and he could feel himself descending on a slight gradient.

His radio crackled. 'What's your position, Ben?'

'Almost there.'

Cooper kept walking and the lights ahead kept curving away to the right, as if he would eventually walk round in a circle and be lost in an endless tunnel for the rest of time.

Finally he saw a distant dot, which grew very slowly to be . . . a cyclist riding towards him from the other direction. Another cyclist behind, both of them wearing helmets. They said hello as they passed him to his right. Cooper didn't know whether to be relieved or not. He kept walking.

And the next light was the real end of the tunnel. He could see it creeping in along the floor and walls, saw the green of the moss and lichen again. Finally, it was the genuine light at the end of the tunnel. He felt slightly disoriented, as if the tunnel had been much longer than five hundred and thirty yards. Had he passed through some strange parallel world halfway along? His mother would have said the fairies owned the middle of the tunnel and only let people through after playing tricks on them and making them feel lost. It was the darkness, he supposed. Human beings weren't designed for it.

When he emerged into daylight, he found a path

to his right leading down to the car park at Monsal Head. A fingerpost pointed him straight ahead to Wyedale. A moment later, he had stepped out on the viaduct.

And he saw Anson Tate standing in the middle, tapping his foot as if getting impatient for Cooper to arrive.

Diane Fry was having to follow DC Villiers. She didn't know where anything was around here. She never had done, even when she was stationed in Edendale. What could you do when there were no roads?

Villiers took her by car up the hill from Monsal Head, as if they were heading away from the incident. Fry kept looking at her, wondering if she'd gone mad. But Villiers seemed to know where she was going. A mile up the hill, she swung sharp left and they descended rapidly down a narrow, winding lane. Fry clung to her seat as they skidded round a corner through a belt of trees.

'No wonder your cars get damaged,' she said.

'It's an occupational hazard around here,' said Villiers, having to raise her voice above the noise of the engine bouncing off the stone walls.

They reached a junction and Villiers turned left, driving along the side of a small river. A few yards further on, she stopped, letting the car slide on to the grass at an awkward angle.

'Where to now?' said Fry.

'Across the bridge.'

It was only a narrow footbridge, but it led directly on to the trail. And there was the other end of the Headstone Viaduct ahead.

'Amazing,' said Fry.

Cooper's voice came over the radio.

'Carol? Diane? Where are you?'

'We're here. Just keep him talking.'

Anson Tate had never needed much encouragement to keep talking. Cooper edged slowly towards him, conscious of the advice never to make a sudden move when dealing with a potential suicide. Tate had seen him, but Cooper didn't speak until he got closer.

'Don't do anything silly, Mr Tate,' said Cooper, guessing from their previous conversations that the phrase would annoy him.

'Silly? Silly?'

'Taking your own life doesn't solve anything, if that's what you were planning.'

Tate shifted his grip suddenly on the parapet and Cooper stopped.

'You call it "doing something silly or stupid",' said Tate. 'But it's not stupid. Sometimes, it's the most sensible and logical thing you can do. What's wrong with taking your own life?'

'It's irrational,' said Cooper.

Tate shook his head vigorously.

'No, I believe in rational suicide,' he said. 'Rational is the important word.'

'There's nothing rational about it.'

Provoked, Tate couldn't resist trying to justify himself. That knowledge was the one weapon Cooper had at his disposal.

'Really?' said Tate. 'Well, you're as ignorant about

363

it as everyone else. For anyone who likes to be in charge of their own life, the final stages of it should be the way *you* choose it to be. We should be in charge at the end of our lives, not helpless babies, dependent on strangers, kept alive by technology, with no say in what happens to us, no knowledge of what's going on around us. No dignity. It turns us into something less than an animal, which is allowed to die in peace.'

Cooper held up his hands in a placatory gesture.

'You're thinking of your mother,' he said. 'I understand.'

'You understand?' snapped Tate. 'No, you don't. No one does. Not until they come to that moment themselves. I've helped a few people to understand. That's the best thing I could have done with my own life.'

'What about all the innocent people who have died?'

'Innocent people suffer all the time. It's nothing new. I'm sure you're aware of that.'

'This is different, though.'

'Different?'

'Yes, of course. You must understand. It's completely different when it's *your* fault.'

Tate shrugged. 'I gave them knowledge. It's the most valuable gift one human being can give to another.'

'What do you mean?'

'Well, we're all going to die one day. Death is an open door. Yet society tells us we mustn't go through that door. And most of us don't. Because we're frightened of what's on the other side. And what *is* on the other side of the door? The unknown, of course.'

'People are always afraid of the unknown. You can't blame them for that.'

'No,' said Tate. 'But I can do something about it. Because knowledge is the best answer to fear. It dispels the darkness of ignorance and puts us back in control of our lives. It gives us a choice. When everything is known and predictable and within your control – well, it isn't frightening any more.'

'You're deluded,' said Cooper. 'You don't know everything. You don't know what happens when you die. You have no idea what it feels like. Because you're still alive, Mr Tate.'

Tate shook his head, the wedge of hair on his forehead gleaming jet black, though he was standing in full sun on the viaduct.

'The stigma that surrounds suicide is wrong,' he said. 'Just so wrong. People should be allowed to make their own end-of-life decisions. How can one person make a judgement on how much another suffers? Whose definition of suffering do you use? And why shouldn't we quit while we're still ahead?'

Down below in the dale, Cooper could see a small crowd gathering, their faces turned up, their cameras and smartphones held aloft.

Tate looked down at them with a smile. He enjoyed being the centre of attention. And there was nothing Cooper could do about it. The location was too open and there were too many people around. Like the incident at the shopping centre in Derby, someone might soon get impatient and begin to shout, 'Jump!'

'Look at all these people,' said Tate. 'They think

they're in charge of their own destinies. Well, death will rob them of control. All the talk about the ethics of dying is really a question of who takes charge of the process – and why should it be the doctors? A dying person can plan the clothes they're buried in, the inscription on their tombstone, the music at their funeral. But there's one last freedom, the one we're constantly denied. We don't get to choose our own way of death. Taking the decision into your own hands can make all the difference to your peace of mind in the final days.'

'Is this the sort of stuff you put on your website?' said Cooper.

'I put anything they needed to hear.'

Uniformed officers in yellow high-vis jackets were going among the crowd below the viaduct trying to move them away. Cooper couldn't hear their voices, but he saw the hand gestures, like shepherds trying to usher reluctant sheep away from their favourite food. The crowd backed off, then edged closer again as soon as an officer's back was turned. And the number of spectators was increasing. It was a futile exercise.

Tate had the nerve to wave at the crowd and some of them waved back. Did he think he was some kind of celebrity greeting his fans? It was hard to know what was going through his mind. Perhaps he really was so deluded.

'I'm helping to bring people happiness,' said Tate. 'Don't you understand that? Doesn't anyone understand?'

'Happiness? That's nonsense,' said Cooper. 'It can't be true.'

'Oh? Tell me, these people you've been finding – don't they always look peaceful? Well, I see you won't answer. But I know they do. It's the ultimate peace, which living people can't understand.'

'Do you really think you've been helping them?' asked Cooper.

'Of course. I told you so.'

'And yet that wasn't your entire purpose, Mr Tate. Perhaps not even your main purpose. I'm thinking it was just a side effect, a bit of useful camouflage.'

'I have no idea what you're talking about,' said Tate stubbornly.

'Yes, you do. I'm talking about Roger Farrell. It's no coincidence that your suicide website was taken down after Farrell's death. You'd achieved your purpose then. The others were just unfortunate, weren't they? Collateral damage. Don't you feel the least bit of guilt about them? Alex Denning and David Kuzneski? Gordon Burgess and Bethan Jones?'

'If they came to me, I helped them to achieve what they wanted most in the world,' snapped Tate. 'I was doing them a favour. People should be thanking me.'

Diane Fry had appeared behind him. She could move very quietly when she wanted to, as Cooper knew very well. She'd crept up on him unexpectedly far more times than he cared to remember. Now he was very glad to see her.

He kept his eyes fixed on Tate's, as if absorbed in what he was saying. Tate loved attention. Even at this moment, he couldn't resist the feeling of power it gave him to have another person's complete concentration.

So the shock on his face was total when Fry grabbed his arm and forced him to the floor, while shouting that he was under arrest. She had the cuffs on him before Cooper could get near enough to assist. But then, she didn't need his assistance. She rarely had.

When Anson Tate had been taken away in the back of a car, Cooper leaned against his Toyota in the viewpoint car park at Monsal Head.

The trail had been reopened and a few people were beginning to walk and cycle across the viaduct again. The valley looked even greener, the foliage denser and more vibrant. The landscape was only just now coming to life. In another couple of weeks, it would be high summer in the Peak District and this area would be packed with visitors, like all the tourist hotspots.

Right now, this was a place he would like to sit and spend some time. He would give anything to be able to stretch out on one of those benches in the sun, eat an ice cream from Hobb's Café, listen to the birds, watch the silver glint of the river as it ran down from Litton Mill and Cressbrook through Water-cum-Jolly Dale. He could close his eyes and imagine the peace of the dale further upstream, the hidden corners of Ravensdale, the cool streams and sunlit rocks. How pleasant it would be to drift off with that all around him and never have to wake up again.

Cooper found himself feeling almost envious of David Kuzneski, the man who had escaped from his own particular torment by doing just that. And Anson Tate had helped him to achieve his peace.

30

The rest of the day was filled with interviews, which went on well into the evening. Ben Cooper and Diane Fry shared the interviewing between them, while Dev Sharma and the team of DCs hit the phones to make background enquiries and check details over and over until the picture began to come clearer. Ella Webster was being brought in again, but she could wait for a while.

Detective Superintendent Branagh came down at some point to get an update, probably just before she knocked off and went home for the day.

'That man, Anson Tate,' she said. 'Were you aware that he made a complaint against you for harassment?'

'No, I wasn't,' said Cooper.

So Tate had been playing the role of the innocent victim to the hilt, trying to persuade Hazel Branagh that he was being persecuted. He was very persuasive too. Cooper expected Branagh to say something about the complaint being referred to Professional Standards, but it didn't happen.

'It was a lot of nonsense he was telling me, though. I sent him away with a polite flea in his ear.'

'Did you, ma'am?'

'Absolutely. To be frank with you, Ben, I thought he was a bit of a creep.'

Fry had stayed in Edendale, but was in constant touch with her colleagues at St Ann's. Cooper overheard her talking to Jamie Callaghan and thought he detected a change in the tone of her voice. It was a tone that had once been familiar to him, but which he'd almost forgotten.

'Simon Hull is still talking about Roger Farrell,' said Fry when she came off the phone. 'I don't think we'll be able to stop him now he's started. Jamie says his solicitor is going hairless.'

'Hull knew Farrell from working at the car dealership in Arnold, didn't he?' said Cooper.

'He knew Farrell very well indeed. They were good friends. When Farrell swapped cars after the murders, it was Hull who bought the old car off him and sold him a new one. But it didn't last. Over time, he came to hate Farrell. Hull told me he found some evidence in one of the cars Farrell got rid of, a Škoda Octavia.'

'Would that be the car he was using when Victoria Jenkins was killed?'

'That's right,' said Fry. 'Hull found some photographs of her in the glove box, which Farrell must have over-looked. Some were taken with a long lens while she was still alive. Some were taken when she was dead.'

'So Hull knew exactly what Farrell was doing.'

'Of course. And he felt used, made guilty by association. He felt betrayed by his old friend. So he decided to get what he could out of the situation. He told me he recruited Anwar Sharif to help him blackmail Farrell, to create a bit of distance so that Farrell wouldn't suspect him.'

'No one likes feeling used.'

'Farrell was certainly a man who used people. And he made the wrong enemies along the way.'

'Well, we knew Hull was an old friend of Farrell's,' said Cooper, 'as well as a colleague. We've got him in the photo. I suppose Farrell had that photo with him in the car because it showed him with his wife, perhaps one of the few photos he had from the time before she died. It apparently didn't occur to him to cut Simon Hull off. Or maybe . . .'

'What?'

'Well, it's possible he might have done it deliberately. Perhaps he was leaving a clue for us, a message. He thought it would lead us to track Hull down.'

'But that was the wrong message,' said Fry.

Cooper sighed. 'Aren't they all?'

Fry sat down in Cooper's office without being asked. She acted as though the chair belonged to her.

'So what next?' she said.

Cooper wondered for a moment why he should tell her what his plans were. But they'd got to this stage together, worked out the answer at pretty much the same time, though in their own way. She did deserve a bit of credit.

'I want to talk to Ella Webster again,' he said.

Fry nodded approvingly. 'Roger Farrell's daughter? Yes, that's logical.'

'I feel sure Tate must have been asking questions of Farrell's family, still claiming to be a journalist,' said Cooper. 'And of course he was, in a way. He had credentials. He still possessed his NUJ card as a free-lance reporter. That's often all people need to open the door. Tate hadn't actually sold a story for months and months before that. He was spending far too much time being obsessed with Roger Farrell to pursue a career.'

'He must have run out of money then, with no income,' said Fry.

'Oh, I think it had probably been difficult for him to make a living for a good while before that. He sold the house in Mansfield because he couldn't keep up the mortgage payments and he used the money to continue funding his enquiries, and his *Secrets of Death* website too.'

'Then he targeted Farrell and probably revealed that he knew the truth about him.'

Cooper nodded. 'Farrell must have been aware that he was living on borrowed time. He would have been expecting someone to come for him sooner or later. Though not Anson Tate, I bet.'

'Probably us,' said Fry gloomily.

'Maybe. Or Simon Hull and Anwar Sharif.'

'So Farrell had nowhere to turn.'

'Nowhere,' said Cooper. 'Between Hull and Sharif on one hand and Anson Tate on the other, and with the knowledge that the police might knock on his door at any moment. His family had turned away from him too. There was nothing left for Roger Farrell. Where else did he have to go? There was only one option left for him. And Tate made sure he knew that.'

'Have you asked Tate about Victoria Jenkins?' asked Fry.

'Not yet. I'm saving that little titbit. He's talking, but not about that. I think he's trying to avoid the subject, perhaps hoping we don't know about the connection with her.'

'So you're going to pull that out of the bag at the right moment.'

'I think when I produce the photo of Victoria Jenkins with her A-level results it will break him down.'

'Personally, I still think he might have been one of her customers,' said Fry. 'They say that can develop into an obsession for the wrong man.'

'Well, whatever his reason for it, he seems to have been devastated by her murder. And with no one being charged for it after all that time? Tate turned into a vigilante. And you can see why, can't you?'

'It was just a question of time,' protested Fry. 'We would have got there in the end.'

'I'm sure you would. In the end.'

'So he was able to identify Roger Farrell as the killer before we did,' said Fry. 'How did he manage that?'

'Don't feel bad about it, Diane,' said Cooper. 'The fact is, journalists can do a lot of things the police aren't able to do. They can ask questions we can't, go places we can't, cut corners, break the rules.'

'All right. There's no need to go on.'

'So Fay Laws needs to be spoken to again.'

Fry made a note. 'I'll get Jamie Callaghan to speak to her. Unless you wanted to do it yourself?'

'No, that's fine.'

'And what else was there?' said Fry. 'Oh, yes, the website. Were you going to give me the details of that?'

Cooper handed her the printouts from *secretsofdeath.org*.

'It was just a question of time,' he said.

'It's horrible stuff,' said Fry after a glance through the printouts.

'Luke found dozens of other websites of a similar nature,' said Cooper. 'One of them has instructions for slitting your wrists that match exactly the method that Bethan Jones used. So whether she used the *secretsofdeath.org* website in particular or some other site, I don't know. But we have a definite connection for Farrell, and for three of the others – Burgess, Kuzneski and Denning.'

'Through the business cards.'

'Yes.'

'Could we find out where they were printed? It would provide some firm evidence against Tate.'

'There are too many possibilities. We could try local companies, but we don't have the resources to extend the inquiry any further than that. I suspect it was probably an overseas printer anyway – it's easy enough to do online and practically untraceable.'

'And the combination of letters and numbers were a password?'

'Yes, providing access to a sort of members' area

where you could get personal guidance. That's where all the more detailed stuff comes from, thanks to Luke Irvine. I picture Tate luring Farrell in, or instructing him to go there.'

'Was Tate trying to blackmail him?' asked Fry. 'If he was, he would have been unsuccessful. Hull and Sharif were already bleeding him dry.'

'Personally, I think it was more than blackmail. Tate wanted to get fun out of it.'

'Fun?'

'The feeling of power,' said Cooper. 'Playing with someone's life. You can only do that if it's someone you're convinced is worthless or deserving of their fate. It wasn't just about money.'

'And the card itself?'

'The card may only have been for one purpose. Yes, it was a message. But it was intended as a message from Anson Tate to Roger Farrell. Imagine that *Secrets of Death* card coming through his letterbox one day. It would have shaken Farrell to the core, the realisation that Tate knew where he lived.'

'It would scare me, actually.'

'Me too.'

Fry smiled. 'We'll go back to Simon Hull. We'll work out all the details in due course.'

'I'm sure you will.'

She looked at him quizzically. 'Were all those other suicides arranged just to camouflage the death of Roger Farrell?' she said.

'No, no. It wasn't as simple as that.'

Cooper had thought about the question already.

Anson Tate had surely enjoyed what he was doing. Given the opportunity, he'd found he couldn't stop. All those potential suicides coming to his website had encouraged him to continue. They had needed him. And he'd been unable to turn them away, because he liked it too much. He liked being needed. It was difficult to imagine the feeling of power it must have given him. The power over life and death. It was the nearest you could ever get to being God.

'What about the others?' asked Fry.

'I've had the team going through them in minute detail. We can't find any connection.'

'Really?'

'Apart from Farrell, it seems Tate didn't contact any of the others directly. He didn't need to, though. David Kuzneski, Alex Denning, Gordon Burgess, Bethan Jones, and probably others – they were already in a state of mind where they'd decided to look for guidance or for information, or just for someone who understood what was going through their heads.'

Fry nodded. 'Not everybody would understand. They probably felt members of their families wouldn't.'

'Exactly. So they went looking elsewhere. And of course they did it online. It's like when you feel ill, isn't it? Everyone goes online to check what disease their symptoms might indicate, before they ever think of visiting their GP. It seems to be the same with potential suicides. They do a Google search one night when they're feeling at rock bottom and they come across these websites.'

'And some of them found Anson Tate's site *secretsofdeath.org*.'

Cooper sighed deeply. 'Yes. So they weren't targeted at all. They were drawn to it, like moths to a flame.'

Ella Webster stared at the photograph of Anson Tate, then laid it carefully on the table.

'Yes, I do recognise him,' she said, as if Cooper had been pestering her with the question for days. 'He visited my aunt when I was over there from Spain a few months ago. I didn't like him, but Aunt Fay wouldn't tell me what he wanted. She said he was a journalist, but not what he was writing about.'

'He wasn't writing a story about anything. He was investigating your father.'

Ella looked away. 'I thought it must be something like that. I just didn't want to get involved.'

'Mrs Webster, did you have any idea what your father was doing?'

'No. Well, there was talk among the family. Disapproving murmurings from Aunt Fay, the odd mysterious hint from Uncle Alan, her husband. I tried to keep out of it.'

'You didn't *want* to know anything.'

'No, I didn't. Does that make me so bad? The father I knew had already gone. Not that he was ever a loving and affectionate dad. But he'd changed so much after Mum died that we couldn't even talk to each other any more. He was like a stranger to me. Whatever it was, I just prayed it would end quietly, without dragging us all into some vile scandal. That would have been awful. I have two children, you know. I need to shield them from things like that.'

Cooper studied her carefully. Like almost everyone he'd ever interviewed, she was keeping something back. Some were blatant about it, but others pretended to be open, sharing some information while holding details back. And Ella Webster had clammed up, just like a suspect in an interview room. Cooper expected her to say 'no comment' at any moment.

'You and your family must have suspected something?' he said. 'Why didn't you come to the police?'

Her eyes flickered, but there was no other response.

'You surely had some idea of what your father was doing?' he persisted.

'How could we?' she said.

Cooper stared at her, frustrated. How could they indeed, if they had never talked to him? The timing of the estrangement in Farrell's family looked to be more than a coincidence. But, since none of them would talk, he had no evidence that he could use.

He would have to leave it to their consciences. In years to come they might reflect that their own inaction, the instinct of loyalty to a family member, could have resulted in the deaths of three young women.

'I think you probably knew what your aunt was talking to Mr Tate about,' said Cooper. 'And you didn't object. You just closed your eyes, crossed your fingers and hoped it would work out in your favour.'

Ella Webster pursed her lips stubbornly. 'All I can say is that it turned out for the best in the end. No long-drawn-out court case, no prurient media coverage, no need for any of the family to get dragged in. And my children can remain oblivious. All they know is that they no longer have a grandfather whom they never met. I'm sorry, Detective Inspector, but that's the way I like it.'

Cooper wanted to tell her that it might all come out afterwards, when they got Anson Tate in court. A not-guilty plea would result in a long, complicated trial with many of the details about Mr Farrell brought out by the prosecution. He didn't feel able to say that with any confidence, though. He wasn't sure that the CPS would go ahead with a prosecution or what charges they could use. And Tate was certain to plead guilty to anything they presented. A quick hearing and a lesser sentence. He could see Tate smiling now.

Instead, Cooper stood up. There seemed nothing more to say to Ella Webster. Chloe Young had been so right, more correct than she could know. Some men had no one to talk to, not even members of their own family.

He couldn't feel pity for Roger Farrell, of course. But how many others were there out there, alone and isolated through no fault of their own, easy prey to malicious outside influences and to their own inner torments?

31

Ben Cooper interviewed Anson Tate again. He was very glad that Tate wasn't the 'goldfish' type of interviewee who responded with 'no comment' to every question. Tate liked to talk. He talked a lot. All he wanted was the attention. It was a bit pathetic to see really.

But after a while Tate's arguments about rational suicide began to grind Cooper down. Tate was trying too hard to present himself as someone with good intentions, claiming that even Roger Farrell had made his own decision to end his life. Anson Tate was just a man who was there to help.

Sitting across the table in the interview room, Tate still looked insignificant, despite everything that Cooper now knew about him, or suspected. His narrow mouth was held in a tight line and his eyes darted around the room. The stiff wedge of hair on his forehead had sagged and lost its shape. It lay against his skull like a damp rag.

'So, Mr Tate,' said Cooper, 'tell me this: what was the nature of your relationship with the murdered student Victoria Jenkins?'

Tate scowled. 'I don't want to talk about her.'

'Why not? Are you ashamed, Mr Tate? Surely not.'

'Why would I be ashamed?'

'A man like you, with a teenage girl . . .'

That hit a nerve. Tate flushed angrily.

'That's a disgusting suggestion,' he said.

'Well, you're a lot older than she was,' persisted Cooper.

Tate leaned forward. 'Yes,' he said. 'Old enough to be her father.'

Cooper frowned at his tone. 'What are you saying?'

'Don't you get it? I *was* her father. Victoria was my own daughter.'

'You look a bit shattered,' said Fry later, sitting across the other side of Cooper's desk without a hint of a knock on the door. 'Mr Tate worn you out?'

'He's depressing me,' admitted Cooper.

'What now?'

'His relationship with Victoria Jenkins,' he said. 'It was more than an obsessive crush on a much younger woman. Tate believed that she was his daughter.'

'What?'

'It seems he had a fling with her mother, way back when he was a dashing young newspaper reporter. When he was sent out on the A-level story, he realised who she was and calculated that her age was a fit.'

'Did he never do anything about it? Speak to her mother, try to get a DNA test?'

'No, not Mr Tate. It was an act of faith for him. He must have seen something of himself in her or convinced himself that she was his, because of her cleverness. He has quite an ego, you know.'

'Doesn't he just?'

'Well, that's his story. Believe it or not, as you like.'

'So what did he do after Victoria Jenkins was killed?' asked Fry.

'He expected there to be an arrest and someone to be charged with her murder. He was hoping for justice, I suppose. And it didn't happen.'

'Well, that would be why Tate made himself busy making his own enquiries around Nottingham,' said Fry, consulting her notebook. 'It seems he talked to the working girls. They gave him information that they wouldn't share with us.'

'I suppose he paid them, did he?'

'Yes, that tends to make a difference. So they told him their experiences. Roger Farrell had been on the scene for some time and word gets around. Even the newer girls knew all about him. They gave Anson Tate enough for him to use.'

Cooper looked at her closely. Fry seemed a bit uncomfortable. Her head was down gazing at her notes, as if she couldn't meet his eye. He knew there was something she deliberately wasn't saying. She was hoping he wouldn't ask the pertinent question. That was why she couldn't look at him. But what was it? He considered what he'd be focusing on if she was a suspect in an interview room and he was probing for the truth.

'Diane,' he said, 'how do you know all that, if the girls wouldn't talk to you?'

Her head came up suddenly.

'What?' she said.

To Cooper, it sounded like 'no comment'. So he asked the question again.

'You've just said that the working girls in Nottingham wouldn't share information with you. Anson Tate would be the only other person who knows what information they gave him and he hasn't admitted it in my interviews with him. Not yet anyway. So how do you know what the girls told Tate?'

'I . . .' began Fry.

'Yes?'

'I used Devdan Sharma,' she said. 'He said he had some relevant experience from his assignment liaising with Immigration Enforcement. So I asked him to use his contacts. They came up with an Albanian girl who'd been working in the Forest Road area. They picked her up earlier this week and she was facing deportation. She talked.'

'And that's it?'

'It seemed a good idea,' Fry said defensively. 'And it worked. You can't deny it worked.'

'No, I can't.'

They sat and looked at each other for a while. Cooper was seething inside, but with mixed emotions. Fry had interfered, but he had to admit that she'd achieved results. Dev Sharma should have told him what Fry had asked him to do. He should have referred the request to his DI straight away, since Fry had no authority here in Edendale. But Sharma hadn't done that. He seemed to have switched loyalties very easily. But he had also got results.

Cooper knew it would be churlish of him to object. He should be thanking Fry. But the words wouldn't come out of his mouth. He mentally filed it away to deal with later, when he could figure out the right response. Now wasn't the time. He could only move on.

'So that's how you know Tate paid the girls for information,' he said finally.

'Yes,' said Fry, visibly relaxing.

Cooper nodded. 'I suppose Tate must have run out of money in the end. That was why he moved into that grotty flat in Edendale. He said it was because he liked it. It should have occurred to me to wonder what he'd done with his money.'

'Well, he had no one to leave it to in his will,' said Fry. 'And I don't suppose he was much into charitable giving. He doesn't seem the type.'

'So he figured out who killed his daughter and the other girls, or he believed he had. Why didn't he report his suspicions? No faith in the police?'

Fry sniffed. 'Possibly.'

'And instead he decided to take things into his own hands.'

'Yes. But not the way some men would have done. Many fathers would have cornered Farrell in an alley somewhere with a few friends and beaten him to within an inch of his life. That's the usual sort of vigilante justice we're used to.'

'Anson Tate isn't that kind of man. He doesn't approve of violence. He said so.'

'Well, that's ironic for a man who's killed half a dozen people,' said Fry.

Cooper had begun to feel very weary now. 'He didn't actually kill them, Diane. He was just partly responsible for their deaths.'

'Just partly responsible? What a woolly expression. I'm sure you don't really believe that.'

'No, not really.'

'And you still don't think he was trying to blackmail Farrell?'

'For money? No. Anson Tate was cleverer and more subtle than that. He didn't want money from Farrell. He wanted his death. That was a pretty good reason for him to sell his house in Mansfield and move into that cheap flat. He had nothing else he wanted to do with his money, except to track down Roger Farrell and end his life in some way.'

'He could have hired a hit-man,' said Fry. 'I believe they're easy enough to find in the city, if you've got the money.'

Cooper shook his head. 'No, that wouldn't have satisfied Tate. He needed the feeling of power and control. He wanted to play God. In this case, a vengeful God.'

'Of course, vigilantism is wrong, no matter what form it takes. Whether it's a baseball bat in an alley or psychological pressure. The outcome is the same.'

'Yes, it's wrong. On the other hand . . .'

'We're not going to spend much time regretting it in Farrell's case, are we?'

'No. Just the others.'

'The collateral damage.'

'I'm not sure they could be described as that really.

Denning, Kuzneski, Burgess. They weren't just accidents. I think Tate got a buzz from it. He got a taste for the feeling of power. For him it was like being God.'

A few minutes later, after Fry had left, Cooper looked up suddenly, as if he had just been jerked out of sleep. Carol Villiers was standing in the doorway and she'd brought him a coffee.

'You looked as though you needed this.'

'You're right. I need it so much.'

Villiers stood and watched attentively as he drank it, like a mother making sure her children ate their greens.

'You were right in what you said the other day, Carol,' said Cooper.

'Was I? When was that momentous occasion?'

'When you said that Bethan Jones was the odd one out. And not just because she was female. As far as Dev and Luke can tell from trawling through her online activity, she may have visited other suicide sites but she had no contact with Anson Tate and his *Secrets of Death* website. She was entirely the wrong sort of victim for him to prey on.'

'She was an ordinary suicide, then?'

'If there is such a thing,' said Cooper.

'She made her own decision and decided to give up the fight.'

'There's a difference between giving up trying and coming to terms with what life has thrown at you. One's fatalistic, the other's realistic.'

'You should never give up trying,' said Villiers vehemently. 'Never.'

Cooper turned over a plastic evidence bag. At least Anson Tate had left a note in his flat on Buxton Road, though it was a strange form of farewell that he'd written. What an irony. A suicide note without a suicide. Finally, Tate's planning had gone wrong. There was an unpredictable factor he hadn't taken into account.

'So what are we going to charge Tate with?' asked Villiers.

'We'll have to talk to the CPS. But we'll never get him to trial.'

'What makes you say that?'

'There's only one way out that Anson Tate will be planning. And you can bet it won't be a long spell in prison, followed by old age and a gradual decline into senility. He'll have to be on suicide watch while he's in the cells. And I doubt even that will be enough.'

'I'm not sure you're right,' said Villiers. 'He thought it all through too carefully. All that stuff about the right to control your own destiny. He's come to terms intellectually with death. But he's a sociopath. There's no emotion in him. You need some kind of emotion behind the act to take your own life.'

'He did have an emotion,' said Cooper. 'He was consumed by the desire for revenge.'

'But Tate's first suicide attempt on the bridge was a fake, wasn't it?'

'Oh, yes,' said Cooper. 'I think he wanted to know for himself what it felt like in that moment, when you stand on the verge of killing yourself. He was preparing himself for Roger Farrell.'

Sadly, Cooper shook his head over the story of Anson Tate. He might still be alive physically, but what he'd done already was a form of psychological suicide. Surely you had to kill something inside yourself before you could kill someone else?

The dregs of his coffee were cold when Diane Fry came and asked to see the note that Anson Tate had left in his flat in Buxton Road.

'You know, I thought of Anson Tate as a victim,' said Cooper. 'But he wasn't, was he?'

Fry raised an eyebrow. 'Really? Is that the way you treat victims these days? If so, you've changed even more than I thought.'

Cooper looked away. Was she right? Had he changed that much? He hoped not. Everyone changed slowly, bit by bit, over the years. It happened while you were busy doing other things. Sometimes you didn't notice yourself that you'd become a different person. And by then the change might be irreversible.

Frowning, Cooper read Anson Tate's note again before he passed it to Fry. He wondered if Carol Villiers was right and Tate would take the first opportunity to end his own life. And, if so, whether Tate's victims would be waiting for him on the other side. And what they might have to say to him.

The note read:

This is the third secret of death. A secret they don't want you to know. That death is actually quite . . . pleasant.

Yes, death. It's a subject I think about often. Not that I spend much time wondering what happens afterwards, whether there'll be something waiting for me on the other side. Eternal life, rebirth, heaven or hell. Whatever. Nor do I waste any effort wondering when it will happen. I don't understand that obsession with how long you'll live, what disease will carry you off, whether you'll survive to see your grandchildren growing up or if you'll face growing old alone. Speculation about the future. None of that interests me.

For me, it's the moment. The actual instant of death. What is that like? How do you feel and what are you thinking? What goes through your brain in those final seconds? Is it like falling asleep? Or something quite different – something unique, which we'll never experience at any other time? What is it like?

I can't wait to find out.

32

Cooper was getting ready to go home now. He didn't dare look at the time. His stomach told him he was hungry, but he didn't feel like eating. Takeaways had been brought in for the team in the CID room and he could smell the spices from here, but they just made him feel sick.

Diane Fry stuck her head round the door.

'Still here?' she said.

'Yes, but I'm surprised you are. Nothing to go back to in Wilford?'

'No, thank God.'

Cooper was puzzling over that remark, but not making any sense of it. He probably wasn't capable of making sense of much in his present condition.

'I thought you'd like to know,' said Fry. 'We've tied both Hull and Sharif in to the break-in at Forest Fields now. When we pulled Sharif in we were able to take prints and DNA, and we got matches for both. Hull has admitted the blackmail. Sharif isn't talking, but Hull has already implicated him on that one. We'll have a tight case against them.'

'I suppose Hull's concern was to remove anything from the house that might still link him to Farrell. They used to work together at the car dealership in Arnold. The two couples became quite friendly, hence the photo.'

'Yes, and, when Simon Hull set up on his own, Farrell continued taking his cars to Hull's garage for servicing.'

'Of course – the invoices and MoT certificates. *Those* were what had gone from that file.'

'If you say so. And, at a guess, he was probably looking for that photo.'

'It wasn't there. It was in Farrell's car.'

Fry hesitated. 'Hasn't this inquiry been the wrong way round somehow?' she said.

'I know what you mean. The perpetrator is supposed to take the honourable way out at the end of the story, not at the beginning.'

'I don't even know what that means,' she said.

'Never mind. It's to do with a study of suicide. The socio-economic factors.'

'Have you been taking night school classes in psychology?'

'No, just talking to someone interesting.'

'Oh, well. I can take a hint. Goodnight, Inspector.'

'Okay,' said Cooper distractedly. 'Yes, goodbye. Goodbye, Diane.'

But Cooper still wasn't finished. Carol Villiers came running in for instructions about the next day. He was the DI, after all. It was his responsibility to decide these things.

'There's the post-mortem on Gordon Burgess happening in the morning,' she said. 'Do you want to go yourself, Ben?'

Cooper hesitated. He wouldn't be at his best in the morning. He was bound to say the wrong thing, blurt out some embarrassing remark. How awkward would that be?

'You could do it, Carol. Or I could send Dev Sharma, if you prefer. Now we've got him back, he might as well be doing something useful.'

'Oh, I don't mind doing it,' said Villiers cheerfully. 'There's a new pathologist there, you know.'

Cooper wondered how she managed to stay so cheerful, even at this time of night. She must have an almost superhuman constitution.

'Ah, yes, I've met her,' he said.

'Chloe Young. I know her family – they're from Sheffield. Believe it nor not, I went out with her brother for a few months. It was years ago, of course, before I met Glen.'

'You already know her, then?'

'Very well. In fact, she got in touch with me when she first came back to the area.'

'Really?'

'As it happens,' said Villiers, 'it was Chloe I went to Derby Book Festival with the other day. She's great company. She's very bright too, you know. She's got qualifications coming out of her ears.'

Cooper's mouth hung open as he watched Villiers leave. The news came as a complete shock. His exhausted mind began to whirl with questions. Had

Chloe Young been hearing all about him from Carol Villiers before she met him that evening at the Barrel Inn? And did that also mean Villiers knew where he'd been on the night his car was run off the road? What had they been saying about him?

Slowly, Cooper put on his jacket and closed the door. Like so many other things in his life, he might never find out.